These men expect obedience!

One Night with Her

BROODING
BOSS

SUSAN STEPHENS
CATHY WILLIAMS
RED GARNIER

One Night with

COLLECTION

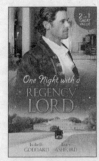

February 2015

February 2015

February 2015

February 2015

March 2015

March 2015

One Night with Her
BROODING
BOSS

SUSAN STEPHENS
CATHY WILLIAMS
RED GARNIER

Published in Great Britain 2015
by Mills & Boon, an imprint of Harlequin (UK) Limited,
Eton House, 18-24 Paradise Road, Richmond, Surrey, TW9 1SR

ONE NIGHT WITH HER BROODING BOSS
© 2015 Harlequin Books S.A.

Ruthless Boss, Dream Baby © 2011 Susan Stephens
Her Impossible Boss © 2011 Cathy Williams
The Secretary's Bossman Bargain © 2010 Red Garnier

ISBN: 978-0-263-25364-1

011-0215

Harlequin (UK) Limited's policy is to use papers that are natural, renewable and recyclable products and made from wood grown in sustainable forests.The logging and manufacturing processes conform to the legalenvironmental regulations of the country of origin.

Printed and bound in Spain
by CPI, Barcelona

RUTHLESS BOSS, DREAM BABY

SUSAN STEPHENS

Susan Stephens was a professional singer before meeting her husband on the Mediterranean island of Malta. In true Modern™ style they met on Monday, became engaged on Friday and married three months later.

Susan enjoys entertaining, travel and going to the theatre. To relax she reads, cooks and plays the piano, and when she's had enough of relaxing she throws herself off mountains on skis, or gallops through the countryside singing loudly.

CHAPTER ONE

MAGENTA yelped with alarm as a scuffed biker's boot slammed onto the ground within inches of her feet. 'What the hell do you think you're doing?' she exploded, frantically clutching the armful of documents threatening to spill from her arms.

Taking off his helmet, the man shook out a mop of inky-black hair. He was exactly the type of man you didn't want to see when you'd had the day from hell and looked like you'd been dragged through a hedge backwards: gorgeous, cool, and commanding. He had 'danger' flashing round him like neon lights.

'Well?' Magenta demanded furiously. 'Do you always ride a motorcycle like a maniac?'

'Always,' he drawled.

'I should report you.'

Eyes the colour of a storm-tossed ocean laughed back at her.

And she would report him, Magenta determined, just as soon as she sorted out the flat on her car, along with a million and one other things.

Such as her father deciding to retire and sell his shares to some stranger without a word to her. Such as saving her colleagues' jobs from this unknown predator. Such as wanting to get back to her team and their fast-moving, retro ad campaign set in Magenta's favourite era, the sixties.

'Do you mind?' she said, trying to skirt around the man's monstrous, throbbing machine. 'Some of us have work to do.'

'Is that why you're leaving the office early?'

'Since when are my working hours your concern?'

The biker shrugged.

Magenta's glance swept the car park. Where was the security guard when you needed him? She had been loading up the car with things she intended to finish over the weekend in her own time—not that she was about to explain that to this guy, who looked like he spent his weekends in bed. And not alone.

'You're leaving me?' he demanded as she made a move to continue on her way.

'Somehow I'm managing to drag myself away.'

What was he doing in the car park of Steele Design anyway? Was he a courier? 'Do you have a package?'

His grin made her cheeks blaze red. She had to watch her words in future, Magenta concluded. They were about the same age—maybe he was a year or two older—but his eyes held infinitely more experience. 'If you don't have anything to deliver, this is private property and you should leave.'

He raised an eyebrow.

Oh, good. He was really impressed by her command of the situation.

The biker's self-confidence was making her edgy—that and his manner, which was cool, when she was fuming. Some men were just comfortable in every situation and this man was clearly one of them.

A sharp flurry of snow kept her hurrying along but the man's laugh was warm and sexy on her back. 'What's so urgent you can't spare a moment to chat?' he called.

She stopped and turned to confront him. 'Not that it's any business of yours, but I am going inside to put on the clothes I wear in the gym so I can change the tyre on my car.'

'Can I help you?'

'No.'

Perhaps she should at least have thanked him for the offer.

Now she felt guilty?

Settling the helmet on his head again, he revved the engine. 'You're going?' she said, perversely wanting him to stay.

Powerful shoulders eased in a careless shrug.

Why exactly was she driving him away, when he was the most interesting thing to have happened in a long time? Because she had more sense than to prolong the encounter, Magenta reasoned, crunching snow underfoot as she started on her way again. But, instead of riding off, the man kept pace with her, scuffing his boots on the surface of the road as he kept the engine purring along in neutral. 'Haven't you gone yet?' she demanded.

'I'm waiting to see you in gym clothes.' He grinned.

She huffed at this, all the time trying to work him out. He was dressed too casually to be a businessman and his voice was low and husky with an accent she didn't recognise. Perhaps he was a mature student; there was a college across the road.

'I could give you a lift.'

I bet you could. A face and body like his could give any woman a lift. But something about him warned her that this was a man who could switch in the blink of an eye from humorous and warm to the modern-day equivalent of Genghis Khan—and she'd had all the aggravation she could take for one day.

'You are one stressed-out lady. Don't you ever relax?'

Was he kidding? Who had time to relax? Plus, she shouldn't even think about relaxing while this guy was around. He looked too fit, too dangerous. 'My car is shot. Bust. Broken. What part of that should entice me to relax?'

'Like I said, I'd be happy to give you a lift.'

She might have given his well-packed leathers a thorough

inspection and found them more than to her liking, but she didn't know him from Adam. 'I never accept lifts from strangers,' she informed him, tilting her chin at what she hoped would pass for an unapproachable angle.

'Very wise,' he said, calmly wheeling along at her side.

'Don't you ever give up?'

'Never.'

Her heart was thundering. Why?

She was heading off towards the side entrance and the employee lockers where her gym clothes were stowed, and was looking forward to closing the door on his arrogant face... right up to the moment when he gunned the engine and rode away.

She stared after the streak of black lightning until it disappeared at the end of the road, feeling...wistful.

Well, she'd blown it, so it was no use crying over lost opportunities now.

Had there been something special about him—an instant connection between them? Or was that the wanderings of an exhausted mind?

Far more likely, Magenta decided. The biker could have insisted on fixing her tyre if he'd really wanted to.

Whatever happened to chivalry? Women like her, Magenta concluded, women who accepted equality as their right and who scowled if a man so much as offered to open a door for them.

Having retrieved her gym clothes from her locker, she threw them on, together with a warm jacket and a scarf. Returning to her car, she lifted the cover concealing the spare...

No spare!

She stared in disbelief at the empty space, and then remembered her father saying something about a puncture a few months back. They had matching cars, which at one time Magenta had thought cute. Not today; her father must have told the mechanics to help themselves to her spare and had forgotten to ask them to replace it.

It was her own fault for not checking.

The business was falling down around her ears, she might not even have a job after Christmas and she was crying over a flat tyre. Pressing back against the car, she shut her eyes, waiting for the tears to stop threatening. Finally, having convinced herself it was no use worrying about something she couldn't change, she decided to go inside, get warm and call a cab. Or she could always catch the underground; there was a tube station near her house.

And here came the security guard. Hurrying over to him, Magenta explained she would call someone to come and rescue her car.

When she returned to the office her father was ready to leave, to sign the deal to sell his shares.

'I thought you'd gone,' Clifford Steele complained, checking the angle of his silk tie. 'No family members muddying the water until this new man has settled in and I have his money in the bank—those are the rules.'

'And I was obeying them. I was just loading up the car when I discovered I had a flat. And guess what?' Magenta added dryly. 'I don't have a spare.'

'Call a cab,' her father advised without a flicker of remorse. 'Can't stay,' he added, wrapping a cashmere muffler around his neck. 'I'm off to sign the final papers. Just make sure you're out of here in case Quinn decides to come and take a look at his latest acquisition.'

She heard the note of resentment in her father's voice and kissed his cheek. It couldn't be easy selling out to a younger, more successful man. Clifford Steele might be high-handed, and his extravagance might have brought the company to its knees, but he was her father and she loved him and would do nothing to risk his comfortable retirement. It was up to her to sort the mess out now in an attempt to try and save her colleagues' jobs.

If the new owner allowed her to.

Gray Quinn might not keep her on, Magenta realised anxiously. Thanks to her father's outdated belief that men ran businesses while bricks and mortar provided better security for a woman, she owned the building but not a single voting-share.

'As you're still here, make yourself useful,' her father instructed. 'I'm sure the men would like a cup of coffee before you go. So you're a senior account exec,' he added with impatience when he saw her face. 'But no one makes a cup of coffee like—'

'A well-trained woman?' Magenta suggested, tongue-in-cheek.

'Like you, I was about to say. You work too hard, Magenta, and you take yourself far too seriously. Stress isn't good for a woman your age,' her father commented in his usual tactful manner. 'If you're not careful it will give you wrinkles. You should take a break—get a decent night's sleep.'

'Yes, Dad.' Her father might have stepped straight out of their sixties campaign, when men had a high opinion of themselves and women were still working out how to let them down lightly, Magenta mused wryly. 'That's just the way it is', her father was fond of telling her whenever she complained he was a dinosaur. 'That's just the way *you* are', she always amended fondly.

He had some parting words for her. 'If you'll take my advice, Magenta—which I doubt—you'll make yourself scarce until the new owner is settled in. Quinn will soon lose interest and leave the running of the company to the old guard.'

'Goodbye, Dad.'

Lose interest? That didn't sound like the Gray Quinn Magenta had read about. 'Dynamic and cool under pressure' was how the financial papers described him—not to mention ruthless and tough. Oh yes, and practically invisible. If there was a good photograph of Gray Quinn in existence, he had managed to keep it out of the public eye. Life under her father's autocratic rule had been bad enough, but Quinn was an unknown quantity, and Magenta's major concern was for her colleagues. Of course, if Quinn wanted a clean sweep, he might fire them all—and if he squashed the zing out of the ad agency's creative personnel it would go down anyway.

If Quinn booted her, she would just have to keep an eye on things from the sidelines, Magenta concluded, going to the window to stare out. If she had to remortgage her house and start a new company to keep everyone in work, then she would.

And what exactly was she looking for now? The biker? She should know better.

She did know better, and pulled away.

Turning her back to the window, she huffed wryly. Business might come easily to her, but where men were concerned she had a long history of failure. She didn't have the right chat, the right look—and the guy on the bike would almost certainly know that she hadn't had a date in ages. He looked like some sort of expert where women were concerned. Magenta smiled as she perched on the edge of the desk to call a cab. The famous orgasm was probably a fiction dreamed up by ad men, anyway.

There were no cabs, at least not for an hour or more. Snow and Christmas shoppers were held to account for the shortage of vehicles.

So, the underground it was.

Having checked she had everything she would need to work at home, Magenta called the garage to come and sort out the car and then brought her team into the office for one last discussion. The holidays were almost on them and she wanted everyone to feel confident about launching the campaign in the New Year before she left.

Would she even be coming back? Magenta wondered as her friends filed into the room. She couldn't afford to think like that. She owed it to the team to be positive. She couldn't let them see how worried she was. This wasn't the end of Steele Design, it was a new beginning, she told herself firmly as she announced, 'I'm going to be working at home for the time being.'

'You can't leave the week before Christmas,' Magenta's right arm, Tess, stated flatly.

'I'll be in touch with you the whole time.'

'It's not the same,' Tess argued. 'What about the Christmas party?'

'There are more important things than that—like keeping our jobs?' Magenta suggested when Tess protested. 'And why can't you organise it?' Magenta prodded gently.

'Because you have the magic,' Tess argued.

'I'll be in touch every day, I just won't be physically sitting at my desk—where, apparently,' Magenta added mischievously, 'I might present a threat to Quinn. Yes, I know I'm scary,' she said when the team began to laugh.

While she had them in a good mood she turned the conversation to business. 'You're a fantastic team, and it's crucial that Quinn sees the best of you guys, so I want you to forget about me and concentrate on making a good first impression.'

'Forget about you?' Tess scoffed. 'How are we going to do that when you haven't even given us a theme for the party yet?'

'Glad to hear I've got some uses,' Magenta said dryly, glancing at her wristwatch. She was starting to feel edgy. She had made a promise to her father to keep out of the way, so there wasn't much time for dreaming up ideas for the party. 'Keep it simple,' she instructed herself out loud. 'What about a sixties theme?'

'Brilliant,' Tess agreed. 'We've got half the props already, and you'd look great in a paper dress.'

'Ah...I won't be at the party this year.'

'Well, that's nonsense. What will it be like without you?'

'Much more fun, I should think.' Magenta was remembering how she'd pulled the plug the previous year when she had thought the men in the office were getting a little out of hand. 'I'm only on the end of the phone.'

'I give you twenty-four hours and you'll be back here,' Tess predicted. 'There's too much going on for you to stay away. And there's another thing,' she murmured, drawing Magenta aside. 'I've noticed something different about you this morning. Can't put my finger on it yet, but I will.'

'I don't know what you mean.'

'Ha!' Tess exclaimed. 'You're on the defensive already. You look wary. No,' she argued with herself, 'not wary. You look alert—excited, alive. Yes, that's it. Have you met someone, Magenta?'

'Don't be ridiculous! I'm only worried about the future here.'

'No...' Tess gave a confident shake of her head. 'There's something else—something you're not telling me.'

Maybe her red cheeks had given her away, Magenta thought wryly as the biker flashed into her mind.

'It's nothing to be ashamed of if you've met someone you like,' Tess insisted.

'But I haven't,' Magenta argued—too heatedly, she realised now.

CHAPTER TWO

TESS hurried to reassure her. 'I know you're worried about the company, and what's going to happen under the new owner, but you're entitled to a private life, Magenta. In fact, as your friend I'm going to be blunt about this—you *need* a private life.'

Magenta paused before continuing. 'All right. This is going to sound ridiculous…'

'Try me.'

Tess was waiting but, though she worked with words for a living, Magenta was suddenly struck dumb. How could she explain the trembling inside her, or the excitement, the awareness, even the outlandish suspicion that she had met her soul mate this morning? The biker had caught her at the worst possible moment and yet with his arrival it was as if everything had brightened. As if the world had suddenly come into sharp focus—and in a freezing-cold car park, of all places. How romantic!

The fact remained, it was as if the sun had shone down just on her, as if her life had opened up to a multi-coloured carousel of opportunity.

If she'd had the courage to seize it, which she clearly she hadn't. 'There was a guy this morning in the car park.'

'I knew it.'

'Shh.' Magenta glanced round, but no one was listening; they were too busy fighting over the choice of music for the party. 'It was nothing—just a good-looking guy. Not my type at all, and he wasn't remotely interested. So now you know.'

'But he excited you?'

'He certainly did something.'

'He made you tingle. He made you feel alive.'

'You're a romantic, Tess. He made me angry.'

'You shouted at him?' Tess frowned.

'I gave him a piece of my mind, yes.'

'And how did he react?'

'He laughed at me.'

'But that's wonderful!' Tess exclaimed. 'What a start.'

'There is no start, it was just an episode.'

'And episodes have sequels.'

'Not this one, Tess.'

'You never know, he may come back. He's seen you now— how could he resist? And when a man laughs with you, well, that's the start of intimacy, in my book.'

'It is?'

'Don't you know anything?'

'Not much,' Magenta confessed. 'After the rush of gold-diggers when I was in my first flush of youth, all the likely contenders lost interest.'

'Only because you frightened them away, dragon lady.'

'They weren't worth keeping.'

'And this guy's a keeper?'

'For someone, definitely, but not me.'

'Why not? What's wrong with you?'

'It's not even worth discussing,' Magenta said wryly. 'He's not going to ask me out on a date. I don't expect I'll ever see him again. It was just a chance encounter that made some sort of ridiculous impression on me because I was feeling tired and vulnerable, and—'

'Lacking in confidence where the mating game is concerned,' Tess supplied. 'Just promise me one thing, Magenta—

if you do see him again, don't shout at him. Try a smile next time.'

They both laughed as Tess demonstrated how to do it.

'Come on,' Magenta said, turning back to the room. 'I need to call this meeting to order or the Mighty Quinn will be here and my father will never speak to me again. So, are we good?' she asked her team. 'Does everyone like the theme for the party?'

'Can we share out the sixties samples for costumes and accessories?' one of the girls asked her.

'Of course. Just help yourselves.'

Magenta was relieved her idea had gone down so well. Everyone needed a boost. They were all on edge wondering what changes the new owner would bring, and the sixties theme allowed them to indulge their fantasies and forget about work for a while. Her team had really been infected by the sixties bug, with quite a few of them trialling the fashions of the time. The sixties styling really suited Tess, Magenta noticed now, with her smoky eyes, long, curving fringe and high ponytail, Tess looked fabulous.

'I still can't believe you're not going to be here when the new boss arrives,' Tess said, seeing she had Magenta's attention.

'I'll leave that pleasure to you. All right, go on,' Magenta said, seeing Tess was bursting to tell her something. 'You've heard some gossip about him,' she guessed. 'What is it?'

'Girls!' Tess exclaimed dramatically as she turned to face the room. 'Will you enlighten this poor innocent about our new owner, or shall I?'

No one was going to deny Tess that pleasure, Magenta suspected.

She was right. Raising a carefully drawn eyebrow, Tess explained, 'They call him the Mighty Quinn because according to the gossip mags—' and here she paused '—Gray Quinn isn't just a giant in business, if you take my meaning.'

Magenta pretended to be shocked. 'But no one knows him, no one's seen him. How do they know?'

'Oh, come on,' Tess protested. 'Don't tell me you don't like a little mystery in your life? And if he's built—'

'Tess, this is a professional environment.' But Magenta had started to laugh. 'Okay, so maybe we have to get him into some tight-fitting flares to find out.'

'There, I knew you wouldn't leave us,' Tess declared. 'You have to stay and see him now. You can't resist.'

Magenta felt a frisson of alarm. She wasn't an experienced girl-about-town like Tess. Business was her comfort zone; it would be far better if she wasn't here if Quinn was some sort of lady-killer. She felt confident behind a desk—writing, dreaming, imagining how other people might react to an advertisement, to life—but when it came to herself…

'Look at this,' Tess said, pushing a magazine across the table. 'And then tell me you're going to stay away from the office while Quinn settles in.'

'There's not much to see,' Magenta complained, though her body reacted strangely to what was little more than a shot of a man's back. What was so arousing about that? For some weird reason, her body disagreed.

Quinn was obviously in a hurry to get wherever he'd been going, Magenta registered, studying the grainy print to try and fathom out her reaction to it. And then she got a bolt of something totally inappropriate for a woman who by her own admission was hardly sexually experienced. Quinn's height, the imposing width of his shoulders, the way he held himself—everything appealed to her. Quinn was different from most men in that he was taut, powerful and exuded confidence, as if he were ready for anything. He looked like the type of man who inspired confidence in others, too.

He wouldn't even look at her, Magenta reassured herself, releasing a long, shivering breath. There were so many pretty girls in the world, quite a few of whom worked here at Steele

Design. Why would a man like Quinn look at an old maid like her?

Theirs would be a match made in hell, she convinced herself, pushing the magazine back to Tess. Imagine adding a man like that to her workload!

'What do you know about Quinn, Magenta?' one of the younger girls asked her. 'We know you did lots of research on him when you started to prepare this project to entice him to invest in Steele Design.'

'I did,' Magenta admitted. 'But I was never able to find any proper photographs. I'm surprised Tess found this.' She glanced again at the magazine. 'I gather Quinn's celebrity-averse. And no wonder, judging by the gossip you've heard about him. A man like that must prize his privacy above everything else. I do know he was orphaned at an early age, and that he dragged himself up by his bootstraps, but that's about it. Oh, and he doesn't suffer fools gladly.'

'At all,' Tess amended, shooting a warning glance around the circle of suddenly concerned faces.

'Which is why you have to be on your mettle whether I'm here or not,' Magenta stressed. Smoothing back her long, dark hair, she wound it into the casual chignon she customarily wore at the office, securing it with a silver clip. 'And don't forget that, unless Quinn sacks me, I'll be back in the New Year when we'll make our final presentation to him as a team.'

'Sacks you?' Tess pulled a face. 'I haven't read that he's crazy.'

'But he may not want a member of the *old guard* working for him, as my father calls us. Here are some documents I drew up—where we are with each campaign et cetera. Make sure he gets them, will you, Tess?'

'Of course I will…' But Tess still looked worried. 'Do you *have* to go?'

'I can't risk screwing up Dad's deal.'

'Well, at least you don't have to worry about the documents. I'll see Quinn gets them.'

'Thank you.' Magenta turned to go. But she should have known Tess hadn't finished with her yet.

'And if you change your mind about the party…'

'I only wish I could.' The end-of-year party was important, but nowhere near as important as keeping Magenta's team in work. The last thing she wanted was to alienate Quinn, or have him think she was trying to split the team's loyalty. She hoped she had made a persuasive case for keeping all her colleagues on in the documents she'd given Tess. To add a little weight to that hope, she had drafted an outline for the next campaign, centred on products she knew Quinn wanted to push and which she hoped would keep his interest in the company going forward.

'You *can't* leave us,' Tess stressed discreetly as Magenta prepared to go. 'You're the heart of the team.'

'You'll do just fine without me—and, anyway, I haven't gone yet. Let's see how it goes. Quinn isn't a fool. Just keep doing what you're doing, and he won't be able to let any of you go.'

But Magenta started fretting before she left the room. The promise to her father counted highly with her, but it went against the grain to walk out on her friends. Her father had his money now and wanted nothing more to do with the company, whereas her colleagues were all desperate to keep their jobs. Maybe Tess was right; maybe she wouldn't be able to stay away.

When Magenta got down to the car park it was full of recovery vehicles with red lights flashing and men in high-vis jackets.

Why was nothing ever straightforward? Magenta wondered, urging herself to remain calm as the mechanics explained to her that, as hers was a vintage car, they couldn't repair it now but would have to order a tyre. They were going to recover the vehicle and keep it in the garage over Christmas and she could collect it some time in the New Year. No, they couldn't be more specific than that, the mechanic in charge told her, scratching his head.

Pulling up her collar against a sudden squall of icy wind, Magenta thanked the men for turning out in such diabolical weather and insisted on giving each of them a crisp new note. Why shouldn't someone enjoy their day?

Wrapping her arms around her body to keep warm, she watched as her car was loaded onto the transporter. She was just bending down to retrieve her bag and briefcase when a familiar roar made her jump, and a familiar boot stamping down by her feet made her scowl.

'Don't tell me,' she managed as the biker lifted off his helmet. 'You didn't get me the first time around, so you've come back to finish me off with a heart attack?'

'Your heart's safe from me.'

Oh…

Was she supposed to feel quite so disappointed? Magenta's brain raced as the biker lifted one ebony eyebrow, sending a tidal wave of hot, feral lust rushing through her veins. Removing one protective leather glove, the man stretched out his hand for her to shake.

'You surely don't expect me to shake your hand after you've frightened me half to death, not once but twice?'

He grinned. 'You're not that feeble, I'm sure. But my apologies, if I frightened you.'

The mock bow made her heart thunder into action. But what exactly did he find so funny?

'Something tells me we're going to be seeing a lot of each other,' the biker said, closing one warm, strong hand around Magenta's frozen fingers.

Yeah, right. In your dreams, she thought.

CHAPTER THREE

As THE biker dismounted his machine and straightened up, Magenta felt her cheeks fire red. He was a lot taller than she had expected and had the type of shoulders that blotted out the light. She had to fight the desire to give him a comprehensive twice-over. She already knew he was an amazing-looking man and that tight black leathers were no respecters of female sensibilities. She dropped her gaze as a dangerous stare levelled on her face.

'Lost your voice?' The voice was low and amused, husky and compelling.

And leather didn't conceal or contain, it stretched and moulded shapes lovingly...

'Well? Have you?' he prompted.

No, but she had been struck by one too many thunderbolts in a single day, Magenta concluded, whipping her head up to stare the man in the eyes. He curved a smile in response that threw her totally, a smile that made his eyes crinkle attractively at the corners.

'I'm glad you think this is funny,' she said, covering her growing feeling of awkwardness with a scowl. 'I don't care who you are, what you just did was dangerous.' Now she sounded like his headmistress and felt old enough to hold the post.

That grin spread from his mouth to his eyes, making her wonder if he'd read that thought.

'You look to me like you badly need a ride.'

Where had that thought come from?

She wished she had the guts to throw him the same grin he had given her earlier. But no, this was how she was, clumsy with men, which made her grumpy and defensive. She might be heavily into studying the sixties for the ad campaign, but it would never occur to her to embrace the concept of free love. And from what she'd seen to date nothing about love was free, Magenta reflected as the biker continued to study her with amused interest.

'I thought I might come back and see if you still needed rescuing.'

'Not then and not now.'

'A man is programmed to play the white knight—it's built into the genes.'

The only thing that was built into his jeans was a warning that she was out of her depth. 'I can look after myself, thank you.'

'And so you prove this by standing out here, freezing your butt off?'

Just the mention of her butt caused her body to heat. 'I haven't been standing outside all this time. And, anyway, I'm going home now.'

'And how do you intend to do that?'

'On the underground, or in a cab.'

'You'll be lucky.'

'Meaning?'

'Delays on the line; buses bulging at the seams. And there's not a taxi to found. Not a free one, at least.'

She tried not to notice how beautiful the biker's eyes were. They were aquamarine with steely grey rims around the iris, the whites very white and his lashes completely wasted on a man. While his tongue was firmly lodged in his cheek, Magenta suspected. 'What are you?' she demanded. 'Some sort of information clerk for the city of London?

'Just observant. Have you worked up the courage to take a ride with me yet?'

Unfortunately, he was right. She could stay here and freeze or she could take her chances with public transport. But hadn't she been lectured on the dangers of taking life too seriously? Shouldn't she at least consider the biker's offer?

Absolutely not.

She turned her back, only to find herself checking the road for black ice. The mystery biker might be the most infuriating, the most arrogant, overbearing and impossible man she'd ever met, but the thought of finding him mashed up in a gutter made her heart race with fear for him. 'Take care—it's slippery,' she mumbled and, putting her head down, she marched towards the exit.

Wheeling his bike in front of her, he stopped dead.

'What are you doing?' Magenta demanded.

'I don't take no for an answer.' His eyes glinted with laughter.

'I can see that. Does everything amuse you?' she demanded, stepping round his bike.

'You make me smile.'

She kept on walking, but as she dragged her jacket a little closer it occurred to Magenta that she was perhaps being a little ungracious. 'If you're looking for someone...'

The biker's eyes glinted.

'I'm just trying to say, if I can help you in any way...'

'Get on the bike.'

No! Yes. What should she do? She had been fascinated by the beacon of freedom women lit in the sixties and talked a good battle when it came to championing the cause—but did she ever seize the moment and take action? Or did she always play it safe?

Too damn safe. 'Helmet?'

The biker produced a spare and then patted the seat behind him.

'You're very sure of yourself, aren't you?' she commented as she buckled it on.

'Sure of you. You can't resist a challenge, can you?'

'And how do you know that?'

He shrugged.

'The helmet seems like it might fit—'

'Then climb on board.'

The husky voice suggested a chastity belt might be a useful piece of kit too.

'Before I change my mind…' He revved the engine.

'Are you always so forceful?'

'Yes.'

The master of the one word answer drowned out the demented timpanist in charge of her heart by taking the revs up to danger level. And now she took a proper look at his monster machine she wasn't even sure she could climb on board, as the biker put it. Did her legs even stretch that wide?

'Chicken?' The smile was masculine and mocking.

'I am not.' She played for time. 'That's a Royal Enfield, isn't it?'

'You know motorbikes?'

Her attention flew to a very sexy mouth. 'I know the brand, thanks to my research into the sixties,' she said primly. She might have known someone as cool as the biker wouldn't ride a pimped-up, over-hyped modern machine. The Enfield was a serious motorbike for serious riders. Big and black, it was vibrating insistently between his leather-clad thighs.

And would soon be vibrating between hers.

No way was she climbing on board.

And she was getting home…how?

Call a cab, the sensible side of her brain suggested. There had to be an empty cab somewhere in the whole of London.

'You are chicken,' the biker insisted, slanting an amused glance Magenta's way.

She laughed dismissively, longing for a way out. But she'd done 'sensible' all her life, and look where that had got her.

'Well?'

'Forbidden fruit' sprang to mind when she looked at him—fruit that was so close, so ripe and so dangerously delicious, she could practically taste it on her tongue. 'How do I know I'll be safe with you?'

'You don't.'

Her pulse raced. But then, she reasoned, it was only a lift home—why the fuss? 'Shouldn't you know my address before we set off?'

'So, tell me.'

She found herself doing so even as she wondered how his strong white teeth would feel if he used them to lightly nip her skin.

'It's time to get on the bike,' he prompted. 'I've no intention of running out of fuel while I wait for you to make up your mind.'

'Could you take my briefcase and stow it for me, please?'

'My pleasure, ma'am.' He held out his hand.

'I suppose I should thank you,' she added belatedly.

'I suppose you should,' he agreed.

'If you're sure it's not out of your way?'

'I'm sure.'

This man would be equally certain about every decision he made. He'd be just as decisive when he left her standing here freezing her butt off, as he'd so elegantly put it, on the basis of her extreme cowardice.

'Would you like some help?' he said, looking on in bemusement as she started hopping into position.

All she had to do was throw one leg across his seat. How hard could that be? 'I'm fine, thank you.'

After one final heave and a lot of unladylike wriggling, she was finally in position—which meant close up to the biker. She tried to shuffle back a bit to maintain the proprieties, but the moment he kicked the stand away, released the brake and gunned the engine she launched herself at him, wrapping her arms as tightly as she could around his waist.

A waist without an ounce of fat on it, Magenta registered, but an awful lot of muscle, and if there was a way to ride pillion behind the biker without allowing her body to mould with his—thankfully, it had escaped her.

By the time they joined the heavy London traffic, she was pretty familiar with the biker's back and the way his thick hair escaped the helmet to caress the collar on his jacket. She was so familiar she had even started shivering…with cold, Magenta told herself firmly. Having consigned her safety to the hands of a man she hardly knew, that was more than enough risk to take in one day.

He really knew how to handle a bike and wove in and out of the congested streets of London like a man who really knew what he was doing, while Magenta was increasingly conscious of the insistent vibrations beneath her. It was almost a disappointment when they rolled up outside her neatly manicured town house. Dismounting the bike shakily, she removed her helmet and shook out her long, black hair.

'That's quite a transformation, lady,' the biker commented as he lifted off his helmet to stare at her.

'You think so?' Magenta laughed as she retrieved her clip as it fell to the ground. She couldn't remember feeling so carefree in a long time. Her hair had been blown to blazes, like the rest of her—and it felt great. *She* felt great. 'Thanks.'

'My pleasure.' His face creased in the now-familiar grin.

Did she imagine the curtains in nearby houses were twitching? For once she didn't care what anyone thought. So she had ridden home on the bike of a tough-looking guy, ditching the power suit and the high-heeled shoes along the way. Short of stripping naked and leaping on top of him in the middle of the street, she was committing no crime.

'Coffee?' she said, still in the throws of enthusiasm. It

seemed only polite. And when would an opportunity like this come round again?

The man's laser gaze was every bit as astonishing as she remembered; she was sure he was going to say, 'why not?' But what he actually said was, 'I should get back.'

'Of course...' What was she thinking?

Where overtures towards good-looking guys were concerned, she was somewhat out of practice, Magenta conceded. But, as this wasn't an overture—not even close—but merely a polite invitation to enjoy a hot drink before making a return journey in the cold, she had nothing to worry about, did she? 'Genuine Blue Mountain coffee.'

'You make it hard to refuse,' he admitted, slanting a smoky grey-green stare her way.

Impossible, hopefully. Having tasted danger, she wanted more. 'So?' she pressed. Pulling out the house keys, she dangled them in front of him.

'I have to get back.'

Of course he did. 'Another time,' she said brightly, swallowing down her disappointment. 'You've done more than enough for me already. Goodness knows how far you've come out of your way.'

'Not far.'

Tess would be furious with her; she didn't even know his name. But she couldn't hold him here while she cross-questioned him without inviting further humiliation. 'It's been good meeting you.'

'And you.' He grinned.

By the time she had lifted her hand to wave him off, he'd gone.

CHAPTER FOUR

WHY did her house seem so quiet and empty, when it never had before?

Because of the biker, Magenta concluded. With his larger than life personality, he didn't even need to speak to command attention; he just had to *be*.

Having changed her clothes, and kicked off her shoes with relief, she picked the mail up and headed for the kitchen. The phone stopped her dead. She picked it up.

'Magenta Steele?' The voice was crisp, deep and very masculine. 'Gray Quinn here.'

Magenta's heart rolled over. 'Gray…'

'Most people call me Quinn.' There was a hint of a smile in the voice, but not enough to reassure. 'I'm in the office tying up some loose ends. I'd like to see you for a discussion on your position going forward with the company first thing tomorrow morning.'

'But my father said—'

'Your father doesn't head up Steele Design now. I do. Nine o'clock okay with you?'

'Of course…' A chill ran through her. Quinn might be a sexy charmer, according to office gossip, but she'd just encountered the Genghis Khan side of him.

'I'll see you tomorrow, Magenta—nine o'clock sharp.'

And it wasn't a suggestion but an order, Magenta gathered as the line cut.

Coffee was needed. The temptation to go straight back to the office to gauge the effect Quinn was having on everyone else was almost impossible to resist. She was worried about her colleagues and felt uncomfortable leaving them.

Plus she had work she could do better at the office, she persuaded herself, and if she got through enough of it her team could have more time off for Christmas shopping. She would get Tess to ring her when the coast was clear.

Now the decision was made, she was all fired up. Forget taking a subtle approach where Quinn was concerned; if she waited until he was bedded in, as her father had suggested, it might be too late to save her friends' jobs. Abandoning the idea of coffee, she ran upstairs to take a shower and freshen up.

Now new doubts set in. Even if Tess rung her when Quinn left the office, there was still the possibility he might return and find her there. The thought of meeting him filled Magenta with excitement, but it also filled her with the type of self-doubt that had always plagued her where men were concerned. She would need a lot more than a freshen-up before she ran into Quinn—a full-body overhaul was called for.

Guided by the horribly honest mirrors in her bathroom, it soon became apparent that she was up against the clock in more ways than one. She would just have to make whatever repairs she could in the short time available.

Collecting up the sixties products she had been hoarding to fuel her imagination for the campaign, she rested the plastic crate on top of the linen basket and started rummaging inside. A queen-sized razor; not a bad place to start.

And what was this? *Myriad sparkles of dewy fragrance will embrace your body in a haze of desire at just the touch of a button…*

A love potion? Well, she could certainly do with some of that.

But after her shower, she decided, stepping beneath the steaming spray.

She had a whole range of retro products in the shower too. She had definitely been infected by the sixties bug. Magenta smiled wryly as she soaped down and thought about Quinn. What would he be like?

That was the only excuse her imagination needed to go crazy. There was only one thing that could make this self-indulgent shower any better, and that was sharing it with Quinn—not that she would; not in the real world. She was better off sticking to work and researching the sixties.

'Soap-on-a-rope, come here to me,' Magenta crooned, capturing the hippopotamus-shaped soap currently swinging on a cord from her shower head.

She glanced through the open door towards her bed, realising how tired she was. The temptation was to just fall into bed after her shower and dream about Quinn, put a face to that grainy back-view in the magazine... Perhaps she'd wake up to discover she had a really big share-holding in the business—power and some cards to play.

But that wasn't going to happen...

Turning her face up to the spray, Magenta knew she would have to take a more conventional route by producing some of her best work and by working her thermal socks off.

Turning the shower off, she grabbed a couple of towels and returned to the bedroom, where a spear of inspiration struck. Why not go the whole hog and dress in sixties clothes? Quite a few of her colleagues had already adopted the fashions and the look, so why not join them?

They always banded together at this time of year and had such fun—decorating the office, sneaking out for warm, full-fat mince pies with thick globs of cream on top—and this year the sixties vibe was adding a special frisson to the holiday celebrations.

She was drying her hair absent-mindedly with a towel as

she started flicking through her wardrobe. Like everyone else in the creative team, she had been scouring the vintage shops for examples of sixties clothing, and had struck gold with a form-fitting cream wool dress. Sliding it off the hanger, she laid it on the bed.

Suppliers had rushed to offer samples of their retro products when Magenta had let it be known that she would be running a high-profile campaign, so she had plenty of accessories to choose from. Fortunately, it hadn't been all mini-skirts and hot-pants in the sixties. There had been the hippies in their flowing, get-em-off-quick clothes, the shock-frock dolly-birds in mini-skirts, as well as a more elegant side to the era. This was where Magenta felt comfortable—though it was the underwear she was supposed to wear beneath these stylish clothes that made her laugh. *Break out of your little-girl body when you're feeling in a big-girl mood*, ran the legend on one pack of matching bra and girdle.

Well, she wasn't a little girl, but she was definitely in a big-girl mood, Magenta decided, conjuring up a vision of Quinn as she broke the seal on the packaging.

It was almost impossible not to think about the new owner of the business, Magenta realised, opening the towel she had wrapped around her body to give her twenty-eight-year-old figure a critical review. She was sitting on the bed facing the dressing-table mirror and she sat up straight immediately. Would he like real women with real bellies, or would his tastes run to something younger and slimmer? Not that she could do much about it in the short time at her disposal. And why worry when her naked body was in zero danger of becoming an issue between them?

She picked up another pack and studied it. *What do you wear under your action-wear? Action Underwear, of course…*

But there wasn't going to be any action.

She put it down, picking up something called the *Concentrate* girdle.

Concentrate on what? Holding her stomach in the whole time?

I don't think so.

And she certainly didn't need the *Little Fibber* bra—one of the only benefits of getting a little older and a little rounder, Magenta thought dryly, tossing the formidable-looking steel-girder-style bra to one side. Strange to think the so-called liberated women of the twenty-first century made so little of her breasts. Breasts were never flaunted at the office in case you were thought of as brainless, as if having lactating glands in common with a cow meant you automatically shared the same IQ. Perhaps that was the reason she had never worn form-fitting clothes to the office before, though she doubted a man as focused on business as Quinn appeared to be would even notice.

She hunted for some sheer tights in her drawer, only to discard them in favour of stockings. Underpinnings were everything, an actress friend had told her—those and shoes. If you didn't get that right, you stood no chance of playing a period piece convincingly.

She picked up another box and quickly disposed of it with an unwelcome shiver of arousal. *Damsel in Undress* was a definite no-no. The slightest hint to a man like Quinn that she was adopting a compliant 'men rule' mindset to go along with her sixties outfit, and she'd be in big trouble. He'd already given her a flavour of his management style. Gray Quinn definitely didn't need any encouragement. He was shaping up to be the original alpha-male. No, this was one occasion when she would be sixties on the outside and bang up to date in her head. But she would consent to wear a provocative cone-shaped bra to achieve the authentic hourglass shape—not forgetting control pants for the belly problem.

And a suspender-belt and stockings were fun…

Having dressed, she slipped on her stiletto heels and immediately felt different. She walked differently too. She tried a few steps up and down the bedroom and found herself sashaying like a famous actress in a hot sixties television programme. She smiled, thinking her actress friend had been right. The shoes and the clothes were like a costume that put her right back in the era, and that was fun.

It was even more fun when she started on the make-up—pale foundation and big, smoky eyes outlined so that they appeared even larger. And some *Un-lipstick*, as it was called, in Shiver Shiver pink.

She certainly shivered as she tasted it. What would Quinn make of that?

Not that he would ever get a chance to find out, Magenta told herself firmly. This was all about dressing up and fantasy. Pressing her lips together, she blotted them in the manner prescribed on the pack and then applied a second coat.

Not bad.

She was ready.

Ready for pretty much anything, Magenta decided as she checked her appearance one last time in the mirror.

She waited for Tess's call and when it came she travelled to the office by taxi to find all the lights were out. Just as Tess had promised, there was no sign of Quinn—exactly what she wanted. Well, it would be, once she had stifled her disappointment. All that effort put into grooming for nothing.

At least she could concentrate on work, Magenta told herself firmly. This was a great opportunity to put the finishing touches to the campaign. Having set out her papers on the large desk in her office, she slipped the lock on the door, feeling safer that way in an empty building. She'd make some coffee later to keep herself awake.

She was halfway through drafting a strap line for a sixties hairpiece when she had to stop. She could hardly keep her eyes open and just couldn't get it right: *the hair fashion that goes on when you go out...*

And drops off when you least expect it to?

Magenta examined the yard-long ponytail made out of synthetic hair and tossed it aside. Some of the products being used to inject fun into the campaign were odd, but this was downright ugly. Surely no self-respecting woman would want to wear a hair-tugger on top of her head that weighed a ton, looked gross and at a guess took a whole card of hair grips to hold in place? If you weren't bald when you started your evening out, you certainly would be by the end of it.

And yet it was a genuine sixties product, Magenta mused, leaning her cheek against her folded arms as she stared at the unappealing hairpiece and waiting for inspiration to strike. She'd been so enthusiastic up to now, seeing only the good, the fun and the innovation of the sixties. But, realistically, how many other things about that time would have got right up her nose?

'Magenta...Magenta! Wake up!'

'What's wrong?' Magenta started with alarm as someone grabbed hold of her arm and shook her awake. Well dressed in sixties style, the girl looked smart and bright—and totally unfamiliar. Magenta felt like she had the hangover from hell—and, not having had a drop to drink, that was a serious concern. 'How long have I been asleep?' Her neck suddenly didn't seem strong enough to lift her ridiculously heavy head from the desk.

'Magenta, you have to get out of here now.'

'Why? Is there a fire?'

'Worse—Quinn,' the girl explained with what sounded like panic in her voice. 'He mustn't find you here.'

'Why not?' Magenta stared in bewilderment around her office, which seemed to have been cleared of all her creature comforts while she'd been asleep. But it wasn't just the flowers, the coffee machine, the bottles of water or the family photographs that were missing. 'Hey, where's my laptop?' she said, shooting up. 'Has there been a robbery?'

'Magenta, I don't know what you're talking about, but I do know you have to get out of here now.'

'All right, all right!' Magenta exclaimed as the girl took her by the arm and physically dragged her towards the door. 'I'm sure I locked this door last night.'

'I used my key.' The girl shook a spare set in her face.

'What's the rush? I'll need my mobile phone, and where's my tote, my handbag, my briefcase?' Magenta demanded, glancing back at the vastly changed room.

'No more questions,' her new friend hissed frantically, tugging at Magenta's arm. 'We don't have time. Quinn will be here any minute.'

A multitude of thoughts and impressions were slowly percolating through Magenta's sluggish brain. This was a new girl, possibly someone Quinn had brought in. She seemed nice, though, confusingly, she seemed to know Magenta when Magenta was certain they had never met before. 'Did Quinn get my list?' she said, clinging on to priorities while her brain sorted itself out.

'What list? You didn't give me a list.'

'No, that's right—I gave it to Tess.'

'Tess?'

This girl didn't know Tess? 'Sorry, uh…'

'Nancy,' the girl supplied, looking at her with real concern. 'Magenta, are you sure you're okay?'

'Yes, I'm fine.' This was growing stranger by the minute; if she hadn't felt so heavy-headed she would have been faster off the mark. 'I gave a list of the list of things Quinn should implement immediately to one of the girls in the office.'

Nancy huffed. 'If you had given me a list like that, I would have seriously lost it on purpose.'

'Has Quinn been bullying you?' She forgot her own confusion; bullying in the office was one thing she wouldn't stand, and Magenta's concerns soared when Nancy refused to answer almost as if she was frightened of being overheard. 'Well, no one's going to bully you while I'm around—especially not Quinn.'

Nancy hummed and started tugging on Magenta's arm again. 'I'm not joking, Magenta, we have to get out of here.'

'But where do you want me to go?' This had been Magenta's office since—well, she could hardly remember; it had been hers for so long now.

'You work in the typing pool, remember?' Nancy told her urgently, poking her head out of the door to check the coast was clear.

'The typing pool?' Magenta laughed. 'Is this some joke of Quinn's to get us all in the right mood for the sixties campaign?'

Nancy gave her a funny look.

'To be more accurate, you *used to* work in the typing pool,' she finally replied, nudging Magenta towards the door. 'The guy who ran the place before hotshot Quinn arrived from the States took his office manager with him, so Quinn promoted you.'

'Why didn't Quinn text me? And what's this?' Magenta demanded as Nancy bundled her towards a mean little desk set to one side of her office door—a door she now noticed with outrage that already bore the legend, 'Gray Quinn'.

'This is your desk now, Magenta,' Nancy explained. 'It's a great improvement to the typing pool, don't you think?'

'Do you want to hear what I think? No. I didn't think so,' Magenta agreed as Nancy shook her head. 'I don't know what's happening around here, but this isn't my desk—and Quinn definitely can't take over my office.'

'But, Magenta, you used to work in the typing pool—you've never *had* your own office,' Nancy insisted, looking increas-

ingly concerned about Magenta's state of mind. 'Don't you
remember anything?'

Magenta swept a hand across her eyes as if hoping everything would change back again by the time she opened them
again. But, to make things worse, people she didn't even know
were staring at her as if she was the one who was mad.

But how could this have happened? She gazed around and
felt her anger rising. Quinn had to be some sort of monumen-
tal chauvinist; men occupied all the private offices while the
women had been relegated to old-fashioned typewriters—
either in the typing pool, where they sat in rows behind a
partition as if they were at school, or at similar desks to this
one outside the office doors. Ready to do their master's bid-
ding, Magenta presumed angrily. She remembered her father
telling her how it used to be for the majority of female office
workers in the sixties. 'Why are all the girls typing?' she
asked Nancy in a heated whisper.

'It's their job!' Nancy said, frowning.

'But why aren't they working on the campaign?' Magenta
noticed now that many of the women, some of whose faces
were adorned with heavy-framed, upswept spectacles, were
pretending not to look at her.

'What campaign?' Nancy queried, stepping back as a keen
teen brushed passed her.

'Wow, Magenta, you look really choice!'

'I do?' Magenta spun on her heels as the young man she
had never seen before gave her a rather too comprehensive
once-over. 'Why, thank you…?'

'Jackson,' Nancy supplied, having cottoned on to the fact
that Magenta needed all the help she could get.

'Jackson.' Magenta raised a brow. 'Stop staring at your
Auntie Magenta and go find yourself a girlfriend.'

Jackson laughed as if Magenta could always be relied upon
to say something funny. 'You're a gas, baby.'

Had Quinn changed all the personnel? Of course, he was

perfectly entitled to, Magenta reasoned. Quinn ran the show now. But what had happened to her friends? And what had happened to their working environment?

So many questions stacked up in her mind, with not a single answer to one of them that made sense.

CHAPTER FIVE

'Look, Magenta, I don't want to rush you,' Nancy said in a way that clearly said that was exactly what she wanted to do. 'But Quinn's only slipped out for an eleven o'clock appointment.'

'So what?' Magenta said impatiently. 'He's got a damn nerve.' She was still looking round, trying to take everything in. She could understand Quinn wanting to live the sixties in order to give the campaign that final fizz of authenticity—hadn't she done the same thing herself? But didn't he know there was such a thing as going too far? 'Nancy, what's been going on here?'

'The usual?' Following her glance, Nancy gazed around the office.

'The usual,' Magenta repeated grimly. 'Is it usual to remove the computers?'

'The what?'

'Okay, so Quinn's got you playing his game,' Magenta said. 'I can understand that you don't want to lose your job—I'm just thinking of all the expense involved in putting this right again—' She had already reasoned that the reorganisation of the office would have been fairly easy if Quinn had copied the layout from the old photographs on the wall, but there were other things she couldn't account for. There was a different feel to the place, never mind the look, which was dated, a little drab and definitely not the right environment to encourage cutting-edge design work. She thought it boring, not to mention inhospitable. There were different phones too, but it was the ergonomically unhelpful furniture that really concerned her—and single glazing? Had Quinn gone mad? Never mind the expense, what about condensation? Cold? If people were uncomfortable at work, productivity would suffer. Didn't Quinn know anything?

And there was a different smell too…

Cigarette smoke?

'Nancy!' Magenta exclaimed with increased urgency.

'Are you all right, Magenta?' Glancing round, Nancy grabbed a chair and tried to press Magenta into it.

'I'm fine.' She was anything but fine. What had happened here? Had Quinn got people in to dress the offices like a sixties stage-set? And how was it possible she had slept through those changes? But it wasn't just the noise element that concerned her; these changes were too thorough, too perfect, too convincing…

Magenta's throat dried. This wasn't some office team-building exercise. This was reality. This was reality for Nancy and for all the people here. It was Magenta who was out of sync. She must have fallen down the rabbit hole, like Alice, while she'd been asleep and landed in the sixties. And now the shock of being trapped inside a dream was only exceeded by her dread of meeting Quinn. From what she'd gathered, he was just the sort of man who would slot right into the sixties, where men ruled. Quinn obviously thought they did.

Magenta took a few steadying breaths while Nancy looked on anxiously. Magenta's heart was pounding uncontrollably, but whatever had happened she would have to manage it.

She looked as much a part of the sixties as everyone else in the office, Magenta reassured herself, with her carefully made-up face, perfect hair and vintage cream wool dress. Though you could have bounced bullets off her underwear, it did outline her shape to the point where her breasts were outrageously prominent. That, believe it or not, was the fashion. It could best be described as 'sex in your face'. No wonder Jackson had commented; she should have known better than to dress like this, but had done so innocently. Back in the real world, it had made her feel sexy—and after the encounter with the biker she had wanted to prove to herself that she still could feel that way. Now she realised drawing attention to herself in a sixties office was asking for trouble.

But, on the plus side, she had been researching the era for quite some time, so even locked into this bizarre dream she wasn't entirely out on a limb. She could even accept and be a little reassured by the fact that the dream seemed to be influenced by her research; there was certainly plenty of raw material here. Although quite how the summer of love, the sexual revolution and the Whisky a Go Go, the first disco in America—which just happened to be Quinn's homeland— would manifest themselves remained to be seen.

She would have to rely on what she knew if she was going to anticipate and avoid some of the problems, Magenta concluded. She would draw on that knowledge now—and her first action would be to open all the windows and let the smoke out.

Predictably everyone complained that it was too cold. 'Well, you can't smoke in here,' Magenta insisted. 'It's against the law.'

'Since when?' one of the younger guys asked, swinging his arm around her waist to drag her close so she had no alternative but to inhale his foul-smelling breath.

'And that is too,' she informed him, removing his searching hand from her tightly sculpted rear end.

'Ooh.' He turned to his friends to pull a mocking face. 'What got into your bed this morning, Miss Steele?'

'No one?' another man suggested, to raucous jeers.

'We all know what's wrong with you, ice maiden.'

'Cut it out!' Magenta said angrily. 'I'm not in the mood.'

'Apparently, you never are,' one of the men murmured to his colleagues in a stage whisper.

As if that were the cue for the main player to enter the scene, the double doors at the far end of the office swung open and every head swivelled in that direction. Some of the women even stood at their desks as if royalty was about to enter the room. To say Magenta was stunned by this reaction wouldn't even come close. 'What the...?'

'Quinn,' Nancy told her tensely, hurrying away.

Magenta turned to say something to Nancy, but everyone including Nancy had returned to work the second Quinn arrived. And Quinn didn't just arrive—he strode across the floor like a conquering hero. To make matters worse, all the women were giving him simpering glances when what he needed, in Magenta's opinion, was a short, sharp, shock and someone to stand up to him. Whatever dream state they were both trapped in, this was getting out of hand.

But could this *really* be Quinn? Magenta's head was reeling. Quinn in the sixties was none other than the gorgeous biker, in a jauntily angled Trilby hat and a dark overcoat that, instead of making him look silly, only succeeded in making him look like the master of the sexual universe.

'Magenta,' he said curtly, shrugging the coat off his shoulder and handing it to her along with his hat.

He knew her?

'That's a better look for you,' he said, giving Magenta the most intrusive inspection yet. 'I like to see a woman in a dress with some shape to it.'

What?

'Keep it up,' he said approvingly. 'And remember, I expect the same high standards from my staff at all times—'

'Yes, sir,' she said smartly, playing along, which was all she could do—other than acknowledge Quinn was a beyond the pale chauvinist—as well as the best-looking man she had ever seen in her life. With his tough-guy body clothed in a sharply tailored dark suit and impeccably knotted tie, he looked amazing.

'I'll need you for a meeting later,' he said, as though they had been working together for ever. There was not a shred of equality between them, Magenta registered with a spear of concern.

'So no gossiping with the other girls in the kitchen when you're supposed to be making my coffee,' Quinn warned.

Would that be the coffee with the extra-strong laxative in it? Magenta wondered.

'And absolutely no lunch break for any of you girls. You'll have a lot of work to get through by the time I finish the meeting I'm going into now—understood?'

Actually, no, I'm a bit confused. Magenta thought Quinn had called a meeting to discuss her position with the company going forward, but perhaps that directive hadn't made it through to the sixties. She decided to prompt him, if only to find out how much had travelled with her in the dream. 'So, you're having another meeting first?'

'What are you talking about?' Quinn demanded impatiently.

'Another meeting before *our* meeting…?'

Quinn had no worries about touching Magenta. Taking hold of her shoulder in a firm grip, he steered her into an alcove out of sight of the rest of the office. 'Not in front of everyone, Magenta…' And then his eyes warmed in a way that made her heart stop. 'Later, maybe—if I have the time.'

Magenta's mouth formed a question, but she was so stunned by Quinn's brazenly sexual behaviour her voice refused to function, and when she did speak it was only to ask Quinn what he wanted her to do with his hat and coat.

'Why, hang it up, of course,' he said as if she were one card short of a pack. 'And when you've done that I'll need plenty of coffee—hot, strong and black. Oh, and when you come into the meeting later, don't forget your shorthand notebook.'

'My—?'

'You're the office manager now, Magenta—that's quite a promotion for you. You'll have to sharpen up if you want to set the seal on this position.'

She'd set something in concrete—the deeds of the building, perhaps, before she dropped them from a great height on Quinn's head…

But someone else owned the building now, she remembered, biting her lip. Steele Design had been called Style Design when her father had bought it. She had no stake at all here.

Now she found herself staring at the back of her own office door as Quinn closed it in her face.

Then it flew open again. 'Magenta?' Quinn rapped. 'My office. Now.'

You could have heard a pin drop behind her. They all anticipated her immediate dismissal, Magenta guessed. She countered that expectation with her sweetest smile. 'Of course,' she replied respectfully; respectful was good—essential—at least until she learned the ropes. Walking inside, she shut the door behind her.

'Let's get one thing clear,' Quinn said, handing Magenta the hairpiece she had left on his desk. 'You do not use my office in my absence for grooming purposes. You do not come in here at all, unless at my express invitation. And, if I'm at work early, you are too.'

'And how would I—?'

'How would you know?' he interrupted, narrowing his eyes. 'I was coming to that. Do you have your notebook? No? Carry it with you at all times? You have a "must do" list, don't you? When I give you a memo to alert you to the fact that I will be in here at six in the morning, I expect you to note it down. Why are you late, by the way?'

Magenta opened her mouth and wondered which of the million and one reasons on the tip of her tongue would work best in Wonderland. 'I apologise,' she said, thinking better of making a fight out of it just yet. 'I just thought you might appreciate a couple of days to become acclimatized.'

'Acclimatised? I've come over from the States, not the moon. What's wrong with you limies?'

Limies? *Whoah*; that was an old term Magenta guessed hadn't been used much since the war. The term was a hangover from the way-back-when days, when British sailors were given limes to counteract scurvy. Surely they were way past that?

'I need you here on time, Magenta,' Quinn continued to rap. 'You're my assistant as well as the office manager. If the job's too much for you, just let me know.'

'It isn't—I mean, yes, sir,' Magenta spat out crisply, stopping just shy of a salute.

This was novel. This was annoying and confusing. And, alarmingly, it was pretty amazing too. Quinn was pretty amazing, with all that dark hair escaping his best attempt to tame it from falling over his brow. And those eyes, steely and fierce—not to mention the *body* currently concealed beneath some pretty sharply tailored clothes. Here at last was a man who was really worth taking on. Had she met her match at last? Forget all that nonsense about not wanting to add him to her workload; she would gladly put Quinn on her 'must do' list.

'Please accept my apologies.' She wanted to keep the job, such as it was, didn't she? 'I forgot you intended making such an early start. And I'll be sure to remember my, er, "must do" list in future.'

'Be sure you do. Just remember, this might be your first day on the job, but it gets you no special favours from me. I expect you up to speed by the end of the day. And any thoughts you might have had about taking time off before the holidays, cancel them.'

She had to swallow her pride. She'd been doing a lot of that recently, but it would only be until she found her feet down this complicated rabbit-hole—or, better still, until she woke up. 'I'll get the coffee, shall I?'

'Yes, you do that,' Quinn agreed. 'And take that dead rat with you.'

'Of course.' She was only too happy to drop the horrible hairpiece in the first bin she found.

The men filed in and sat around the boardroom table as Magenta set the coffee down in front of Quinn. Her team, nearly all female, could have run rings around them, she concluded five minutes into the meeting. What were the women doing sitting outside typing? Surely some of them had flair?

She glanced at Quinn as he rubbed a hand across his eyes, as if he had forgotten something. Was it too much to hope he had intended to include some of the women in the meeting?

'I should have asked for coffee for everyone,' he apologised—to the men. 'Magenta?' he added brusquely, shooting an impatient glance her way.

She wasn't going to snap back in front of the men, she decided. Quinn might have lost all sense of business protocol by speaking to her so rudely, but she hadn't. 'No problem at all,' she said pleasantly, sweeping out of the room, surprised by the openly admiring glances she was attracting. She would gladly exchange those looks for a return to the casual acceptance of her gender she was used to. The men's gazes burning a hole into her back made her really uncomfortable, though she was pleasantly surprised when one late arrival rushed to hold the door for her. Were her sensibilities changing too?

No. She bridled outside the room, hearing some very male laughter erupting behind the door. Quinn barked a command and there was silence, but Magenta got the distinct impression that the laughter had been directed at her.

She made the coffee and took it into the men, but held back from serving it. If they wanted a coffee, then one of them would have to pour it. She left the room and returned with her notebook as instructed. She didn't know shorthand, but she could write fast.

And she had to. Quinn wasn't short of ideas, most of which she agreed with, but it would have been nice if he consulted his team along the way, rather than issuing instructions. He ignored her completely. She might have been invisible. 'Can I ask a question?' she said at one point.

'If you want to leave the room, you don't have to be coy,' he said while the men sniggered and Magenta's cheeks flamed red.

'I don't want to leave the room,' she said, conscious of the other men looking on with interest as the little drama unfolded.

'Then please be quiet,' Quinn rapped impatiently. 'Can't you see we're having an important meeting here?'

And clearly it was a meeting she wasn't up to taking part in, according to Quinn, who seemed stuck in a chauvinist mindset.

What to do? She could argue her point, but it would only be counterproductive in this company. She wanted Quinn to listen to her and to take her seriously. She would have to play this subtly for the sake of the team she had already decided she must build—at least until she got the hang of the workings of this strange new world.

But as she sat through the meeting, Magenta's anger grew. As she'd thought, many of the men weren't up to much, while she was increasingly certain that the women currently wasting their talents typing up dictation were being held back. Everything was upside down. She sighed, frustration beating at her brain. She was impotent to do anything about it until she'd worked things out.

'Magenta?'

She jumped with surprise as Quinn rapped out her name.

'If you find it so hard to pay attention, I can always get someone to replace you—'

Quinn wasn't joking. She was in imminent danger of losing her job. And this might be a crazy dream-world, but right now it was all she had got.

CHAPTER SIX

WHEN the meeting ended, Quinn asked Magenta to remain behind, and her heart sank as the last man out of the room threw her a pitying look. But even if this was a dream she had to defend her corner. Was Quinn content with a weak team? Wouldn't he at least evaluate the skills of his female workforce and give them a chance? The more she thought about it, the more fired up she became. 'This is quite an experiment you've got going on,' she commented lightly as she shut the door.

'An experiment? This is no experiment, Magenta. This is my company, and you work by my rules or you walk out that door and you don't come back.'

'You can't just fire me.'

'Watch me.'

Was she *au fait* with sixties employment law? No. And what good would she be to the girls she hoped to recruit if Quinn threw her out?

'For someone so recently promoted, you have a disappointing attitude, Magenta—which is why I want to speak to you.'

'I'm just surprised by the quality of the team you've drawn around you.'

'Firstly, it's not in your remit to pass comment on my decisions. And secondly, that's not my team. That's a batch of individuals I am evaluating.'

Like battery hens. 'Ruthless' didn't even begin to describe Quinn. She was almost sorry for the men.

'I'm evaluating everyone's performance—and I have to tell you that you are my biggest disappointment to date. Instead of being thrilled by your promotion, you seem discontented.'

'That's not the case at all.' Above all she had to hold on to her job. How else would she fight for recognition, not just for herself but for her colleagues? 'I'm overwhelmed by my new role, and your trust in me.' She held back from batting her eyelashes. 'You won't have to wait until close of play today. I'm up to speed now and I promise I won't let you down again.'

Suspicion flared in Quinn's incredible eyes, which she quickly took care of. 'I hope the notes I've taken down are what you require?' She offered them for his approval.

He ignored them. 'I'll let you know when you've typed them up. And one more thing, Magenta.'

'Yes?'

'Your duties include running the office and managing the cleaners, the girls in the typing pool and those on the switchboard. They do not include interfering in my business meetings. Is that clear?'

'Even if I have an idea I'd like to put forward?'

Quinn's expression would have sent grown men scurrying for cover, but Magenta pressed on. 'There are a couple of things I'd like to suggest for the good of the company—and I only mention them as your office manager and secretary to save you unnecessary aggravation in the future.'

'Spit it out.'

'Take smoking.' Quinn was an overwhelming presence in the room—a fact her body refused to ignore however she felt about it. Determinedly, she pressed on. 'Nancy mentioned you have people working here who suffer from asthma, heart conditions.'

'And you think I should get rid of them?'

'No!' Magenta exclaimed, wondering how two people could be so far apart in their thinking. 'I want you to ban smoking in the office.'

Quinn laughed as if she had said the funniest thing that year. 'Tell you what,' he said. 'I'll let you handle that.'

'Okay, I will. It's either that or I'll have to open all the windows wide—and I don't think you would want the girls' work-rate to drop if their fingers seized up with cold. Didn't you say there would be a lot of work coming down the line for them?'

Quinn's face creased in a deceptively attractive smile, but his eyes were dangerous. 'Nicely done, Magenta, though I must admit I prefer my secretaries decorative rather than combative.'

A shiver of worry crept down Magenta's spine when Quinn added brusquely, 'Are we finished here?'

'Yes. Yes, of course we are.'

'You're sure I've heard all your complaints?'

So now he had her down as a moaner. *Great.* 'I'll get started on those notes for you, shall I?' she said brightly.

'You do that,' Quinn said, turning back to his work. 'Oh, and don't forget to take the coffee tray with you when you go.' He didn't even bother to look up from the document he was studying.

'I hope this is satisfactory?' Magenta asked Quinn later that day, handing him the typewritten notes she had prepared. It was a long time since she had typed anything without the option of making corrections on a computer.

'Don't deviate from this standard.' He handed the document back again.

Could she survive this level of praise? She had only spent most of her lunch hour mastering the art of using a cranky typewriter with a ribbon that came off and keys that stuck. From what she'd seen, all the office hardware needed a thorough overhaul. This might be the sixties, but surely they didn't have to use faulty equipment? She put her concerns to Quinn.

'You've just put yourself in charge of repairs and renovations. I hope you can handle that on top of your other new duties?'

She would have to. But she was so eager to get stuck in, she was taking on more and more, when what she really wanted to do was form a team. To call together and convince those girls in the typing pool that they could do a lot more than type up lists and letters for the men.

'Dinner tonight?'

She stared at Quinn. 'Would you like me to book a dinner reservation for you?'

'I'm prepared to make a few allowances until you get up to speed, Magenta, but if you don't start paying attention when I speak to you my patience will very quickly run out.'

Quinn's *patience*? Had she missed something?

'I believe I just asked you if you would care to join me for dinner tonight.'

Her heart raced. Her mind said no. But how could she refuse him without causing offence?

How could she accept Quinn's invitation to dinner without compromising her position? Since falling down this rabbit hole he had shown her no warmth at all—though he had shown the occasional flicker of another type of interest; if her heart would stop hammering long enough for her to say anything remotely intelligent, she must find a way to refuse him. 'I'd love to have dinner with you, but unfortunately I have so much work to do…'

'You have to eat.'

His charm offensive was overwhelming. 'I'll probably have a sandwich here. I'm conscious of the tight deadline you're working to as far as launching the ad campaign in the New

Year is concerned, and I'm also working on some ideas of my own.'

'You're doing what?'

'Trying a new angle.' Her voice was starting to shake. Quinn's expression wasn't exactly encouraging. He couldn't imagine a lowly woman coming up with a single original idea. She owed it to the team she was now determined to build to prove him wrong.

'I take it these ideas you mention have nothing to do with the work you do for me?' His tone was critical.

They had everything to do with the creative work she wanted to do for him. 'Correct, but—'

'If the work you do for me suffers…'

'It won't suffer.'

Standing up, Quinn propped one hip against the desk, managing to look both formidable and desirable at the same time. 'It had better not,' he said.

Half-man, half-beast—all male… The shout line on a sixties massage-cologne rushed into Magenta's mind. The thought of massaging it into Quinn was quickly stifled. She held her breath as he stared at her thoughtfully.

'Let me see those ideas when you're ready.'

Did she have to feel so gratified at his grudging concession?

'And don't tire yourself out working on personal projects to the point where you're no good to me.'

'I'm only too happy to stay behind and work.'

'You should have asked the girls to help you.'

The girls had enough to contend with from the men during normal working hours without Magenta asking them to stay behind and do more work for her. 'I'm fine—honestly. You go.'

'*May* I?' Quinn demanded ironically. 'That's very good of you.'

'I'm sorry—I didn't mean—'

'Goodnight, Miss Steele. Remember to lock the door behind you when you leave.'

Watching Quinn stride towards the exit made her wish that just for once she could be a *femme fatale* that no man could walk out on.

Dream on, Magenta thought wryly, turning back to her work.

She was stiff from sitting at her mean little work-station for hours on end, working on the final tweaks to the campaign, when the sound of the lift arriving made her tense with alarm. She felt exposed and vulnerable without an office door to lock and sat bolt-upright as the lift doors slid open.

It was almost a relief to see Quinn emerge, but what was he doing here?

Her heart thundered with anticipation. 'Have you forgotten something?' She hurried to greet him. However much Quinn infuriated her, there was no doubt he injected life and vitality as well as a sense of security into the empty, silent office—though she still felt uncomfortably like a soldier on parade.

'Miss Steele.' Quinn's eyes were sparkling in a very un-Quinn-like way—which was to say his expression was both warm and amused, leaving her a very confused and shaken-up soldier. 'Can I get you something?' she pressed.

'Coffee?' Quinn suggested.

'No problem.' She could smell the night air on him, cold, clean and fresh. There was snow on his collar, and ice crystals sparkling like diamonds on his thick, black hair. It was a change to see Quinn looking so windswept, a good change that took her back in time—or was that forwards?—to a young biker removing his helmet and shaking out his unruly mop of inky hair.

'You didn't expect me to come back tonight,' Quinn guessed correctly. Shrugging off his overcoat, he tossed it over the back of a chair and walked with her to the kitchen. 'I saw the lights from the street and took pity on you.'

'How kind,' she murmured. 'Strong and hot?' she said, pushing the kitchen door open.

Quinn's laugh was low and sexy. 'If you say so.'

Were they flirting? 'I'm talking about coffee.'

'And so am I,' he assured her. 'Put a dash of this in it.' He produced a bottle of very good whisky. 'You looked worn out earlier, so I thought I should bring you something to get your blood flowing again. Something told me you might baulk if I offered you fortified wine.'

'Whisky is my drink of choice, as it happens. You know me well.'

'I don't know you at all, Miss Steele, but that is something I intend to put right.'

It was a tiny moment of connection between them, and she wanted to protect and nurture it like a candle flame.

Quinn was way ahead of her.

'Apologies in advance for contravening one of your feminist by-laws.'

She gasped as his lips brushed hers. In the same instant, he pressed her back against the kitchen counter and, with one powerful thigh nudging her legs apart, he drew her close. 'Forget the coffee,' he murmured, teasing and nuzzling her neck and mouth in a way that delivered a powerful charge to every sex-starved part of her. 'You need this more.'

Oh yes, she did, Magenta realised as she wound her arms around Quinn's neck. What her sensible side would have to say about it when she woke up in the morning was another matter. But she was dreaming and, according to the law of dreams, anything was possible, even forgetting her inhibitions where sex was concerned. She would just have to put up with Quinn kissing her like a god.

Quinn's hair was thick and lush, his body was hard and strong, and she was instantly aroused. Quinn's heat was iced with night air and the taste of mint was on her tongue. He had splashed on some cologne—musky, spicy, warm and clean—and his stubble was an unaccustomed rasp against her face. He was an expert in the art of seduction who knew just how to tease, stroke and nip, until she was pressing herself against him, writhing, sucking, biting, practically demanding the invasion of his tongue as she showed him in no uncertain terms that she had fully embraced the concept of free love—at least in her dreams.

But somewhere deep inside her a warning bell was ringing, and that bell was determined to spoil everything. It said that she might be on a fast track to pleasure, losing all sense of right and wrong, but Quinn was still firmly in control. She was strong in everything else she did, except this. Free love was one thing but it had to be on her terms. She'd put a price tag on it, Magenta decided, and that price tag might just buy a chance for the team she planned to build.

Using every bit of mental strength she possessed, she pulled back. 'I'll make that coffee for you.' Turning away, she continued to prepare their drinks with hands that shook slightly. 'Do you think you could spare the time to look at the ideas I'm putting together?'

'Would I like to see what you've been doing when I'm paying you to work for me? I think I should, don't you?' Propping his hip against the counter, Quinn waited until she had finished and then he led the way back into the office, where he swung her ideas book around. 'This is good. What gave you the inspiration?'

'Research.' She could hardly say, the benefit of living fifty years from now. 'I'm keen to push the campaign to the next level.' She had never cheated in her life before, never needed to.

'Your idea certainly moves things somewhere,' Quinn agreed dryly. 'Do I take it you weren't impressed with the team you saw in action earlier today?'

'You could say that,' Magenta admitted as Quinn stared at her keenly.

'Maybe they just need time to settle in.'

'There is no time to settle in if you want to launch in the New Year.'

'So you're suggesting I accept a campaign designed by a woman?'

'Is that so crazy?'

'You've forgotten the natural order of things, Magenta. Men lead at work so that women can enjoy a certain lifestyle.'

'Women can do that for themselves, given half a chance.'

'And I don't let them—is that what you're saying?'

'Maybe men feel threatened—'

'Not this man.' Quinn cut across her.

She took her courage in both hands and went for it. 'Then prove it by allowing women to play a part in your campaign.'

His lips curved; he took it well. 'How do I know that there's anyone working for me, other than you, that has this flair?'

'You'll never know until you give everyone an equal chance to prove themselves.'

'If there's so much latent talent here, why has no one put themselves forward before now?'

'Because women want to keep their jobs, so they keep their mouths shut. Is there any reason good enough to make you ignore a possible seam of in-house talent? I think we must consider our female audience when we design a campaign.'

'What do women want?' Quinn didn't even pretend to think about it. 'Who cares when men pay the bills? This is business, Magenta, not some feel-good society for you to float around in. Men earn the money women spend—remember that. So men are our target audience.'

She hated herself for trembling with awareness of Quinn when he was preaching this heresy. But Quinn was a product of his time, Magenta remembered, which made what she had to do while she was a visitor in this dream world all the more important. 'But you've just admitted women do the shopping, so they have control of the finances.'

'Nonsense. Are you the most argumentative woman I've ever met?' he demanded. 'Who tells a woman what to buy, Magenta? Her man.'

'Not this woman.'

Quinn looked at her and almost laughed. He controlled it well, but at least he'd lightened up. That was a small victory of sorts, Magenta supposed, wondering if her heart would reach some critical point where it would have to slow down.

'All I'm asking you to do is to tune in to your audience, Magenta, but sometimes, I think your head's elsewhere—like another century, maybe.'

Close. But she couldn't stop now. 'If you go on with this belief that we only have to sell to one sector of the community, then this company will sink like a stone, taking your investment with it.'

There was silence, and then to Magenta's relief Quinn's face relaxed as another idea occurred to him. 'Why don't you illuminate me on the correct way to reach every member of our target audience?' Challenge turned his steely gaze to fire.

CHAPTER SEVEN

'I'D BE pleased to explain,' Magenta said, facing up to Quinn. She had to look up at him; he towered over her. 'There are plenty of women in the workplace trying to keep a family afloat.'

'You think I don't know that?'

How attractive was that crease in his cheek? And how determined was she not to be distracted by it? 'Women have always been fighters, Quinn—they've had to be—and if you want to know what appeals to them you capture the whole of the market—their men and the next generation, too.'

'And if I want to know how to appeal to women I should ask you?'

Like Quinn didn't appeal to every woman he met. But he didn't face up their ads. 'You could ask any of the women who work here for their opinion. Use the resources you have, don't ignore them. Ask them what they like to buy, to use, to experience.

'You're suggesting we run a series of trials?'

'Why not?'

'Involve women in our brainstorming sessions?'

'Of course.'

'Persuade me.'

Quinn's eyes were dark and smoky; how she longed to. But this was her chance; she couldn't blow it. 'Okay. So, women want to buy your products because they're dependable, exciting and they can trust them—but women want to command attention too. They want to look sharp—they want to be in control.'

'And they want to do all this while they're sitting behind a typewriter knocking three bells out of their expensive manicure?'

'And so the ad has to say to them,' Magenta drove on determinedly, *'You're in charge!'*

'That's a dangerous line to take.'

'Are you telling me men are so fragile they can't survive a challenge from a strong woman?' She held Quinn's gaze. Feeling strong whilst pulsating with lust was confusing, to say the least.

'You're a strong woman, Magenta.'

'Yes, I am.' She knew Quinn was testing her, looking for cracks in her defences. He knew she wanted him to yank her close and devour her with kisses. 'But I'm only one example of a strong woman,' she told him coolly. 'I'm sure there are many others right here in this office.'

'Some men don't find strong women attractive.'

And you, Quinn? Magenta longed to ask him, but she already knew the answer. Quinn was highly sexed—hot, feral, dangerous. Her body was ringing proof of that. Of course he liked strong women. Quinn would like the challenge of subduing them.

'I never discount a woman's needs.'

'If you do, it's your loss.' She had thought he was talking about business, but as Quinn's lips curved she realised he was teasing her and that his mind was on anything but business. It was time to sharpen up that sleep-deprived brain of hers and take this battle to the next level.

'Why don't you get two glasses and we'll have a drink?' Quinn suggested. A sexy grin played around his lips. 'You should take some down-time occasionally.'

Yes, she could go with that—she could let drink fuzz her

mind and make that her excuse for giving the green light to Quinn's white-hot charm offensive—but she wanted more out of life than fleeting satisfaction. 'I'm good. I'd like to finish this work so it's ready for you to see in the morning.' That was the right thing to do. She should remain strong.

She should do a lot of things, Magenta reflected as her body melted like butter when Quinn closed his hands on her arms. Business was one thing, but this was something very different, and she was tired of keeping up a front. She was tired full-stop, and felt dreamy and reckless... And Quinn was...Quinn.

'Better?' he murmured, curving a smile as he dropped a kiss on her mouth.

She sucked in a ragged breath, exclaiming softly somewhere deep in her throat as Quinn deepened the kiss. This was some dream. His hands were lazily coasting down her back while her responses were quickly changing from tentative to hungry and on to greed.

She almost staggered when he stepped back.

He steadied her and then gave her a mocking look.

'Why?' she said, feeling hurt and confusion overwhelm her. She never lost control, except for this one time.

'Because you're tense.'

She got what she deserved. Magenta passed her hand across her lust-swollen lips and then kept it there as if she could hide her arousal. They both liked to be in control, but Quinn was far better at this than she was. She was hardly a practised siren, and even in a dream her skills hadn't improved in that direction.

Quinn moved behind her and she tensed as his warm hands found the tender spot on the nape of her neck where all the stress had collected.

'I told you there was tension,' he said, proving how skilled he was at clearing her mind of anything but sensation.

She didn't argue as he began to massage the stiffness

away. She doubted anyone could move away from that touch. Quinn's breath was warm on the back of her neck and his body was only a breath away. She exhaled unsteadily. Quinn was making it impossible to think. Did he know how powerfully he affected her, how her body yearned for him? She wanted him. She hadn't even thought about her curves before, let alone that they would fit Quinn's hands so well—if only he would touch her.

'Why don't you talk me through your work plan for the rest of the week, Magenta?'

He could switch tracks in an instant, leaving her reeling in his wake. She'd been right to be wary, and now it took several valuable seconds to get her brain in gear. 'I've typed up a work plan which I've left in your office. Shall I get it for you?'

'That won't be necessary.'

Quinn liked this game. He liked playing with her. And from what she'd seen of him so far Quinn only ever played to win. 'I'd like you to see it,' she said, breaking away. 'I want you to know I won't let you down.'

'You won't get the chance. There can be no special favours because you're new to the job, Magenta. I expect the same productivity from you that I expect from the other girls. More, in fact, because I made the decision to put you in charge.'

Which was why she had made sure to be prepared. Going into the office, she retrieved her list and passed it to Quinn, who scanned it briefly before handing it back to her.

'You're going?' She watched Quinn shrug on his overcoat.

'Did you expect me to stay?'

Anger consumed her. Quinn knew just how to work her. She would have to move a lot faster if she were to avoid becoming his puppet—the woman who could not only knock up an excellent coffee on demand, or a spreadsheet or two, but who could also oblige Quinn in more personal areas of his life. What he needed was a strong woman to take him in hand, Magenta concluded. She had always believed she was strong—but was she strong enough?

Quinn's laughing eyes put that challenge directly to her. 'We'll have a lot on tomorrow, Magenta. I'll expect you in the office first thing, and I will make no allowances for the fact that you're working late on your own project.'

'Of course not.' *You unrepentant barbarian,* she thought, smiling pleasantly.

'Sleep well.'

'I will.' *And I wouldn't go to bed with you if you were the last man on earth,* she thought, holding the smile. *Unless you asked me nicely.*

She refused to notice how attractively Quinn's lips pressed down. 'I almost forgot this,' he said.

'What is it?' she said, gazing at the plain-brown paper bag.

'A sandwich. In case you get hungry while you're working.' One last amused glance, and Quinn stepped inside the lift doors.

He knew she wanted him, Magenta realised. He no doubt also knew she was a complete novice where men were concerned. This was shaping up to be one hell of a fight. Whichever world they inhabited, she always liked a challenge.

Fortunately you could still flag down a cab in the sixties. If anything, the streets were calmer and the traffic far less frantic. Even the pavements were in better repair. And for a sixties buff like Magenta even the smallest detail, like a billboard featuring a youthful Elvis Presley in his latest film, was a source of the utmost fascination. But there were some things she couldn't get used to: the lack of central heating in her house, the ice on the inside of the bathroom window, a bed that made her feel like the filling in a particularly well-chilled sandwich.

Tucking herself in beneath a cumbersome sheet, and several thin blankets with a ridiculously small eiderdown perched precariously on top, she realised that her passion for the sixties had made her overlook the privations that had existed then. She had taken the best parts—the comfortable and exciting parts—and had romanticised them to fit in with how she thought the sixties should be. But the truth was somewhat different, as she was rapidly finding out. And now she only had a couple of hours in this frigid room to rest her head before getting up for work again.

The phone rang, annoyingly. Without opening her eyes, she risked one warm arm to reach into the chilly air and pick it up. The voice on the other end of the line was deeply male and instantly recognisable. 'Magenta? Are you awake?'

'Wh…wh…?' How long had she been asleep? Five minutes? Less? 'Yes?' Magenta realised she was sitting bolt-upright and practically saluting.

'Aren't you out of bed yet?'

Quinn's deep, sexy voice lacked all vestige of charm. 'Of course I am,' she huffed, getting tangled up in the phone cord as she rolled out of bed.

'Good, because I'm at the office, and you should be too.'

She stumbled over the cord.

'Magenta, what's happening there?'

'Nothing. Why?' she demanded, untangling herself.

'I can hear a lot of banging about.'

'That would be the front door closing,' she covered for herself, stretching the curly phone-cord to its limit as she peered through the open bathroom door. 'Just getting the milk in.'

Quinn hummed. 'Forget breakfast and get in here, will you? A national newspaper has announced that its first colour supplement will be launched in the New Year, and—'

'And we're going to be in it!' she exclaimed excitedly.

'That's the plan.'

'Fantastic!' It was fantastic. And would be even more so if

Quinn could only bring himself to trust her with the smallest detail, rather than expecting her to type up the minutes of his latest meeting. But first things first; the sooner she got herself back to the office, the sooner she was back in the game. 'I'm just putting the phone down for a second,' she said, knowing the phone cord wouldn't stretch far enough. 'Hang on.'

Rushing into the bathroom, Magenta looked in vain for the shower. She would have to take a quick bath—a cold bath, as it turned out. Too late now to notice the switch on the wall and realise she'd have had to turn it on some hours earlier if she wanted the luxury of hot water.

'Fantastic?' Quinn bellowed as she picked up the phone again. 'Is that all you have to say about it? I can't believe you're awake yet, Magenta. This is a national first and I want a big, visual splash for Style Design in that first supplement— Magenta? Are you still there?'

Barely. She had stepped into the frigid water and made a big splash of her own. Down, up and that would have to do it. Teeth chattering, she reached for a small, scratchy towel.

No fluffy bath-sheet warming gently on a heated towel-rail.

No bath sheet, full-stop.

Lodging the phone between her shoulder and chin, she jumped about to keep warm as she flung open the single wardrobe door. Now here was a thing—a disposable paper dress in a black-and-white op-art pattern. Paper clothes would be put to good use in clinics in the future, though not in this flamboyant design. She smiled wryly. Goodness knew how, but dresses like these were making it to the fashion pages of the sixties, judging by the magazines she'd seen in the office. This particular company's bold claim was that they were not only at the cutting edge of fashion, but were ready to supply disposable clothes for space flight and settlements on future moon-colonies.

How high would Quinn take her?

Thoughts like that definitely belonged in the realms of fantasy, Magenta decided as Quinn uttered a phrase that was bang up-to-date in whichever era he lived.

She settled for a safe wool dress, deciding to keep the outrageous paper mini-dress for the Christmas party. Why shouldn't she break out that one time and surprise Quinn? Tradition demanded everyone let rip during the holiday celebrations, and surely that had been no different in the sixties? And wasn't she incredibly comfortable around paper these days? She would just have to hope Quinn would see the irony in her choice of outfit. But that was for later. The sleek wool dress she chose for now was in an attractive shade of coral and had a wide, form-enhancing belt, which Magenta buckled securely. She looked the part and was determined to work the role fate had given her to the very best of her ability.

What else could she do? she reasoned as she soared upwards in the office lift. At least she'd get to see Quinn again—and, in spite of his manner towards her last night, she felt the customary buzz of anticipation as she walked into the office. She was already looking for him, practically scenting the air like a doe on heat searching for the buck. Yes, Quinn was a bad-boy, but would she seriously want to change her dream lover into a weed?

CHAPTER EIGHT

THIS sixties version of the office where she worked was more like a stark, bare stage than the technology-crammed work setting Magenta was accustomed to, with its anonymous banks of twenty-first century computers and purposefully androgynous personnel. Here in the sixties everyone dressed to impress and showed off their assets to best advantage. Fortunately, she had adapted quickly to her new role as office manager, and found that her natural air of authority even had most of the men begrudgingly following her orders. Not Quinn, of course. The only orders Quinn followed were his own.

'Always liked a strong woman,' one of the men who had teased her earlier declared as she took the cigarette from his hand and stubbed it out.

'No more of that,' Magenta said firmly, realising that, the firmer she was with these men, the more they seemed to like it.

All except for Quinn, who when she did see him chose to ignore the fact that they had spent a large part of the last evening flirting—or verbal jousting, as Magenta preferred to think of it. He repeated his warning—with his lips very close to her ear—that she would pay the consequence if outside interests detracted from her work for him. Quinn had otherwise left her alone with a pile of work she was sure he had added to in order to punish her for oversleeping that morning. Not that her lips cared about that. They were too busy tingling from the memory of his kisses.

The day passed quickly, the only down side being the lack of Quinn. Magenta let Nancy and the rest of the girls leave early again, feeling they had spent another day under the heel of unreasonable men; she was equally determined that all that would change soon. If there was one thing she was determined to do before she woke up again, it was to make a difference for those girls.

Would she wake up if she fell asleep at the office? Magenta wondered, resting her chin on the heel of her hand. After all, she had woken up here at the office. Who knew what might happen in such an upside-down world? She glanced across at the group of men hanging around in the hope of being able to say goodnight to Quinn—and possibly kiss his backside too, Magenta reflected waspishly. It was nothing short of a miracle that women had found the energy to prove themselves in the sixties, in her opinion. And on top of that they were expected to run a home.

So what had changed? Magenta wondered wryly. Things were pretty much the same in the twenty-first century.

Quinn appeared and everyone straightened up. Even Magenta was guilty of trying to give a good impression. There was no harm in looking; Quinn was one good-looking man.

'Still working, Magenta?'

She was surprised when he came over to her rather than heading for the men.

'This is good,' he said, scanning her latest idea.

'And when it's finished you can see it.' She covered her work protectively.

'You should share your ideas,' Quinn told her.

'And I will,' she said. Just as soon as she had organised a team. She was determined to recruit from the typing pool and the switchboard. She had to get those girls believing in themselves so they could leave the corral behind for good.

'When can I see it?' Quinn's gaze sharpened.

'As soon as we're ready.'

'We?' he said suspiciously.

'This type of work is usually undertaken by a team.' As his eyes narrowed she could tell she'd gone too far. 'What I mean to say is, with your approval, I would like to canvas opinion in the typing corral.'

'The typing corral?'

Why was she staring at his lips? 'I mean the women who type,' she said carefully. It wouldn't do to put his back up. Not yet. 'They're closed off from the rest of the office as if they're in a corral.'

'And?' Quinn queried.

'We're losing out on their opinions. I just thought that maybe their thoughts on the various products you're promoting could be useful to you.' She spoke mildly but felt like a tigress defending her cubs.

'Perhaps…' Quinn thumbed his sharp black stubble.

'And I have another idea for you.'

'Why aren't I surprised?'

Was Quinn trying to overwhelm her with that incredible stare? 'I realise I'm only the office manager, but I thought if you would allow me to build a team—in my own time, of course—perhaps we could test our ideas, one team against the other?'

'Men against women?' Quinn looked immeasurably smug, as if the end result were a foregone conclusion. 'You're serious about this?'

'Never more so.' She held Quinn's stare, feeling her body's response to him like a flame of heat that brought her blood to boiling point. But she had to ignore those glorious eyes and focus on her goal. 'I've heard that slots for advertising in the new colour supplement are so sought-after they are going to be decided by a team of style-setters.'

'I've heard that too. We have to be at the top of our game.'

'Which is why I thought if everyone was involved you could cherry-pick the best ideas to produce the final, winning scheme.'

'You don't give up, do you?'

She knew better than to respond to that.

'I hope you don't make me regret this.'

'So you agree?' Holding Quinn's gaze was dangerous, but she was fast becoming an adrenalin junkie.

'If this is a wind-up, Magenta...'

'I promise you, it isn't. I just know that some of those girls are going to want to be involved, and that some of them are bound to be good.'

'You like a challenge,' he said.

'Doesn't everyone?'

'No. Most people like to play it safe, but not you. You seem to thrive on living dangerously—which is good,' he added when she was about to say something, 'because I have plans for you.'

Magenta's heart leapt for all sorts of reasons, any of which she'd settle for.

'I'm going to give you the chance you've asked for. I've got nothing to lose,' Quinn pointed out with a shrug. 'I'm going to give you the running of the year-end party too. That's coming up fast—do you think you can handle the pressure?'

'I'll handle it.' Here in the sixties it was some way to Christmas, so she had plenty of time.

'And don't bring me any old ideas. Think outside the box, Magenta.'

Which was exactly what Magenta and her twenty-first-century counterparts were renowned for. Now she just had to adapt that flair to a different era.

'Well, don't just stand there—go work on your ideas. We'll have another chat in the morning.'

'Yes, sir.'

Magenta was thrilled to think Quinn might let the girls have a chance. But had she taken on too much? She would have to get a credible team together as fast as she could and be ready to present to a judging panel of one.

'Those trials you mentioned?' Quinn said, turning at the door.

'Yes?'

'Warn the girls I'll be looking for their opinion on a selection of new products.'

'I will.' This wasn't a victory—not even close—but it was a great improvement on how she had felt when she'd first fallen down the rabbit hole.

The following morning Magenta put her plan to the girls. She'd fully expected them to look at her as if she were mad. What she couldn't have expected was that they would warm to her ideas quite so quickly. She guessed that had everything to do with her explanation that it would mean going head to head with the men.

'But Quinn has the final word,' Nancy observed. 'How does that work?'

Magenta slipped down from her perch on top of the table in the ladies' room, which was where they had assembled to be sure of being out of earshot of the unfair sex. 'If there's one thing I know about Quinn it's that he's first and foremost a businessman.'

'A warrior with the eyes of a lover,' one of the girls argued, shivering deliciously as the others murmured their agreement.

Why was she so jealous, suddenly? Magenta wondered, quickly smothering that thought. 'He'll certainly fight for the company.' She had to believe that. 'And he wants that contract. You're wrong to be concerned, Nancy. Quinn might be tough, but he's fair.'

She was sticking up for Genghis Khan now! But the girls were agreeing with her, so she'd stick with that line for now.

'Is it going to be a fair fight, or is this just a ploy by Quinn to keep us quiet?' Nancy demanded.

'It's a genuine competition—just as the competition for inclusion in the new journal is genuine. I wouldn't waste your time otherwise. Put a challenge in front of Quinn and he can't resist it—neither can I, neither can you. And I'm as sure as I can be he'll play fair.'

'But would he ever go for our ideas over those of the men?'

'Why not if they're better ideas, Nancy? And what do we have to lose? This is a fight to better our jobs.'

'And smash the men!' Nancy's cheeks were already glowing at the thought.

'Don't forget the pleasure it will give us,' Magenta reminded her.

'When we bury those worker bees?' a girl with sweeping glasses suggested to agreement from her friends. 'We're with you, Magenta.'

'There's just one more thing.'

'Which is?' Nancy said suspiciously.

'We have to do something first to help Quinn, to demonstrate how cooperative we can be.'

'I might have known it,' Nancy exclaimed to a background of groans.

'You might enjoy it,' Magenta said hopefully.

'If it includes typing, cleaning or extra coffee-making duties, I'm out,' Nancy assured her.

'Are the men expected to pre-qualify too?' one of the other girls asked.

'I think we all know the answer to that question,' Magenta admitted. 'But let's concentrate on things we *can* change rather than worrying about those we can't.'

'So, what do we have to do?' Nancy demanded, hands on hips.

'Trial a few products?'

'Oh, that sounds nice,' Nancy said sourly. 'Let me guess—pan scrubs, sweeping brushes and limescale-removal cream?'

'Make-up, beauty products and clothes, actually. And you get to keep the samples.'

'Quinn's buying us,' Nancy observed sceptically as the other girls exclaimed with pleasure.

'No. I believe Quinn genuinely wants our opinions,' Magenta argued. 'It's as simple as that.'

'Nothing is ever as simple as *that*,' Nancy commented, studying her nails.

'Maybe not,' Magenta agreed. 'But are we going to let a few tubes of lipstick stand in our way?'

'No,' the girls shouted, while someone else chipped in. 'This is bigger than lipstick. This is a fight for freedom.'

'To the barricades!' Nancy exclaimed as everyone laughed. 'But don't forget to put your make-up on first.'

'So, are you with us, Nancy?' Magenta asked, turning serious.

'You bet I am. After what I've taken from those men today, I'm itching for a fight.'

She might have known, Magenta thought as she entered the room where they were to trial the products at the head of her girls. Sweet little dressing-tables had been set out for each of them as if they were life-sized Barbie dolls. On top of these was spread an array of high-end beauty products guaranteed to make any woman's heart beat faster. Fortunately, both Magenta and her newly formed team knew how to play it cool—which was just as well, seeing as Quinn's team was standing ready with their clipboards waiting to take down their thoughts.

'How nice,' Magenta murmured, as if trialling nail varnishes and lipsticks was all her candy-floss heart had ever yearned for. She gestured that her team should choose a seat, and the girls smilingly obliged—but then they were in on the surprise Magenta had in store for the men.

Said men could hardly keep the smiles from their smug faces, though Quinn appeared quite relaxed about the trial he'd set up. And gorgeous, Magenta registered, with his crisp, white shirt rolled up to the elbows and beautifully tailored black trousers moulding the shape of his muscular thighs and hips with obscenely loving attention to detail. Undressing such a spectacular specimen would be a privilege…

'Aren't you going to sit down, Magenta?'

'If there were enough chairs.'

'Here, take mine—I won't be needing it,' Quinn explained as he held out a chair for her.

There was a distinct rustle of expectation in the air as the men adopted serious expressions. Once again, they were ready to jeer and jibe at the slightest cue from Quinn, but he remained brooding and unmoved. And now all Magenta had to do was to discover if she was as bold as she had promised the girls she would be on their behalf. Picking up a lipstick, she pursed her lips. 'Glittering Fool's Gold,' she murmured, straightening up again. 'What do you think of it?'

'What do I think of it?' Quinn said, frowning.

'Yes. What do you think of it?' Magenta repeated, standing up. She had everyone's attention now. 'According to men, women do everything for their benefit—so surely your opinion matters more than ours?' She tipped her chin to stare Quinn in the eyes, all the while smiling pleasantly. 'Would you like to taste it?' An audible intake of breath rose around her, but before there could be any misunderstanding she handed the lipstick over to Quinn. 'You don't have to put it on. You could lick it, or suck it.'

Taking her arm, Quinn drew her out of earshot of the others.

'This is a serious trial and you're a disruptive influence. What the hell do you think you're playing at, Magenta?'

'Conducting a serious trial,' Magenta insisted in a heated whisper. 'This lipstick looks as good as the one I use, but it tastes like medicine mixed with pond swill. Would you kiss a girl wearing something like that twice?'

Quinn's eyes narrowed dangerously and it took all her strength to hold his gaze without flinching. The glint in his eye said she'd gone too far again, but he couldn't argue with her motives. 'I'll give you the benefit of the doubt this time,' he said. 'But keep it straight from here on in. No jokes. No *double entendre*. Don't try any more tricks. Understood?'

'Perfectly.'

When the girls had finished testing the make-up, Quinn eased away from the wall. 'Thank you, all of you, for your co-operation. Please take anything you like.'

'Excuse me…?'

'Yes?' Quinn's head shot round when Magenta spoke up.

'We girls didn't want to be passive observers in the trial, and though we've enjoyed the experience enormously we do have some products we'd like you men to trial.' She almost had to shout over the ensuing uproar. 'We thought it could only benefit the campaign to get some insight into male products too, to cover all the market,' she said quickly, seeing Quinn's expression turn thunderous. He had granted her one favour and now she was stretching his patience to the limit, while the men were baying for her blood. After all, what could a woman possibly know about a man's world?

Quinn silenced the roar of protest.

She had to risk everything on one final throw of the dice. 'I wouldn't have thought of it,' Magenta said innocently. 'I have you to thank, Quinn, for pointing out that our advertising efforts are largely directed at men. As this is the case, the girls and I thought it only prudent to be sure we're on the right track by trialling some of the new male products and getting your thoughts on them.'

'Yes, yes, yes,' Quinn interrupted impatiently as the other men around him started to complain. 'Magenta's right,' he added to her amazement. 'I said we'd have a fair trial, and we will, which means the results cannot be assessed until we have views from both ends of the spectrum.'

With men at the top end of that spectrum and women nowhere, presumably, Magenta thought. But this wasn't the time to be greedy—not while everything was going to plan. 'Would you give us a minute to set up?' she asked before Quinn had a chance to change his mind.

'Take all the time you need. More than a minute and I'm out of here. What's this?' Quinn demanded when Magenta returned at the head of her team.

'A shaving chair I borrowed from the local barber.'

Quinn shook his head in cynical surprise, but insisted on lifting it out of her hands all the same. 'Where would you like it?'

'In the centre of the room, please.' The men weren't smirking any longer, Magenta noticed. 'All we need now is a volunteer. What, no one? Won't anyone help us with our trial?'

Someone sniggered.

'I will.'

All eyes were on Quinn, who was already loosening his tie.

CHAPTER NINE

'THANK you, Quinn.' She only had to hold his gaze to realise it contained all sorts of messages that made her yearn inside, most of which were, thankfully, indecipherable to anyone else in the room.

Everyone held a collective breath as Magenta helped Quinn take off his jacket. She could feel his warmth through the cool of his cotton shirt and an array of muscles flexing beneath her fingers. The spread of his shoulders was a challenge in itself, and though she wasn't small she had to stand on tiptoes to slide his jacket off them. She gave it to one of the girls to hang up.

'Would you like me to take my shirt off too?' Quinn suggested.

'That won't be necessary, thank you.' He really knew how to make her heart thunder. 'If you would care to sit down…?'

Quinn arranged himself on the leather seat, and before she lowered it she secured a protective cover around his neck. Then, tipping him back so she could reach the sink, she stood over him. Their stares connected. Lying flat on his back, Quinn's was amused, while hers could only have shown how much she was enjoying this moment of domination. To have Quinn's strong, tanned face beneath her fingers and his gaze, laced with irony, daring her to do her worst was the best challenge she could have dreamed of. 'Would you be more comfortable with your shoes off?'

'I'll keep them on, thank you—I might want to make a quick getaway.'

Quinn's comment lifted the atmosphere at a stroke and even Magenta laughed.

'Get on with it,' he warned. 'Remember, I want all those reports on my desk before lunchtime today. In fact, everyone,' he said swivelling round in the chair, 'you can go now. There's no need to hang around while Magenta conducts her trial. I'll file my own report.'

And if that didn't cause comment in the office, nothing ever would.

'Would you have preferred an audience?' Quinn demanded as their colleagues filed out.

'It doesn't matter to me either way.' She would carry through with this whatever happened, though a few-dozen chaperones would have been nice. And safer.

'So? Where do we begin?' Quinn demanded.

'With a warm towel to soften your bristles before I shave you.'

'You'll be using a safety razor, I presume?'

'Would you prefer I used a cutthroat?'

Quinn laughed. Magenta doubted anything qualified as 'safe' if Quinn had anything to do with it. The thought of touching him, let alone massaging him with her inexperienced fingers, was a mountain she had to climb without a safety rope in sight. 'There's just one thing.'

'Which is?'

'You won't—'

'I won't what?' Quinn demanded.

'You won't try to kiss me?' Magenta blurted awkwardly.

'You don't want me to?'

'I don't want any surprises—I don't want my hand to shake, or I might cut you.'

'You really know how to charm a man, don't you?'

No. That was one thing that was completely outside her area of expertise.

'I don't plan to surprise you, Magenta.'

'Good.'

'I don't plan to kiss you either.'

Bad.

'Are you ready?' Quinn demanded. 'I don't have all day.'

The damp towel had been warmed in the prescribed manner and she took the greatest pleasure in winding it tightly around Quinn's face.

'It helps if I can breathe!' he exclaimed, rearranging it.

'Sorry.' And now she had a dilemma, Magenta realised as she rummaged through the products. Should she choose the *Head Man* toiletries, for the man who was a man's man from nine to five and a lady's man after six? Well, Quinn was hardly a nine-to-five man, and so far there had been no sign of any ladies.

So, how about men who wore *English Leather* or nothing at all?

Magenta's appreciative gaze swept down Quinn's muscular form. She mustn't even think that way.

How about something called *Inferno*? The shout line was enough to put her off: *if she doesn't give it to you, get it for yourself.* Cologne seemed a poor substitute for the type of gift that ad was hinting at.

'Well, have you chosen a product range to trial on me yet?' Quinn demanded impatiently.

'Yes, I have, actually. Something called *Forbidden Fruit*.'

'Sounds reasonable.'

'"The Lime of Least Resistance".'

Quinn's lips tugged and Magenta could hardly keep her face straight. The sixties ad lines were really corny. If she couldn't come up with something better, it was time to get out of the business—though, of course, her knowledge of the future should give her team a head start.

Was that cheating? Not really; it was just good business sense, Magenta reasoned. 'Ready?' she asked Quinn.

'As I'll ever be,' he told her dryly.

Soaping Quinn was fun, shaving him less so, but only because he put her on edge and she was genuinely frightened of cutting him. And, far from being softened by the hot towel, his stubble remained just as dense and sharp as it had been when she started the process. Plus, she had to lean in very close, which made her even more aware of him, especially when each time she pulled back it was to find Quinn's disturbing stare levelled on her face. He had the most beautiful face—strong, clean lines and a healthy complexion. And those lips…

She had never been so intimate with a man before and felt her whole body respond as her hands adopted a new, caressing touch as she positioned Quinn on the padded head-rest. She couldn't help her breasts brushing his arm as she worked and the feel of Quinn beneath her hands was intoxicating. She had to concentrate very hard indeed on this trial.

'Not bad,' he admitted, testing his chin when she'd finished. 'I might keep you on.'

'You should be so lucky.' She laughed nervously, only now realising how tense she had become.

'Don't forget the massage—that's my favourite part,' Quinn insisted. 'And I can hardly be expected to give my verdict on the products until I've sampled all of them.'

'Of course.'

'Warm the cream in your hands first.'

The air stilled between them as she picked up the container and poured a little of the cream onto her hands. She warmed it between her palms as Quinn had suggested, and the sliding sound of cream on skin was yet another reminder that she was batting well out of her league.

'Don't be shy,' Quinn advised her dryly.

'I'm not shy.' She started tentatively at first and then grew bolder. She closed her eyes, allowing her fingers to map the shape of Quinn's face. She wanted to imprint every detail on her mind so she could remember this moment whatever happened next. Quinn's brow, his ears, his neck, his lips—nothing was forbidden to her and she indulged herself to the full.

It was Quinn who brought the session to an end. Operating the lever at the side of his chair, he sat up. 'I always suspected you were a dark horse.'

'Did I do something wrong?'

'On the contrary, that was the most sensuous massage I have ever experienced.'

'But what about the product?'

'What about the product?'

'You're supposed to be assessing it.'

'I thought I just had. Write it up,' he said, removing the protective sheet from his neck and handing it to her. 'Give yourself full credit. I'll expect your report on my desk by lunchtime today, Magenta.'

'And you'll listen to the ideas of my team now?' She held her breath.

'I gave you my word, didn't I?'

She wanted to leap up and kiss him, but of course she had more sense.

'Anyone stand out for you?' Quinn demanded on his way out of the door.

So many of the girls had flair she hardly knew where to begin. 'Nancy, Maria, Josie—' *Oh, to hell with it.* 'If you could just give them all a chance.'

'And?' Quinn said, suspecting there was something more.

'Equal pay with the men?'

'You don't want much,' he said wryly.

No, but while he was in a good mood she was going to ask for it.

'All of these things have to be earned,' Quinn observed.
'Regardless of gender.'

'So you'd consider making changes?'

'When I do, you'll be the first to hear.'

'Thank you.'

'Don't thank me—you'll be typing up the memos. If
you can't take the heat, you'd better get out of the kitchen,
Magenta.'

'I can take it.' Yes. *Yes*! Oh boy, could she take it. This
was an incredible turnaround from the most intransigent of
men.

'Good, because you'll be adding all this new work to your
regular duties.'

Would there come a point where she crumpled beneath the
pressure? Well, if there did, Quinn wouldn't care—so she had
better not. Getting that break for the girls was the only thing
that mattered.

Magenta could barely wait for Quinn to leave the room
before flinging the protective sheet he'd handed her into the
air with a whoop of excitement. The next step would be planning a new ad campaign with her team.

The girls were giddy with excitement just at the thought of
being taken seriously. The sexism and chauvinism in the office
knew no bounds and Magenta could hardly believe that such
intelligent and vital individuals had been disregarded solely
on the basis of gender. How could these women have been
kept down for so long, subjugated by the men? How could any
manager afford to waste such a valuable resource?

Having assured her new colleagues that their ideas really
were going to be listened to, she got down to writing up her
report and delivered it to Quinn before lunchtime as instructed. To her amazement, he handed her a typewritten sheet.
'My report,' he said.

'Thank you…' Perhaps they were getting somewhere after

all. Holding the sheet of folded paper close, she left the room feeling warm inside. And, yes, even a little triumphant. If all the battles ahead of her would be so easily won...

'Leave my door open, will you?' Quinn called after her.

'Of course.'

Quinn wasn't so bad, Magenta decided, settling down at her desk. He just needed handling. She was in charge of collating the results for the trials and, now she had Quinn's report, she could make a start.

Studying the sheet of paper he'd given her, Magenta's eyes widened.

Dinner tonight, Quinn had written. *Pick you up at your place at eight—no excuses.*

It was less of an invitation and more of an instruction.

Magenta tensed. Reports forgotten, she stared into space. Kisses were one thing, but anything more... She had just experienced a prolonged sensory experience with Quinn and now he was calling her bluff. Was she up to a one-on-one meeting after work?

'Did you want to talk business tonight?' She turned with the note in her hand to speak to him through the open door.

'What else?' Quinn said impatiently, waving her away.

A business meeting. Well, that was all right, and would give her a chance to learn more about Quinn. She felt a thrill of anticipation. Of course she could handle it. She was a big girl, wasn't she? She could always say no. How could she turn Quinn down without offending him? That might put the girls' future prospects in jeopardy, which she would never do.

Turning in her chair, she flashed Quinn a faint smile and a nod. It didn't do to look too eager.

Hemlines were getting shorter, according to the fashion magazines the girls kept around the office. Venturing into one of the tiny boutiques, that had sprung up down a street Magenta knew would one day be turned into office blocks, was a temptation she couldn't resist. Armed with cash from her wage packet, she was ready to shop. The chance to wear one of the daring outfits for Quinn being showcased in the shop windows was slightly less appealing—she'd feel safer in a sack—but she guessed he might baulk at that for their evening out.

Swinging London was the first headline she noticed on a news stand as she walked along, together with a picture of the Beatles. She definitely had to make some sort of effort to be stylish. Dragging her gaze away, she saw a hairdressing salon and decided to make that her first stop.

A stylish young man with floppy hair and tight, flared trousers arranged Magenta's long hair so that it hung loose down her back and was dressed fairly high at the top. Taking it up at the sides, he gave her a fringe so long it caught on her eyelashes.

Realising she could buy make-up at the salon, she chose some smoky eye-shadow, passing on the pale foundation with the option of white lips. She had to contend with the lady behind the counter giving her some strange looks as she battled with the unfamiliar pre-decimal currency. She finally managed to get it right and handed over what seemed to her like a very small amount of money before leaving the shop.

Now she had to hunt for an outfit to wear that evening. She had fun trying on all the vintage clothes and realising they were new. There was nothing subtle about sexiness in the sixties; she already knew that. Though she didn't want Quinn to think her a frump, a couple of inches above the knee was as far as she was prepared to go. Rejecting a cobwebby, crotcheted dress, she chose a high-necked, soft turquoise silk with trumpet sleeves that flattered her figure without exposing too much of it.

'You could go bra-less,' the shop assistant informed her. 'You've got the figure for it.'

What and show off her nipples? Give Quinn a handy

barometer to go by? He hardly needed that sort of encouragement. 'I'd prefer to wear a bra.'

'What about this no-bra bra?' the assistant suggested. 'It's almost sheer, but it does offer some protection...' She weighed Magenta up. 'If that's what you want.'

'It is pretty,' Magenta agreed and she definitely wanted all the protection she could get.

'You could try these hip-huggers to go with it. Or some matching bikini-pants in the same flesh-coloured lace?'

'They're very flimsy.'

'That's the idea.'

'I'll take them.' She just wanted to get out of the shop now. The girl's close scrutiny was beginning to make her feel uncomfortable.

'Which one?' The girl was holding up a pair of knickers in each hand.

'Both.'

'You're sure they're not too flimsy for you? I do have some heavy-gauge serge in the back.'

Was it so obvious that Magenta's twenty-first-century lifestyle meant her choice of underwear depended on what washed well on a short cycle and lasted longest?

CHAPTER TEN

MAGENTA braved her freezing bathroom to take a bath and then dressed carefully. When the doorbell rang, her heart went crazy. If this was a dream she was certainly taking her time waking up, she thought as she hurried downstairs.

And now she didn't want to wake up. Quinn looked amazing. Standing on her doorstep wearing a heavy overcoat over his suit, and with a long, silk scarf slung casually around his neck, he was unreasonably handsome—like a hero stepping out of a dream. In full sixties hero-about-town rig, he really was something else.

'Ready to go?'

'I am,' she confirmed, trying not to notice the silver-grey Aston Martin DB5 parked behind Quinn on the road. She'd half expected to see a motorbike parked at the kerb.

It didn't do to mix up dreams with reality, Magenta resolved, still gazing at Quinn's fabulous car. 'I can't believe it's in such immaculate condition,' she murmured, hardly realising she was speaking out loud.

Quinn looked at her curiously. 'Do you mean the car? Why wouldn't it be?'

Of course, it must be brand new; she had almost betrayed herself. 'I love it. You're a very lucky man.'

'And the harder I work the luckier I get,' Quinn said dryly. 'Have you forgotten something, Magenta?' he added. 'Your earrings?'

It wasn't as if *she* felt naked without earrings, but as she touched her earlobes Magenta remembered that no self-respecting sixties woman would be seen without them— whether they were colossal hoops or feathers trimmed with bells, not to mention the all-important chandelier for the woman who considered herself a cut above the rest. 'I'll be right back,' she said. 'Come in out of the cold while you wait. Close the door.' She flung this over her shoulder as she raced upstairs.

Neat pearl-drops in place, she returned to the hallway.

'Perfect,' Quinn approved, looking her up and down.

His assessment was a bit intrusive for a business meeting, Magenta thought, but she'd let it pass. Quinn escorted her to the car and, opening the door for her, saw her settled inside.

'Where are we going?' she asked with interest as he took control of the high-powered machine.

'I haven't decided yet. What kind of food do you like?'

'Anything, pretty much.' She was curious to see if Antonio's was open. The restaurant was situated in this direction and was one she knew. Antonio's was famous for injecting the serious up-market restaurant quarter in London with Italian sunshine and some much-needed *joie de vivre*. It had been in the same family since the late fifties, being one of the first to bring spectacular ice cream and the art of curling spaghetti around a fork to London. So it should be a bustling concern in the sixties, Magenta reasoned, peering expectantly out of the window. 'But this isn't the way to Antonio's,' she said with concern as Quinn took a turning that led to a leafy and exclusive London suburb.

'Antonio's?'

'Sorry, I was just thinking about an Italian restaurant I used to go to round here. So...' She tried for light, and predictably ended up with an anxious wobble in her voice. 'Have you decided where you're taking me yet?'

'I thought I'd show you my etchings. *Joke*,' Quinn said

dryly when he heard Magenta's sharp intake of breath. 'I thought we'd go to my house.'

'Your house?' Her mouth dried. 'Should I be worried?'

'Do you want to be?' Quinn threw her a glance.

'Of course not,' she said, crossing her legs.

'Good—but reserve judgement. Remember, you haven't tasted my food yet.'

'You're going to cook for me?'

'Is that a problem?'

'No.' *Just a surprise.* Genghis Khan in a pinny was quite a thought.

What was she getting into? Magenta wondered as Quinn swung into the drive of a grand, porticoed house. Was this where he usually brought his business associates for a chat? She'd had him down as a very private man who would never mix business with his private life.

She tried not to act like Quinn's country cousin as he showed her round his house. Magenta's father lived in some style, but nothing close to this. The music room on the first floor, with its full-sized harp and selection of valuable period instruments, was like something out of a palace. Quinn was a connoisseur as well as a warrior in business. The thought of how that combination might translate in the bedroom made her senses roar. When Quinn slipped her coat from her shoulders and his fingers brushed her neck, she betrayed herself by shivering.

'Are you cold?'

She stared into Quinn's amused gaze. They both knew the opposite was the case. Why was she feeling so embarrassed and unsure of herself? Sexual attraction between a man and a woman wasn't unheard of, was it? Whatever their respective positions in life and whatever the era.

To the sex-starved it was. She moved a sensible distance away from him.

Shrugging off his overcoat, Quinn left her for a moment

and when he returned it was with two glasses of amber liquid that glowed seductively in the cleverly designed lighting.

'What is it?' Magenta said as Quinn handed her the glass.

'Single malt.'

She laughed and lightened up. 'You remembered. Do you know many women who drink whisky, Quinn?'

'Does it matter?'

'Not at all—I just wondered if you liked non-conformists.'

'You're not a non-conformist, Magenta.'

'How can you tell?'

'Because non-conformists all look the same.'

'Like hippies?'

'Exactly.'

Now they were laughing together, and against the odds she was beginning to relax in Quinn's company. She really liked him—too much. She couldn't afford to let her guard down and expect to survive the experience unscathed.

'Shall we get down to business?' she suggested, putting her glass on the table.

Quinn's lips pressed down with amusement as he put his glass next to hers. 'I'm ready if you are.'

This was business?

Quinn dragged her into his arms and his kisses were a brushing, teasing, honeyed reminder. 'I shouldn't...'

'You should. You must.'

Quinn's dark eyes glinted with humour and then he deepened the kiss. The chance to experience everything she had ever dreamed about with Quinn—a man who exuded power, raw and unrepentant—was now a very real possibility. She had always been awkward with men before, concerned she'd get it wrong, but the way Quinn was kissing her, binding every part of her to him, left very little to chance.

Best of all, Magenta reasoned, nothing could go wrong in a dream—there were no consequences. She was free of inhibition and embarrassment. Her twenty-first-century world of metro-males and smooth-cheeked mummy's boys had never seemed further away as Quinn persuaded her this was one sixties experience she shouldn't miss out on.

Now his tongue was teasing her lips apart, leaving her in no doubt as he plundered her mouth what he would like to do to her and how very good he'd be at doing it...

She exclaimed with shock when he pulled away.

'Do I frighten you?'

'*You* frighten *me*?' The awkward laugh was back again; she was more frightened of her own feelings than Quinn.

Quinn hummed. 'You play it tough,' he said. 'But I'm not so sure.'

'You mentioned supper?' She was out of her depth and sinking fast. Quinn was compelling, and had drawn her to him like a magnet, but his insight had left her feeling exposed and vulnerable. For all she knew, Quinn had caveman morals wrapped in an Ivy League veneer. He certainly promised pleasure with no price to pay, but life was always more complicated than that. Was it possible dreams were more straightforward?

'Omelette good for you?'

Quinn had changed into jeans and a shirt, which made him look dangerously user-friendly as he led the way into his kitchen. 'Yes. Perfect, thank you.'

She found it bizarre that they were talking about food while she was still shimmering from the effect of Quinn's kisses.

Quinn appeared unaffected. 'Cheese? Plain? Herbs? That's the selection I have on offer tonight.'

She inhaled swiftly when he levelled a keen gaze on her face. 'Cheese would be good.' Why must she always feel as if Quinn knew everything she was thinking? Did she need to be so sensitive? Quinn was a hot-blooded man and it was she who was out of sync here. She wasn't embracing the sixties vibe; free love, free from commitment, was the norm.

'Would you like your omelette well done, or a little soft and liquid inside?'

She swallowed convulsively. Must that deep, sexy voice make everything sound like an invitation? 'Moist and not too well-done, please.'

Would she disappoint in the sexual-performance stakes? Quinn was highly sexed, while she wasn't exactly a well-oiled machine. In fact, she was probably starting out at a lower point than a virgin—she knew what to expect and how badly she could disappoint.

'Are you frightened of all men or just me, Magenta?'

'I'm not frightened of anyone,' she protested. 'If I was frightened of you, I wouldn't be here.'

'But you don't think much of men, do you?' Quinn observed as he reached inside the cupboard for a bowl and a whisk.

'That depends on the man in question.'

'Tell you what we're going to do.' He swung around to face her. 'I'm going to make supper, and while I do that we'll talk through your plans for the Christmas party and anything else connected to the business. Then I'm going to make love to you. Does that sound reasonable?'

Her intake of breath was swift and noisy. 'You are one arrogant son of a bitch.'

'Guilty as charged,' Quinn acknowledged calmly.

'I'll eat, we'll talk business and then I'm going home.'

'Whatever you like.'

Couldn't he show a bit more disappointment? She was more mixed up than the egg was about to be, Magenta felt as Quinn reached inside his large and very stylish refrigerator. It must have come over from America with him; this was a time when many people still stored their perishables in a meat safe in the cellar. 'What?' she said defensively when he started to laugh.

'You're as bad as me, Magenta Steele.'

No one was that bad, Magenta mused, taking in the hard-muscled package that was Gray Quinn. 'Explain.'

'You do nothing by chance.' Reaching inside a drawer, he found a pan and tossed it, catching it niftily by the handle. 'You plan carefully and you do your homework. You've proved yourself to be an effective team leader in a short space of time. You know where to locate the rich veins of business and how to mine them. You're wasted behind a desk, Magenta.'

'You've noticed,' she said dryly.

'I notice everything,' Quinn assured her, breaking eggs in a bowl. 'I brought you here because I know you'll be good for the business and I want to talk to you about that.'

She should be pleased. But female vanity, however fragile—and, boy, was hers fragile—demanded more. But Quinn wasn't going to give her anything more. Sex and business was for him the perfect combination—with an omelette on the side.

'Your team will sit in on the next board meeting. If there is an untapped resource in-house, I'm going to use it.'

She struck while the iron was hot. 'So you're going to take down the partition?' she enquired. When Quinn gave her a warning glance, she added, 'As you said yourself, sharing ideas in an ad agency is paramount.'

'Anything else?'

Magenta listed everything she thought might give the girls an even playing-field at work—including banning sexist comments.

'You are turning into quite a force to be reckoned with.'

His thoughts on that were unreadable. Would he crush her, or would he give Magenta and her team a chance?

Quinn pushed a bowl of salad towards her with the instruction to add dressing and give it a toss. She did as he asked and then sat down across the polished-steel breakfast bar from him.

Quinn's gaze remained steady on her face. 'You sure don't go for gentle change.'

'Gentle might not be enough.'

'You want things fast and now.'

Intensity had drawn their heads closer to the point where she could see the flecks of amber fire in Quinn's eyes. It was warning enough, and she started to draw back, but Quinn caught hold of her wrist, stopping her. 'Don't back off now, Magenta.' His voice dropped low. 'You know there's nothing more you love than a challenge.'

Just when she thought she was safe, Quinn reminded her there was another tension between them, and one that had nothing to do with business. Part of her longed to go along with this, to soften and invite as Quinn expected her to. Fortunately, that part was firmly under control.

'You're blushing,' Quinn observed.

Yes, because he had no inhibitions and she had plenty.

The breath hitched in her throat when Quinn ran one firm fingertip very slowly down her heated cheek until it came to rest on the swell of her bottom lip. 'Why are you blushing, Magenta?'

'No reason,' she said, pulling back. 'The heat of the kitchen, probably. I'm impressed you can cook,' she added, moving out of range.

'The men you know don't get hungry?'

'I don't know many men.'

'I taught myself how to cook.'

'That's good.'

'More like necessity.'

She relaxed a little. 'I didn't mean to offend you. It's just, you don't look the type.'

'To cook? What type of man doesn't like to eat, Magenta?'

'Most men have someone to cook for them.' *Yes, even in the twenty-first century*, Magenta thought wryly.

'More fool them. I'd rather trust my own abilities.'

Than those of some woman—was that what Quinn had left unsaid? How much leeway would he give her, or any woman in his business? 'I'm sure you have all the skills required,' she said recklessly.

How was she supposed to concentrate on her concerns at work now when Quinn's eyes had darkened to smoky black?

CHAPTER ELEVEN

SHE was operating on two levels, Magenta realised as she watched Quinn's skilful hands at play on the second omelette. Whether the cautious part of her approved or not, she was violently aroused. And this was the best chance she was ever going to get to discuss business with Quinn, that sensible side reminded her.

'Sit. Eat,' he said, putting a perfectly prepared golden omelette on the table in front of her.

The aroma alone was enough to make her salivate. 'This is delicious,' she said, forking up a feather-light morsel of buttery, golden egg.

Quinn joined her at the table and dumped some salad on both their plates. 'Tell me more about your ideas.'

He never wasted a moment; she liked that about him. It encouraged her to confide more. Quinn was an attentive listener. He asked her about the Christmas party. She took him through her plans as far as she'd got. 'I'm pleased you trust me to take care of it.'

'If I can't trust you on any level, Magenta, you'd better let me know now.'

And there it was again—the change in Quinn from charming host to uncompromising employer in the blink of an eye. She would have to be more circumspect in future, Magenta warned herself.

'I just make these stipulations for the party,' Quinn continued. 'No clichés. No glitz. No threadbare traditions. And, of course, no unnecessary expense. And I love surprises,' he added, having wiped out most of her plan in a matter of seconds. 'Eat,' he insisted.

No one had said this was going to be easy.

'That was delicious,' Magenta told Quinn as she helped him to clear up.

He nodded briefly. 'Let's get on to your talents, your ideas.'

'I work in a team.'

'But it's your brain I want to mine. Whoever came up with those ideas, it was your drive and initiative that brought them to my attention.'

'I can't claim all the credit.'

'Why not?'

'Because that's just not the way we do things.'

'Do things where?'

Ah. That was a little harder to answer.

Quinn shook his head. 'If you want to get ahead you'll have to toughen up, Magenta—unless you want to be stuck outside my door for ever.'

'I don't want to be there any more than the girls want to be stuck in the typing pool.'

Quinn's eyes narrowed. 'Don't push me, Magenta.'

'You make me sound like the most exasperating woman you ever met.'

'By far.'

Now they were both smiling.

Feeling Quinn's heat shimmering on her senses, she glanced at her wristwatch. 'I'm not sure it's sensible for me to be alone with you here late at night.'

'You think you're in danger?'

'I think you could charm the pants off anyone.'

'What colour are they?'

'What?'

'Your pants. If I'm going to charm them off you, it would be useful to know what colour they are.' Quinn's lips curved wickedly.

Magenta's cheeks fired red, remembering her flimsy, flesh-coloured almost-pants. They wouldn't take much thinking away—one tug and they'd be off.

'Why, Magenta Steele, I do believe you're blushing again,' Quinn murmured as he brushed a strand of hair back from her brow.

'It's hot in this kitchen,' she said stubbornly.

'Oh no,' Quinn disagreed. 'I don't think it's that.'

His mouth was just a whisper away. 'Coffee?' she suggested weakly. Pressing her hands on the surface in front of her, she forced herself to push away from him. Glancing round the kitchen, she hurried to collect cups, coffee and spoons.

'Here, let me make it before you scald yourself.' Quinn covered her trembling hands with his.

'Are you trying to persuade me to stay?'

'I don't need to go to those lengths.'

'You're very sure of yourself.'

'Yes, I am,' Quinn agreed.

The breath caught in her throat as he drew her close. Her back was to the table and Quinn's firm thigh was between her legs. She was so aroused, his lightest touch was all it took to make her tremble with awareness. 'I should go.'

'No, lady, you should come.'

As Quinn moved against her, she groaned deep down in her throat. What was the use of pretending she didn't want this? Quinn's touch was firm and sure, and he gave her the kisses she was aching for, stoking the hunger inside her until she was moving urgently against him in the hunt for more contact, more pressure, more sensation. The aching need grew inside her until it dominated her thoughts and occupied her womb where she longed for Quinn to fill her. He had woken a slumbering appetite and it was clamouring to be fed.

'I want you,' she gasped, winding her fingers through his hair so she could pin him to her. Thrusting her body into his, she relished the sensation of his steel against her silk, his muscle against her softly yielding flesh. She was greedy for his lips and rubbed her cheek against his, loving the rasp of his cruel black stubble against her tender skin.

'Not here. Not now,' he said huskily, lifting her.

'Where are you taking me?' Though she was sure she knew. Not in the kitchen, not the first time. The first time was far too special for that.

When Quinn dipped his head and kissed her again, the question became redundant. He took her mouth with a breath-stealing lack of urgency as if he had all night to tease and arouse her. 'Do you remember what I promised you?' he murmured.

That he would make love to her? She would hardly forget a thing like that. She might have had her hang-ups back in the real world, but here in the sixties her body ached for Quinn all the more, knowing his plan. 'Just promise me one thing.'

'I promise to pleasure you until you fall asleep exhausted in my arms.'

One final thud of anxiety beat in her heart at the thought of disappointing him, but she pushed it aside. 'I want something else.'

'Greedy.' Running the palm of his hand lightly over her hair, he continued stroking her, from cheek to neck, before brushing the swell of her breast and the imperative thrust of her nipple with a tantalisingly light touch.

'Whatever happens between us,' Magenta whispered, trying to catch her breath, 'you won't let it interfere with your plans for the business—the chance you've given the girls?'

'They mean a lot to you, don't they?' Quinn murmured against her hair.

'Loyalty means everything to me.'

'Aren't you concerned about your own position in the company?'

'Of course I am, and if I fall short in any way I would expect you to ask me to leave. But not because of this—not because of us.'

'Us?'

Quinn's lips curved. Who knew what he was thinking? The only thing she could be sure about was the way she felt about Quinn.

He gave a dry laugh. 'Do you really think I'm going to mark you out of ten and take that score forward from the bedroom to the office? Your job's safe, Magenta; the company needs you. And, whatever happens between us, I'd be a fool not to consider what your colleagues have to offer. Reassured?' Quinn demanded. 'You should relax more and worry less.'

That might be possible if she had any useful experience in the bedroom department. 'I won't be any good.'

'You're going to be *very* good,' Quinn argued. 'I'm going to make sure of it.'

Quinn's lips were firm and tempting and the expression in his eyes reassured her. She wanted everything he had to give her, starting with tenderness, Magenta decided as Quinn nuzzled her neck. No—starting with fun, she amended when he pulled back to smile his sexy, curving smile. No. That was wrong too. She wanted to feel safe like this, to feel the strength of a man as he lifted her in his arms.

Oh, to hell with it—she wanted sex with a man who knew what he was doing, Magenta conceded as Quinn carried her up the stairs.

Quinn's bedroom was huge, warm and cosy, and was both neat and scrupulously clean. The scent of sandalwood hung in the air and the decor was tasteful—shades of cream, honey and chocolate—the perfect frame for Quinn, who kissed her firmly, skilfully, deeply. He lowered her onto linen sheets without pausing one instant. 'Where did you learn to kiss like that?' she demanded, smiling as she marvelled at his strength combined with such subtlety.

'They produce some great self-help manuals these days.'

This was some dream, Magenta thought, laughing with him; she was going to enjoy every minute if it. Reaching up, she started on Quinn's buttons. Pushing the shirt from his shoulders, she paused a moment to drink him in and wonder what she had done to deserve a dream like this. Quinn's torso was lightly tanned and heavily muscled. He was magnificent—perfect. If she could bottle this dream and sell it on the open market, she could save her company back in the real world without any help from anyone.

'You're so beautiful.' And she was so greedy for him. She tugged Quinn's shirt from his waistband to feast her eyes on his belly, banded with muscle. All men should be like this, and if women ruled the world they would be.

Kicking off his shoes, Quinn joined her on the bed. Stretching out his length against her, he ran his fingers lightly down her arms.

Could anything else feel this good? But when Quinn dipped his head to kiss her she pressed her hands against his chest and made him wait. 'Not yet. I want to look at you; I want to touch you—explore you.' She was finding strength she'd never known she had and, luckily for her, Quinn was willing to indulge her.

She smiled as he tucked his arms behind his head. Inhibitions? Quinn had none. And if Magenta was ever to lose her own hang-ups it was here with this man, and it was now.

She knelt over him, brushing his naked chest with her hair. 'Stay where you are,' she commanded softly when he made to move. Trailing her fingers across his chest, and down over that hard band of muscle to the waistband of his jeans, she teased Quinn as he had teased her. Hearing his shuddering breaths aroused her even more.

'And now it's my turn.'

She gasped as Quinn swung her beneath him.

'Trust me,' he said, seeing her apprehension.

The bond between them was growing, Magenta realised, and she did trust him. She groaned as Quinn caressed her. He was so intuitive; his hands knew everything about her body and sensation was already throbbing between her thighs.

'Is this your first time?'

She turned her face away from him. 'No.'

'Convince me,' Quinn demanded.

'I am worried.'

'About what?' he said. Cupping her chin, he made her look at him.

'I might have healed up...'

He laughed; they both laughed.

'You're frightened I might hurt you?'

I'm more frightened of the way you make me feel, Magenta thought. 'Not that—but I am frightened of losing control. I'm frightened of the sensation that builds inside me each time you touch me. I'm frightened of falling over the edge and never coming back. I'm frightened of experiencing something I can't begin to cope with.'

'Can you be more specific?'

'This is going to sound so stupid to you.'

'Try me,' Quinn suggested wryly.

'I have never—' She swallowed and started again in a firmer voice. 'I have never...'

'Had an orgasm?' Quinn supplied, making her blush.

Her face was on fire. She couldn't speak.

'And you want me to show you?'

'I'm not sure I do,' Magenta admitted.

'Only because you don't know what to expect. When you do, you won't want to stop.'

Her body responded with outrageous enthusiasm to Quinn's proposition.

He took his time undressing her, smoothing his hands down her body while she responded eagerly to his touch. Her desire was reflected in Quinn's eyes. She wanted everything he had to give—more sensation, more caresses—but she suspected Quinn would make her wait now he knew her secret. He would draw this out, allowing her time to think about the magnitude of the pleasure to come—pleasure he would bring her.

He proved this theory now. The more she tried to hurry him, the more his lazy smile assured her that he would set the pace.

'Why?' she demanded finally on a shaking breath. 'Why are you making me wait like this?'

'Because it will be worth waiting for.'

'I've waited long enough.'

Quinn's words and his stern expression, the note of command in his voice, all drove her to the pinnacle of lust—which he knew only too well. Quinn understood everything about her needs. He knew how to make her hungry for him and was shameless about using that power. Cupping her breast, he chafed her nipple through the flimsy fabric of her bra while his hot mouth attended to her other nipple. Her new lacy underwear concealed nothing; she could see that her nipples were no longer modestly pink, but were livid and erect. Her cobweb-fine briefs did even less to conceal the brazen swelling of a body that had to know Quinn's touch—and soon.

He had slipped a pillow beneath her buttocks and now she realised why. He wanted her to see the pleasure he was bringing her—he wanted her to have clear sight of all her erotic zones responding to him as he coaxed them into pleasure.

'I think you like that,' he observed when she sucked in a noisy breath.

'I don't like you teasing me,' she complained, writhing

beneath him as she tried in vain to capture some elusive pressure from his hands. 'How can you do this? How can you wait like this?' She arced towards him, but Quinn was too fast for her, and had already moved his hands away.

'I can't bear it!'

'Well, I can—and you are going to learn the benefit of delay.'

She reached for his belt.

'I refuse to rush.'

'You must—you have to help me,' she insisted. It was then that Quinn pressed his lips to her ear.

'When you're swollen and ready to the point where you can't hold on, then I'll help you.' Lifting her, he deftly removed her bra and tossed it aside. She moved to cover herself, but Quinn wouldn't let her. 'It's my turn to look at *you*,' he said.

She loved the note of command in his voice and, resting back on the pillow, she raised her arms above her head, displaying her body for his approval. Her breasts were full; Quinn approved, she gathered, as he caressed them. When he had suckled to his heart's content, he buried his face in them. 'You were made to be loved, Magenta Steele.'

By you. Only by you. 'Has anyone ever told you you're very good at this?' she said, easing her head on the pillow to look down at him.

'How would you like me to answer that?' Quinn demanded softly, staring at her with amusement.

'With the truth?'

But Quinn just laughed and moved farther down the bed.

She cried out softly, feeling his hot breath on her thighs. 'Oh *please*,' she begged as his strong, white teeth teased and tormented, sharp against her hot flesh. Arcing her body, she made it easier for him to remove the scrap of lace, which was all that was left between them, and then whimpered when he pressed her to him flesh to flesh. She should feel embarrassed—awkward, apprehensive—but instead she was lifting her hips for him. She was ready, more than ready, for the pleasure Quinn had promised her.

And then he touched her.

CHAPTER TWELVE

SHE went quite still. She didn't want to breathe or move in case she did anything to distract Quinn and make the pleasure stop. Time was suspended as he began to touch her in a more purposeful manner. His movements were leisurely so she had a chance to relish each studied movement. Delicately parting her swollen lips, he touched her with his tongue. Rough tongue, hot flesh, warm breath and the steady but dependable rhythm he set up soon brought her to the edge. 'Lie still,' he commanded. 'Let me do everything. Do you understand?'

She could only gasp something unintelligible in reply. She wanted to keep her focus on Quinn and the pleasure he was bringing her.

He began again.

'Oh, no, no, no!' she exclaimed, thrashing her head about on the pillows when he stopped. 'You can't stop now. Even you couldn't be so cruel!'

'Cruel?' Quinn demanded softly, moving back up the bed. 'I'm not cruel. You have no idea how considerate I can be—especially when you follow my instructions to the letter.'

'You are so bad,' she breathed. 'But I will. I will…'

The last thing she saw was Quinn's lips curving and then he was moving down the bed to start again.

'I can't hold on,' she wailed as the tidal wave rushed towards her.

Quinn might have answered; she wouldn't have known. She

bucked convulsively as the first climactic throb of pleasure claimed her, and only heard herself crying out his name when the violent surges of pleasure began to subside. Quinn held her as she writhed beneath his firm touch until she quietened. 'That was…amazing.'

'More?' he suggested.

'I have to undress you.'

'You have to?' Quinn curbed a grin.

'Absolutely. Now I know what I've been missing. Like you said, I have plans.'

Sitting up in bed with her long, dark hair tumbling over her shoulders, she started on Quinn's belt. She hated the thickness of the leather and the stubbornness of the tine. His erection thrust imperatively against the denim, tantalising her, taunting her, and when she finally released the zip it flew back under enormous pressure. 'Lift your hips.' Her voice sounded harsh and primitive, matching the hunger inside her. Inhibitions meant nothing to her now. She was claiming her mate.

Boxers followed Quinn's jeans to the floor, and only now did she hesitate. Quinn might have prepared her to the point of no return, but seeing him naked like this for the first time startled her. Could she possibly take him inside her? He was so much bigger than she had imagined, more brazenly masculine in every way, and utterly unselfconscious about it. Powerful and virile, this was a man in peak condition, muscular and tanned, and right now he was formidably aroused.

'Is something wrong?' he said.

'I want you.' She held his gaze, and Quinn knew from her expression that at this point she needed him to take over.

Reaching out, he brushed the hair back from her face. She felt awkward momentarily, even surprised that Quinn would make sliding on a condom part of the love play between them.

'Can I?' she said shyly.

She had everything to learn and now was her chance. Covering her hand with his, Quinn guided her.

She had always thought it would be embarrassing to manage the mechanics of love-making but nothing was awkward with Quinn. He was so open about everything it made her feel the same way. And this opportunity to explore him, to feel him beneath her hands, warm, hard, veined and smooth, thick and pulsating...

Closing her eyes, she relished the simple pleasure of touch, but then Quinn brought her down to the bed and she was soon distracted. Their kisses grew in heat until they were tumbling over each other as if no touch or kiss, no tangling of limbs or wild, raw, heated embrace, could ever be enough for them. Quinn's body was a passport to pleasure and hers was his to use as he pleased.

But right at the moment, when she should have been at her most receptive, the doubts swept back in. Sensing the change in her, Quinn stilled immediately.

She moved away.

'Are you still afraid I might hurt you?' Bringing her back into his arms, Quinn dropped kisses on her brow, on her eyes and on her lips.

'I'm more frightened of disappointing you.'

Quinn smiled his reassurance against her mouth. 'You could never disappoint me. But if you don't want this...'

'I definitely want it.'

'And I definitely want it. So it seems to me we're riding the same wave here.'

Quinn's lips pressed down attractively as he cupped her face, caressing her cheeks with his thumb pads. From there his hands continued to soothe as his kisses migrated down her neck to her breasts, and from there to her belly and the inside of her thighs. He moved lower, kissing her ankles as he massaged her feet until she thought she would faint with pleasure, before moving on to caress her calves and lick the back of her knees—a place she could never have imagined held such potential for sensation. 'Don't you dare stop,' she ordered him huskily, linking her hands behind her head as he rested her legs on his shoulders. 'Do I please you?'

'What do you think?' Quinn murmured.

She sighed and pressed against him, pressed against his mouth. She didn't want to hold anything back. She wanted to experience everything Quinn wanted to give her to the full. And after he'd brought her to the edge again he straightened up to brush himself against her. He teased her with the delicious foretaste of the pleasure to come until she cried out in complaint. His answer to this was to tease her again, drawing himself more slowly this time over each moist and swollen part of her, until she was relaxed enough for him to stretch her with just the tip.

The sensation was so extreme, so good, that when Quinn made to withdraw this time she thrust her hips towards him, claiming him.

The breath shot out of Magenta's lungs in a rush. She wasn't even sure if she could take all of him; sensing her shock, Quinn worked some magic with his fingers and, with that and his kisses to distract her, he took control. It was only moments until he inhabited her completely.

Quinn moved and she moved with him, marvelling at the lack of pain, the lack of fear, even though he was stretching her beyond anything she would have imagined possible. He filled her in the most pleasing way, massaging her most effectively, and it wasn't long before she was working frantically with him towards the inevitable conclusion. Digging her fingers into his buttocks, she pressed her hips down until she was certain that no part of them was left unconnected, and moments later the first spasm hit her. Crying Quinn's name, she abandoned herself to pleasure, bucking uncontrollably yet registering somewhere in the depths of her mind that her first orgasm with Quinn had just been utterly eclipsed.

It took ages for her to recover and ages for the delicious little aftershocks of extreme pleasure to subside. Quinn rested deep inside her, waiting until he judged her sufficiently recovered, and then he began to move. Rolling his hips slowly from side to side, he brought the hunger back again and the next climax hit her before she even knew it was building. Screaming out his name, she thrust her hips convulsively while Quinn held her firmly in place, making sure she enjoyed every moment of it.

'You're spoiling me,' she managed groggily as he moved to take her again.

'We're only getting started,' Quinn assured her. 'I'm taking the edge off your hunger.'

'Taking the edge off!' Magenta laughed, but Quinn confirmed his intentions, dropping kisses on her swollen lips. 'And when I've done that,' he said, 'just as I promised I would, I'm going to make love to you.'

'Haven't we been doing that?'

Quinn's laugh was low and sexy. 'Come on, Magenta,' he murmured in her ear. 'We both know that neither of us is cut out for a diet of canapés.'

As Quinn was already moving deep inside her she had no intention of arguing with that. Holding her secure in his arms, Quinn was rocking her. 'Harder,' she begged him greedily. 'Take me faster, Quinn.' Then speech was no longer possible. 'Hold me!' she cried out in the last few ecstatic moments.

Cupping her buttocks firmly, Quinn kept her in position as she thrust her fists against his chest. She needed something to brace herself against as her mind was ripped from her body and flung into a world of unimaginable colour and sensation. She explored it to the full, knowing that when she finally quietened Quinn would be waiting to soothe her with reassurances that she was safe.

This was definitely the way forward, Magenta decided, practically purring with contentment as she woke slowly the following morning, thankfully still in the sixties, in Quinn's huge bed. They had made love through the night and only dawn had interrupted them. At the first faint glimmer of light, Quinn had sprung up and left her side.

Her heart filled when he returned from taking a shower. It was no use pretending this was anything casual. She couldn't get enough of him—and no wonder. With a towel slung around his hips like a loin cloth, Quinn was quite a sight to wake up to in the morning. He was the full package, she reflected contentedly, easing her sated limbs. Quinn had the body of a gladiator and a mind like a steel trap. He was funny and tender, and had an appetite for sex that knew no bounds. He was *the* dream lover.

She could so easily make a habit of this, Magenta mused as he strolled towards the bed, drying his wayward hair on a towel.

'It's time to get up.'

'Already?' she complained.

'Work?' Quinn reminded her.

'Work?' she echoed without any of her usual enthusiasm. 'Can't we stay here a little longer?' For the first time in her life, there was something a lot more important than work— such as being with Quinn. Gazing up into his face, she only found it disappointingly resolute.

'Work,' he confirmed, turning on his heels. 'Take a shower; there's plenty of hot water.'

Take a shower—alone? Mageneta frowned, wishing she hadn't heard the distant note in Quinn's voice. After last night she had expected things to be very different between them.

She waited until she was sure he was busy dressing before creeping out of bed. Grabbing her discarded clothes, she held them in front of her. She felt self-conscious suddenly. Quinn made her feel as if she had overstayed her welcome—a sense that only grew when he asked if she wanted a lift to the office.

If? He hadn't even turned to look at her yet.

'I don't want to be late,' he explained. Stepping inside his open-plan dressing room, he started the process of selecting a tie. 'I've got a lot on this morning.'

She mustn't think the worst of him. 'You've called a meeting of the team?' she guessed hopefully.

'Yes, I have,' he confirmed.

If this was an opportunity to get those girls out of the typing pool, she'd forgive him anything. 'Great. I'll be as quick as I can,' she promised, springing out of bed.

She had to be positive about this, Magenta told herself firmly as she stepped into a proper shower beneath steaming spray. She might have known that even in the sixties Quinn would enjoy state-of-the-art plumbing. She had to put her personal feelings to one side and recognise the meeting Quinn had called for the victory it was. And what had she imagined—that Quinn intended to progress their relationship? It was time to get real, time to come to grips with the era in which she found herself, however much that hurt.

But as they drove to the office, and she stared out of Quinn's car window at the sixties cityscape of concrete and high-rise grey boxes, there was nothing she wanted more than a return to real time, real relationships, and an end to this confusing dream if that was what it was. She had expected to be intrigued by everything she saw. She had also expected to be set free to enjoy a whole new set of rules. What she had not expected was those rules leading her to feel so deeply about Quinn, or to find that sexual freedom came with quite such a heavy price tag.

Quinn remained aloof and unspeaking throughout the journey, while Magenta tried to persuade herself that he was mentally preparing himself for the day ahead. Whatever had happened between them, she was determined to show a bright face at the office. There was enough uncertainty there without her adding to it, and the most important thing she had to do today was to tell the girls the good news.

Magenta felt even more positive when she entered the office to discover that the partition around the typing pool had been removed; Quinn had kept his word. Even if the girls were still sitting in rows typing, at least they could see what was going on around them now. And, most importantly, they felt good about the changes, judging by the smiling faces that greeted her.

Her feelings of elation grew when Quinn invited her and the girls to join his team in the boardroom that morning. She had suspected he might, and had briefed the girls beforehand, urging them to speak out and ignore any slights the men might throw their way. 'We have to be professional, even if they aren't,' she'd warned. 'If we want Quinn to involve us in the campaign, it's crucial that we keep emotion out of it. We have nothing to prove in there other than the fact that our ideas are better than theirs.'

'You bet they are,' Nancy had agreed. 'We're behind you all the way, Magenta.'

One of the girls still made coffee for everyone, Magenta noticed. But she told herself she mustn't be greedy. Quinn was right in that lasting change took time to implement. One small step at a time would suit her, so long as that step was in the right direction.

She led the way into the boardroom and acknowledged Quinn as if they hadn't spent the night in each other's arms.

'Magenta,' he greeted her in much the same way. 'Would you and your team like to sit down?'

'Thank you.'

Ever the gentleman, Quinn remained standing until he and his team had seen all the women comfortably settled around the table. Quinn had clearly briefed his team in advance, as Magenta had, and she took this as a good sign. Quinn had also recognised that nothing could be achieved in an atmosphere of taunts and sneering remarks.

'Would you care to begin?' he said. His eyes reflected nothing more than professional interest.

She had to ignore the ache of disappointment inside her and do her job. 'Nancy?' she prompted. 'Would you like to begin by explaining what we have here on the easels?'

Magenta had never wanted to hog the limelight, and couldn't help but be thrilled by the audible gasp of surprise from the men when Nancy revealed the team's first idea. Vivid, graphic imagery and clever text was a winning combination—no one could deny it, not even the men around the table. The general theme was irony, suggesting men must be catered for and even spoiled a little so that women were free to do their own thing.

'You're suggesting we should be pampered and cosseted so we work harder and stay out of your way?' one of the men queried, glancing at Quinn—who had remained carefully neutral up to now—to see his reaction.

'With more women in the work place year on year, I'm sure that's a message that resonates with everyone,' Magenta said, defending her team's premise good-humouredly.

'I think we can see that Magenta's group is coming up with some sound ideas,' Quinn observed. 'Not all of them will fly,' he added, 'but I'm sure we can tailor them to suit our purposes. They will enrich the project—and we shouldn't close our minds to a new approach,' he added when there were murmurs of discontent from the men around the table.

What did Quinn mean? Magenta wondered. She didn't want to rain on her team's parade—the women were all excited that at last they were being taken seriously—but having their ideas 'tailored' to fit in with those of the men didn't sound like the end result Magenta had been aiming for.

CHAPTER THIRTEEN

MAGENTA'S worst fears were soon confirmed.

'Jackson, you take the graphics and work on them,' Quinn instructed. 'And Michael, you handle the fashion side of things. You're more in touch with your feminine side than the rest of us.'

As if a dam had burst, the tension between the men at the table relaxed and they all burst out laughing; it wasn't kind laughter. It was laughter directed at the women in their midst, as if to be a woman was somehow contrary to the laws of business.

Or at least business under Quinn, Magenta thought, feeling betrayed. She could only watch in impotent horror as one by one the ideas her team had worked so hard on were handed over to a member of Quinn's team to progress. The good of the business had to be her only concern if everyone was going to keep their job, but how was she going to explain this to the women who had trusted her? She could feel their shock as well as their disappointment. They would become resigned soon and she couldn't wait around for that to happen. 'May I have a word with you—in private?' she asked Quinn when he brought the meeting to a close.

'About business?'

'What else?' Her gaze drilled into him, telling him in pretty blunt language what she thought of both his question and his manner.

'Won't you sit down?' he said when the last man had left the room.

'I prefer to remain standing, thank you.'

'As you wish.'

Getting up from his chair, Quinn went to stand beside the window, staring out. It had started snowing, Magenta noticed, but that was nothing to the sheet of ice that had closed around her heart. 'I thought we had an agreement.'

Quinn turned to face her. 'And as far as I'm aware,' he said, 'I have fulfilled my obligation to you.'

'I don't understand what you're doing,' Magenta admitted.

'It's clear enough to me.'

'Well, not to me. My ideas and those of my team—I thought you were prepared to consider them, to incorporate them. I never imagined for one moment that you, of all people, would steal them.'

'Steal them?' Quinn demanded. 'What are you suggesting?' His eyes turned black.

Her job, her future—everything hung in the balance, Magenta realized. But this was a battle that had to be fought. 'You took ideas the women have been working hard to perfect and handed them over to the men when all the hard work has been done. I wouldn't mind, but those men don't have an original idea between them. Why should they claim credit for work that isn't theirs?'

'We all work for the same company.'

'Well, of course we do,' Magenta agreed, trying to remain calm. 'But why do you trust the men here more than the women? What makes you assume they have more ability? Quinn, I don't know what's happened to you!' she exclaimed finally, as exasperation got the better of her.

The expression in Quinn's eyes gave her no hope at all.

'Don't ever make the mistake of thinking that what happens between us in our off-duty moments is a green light in the office.'

'I haven't,' Magenta protested. 'I wouldn't—'

'But that's exactly what you're doing,' Quinn cut in. 'Since last night, you have had expectations that go far beyond the bedroom. Well?' he demanded harshly. 'Don't you, Magenta?'

'I thought I could trust you, yes.'

'You can trust me. You can trust me to keep a consistent line. You can't walk in here hours after your promotion and think you can order this business to your liking. New systems have to be tried and proven first. I don't operate a business on a whim—not even my own whim, and especially not yours.'

As each hammer blow landed on her heart, Magenta wished one of them would be violent enough to wake her up. How could anyone share what she'd shared with Quinn last night and feel nothing? How could he switch off from her like this? And, as for the green light, the only light she was aware of was flashing in her brain, telling her she'd made a fool of herself. And their 'off-duty moments'? Quinn made their love-making sound like a useful alternative to counting sheep.

She'd let her team down, and wouldn't make things right by handing in her resignation. And, even if she waited for this nightmare to pass, what if it didn't pass? What if this was her life now?

She had to stay and fight. It didn't matter whether this was a dream or her reality now, her internal dial would remain tuned to the same setting it was always on, which was survival and the determination to defend those she cared about.

She couldn't have felt worse when she called the girls together. 'You're far more supportive than I deserve,' she told them, feeling dreadful when she noticed the small bunch of flowers someone had arranged in a vase on her desk. 'I've let you down, misled you. I can't apologise enough for what happened at the meeting. I had no idea Quinn would take that line. I really thought he was going to involve all of you in the steering group for the campaign. But this isn't the end,' she promised. 'I won't allow your ideas to be squandered or diluted by anyone—and we're not going to sulk or cause a problem,' she added decisively. 'We're going to win this battle by being the very best we can and by selling direct to the customer.'

'Quinn,' Nancy supplied.

'Yes, that's right, Nancy—Quinn,' Magenta agreed. 'Quinn is the only person we have to convince.' She exclaimed with shock as a familiar hand took hold of her arm and firmly moved her aside.

'I was trying to warn you,' Nancy explained discreetly as Quinn went into his office and shut the door.

Could the girls hear her heart hammering? Magenta hoped not. It was crucial that they still believed in her or those typing-pool partitions would soon be up again. 'I'm going in to see him now, to convince him he's made a mistake and needs us on board. I had a word with him after the meeting, but I was too angry to think straight, and so of course Quinn took advantage.'

'That's not such a bad thing, is it?' Nancy said, injecting some much-needed humour into the tense mix. 'We've all seen the way Quinn looks at you.' Nancy glanced around the other girls for confirmation.

'Please stop.' This was absolutely the last thing Magenta wanted to hear. 'I can assure you there is nothing going on between Quinn and me.' Not any longer there wasn't—nor was there ever likely to be again. 'We're as different as two people could be.'

'We all saw the way he touched you just now,' Nancy argued. 'And you never know when a hand on your arm leads to a night on your back,' she added, which made the other girls laugh.

Magenta blushed furiously as the girls continued to tease her, but she was glad they were laughing again. 'Quinn's probably watching us,' she warned. 'We'd better get back to work. We don't want to give him any reason for complaint. Just pick up where you left off,' she said, exchanging meaningful looks with the girls. 'We're not going to give up on this.'

Playing by Quinn's rules, Magenta took him his morning coffee and remained calm as she shut the door. But the moment he looked up at her all her protective instincts for the girls rose up and poured out. 'You've made a mistake cutting the girls out of the equation.'

'Well, thank you for your opinion, Magenta, but I've made the right decision—and you've just proved it.'

'What do you mean?'

'There's no place for emotion at the office, and if I encourage women to seek promotion it would open the floodgates.'

'To feelings?' Whatever she said now would influence every woman's future at the company. 'Isn't that exactly why my team's ideas are more likely to connect with the public than yours? Or do you really think the market deserves another macho ad-campaign dreamed up by men?'

'There's nothing wrong with passion.'

'But no to emotion? How does that work, Quinn?'

'Magenta.' He sighed. 'I have work to do.'

'Allow the girls to work on their projects without consulting the men at every turn and they'll work faster,' she pleaded with him. 'Let them do that, and then you judge which campaign you prefer. Or is that too big a risk for your male ego to take?'

There was a glint in Quinn's eyes as he leaned back to stare at her.

'This is all about you running a successful business, isn't it?' Magenta continued. 'Or did I miss something? And there is one question I would like you to answer.'

'Which is?' Quinn's eyes turned hard.

'What difference does gender make to a successful team?'

He relaxed, making her wonder if Quinn had expected her to attack him on the personal front. 'That's for you to prove and for all of us to find out,' he said.

'We still get our chance?' She kept the pressure on. She had no intention of walking away from this and making things easy for him.

'Don't push me, Magenta.'

'So, that's a yes?'

'That's a maybe,' he corrected her.

She counted it as a victory—however small—and, knowing she'd pushed things as far as she could, she turned to the subject of the end-of-year party. How many more of these cold-blooded meetings with Quinn could she take? It was better to get through as much as she could now, Magenta reasoned.

Quinn was looking at her as if assessing how much she could take on. 'It will be held at the end of this week, well before Christmas,' he said. 'Not much time for you to arrange things, but that suits my schedule better. Well? Don't you have work to do?'

Magenta's head was reeling with all the things she had to do. Quinn had just brought the party forward with no warning at all. She could throw up her hands and admit defeat, or…

'If you can't handle it,' he said, 'just let me know.'

'I can handle it,' she assured him.

'Do you have a theme?'

Did she have a theme?

'If it's good enough, it might buy your team a second hearing.'

In that case, she definitely had the theme. 'I've got the theme.'

Well, she would have in a minute.

'I'm listening.'

'The theme is…' She had to come up with something mildly original or go to the bottom of the class, risking the girls' opportunity to advance in the business in the process. 'Back to the future,' she said as inspiration struck. Okay, it was not so original, but Quinn wouldn't know that. 'It can be interpreted any way people like—but, as we've had the first man in space, and the race is on to land a man on the moon…' Ideas were tumbling over each other in her brain.

'Could be different,' Quinn admitted.

'Could be fun.'

'Could be.'

'I'm interested to see how you interpret it. And Magenta?'

'So…?'

She turned at the door.

'I'm going to trial some of your ideas.'

'You are?' All her personal battles with Quinn were put on hold. She felt like hugging him. Fortunately, after what had happened, she had more sense.

'Tell your team to get back to work on the ad campaign right away.'

'They never *stopped* working on it,' she said quietly.

CHAPTER FOURTEEN

'WHAT are you complaining about?' Magenta heard one of the men, who she'd heard others address as John, taunting Nancy in the main office as she closed Quinn's door. 'You've still got a job, haven't you?'

The men hadn't waited long to resume their bullying tactics, Magenta reflected angrily. It was vital the girls won this battle or there would always be conflict between the sexes in the office. But at least Quinn had agreed to give them a chance. She had even persuaded him to let them use the old boardroom as their temporary campaign-headquarters, and she'd planned to call an emergency meeting there now. But overhearing the exchange between Nancy and their male colleague reminded Magenta how far they had to go—that and the fact that she could wake up at any moment, leaving her new team in the lurch.

'It's tradition,' John was saying. 'You women are supposed to make all the homey, holiday preparations. Just because you have a few letters to type, that's no excuse. We need our mince pies and treats while we handle the real work around here.'

If any useful work was going to get done, they all had to calm down. 'I'm afraid the girls won't be free to run errands for you,' Magenta explained, shooting a warning glance at Nancy.

'Oh?' John demanded. Glancing at his cronies, he sat back, staring at Magenta as if he were a headmaster forced to deal with a child he considered very much his intellectual inferior.

'We're all going to be busy, because we're all back in the race,' Magenta explained. 'Quinn is going to judge both campaigns and choose the one he prefers.'

'But we've got all your ideas,' John said with a laugh in his voice as he traded smug glances with his friends.

'It's what you do with what you've got that makes the difference,' Magenta argued, stealing a glance at Quinn through the office window. 'Girls, follow me to our new headquarters.'

They worked until the end of the day on finessing their campaign, and then the girls insisted on staying behind to help Magenta plan the Christmas party.

'Quinn had a few stipulations to make. Beyond that, we're free to interpret the theme any way we choose.'

'Within a tight budget?' Nancy guessed shrewdly.

'This is hardly the best time to go overboard,' Magenta agreed. 'But I'm happy to cover any shortfall.' Though quite how far her office manager's wage packet would stretch...

'Am I right in thinking you have come up with an idea?' Nancy prompted.

'I have,' Magenta confirmed, revealing her theme for the party.

'But no space-food,' Nancy insisted. 'The only thing I'm prepared to drink through a straw is a cocktail.'

'You don't have to follow a space theme at all,' Magenta explained. 'All I'm suggesting is that each of us interprets the future as we see it.'

'No long hair, caftans, beads or beards!' Nancy exclaimed with relief.

'Not if you remember to shave,' one her friends added with a laugh.

'But the food stays how we like it,' another member of the team insisted. 'All the usual, with my favourite, cheese-and-pineapple on sticks. I'll even volunteer to cover the cabbage with foil.'

'Hang on,' Magenta protested. 'I'm good with cheese and pineapple, but since when do we eat cabbage at a party unless it's in a bowl of coleslaw?'

'We don't eat it,' Tess said, giving Magenta a sideways look. 'We cover the cabbage in foil and stab sticks loaded with the cheese and pineapple into it. Surely you've seen a finished hedgehog before?'

'A hedgehog?'

'Oh, never mind. You'd better handle the cocktails.'

'My pleasure,' Magenta agreed, mentally wiping her brow. Her knowledge of sixties food-fads was non-existent.

'It's just a pity the men are going to be there,' Nancy observed as the girls started working out who was going to be involved in dressing the office and who would arrange the music.

'I'm glad they'll be there,' Magenta argued. 'I want this year's party to bring everyone together. We need something to stop this silly bickering. We have to land this colour-magazine job, and to do that we have to work as one.'

'That'll be the day,' Nancy snorted.

'Well, at least let's give it a try.'

'I suppose there could be worse things than spending the night with a crowd of randy ad men,' Nancy agreed thoughtfully.

'Can we put sex to one side for a minute and concentrate on planning?' Magenta suggested.

'If we put sex aside for as long as that, it will all be over.'

'Give those poor men a chance, Nancy!' Magenta exclaimed, choking back a laugh.

She caught Quinn glancing at them through the window as he walked past. Their eyes might only have clashed briefly, but it was enough to tell Magenta that there was still a live spark between them. Interesting. According to some market research she'd been working on, fifty-nine per cent of men rated women who stood up to them as having the ideal qualities they looked for in a mate. Excellent. *En garde*, Gray Quinn...

Tamping down the rush of heat inside her, she called the meeting to order. 'Can we get back to work, please? There's very little time to do this and we have the campaign to work on during the day—which, by the way, is more important. We're going to give those men a real run for their money when we submit our final ideas to Quinn.'

'And we're going to have the best Christmas party ever,' Nancy added.

Magenta smiled back. 'This is one party that is definitely going down in history.'

How she missed the computer! She never thought she'd say that, Magenta realised, checking the mock-up of the party invitation she had designed. But finally the invitation was ready to go to the printer's and the Back To The Future party was on its way.

'Still here?' Quinn commented, peering round the door.

I could say the same about you, Magenta thought. They were both workaholics.

As Quinn came into the room, her skin began to tingle with anticipation. It was no use pretending she could somehow make herself immune to Quinn. There was a connection between them and she wasn't prepared to let go of it yet. The air had changed—she had changed. She was like an animal scenting her mate. Every breath she took was drenched in Quinn's energy and his clean, distinctive scent. All the more reason to get out of here, her inner alarm advised her. 'I was just leaving, actually.'

'Can I buy you a drink?'

Was he joking? 'It's been a long day.' She kept her back turned so Quinn couldn't see her cheeks flushing with the memory of humiliation. His idea of free love wasn't hers. She was better off without him.

'Are you sure?'

'I'm quite sure, thank you.'

She hadn't realised Quinn was right behind her and bumped into him when she turned around. He showed no sign of moving. She could only get past him by brushing up against him—something which no doubt would give Quinn great amusement. 'Excuse me, please…'

She didn't want this; she didn't want to feel Quinn's heat warming her, or the power in his body reminding her of what they'd shared. She certainly didn't want him towering over her, or his hard, muscular frame awakening memories better left undisturbed.

She exhaled with relief when Quinn stood back. 'I would prefer it if we could keep everything between us on a professional level,' she said, staring into eyes that were nowhere near convinced.

'Suits me.' A faint smile played around the corner of Quinn's mouth.

'We'll have the presentation ready for you very soon. My girls are ready.'

'And you, Magenta?'

'I'm ready too,' she assured him.

The crease in Quinn's cheek deepened. 'Any chance you might have lightened up by the time the party comes around?'

'I'll be on the cocktail bar,' she said. 'And I'll mix you anything you like.'

Quinn hummed. 'I take it you have something appropriate to wear?'

'An apron?'

'I was thinking of something a touch more glamorous than that.'

'Something you'd approve of?'

'Pleasing me would be a first.'

Short memory, she thought. 'I won't be trying to please anyone—I'll be wearing one of the products your team is eager to push in the campaign.'

'Now you've got me worried. Are you going to give me a clue?'

'Paper?' She kept her face admirably straight.

'Paper?' Quinn frowned, but then his eyes began to dance with laughter. 'You're going to wear a paper dress?'

'Apparently they're going to be the next big thing.'

'Is that right?' Quinn said. He even held the door for her, and was still smiling when she left the room.

The day of the presentation dawned bright and clear. Quinn kept everything close to his chest. He hadn't been in the previous day, and Magenta had missed the electricity between them as well as Quinn's ironic glances and challenging stares. The office had ticked over while Quinn had been away, but had lacked some essential spark. Now he was back.

Magenta's heart rate soared when Quinn strode into the office, and she wasn't the only one to be affected. He had changed the mood in an instant from diligent to enthused—and no wonder; Quinn looked like a film star with his tan, his build and bearing.

Magenta was pleased she had gone the extra mile with her appearance for the all-important meeting. Jackie Kennedy had set the pace for the elegant woman of the sixties, with the clean lines of her Oleg Cassini fashions, and this morning Magenta was wearing a copy of one of the beautifully tailored suits the girls were keen to feature in the ad campaign. A better bet than paper, Magenta thought wryly. The men didn't stand a chance if they were pushing things like that. She had made sure the girls had the first choice from the rail of stylish garments which the photographer had left in the staff room, but she couldn't have been more delighted with the soft red suit Nancy had kept to one side for her.

'Nice,' Quinn said briefly, looking Magenta up and down. 'Call everyone in, will you?'

Would he ever change?

Never, Magenta concluded.

Would he ever pause to take breath? Rarely, she thought, remembering the non-stop action in his bed—which was the only encouragement her cheeks needed to fire up to the same shade as her jacket.

Oh yes, it was a triumph, Magenta agreed with the other girls later. Quinn had chosen their ideas hands down. 'But no crowing,' she insisted. 'Especially not if there's someone in the office you like. Remember, no man likes to be put down.'

'Like we've been for years?' Nancy countered, still glowing from her promotion to assistant account-executive.

'Men are more fragile,' Magenta said thoughtfully. 'We have to protect their egos if we want the best out of them.'

'Just as they have to treat us as equals if they want the best out of us,' Nancy put in.

'You're right,' Magenta agreed. 'Respect has to be earned on both sides.'

'And you have to lighten up.'

Magenta huffed wryly at Nancy's comment. 'Someone else said that.'

'Let me guess…' Nancy murmured, sucking her cheek.

'Never mind who said it. We're fighting for equality, and that's a serious business.'

'So is partying,' Nancy insisted. 'So we're going to put our concerns about the men's ability to contribute anything remotely useful to an ad campaign to one side for now and give them chance to schmooze us. But if we're going to party you have to, too. And you have to be nice to Quinn, Magenta.'

He's given us this chance, so now you have to give him a chance.'

Now everyone started teasing her. 'All right, I give in!' she exclaimed. 'I will give him a chance—a tiny, miniscule chance.'

'Yeah, right,' Nancy said to a chorus of disbelieving jeers.

CHAPTER FIFTEEN

THE night of the party turned out better than Magenta had dared to expect. Her colleagues forgot their differences and started to mingle and get to know each other. Friendships were forged across the sexes, which was exactly what she had hoped would happen—and some of those friendships were heating up, which couldn't hurt. But when Quinn called her into his office she soon realised that not everything was going to plan.

She should have thought this through, she realised as Quinn gave her outfit a scorching review. 'That dress is shapeless.'

And thin. And she was only wearing paper knickers beneath her paper dress, while Quinn—alarmingly, surprisingly, incredibly—was dressed exactly as she would expect a sexy guy to dress for an evening out in the twenty-first century. He wore a crisp, white shirt with the sleeves rolled back to reveal his muscular, hair-shaded forearms, sharp jeans with an understated belt and the cleanest black shoes Magenta had ever seen. This, together with the craziest-coloured socks, she noticed now as he crossed his legs at the desk to lean back and stare at her—red, fuchsia-pink and black stripes—quirky, sexy, different. 'Let me explain.'

'Please do,' Quinn invited dryly.

'It's a paper dress,' she explained, running her hands down the offending garment. 'So you can't expect it to be cut in a sharp design. It's meant to represent practicality.'

'Well, I doubt it will ever take off in a big way, other than into a niche market. Something as ugly as that doesn't deserve to last in the realms of fashion.'

'Thanks for the vote of confidence. It's one of the products your team was keen to promote, by the way.'

'I hadn't forgotten.'

Quinn's eyes had lit—was that humour?

'Personally, I agree with you. I don't think paper fashion will fly for long, however fiercely we promote it.' But, eerily, Quinn was correct; disposable paper-garments would have a niche market in clinics, beauty salons and other places where a single wear was all that was required. Of course, she had the benefit of knowing this for sure while he could only be using his intuition. She dismissed the shiver down her spine. Quinn couldn't be aware of the future. 'At least I'm there with the theme,' she said, eager to distract herself from questions with no answers as she looked him up and down.

'As am I,' Quinn said, standing up. 'I'm guessing this is exactly what I'd be wearing if we were living in the twenty-first century.'

Magenta paled. The shiver was back again. Why had he chosen the twenty-first century in particular?

'You've done well,' he observed, lifting the slats of the blind covering his window. 'Everyone appears to be enjoying themselves.'

'I'm glad you're pleased.'

Quinn's appreciative glance sent heat dancing through her.

'You look hot, Magenta.'

'Do I?' Magenta's hand flew to her brow. 'Perhaps a glass of water…'

'Or a jug full?'

She shrieked with shock as Quinn slowly poured the jug of water on his desk slowly down the front of her dress.

'I can't believe you did that!' she exclaimed. 'You've—'

'Ruined your dress?' Quinn hummed. 'You know, I think you're right; this will never catch on.' Taking hold of the front of it, he peeled it off her.

She was shivering with a combination of shock, anger and arousal as Quinn continued his unrelenting survey. 'Stop that,' she said. 'You can't just—'

'Trial a product?' he suggested.

'I am not a product.'

'If you were, I'd buy you.'

'Like you'd get the chance,' she huffed, but fighting off images of Quinn in his role of sexual master of the universe with a shopping list in hand wasn't quite so easy. 'And what am I supposed to do now?' Crossing her hands and arms over her sodden paper-bra and pants, she glowered at him. 'Should I staple a few sheets of A4 together and go as a galleon?'

'Lucky for you, I bought a dress.'

'You bought a dress?' she queried. 'Good for you. I'm sure you'll look very nice in it.'

'For you, idiot.'

And now she *was* shocked. 'What type of dress?' she demanded suspiciously. 'I'd better warn you now, I don't do caftans.'

'Or micro-minis, apparently.' Quinn stared at her legs, where to Magenta's horror she realised her hold-up stockings were slowly slipping down and wrinkling unattractively around her ankles.

'Shame about the underwear,' he murmured, drawing Magenta's attention back to his sexy mouth. 'I guess that's gone south too.'

She tipped her chin in the air and refused to look at him. Quinn had probably bought her a prim little school-ma'am dress, complete with a coy little Peter Pan collar, long sleeves, full skirt, and a nipped-in waist—and she'd hate it.

Or not.

She stared in surprise as Quinn produced the dress.

Now she was thrown into total confusion, because this was a dress that perfectly complemented Quinn's twenty-first-century clothes. It was a figure-flattering navy-blue column of silk cut just above the knee—but the finishing touch really floored her. 'Where on earth did you get these?' she gasped as Quinn handed her a pair of sexy black suede shoes with tell-tale red soles.

'Not only am I well prepared,' he said dryly, 'I am also way ahead of my time.'

A feeling of light-headedness passed over her. She could hear the music playing outside Quinn's office. A selection of Beatles hits was just coming to an end, and the following track was some raunchy Rolling Stones.

'You seem bewildered, Magenta,' Quinn murmured as he ran the palm of one warm hand very lightly down her naked arm. 'Why is that?'

Because she wanted Quinn, with his dangerous smile and sexy eyes, in spite of the fact that he had treated her no better than a novelty product to be tested, trialled and put aside when he grew tired of it. And because there was no longer any place for reasoned thinking.

He lifted his hand away, breaking the spell. 'I'll turn my back while you get changed, shall I?'

'Yes, you do that,' she told him.

Magenta was willing to bet she had never thrown clothes on so quickly in her life. 'It sounds noisy out there,' she said as she made the final adjustment to the tights Quinn had also thoughtfully provided, along with some underwear that proved that he had both good taste and the ability to judge her size down to the nearest millimetre. 'I think I should go and check.' She didn't wait for Quinn to answer; she knew how fast he moved.

When she returned to the main office, she saw the party had really livened up. All the desks had been pushed to one side to create a dance floor, and if dirty dancing hadn't been invented yet there were certainly some hot contenders for stealing the crown. The boys and girls in the office were definitely getting to know each other a whole lot better....

'You look like you're missing out, Magenta.'

She tensed as Quinn's shadow fell over her. 'If I were looking for a partner, you might be right.'

'I am right,' he said.

Did the music have to change that very moment from heated to cool? And did Quinn have to pull her into his arms? 'Did I say I wanted to dance?'

'You didn't say no.'

The psychedelic classic *A Whiter Shade of Pale* was hardly conducive to tension, but she held herself aloof.

'Oh good—you've relaxed,' Quinn murmured against her hair.

She knew he was teasing her; she could hear the smile in his voice. 'Do you seriously expect me to relax after everything that's happened?'

'I know a way.'

They both knew a way, but whether she was ready to play with fire again was another matter.

'Do you want to go home with me? Or would you rather live dangerously in my office?'

Quinn always got right to the point. She should say no; she should do a lot of things. But the heat rising inside her was making sensible decisions impossible. And what did she have to lose? This was a dream, wasn't it? Any self-respect she might lose in the short term would be restored the moment she shook herself awake.

She wanted more than this...

But sometimes in dreams, as in life, you had to settle for what you had, Magenta concluded as Quinn led her by the hand through the press of people. The promise implicit in his grip had quickly reduced her to liquid fire, and she could only be relieved that no one turned to look at them, though the party had reached that stage where they could have walked through it naked and no one would have noticed.

'It's a huge success,' Quinn observed, shutting his office door and leaning back against it. 'And that's all down to you.'

'Hardly.'

'What have I told you about underplaying your skills, Magenta? If you don't believe in yourself, why should I? Stop with all this negative and give me something positive.'

'Will this do?' Going for broke, she wound her arms around Quinn's neck.

'It's a start.'

She heard the door lock.

Quinn's hands quickly ignited an inferno. The memory of pleasure mixed with the anticipation of more was an explosive recipe. It made her reckless, made her want to hurry things along.

'Hey,' Quinn murmured, taking hold of her hands when she tugged at his belt. 'Not so fast—haven't I taught you anything?'

Who was backing who towards the desk?

'Same underwear as the dress?' Quinn demanded, thrusting one hard thigh between her legs.

'If you mean that paper stuff that disintegrates at a touch, then yes.'

'Excellent. Let me know if this is going too fast for you.'

'I will.'

'You're on the pill?'

'Of course I am.' She blushed. Strange to think she'd been so intimate with Quinn and yet could feel so awkward and exposed when he asked her a perfectly reasonable, if unexpected, question.

'I only ask because I heard some clinics in this country will only prescribe the pill to married women.'

'But that's ridiculous.' *And quite possibly true.* This was the sixties, after all. And, though almost a week had passed in dream time, she was methodical about taking her pill each morning in the real world—even though there wasn't the slightest chance she would ever put it to the test.

Needless to say, she hadn't brought her pill with her on this crazy time-slip adventure, but that hardly mattered when she had probably only been asleep a couple of hours.

And that was her last rational thought before Quinn sank deep inside her. She had forgotten how good he was, and now she discovered that his desk was at the perfect height. He helped her up; she drew her knees back and he moved in close. Testing her, he found her more than ready. She climaxed immediately. But she hadn't finished with him yet. 'Fill me,' she commanded hoarsely. Nursing him, she worked her muscles. 'I want all of you.'

And that was exactly what she got, only now realising that neither of them had paused long enough to use protection.

They returned to the party together and Magenta soon forgot her moment of concern. None of this was real. It was wonderful, but it was still only a fantasy, and all she'd cared about while she was living the dream was that Quinn lost his brusque business-manner. He'd done more than that, Magenta realised when Quinn put his arm around her waist. Something had changed between them, bringing them closer.

Quinn remained at her side from that moment on, and everyone accepted them as a couple—though, in fairness, everyone had had quite a bit to drink by this time. The spacemen were barely distinguishable from the aliens, she noted with amusement as Quinn forged a passage through the heaving throng of green-smudged silver people and silver-streaked green folk.

But at least she wasn't on her own when it came to the way she felt about Quinn. If anything, he was more outwardly affectionate in front of the other people than she was, and when the party finally drew to a close their destination was in no doubt.

They seemed to laugh all the way back to his house. Quinn drove smoothly and fast, and still found time to regale Magenta with stories of how far the party had gone in loosening everyone up. 'You're definitely in charge of office parties from here on in,' he told her. 'You have the knack of bringing people together.'

Never more so than now, she hoped when Quinn swung the car into the drive and they both climbed out.

They barely made it through the front door before they fell on each other, kissing and touching, as if tomorrow with all its uncertainties was almost upon them and the here and now was a fragile, unpredictable thing that refused to be captured or slowed down.

They made love on the hall rug, which fortunately was thick enough to cushion them, and wide enough so they didn't have to test the cold, hard marble floor. If there was anything nicer than snuggling up to Quinn, she had yet to discover it. When they were both briefly sated, Quinn suggested they go to bed. 'Now there's a novel idea,' she observed, laughing with happiness as he swung her into his arms.

She should have known that happiness was as fragile as time—and that it didn't do to be too greedy where either was concerned.

CHAPTER SIXTEEN

THE idyll lasted for a matter of weeks. During this time, they visited a fun fair; Quinn won a lop-eared rabbit on the shooting range and held Magenta tight when they rocketed through the candy-floss-scented air. Playing it serious, they went to an art gallery one day and to a concert the next, before Quinn changed the pace, taking her down into a cellar for some alternative musical entertainment, where the throbbing beat rang off the walls along with the sweat.

Switching styles, he escorted her to an up-town disco where they danced on a mirrored floor beneath coloured lights. On another night they saw *Breakfast at Tiffany's* at the cinema with an exquisitely beautiful Audrey Hepburn in the lead. One evening they decided to stay at home and cuddled up in front of the television, watching Goldie Hawn playing the ditsy blonde in *Rowan and Martin's Laugh-in*. Then late one night they discovered a mutual love of jazz, and ate hot dogs at a late-night cab stand after the jazz club, sharing anecdotes with friendly cabbies as they licked mustard and ketchup off each other's fingers.

She was falling in love, Magenta realised as Quinn walked her home along the embankment, where the river Thames stretched wide and silent at their side like a black-satin ribbon sprinkled with stars.

It was a wild, funny, tender, rollercoaster time, during which they grew as close as two people could grow. Now tomorrow was Christmas Eve, a time for presents, fun and celebration.

It was definitely not a time for Magenta to be clutching the edge of the sink in the ladies' room at the office, while wondering if she was going to pass out or be sick.

I'm pregnant, she thought, staring at her green-tinged reflection in the mirror.

It had only been the one time without protection, but one time was enough. And she was sure. She had never been more certain of anything in her life—she was expecting Quinn's baby.

But how could this happen in a dream-world?

Anything could happen in a dream, Magenta reasoned, though dreams didn't usually feel as realistic as this, nor did they usually last as long. She was growing increasingly concerned—or was that hopeful?—that perhaps she really was in the sixties. There was no need for her to buy a pregnancy kit to confirm what she already knew. The changes in her body had been swift and all-consuming. She was late, sick and, more important than all of that, had the overwhelming sense that she wasn't alone in her body any longer, a fact which thrilled her beyond belief. She felt instantly protective of the tiny life inside her, even though motherhood wasn't part of her life plan, or even her dream plan. And, yes, it might have taken two to tango, but she had never asked anything of Quinn and she didn't intend to start now.

The rest of the day passed quickly, with everyone tidying up the loose ends of the campaign in preparation for the launch after the holidays. Magenta stayed behind to make sure the new top-flight team of men and women had everything they needed before she left. Quinn was still working in his office when it came time to lock up. She had some chilly hours of uncertainty ahead of her, she reflected, picking up her coat in the staff room. She was the only one who knew about her baby—Quinn's baby—and, though she could happily cope with a pregnancy, she would prefer to do so in a world she understood. 'Oh, why can't I wake up?' she murmured, without realising Nancy had joined her in the room.

'Long, hard night?' Nancy suggested with amusement. Opening her handbag, Nancy began to touch up her make-up.

'A great night,' Magenta admitted honestly. She hadn't spent a night without Quinn since the party, which was weeks ago now, and they had all been great.

'Is there something wrong?' Nancy said, turning to look at her with new interest.

'No,' Magenta said with a laugh in her voice. 'Long, hard day, that's all.'

'Are you sure that's all? You look to me like you're hiding something.'

'No, I'm not.' She was a hopeless liar. Nancy had become her best friend in this strange dream-world and Magenta was eager to share her news with someone. 'Except…I've got something amazing to tell you.'

To Magenta's dismay, Nancy paled. 'You're not pregnant, are you?'

'Why do you say that?'

'It's the first thing that popped into my mind.'

And if I am? Would that be so terrible? From the expression on Nancy's face, Magenta realised she was clinging by her fingertips to cloud nine—that as far as Nancy was concerned it was that bad.

'If you're married, that's fine. If you're engaged, that's almost acceptable—though it would raise eyebrows and cause a whole world of unwanted comment here.'

Magenta laughed incredulously. 'Are you saying only married women can have children?'

'That's the usual way, isn't it?'

Dumbstruck, Magenta stared at Nancy, a girl she had thought so feisty and up to the mark in everything.

'You're having Quinn's baby, right?' Nancy demanded in her usual forthright way.

She nodded.

'And you're seriously considering going ahead with the pregnancy?'

'Of course I am. What else would I do?'

'How long have I got?' Nancy murmured under her breath.

'You disapprove?' Magenta couldn't have been more surprised.

'*I* don't, but everyone else will.'

'But it's no one else's business. I'm not asking for help. I won't be a burden to anyone. I won't even expect Quinn to take an active role in bringing up his baby if he doesn't want to.'

'Boy, are you naïve.' Nancy was full of concern now. 'Honestly, Magenta, I always thought you were smart, but now I'm not so sure. Can't you see what this will do to your reputation? Oh, forget that,' Nancy said, shaking her head in exasperation. 'You won't be able to work, so what will your reputation even matter?'

'That's a little dramatic, isn't it?' Magenta demanded wryly. 'I can't see why it should change anything.'

'And how many unmarried mothers do you know?'

'Well, none in this—' She had been about to say 'this world' but quickly held her tongue.

'Do you have family who can care for the baby while you work?'

'No, but what about childcare?'

'Childcare!' Nancy exclaimed. 'What planet are you living on? And without money to support yourself you're going to be in a real bind, Magenta. You have no idea what's ahead of you, do you?' Nancy demanded, staring her in the eyes. 'If you did, you wouldn't want this baby.'

'Nancy, no, stop it. I can't believe you mean that.'

'You'll be finished in advertising,' Nancy said in a calm voice that really frightened Magenta. 'And all the men here will have a field day.'

'Then we won't tell them.'

'Not even Quinn?'

'I'll choose my time.'

Nancy laughed, but it was a hollow sound. 'Yes, you do that,' she agreed.

'And as for being finished…'

'It's not you, Magenta,' Nancy was quick to say. 'It's what everyone will think of you.'

'And what will you think of me?'

'I'm sorry you even have to ask that question,' Nancy told her, meeting Magenta's stare. 'My feelings won't change—and I'll help you all I can. You just can't expect Quinn is going to step in, or that he'll even acknowledge the baby is his. He only has your word for that. I'm sorry, Magenta, but that's the truth and I'd rather I say it than you hear it from someone else…'

Of course—no DNA tests, no proof. No help of any kind for single mothers in the sixties—that was what Nancy was telling her. How had women managed? Magenta felt as bad as she had ever felt in her life—not for herself, but for all those women who had been treated so shabbily. 'And what if I don't care what people think? What if I make a go of it?'

Nancy said nothing, which was an answer in itself.

Magenta shook her head. 'I'm not ready to have this conversation,' she admitted. 'It's too soon. I'm still getting over the thrill of discovering I'm pregnant. I hadn't thought of it as a problem, or anything remotely close. I'm sorry, Nancy, I shouldn't have burdened you with this.'

'Who else can you confide in?' Nancy pointed out with her usual pragmatism. 'Don't worry about me. It's you I'm worried about. You should take some time off work, try to come up with a plan. I'll help you.'

'I don't want to take time off work—I'm pregnant, not ill.'

'But when you start to show?'

In the sixties, that would be her cue to feel ashamed, Magenta presumed, imagining the reaction from the men in the office. But would she even be here that long, or would she wake up long before then? Uncertainty hit her like an avalanche. What could she count on in this strange, disjointed world?

Sensing her desperation, Nancy gave her a hug.

'I'm all right,' Magenta insisted, pulling herself together. She would have to be. There was some irony in the fact that she had researched most things about the sixties except for this. But, if Nancy's concern was anything to go by, impending motherhood must have been a nightmare prospect for a single woman in the sixties.

But that was no reason to give up. She had a baby to fight for now, and if people were as narrow-minded as Nancy suggested then she'd find a way to start up her own ad agency— working from home, if she had to. She would make this work and support her child whatever it took.

But then another, bigger problem hit her: would she still be pregnant in the real world? And, if the answer to that was no, did she want to wake up?

Maternal instinct was a formidable force, she realised as Nancy continued to offer advice. 'Some women have no alternative but to have an abortion or give their child away.'

'Then I feel sorry for their unimaginable plight, but I'm not one of them.' Discovering first-hand what it had been like to exist in an era where the single mother had been stigmatised made Magenta long to be able to go into battle for each and every one of them.

'And when some men find out you're pregnant,' Nancy went on, 'they'll assume you're easy meat.'

'Then they'll soon learn they're wrong. I'm sorry, Nancy—I

don't mean to have a go at you. It's just that this is all so new to me. But don't worry; I will sort it out. And I'm going make a start right now by telling Quinn.'

'Good idea,' Nancy agreed. 'You should before you pass out, or you're sick on someone's shoes.'

Magenta managed to wrestle up a smile for her friend at the door. 'I'll try not to be sick on your shoes.'

'That's all I ask,' Nancy said, playing the same game with a faint smile in return.

Quinn was packing up his things when Magenta knocked on his office door and walked in. Before she had found out about the baby, they had agreed to meet in town for something to eat, but events were moving too fast to wait for that.

'Hey,' he said, looking up. 'Hungry already?'

She stood for a moment just drinking him in. Quinn had announced that the last day before the holidays would be a dress-down day. No one did casual better than he did and, in faded jeans and a leather jacket left open over a close-fitting top, he looked amazing. But it wasn't Quinn's physical features that drew her; that was the least of it. It was the warmth in his eyes and the curve of his mouth. She wanted to frame that and remember it, as if tomorrow was coming round a lot faster than she wanted it to, and then everything would change.

'Well, come on,' he said. 'Spit it out. I know that look.' Still leaning over the desk, he gave her the Quinn smile, the one with warmth, fun and trust in it.

She took a breath and began. 'I know I told you I was on the pill.' She didn't need to say anything else. Quinn's face had already changed. Frown lines had deepened between his eyes. 'I know it was only that one time…' she went on.

'When circumstances overcame us?' Quinn straightened up.

That's one way of putting it, Magenta thought as anxiety

started to build inside her. She couldn't read Quinn. She didn't have a clue what he was thinking.

'You're pregnant?'

'Yes, I am.' They had grown so close, yet suddenly Quinn was like a stranger standing in judgement on her. 'I don't want anything from you.'

'Why not?'

That was the one question she hadn't anticipated. 'Because I can manage this on my own.'

'So, you're cutting me out?'

'I just don't want to be dependent on anyone.'

'Sounds to me like I'm going to be a father but you'd prefer I didn't interfere.'

'I'm sorry if it came out that way, it's not what I meant.'

'How do I know that?'

'You'll just have to take my word for it.'

'Like I took your word for the fact that you were on the pill?'

'Aren't we both equally responsible?' Now she was getting mad.

'Well, of course we are, Magenta, and I'm happy to accept full responsibility. I only wish you could be as straight with me.'

'I am being straight with you.'

'Are you? I feel like I don't know you—like you're hiding something.'

'I can explain.'

But she couldn't. How could she explain what she couldn't understand? How could she tell Quinn that this was a dream and that she might wake up at any moment to find out that none of it was happening?

Quinn's sound of exasperation forced her to refocus. 'Why don't you tell me what's really on your mind, Magenta?'

Quinn was waiting for answers and she had none. *This is a dream*, she wanted to blurt out. *I'm locked in a dream and*

I can't get back. 'The pregnancy was a shock to me,' was the best she could manage.

'A shock to you?' Quinn queried. 'This is a baby we're talking about. How can you talk about the creation of a child as a shock and expect me to be reassured?'

'Because I can handle it.'

'You can handle it,' Quinn repeated angrily. 'This is my child too, Magenta. Do you seriously expect me to take a back seat and leave every decision to you?'

She hadn't factored Quinn wanting a child into her thinking. She hadn't thought about shared responsibility at all.

'What gives you the right to do this on your own?'

She knew no other way. Since forever it had been Dad and her—the two of them. She had been raised in a single-parent family. 'I love my baby,' she said simply. 'And I never intended to hurt you.' Some things were impossible to lie about or to hide.

CHAPTER SEVENTEEN

IT WAS the first time Magenta had heard Quinn so impassioned on any subject. He would fight for his family and stand firm as a rock in the face of any difficult decision. Under any normal circumstances, that was just the kind of father she would want for her child. But she couldn't make any promises to Quinn in this strange world of imagination and dreams.

'Have you nothing to say?' he said sharply. 'Why is that, Magenta? Have you got what you came for?' he said suspiciously. 'Are you planning to leave now and take our child?'

'Please don't make this ugly Quinn.'

'It is what it is,' he rapped. 'A woman I thought I could trust—a woman I care about—cannot be honest with me. What am I supposed to think? That you're a single woman who has always longed for a child, maybe? Who knows what lengths you'd go to?'

'Don't!' Of course she had heard of men being used as sperm donors—usually with their full permission—but doing such a thing herself had never occurred to her. 'I could never be so cold-blooded.' And when Quinn made a sound of contempt, she exclaimed, 'I love you, Quinn! How is that using you?'

'You love me?'

The tone of his voice chilled her to the bone. 'Yes, I do.'

'Then your idea of love and mine are poles apart. To me, love means trust—sharing.'

'I love you and our baby.'

'Words come easily to you, Magenta.'

She exhaled in a rush, shock hitting her in the chest like a punch.

'Let me replay this for you,' Quinn said in a chillingly calm voice. 'You come into my office and announce that you're pregnant—then you barely draw breath before telling me that you don't want anything from me. How convinced would you be of my integrity if the tables were turned, Magenta? What gives you the right to make the rules?'

She didn't want to fight, but she was in no position to make promises of any kind when she inhabited a parallel universe. And, even supposing she could revisit this world in her dreams, would a hook-up on some cosmic interchange ever be enough for them? It was hardly a sound foundation for a family.

'Good to see you're ready with your answer,' Quinn snarled.

She blocked his path to the door. 'Please don't walk out on me, Quinn.'

'Don't lie to me.'

'I have never lied to you.'

'Then open up, Magenta!' Quinn roared this as he seized her arms. For a moment she thought he was going to shake her, but instead he loosened his grip and whipped his hands away, murmuring furiously, 'What's happening to me?'

You too? she felt like saying. But if Quinn was also a visitor to this strange dimension it really would be too much to take in.

Exhaling heavily, Quinn turned away, and he remained aloof from her for a long while. When he finally turned back to face her, he was calm again. 'Forgive me,' he said levelly.

'There's nothing to forgive.'

'Shock, surprise—the force of my feelings. Whatever the excuse, I shouldn't have lost it like that.'

'We're both on a steep learning-curve here.'

'And I like to think I have all things covered.'

'But not babies?' Magenta suggested softly.

'Not babies,' Quinn agreed, giving her an assessing stare. 'Are you going to be all right?'

'Of course I am. I'm going to be a mother.' She couldn't keep the joy out of her voice. Just saying the words made her feel privileged, happy—ecstatic. The difficulties could be overcome, *would* be overcome.

Sensing her inner strength and determination, Quinn shrugged. 'Looks like you've got it all in hand.'

Magenta smiled. 'There still room for a father in the picture—if he wants to be included, that is. I can understand this has come as a shock to you.'

'To put it mildly,' Quinn agreed.

'And I'm sorry if you think I've been keeping things from you.'

'Aren't women supposed to be enigmas?'

'Like the sphynx?'

'Like Magenta Steele,' Quinn said, eyeing her keenly. 'You're definitely a one-off.' He shook his head. 'No one could deny that.'

She smiled at him a little hesitantly. With the bounce of joy when they talked about their baby came the dread of separation. And now Quinn had just made that worse by caring so much.

'Whatever you want to do, I'll be here for you, Magenta.'

Quinn couldn't know how poignant a statement that was. *And I'll always love you*, Magenta thought, staring deep into his eyes. If she could only bind this moment and keep it just the way it was for ever.

'You're sure you want this baby?'

'Absolutely sure,' she confirmed.

'Good.' Quinn stared at her for a moment, and then he drew her close. 'Now all you have to do is tell me what you're hiding from me, Magenta.'

He knew her too well. She might have known he would ask, and what could she tell him? If she told Quinn the truth he'd think her mad—and, worse, he'd think her incapable of looking after their child. 'Can't we just have now?'

'Now?' Quinn pulled back to stare at her with eyes that were shadowed with as many secrets as her own. 'What is "now", Magenta? This breath? This day? This dream we call life?'

She could feel him pulling away from her, feel the distance growing between them as surely as if Quinn had removed his hands from her back and his breath from her face. She wished she could find the words to heal the broken bond between them, but there were no words. Now Quinn was walking away from her, closing himself off in every way there was.

But then he stopped and turned. 'We have to make this work,' he said. 'I'm not sure how we're going to do that yet, but I'll find a way.'

The breath caught in her throat. She knew she should be happy, and she would have been if she hadn't known theirs was a problem Quinn couldn't seize hold of and fix.

'Don't look at me like that,' he said, sensing her concern. 'This won't come together unless you believe in me.'

Quinn was a warrior who refused to accept defeat, and for one crazy moment it occurred to Magenta that he might be wrestling the same mysterious forces that she was. That was too much for her bruised and battered brain to take in. But he did seem to be staring past her to some place she couldn't see, and she let out a relieved breath when his storm-dark eyes focused on her face again. 'You don't have to be part of this, Quinn.'

'I'm determined to be.' A faint smile touched the corner of his mouth. 'Who'd have thought?'

Yes, who'd have thought? But she could no more plan for a future with Quinn than she could wake up. And how long could she keep up this deception? Could she lie to the father of her child? 'Quinn, there's something I must tell you.'

'Not now, Magenta. I know you're worried about the future and I can understand why. I know you want me to tell you where this will lead, but truthfully I don't know.'

How could he know when she was nothing more than a sham, an illusion, a figment of her own imagination? 'This isn't what you think.'

'You're pregnant with my baby. How different can it be?'

You have no idea, Magenta thought.

'Unless it's not my baby?'

Quinn's stare frightened her. 'Don't say that.' She couldn't bear to see the doubt in his eyes.

'Is this my baby? It's a simple question. Is the child you're carrying mine, Magenta?'

The air between them was suddenly charged with fury and passion, but she stared into Quinn's gaze without flinching. 'Yes, I'm carrying your baby. And realising that was a shock to me to begin with,' Magenta admitted. 'But now I can only think of my pregnancy as an unexpected blessing.'

Quinn stared at her in silence and then he said, 'You are the mother of my child, and as such I will always protect you.'

'I can look after myself, Quinn.'

'You won't have to. You're not alone.'

For that she was grateful. Becoming a single mother in a world she understood was one thing, but here?

'You should be smiling, Magenta.' Quinn said, sensing her doubt. 'This is a happy day, isn't it?'

'Of course.' And now she felt guilty. She didn't deserve this man, and she certainly didn't deserve the gift of a child. 'Quinn...' She didn't know where to start, but she had to tell him. She had never imagined Quinn would be so deeply loyal or so complex. She had underestimated him in so many ways, but he was right to say today was precious. She wanted nothing more than what she had here and now. Surely it was a small thing in the scale of the cosmos to be with the man she loved so they could bring up their baby together? To make a home for it surrounded by love? Knowing that it was an impossible dream was killing her.

'Why so serious?' Quinn demanded.

The last thing she wanted was to add to his suspicions by allowing a moment to pass, and then another, when she could have told him—when she *should* have told him. It was getting to the stage where she wished for his sake that she could just close her eyes and wake up in a world she could make sense of.

Misreading the signs, Quinn embraced her, and the moment when she might have told him passed. This was what she wanted more than anything—to be with Quinn—and it was the one thing she couldn't have.

She clung to him in desperation and when he released her she saw a different expression in his eyes. It was an expression she knew, an expression her body responded to immediately.

Quinn's lips curved. He was an unrepentant hunter; he was hungry and so he ate. 'You're the mother of my child.' He stared her in the eyes. 'And you just reminded me why...'

'Quinn...' She was already responding.

Quinn was aroused, hugely aroused. This was a private joke between them—that she barely had to look at him to provoke this response. She had to be careful about looking at him in public, Quinn had warned her with amusement when they'd been dancing in a club. 'Have you no shame?' she asked him now, already working on his clothes.

'None at all.'

'Just as I thought.' The ache inside her had spread like a delicious heat to encompass all her body, but Quinn shushed her and steadied her hands.

'Gently,' he said. 'I'm going to be gentle with you.'

'Because I'm pregnant?' Magenta demanded. 'Pregnant women love sex.'

'I'll bear that in mind.'

Now they were both yanking clothes off and tossing them aside. But even now there was a shadow. *Carpe diem*: seize the moment. Who knew how many they had left?

Quinn steered her back against the wall, lifting her and tugging off her underwear at the same time. She was as bad, breaking her nails on his belt in her hurry to undress him.

Locking her legs around his waist, she angled her body to make it easy for him. There was no foreplay this time, no finesse or teasing, no wasting a single precious moment.

Quinn's first thrust was enough to make her lose control, but he had taught her well, and she knew the power of delay. She held on as long as she could as he pounded her against the wall, but even as she hovered on the exquisite plateau of sensation she knew she couldn't stay there for ever. She must fall. It wasn't just the strength of the approaching climax she feared, but the feeling—the sense, the premonition—that when she fell this time it would be for good. The thought of being thrown back into a world without Quinn, without their baby, was a prospect she dreaded beyond all things. 'No, Quinn, stop,' she begged him, pressing her clenched fists against his chest.

'Am I hurting you?'

'No.'

'What, then?'

He was already moving, steadily, deeply and slowly as he stretched her, massaging her in a way she couldn't resist. 'Quinn, I can't. It's too big, too wild—too dangerous.' But as she punctuated each of these declarations with a groan of pleasure, Quinn took no notice. 'I'm locked in a dream and I don't want to lose you,' she managed to gasp out in one fleeting moment of lucidity.

'If you're locked in a dream,' Quinn said fiercely, 'then I am too.'

'No,' she begged shaking her head from side to side. 'We can't do this together.'

'Haven't I always promised to keep you safe?' Instead of slowing, Quinn adjusted his grip on her buttocks so he could take her more deeply.

The last thing she heard before she screamed out his name was Quinn's husky laugh against her neck, and then there was a fire-burst of light behind her eyes and her world was all sensation.

As the violent pleasure washed over her, she clung to Quinn as if her life depended on it. But the firmer her grasp the more illusive her hold on him became. Their reality was fading, Magenta realised in despair, and there was no way to call it back. The moment she had dreaded was here—was now. She was leaving Quinn, floating away from him, floating out of his reach...

'Quinn, save me!'

But even as she cried his name she knew he couldn't hear her.

She made one last desperate attempt to reach him, but the more she strained to stay where she was the more the yawning chasm between them grew. The last thing she saw was Quinn stretching out his hands as if he had the power to defeat time, space and dimension and could snatch her back again. But it was too late. She was already being sucked into the void from where there was no return, and as she tumbled helplessly from one world to the next she was dimly aware of Quinn calling out to her. But then even his voice lost its power to hold her and she slipped away.

CHAPTER EIGHTEEN

'DAMN the woman!' Gray Quinn's face was thunderous as he hammered on Magenta's office door with his fist. 'Magenta! Answer me! Magenta, are you in there? Are you all right?'

The silence was deafening. Straightening up, he braced his shoulder.

Within micro-seconds of him preparing to take action, the door opened and a wan face peered out.

'What the hell are you playing at?' he said, pushing past her. 'Have you been here all night?' He heard the door close behind him and wheeled around. 'You look awful. We've all been worried to death about you—me in particular.'

'Why you in particular?'

Her voice was like a feeble reed, which only added to his suspicions. 'We had a meeting at nine o' clock sharp. Remember that?'

Raking her hair, she looked at him in bemusement. 'Oh, I'm sorry,' she said as reality dawned.

'You don't show for the meeting,' he rapped out. 'And then I hear you're locked in here.'

'But Tess keeps a spare key.'

'Tess had a dental appointment this morning. So why the locked door, Magenta?'

'I felt safer.'

'Safer?'

She didn't answer. Rather than acting like the sharp

executive, with the smart line in repartee to match the sassy copy she wrote for her ad campaigns, Magenta was staring at him as if he was an apparition—as if she didn't know what day it was. Even odder to him was her bemused acceptance—he'd expected the woman he'd met and flirted with yesterday to be furious to learn the biker she'd dismissed, and possibly even flirted back with the day before, and her new boss had turned out to be one and the same. He gave the office a thorough scan. 'Have you been drinking?'

'I have not!' she exclaimed indignantly. 'I've been working.'

'Commendable.' There were no bottles, but he saw the work laid out on the desk. She had been working and now she looked ready to pass out. 'Lucky for you I have the bike here.'

'The bike...'

Her eyes slowly cleared, but she was still looking at him as if she didn't know what century it was, let alone what day. 'I'll take you home,' he explained in clear terms. 'You can shower, eat, dress and get back here with your brain in gear. Okay with you?'

'Do I have an option?' Colour was coming back into her cheeks.

'No. Just grab your coat.'

'I can't ride a bike dressed like this.' She stared down at her crumpled dress.

'Are your workout clothes still in the gym?'

'In the basement? Yes.'

'Then change into gym clothes. I'll wait.'

She started to say something, but he was already out of the door. Magenta might be a first-class creative, but if she proved to be unreliable there was no place for her in his organisation. There was just something nagging at the back of his mind that said he shouldn't let her go yet.

And if he did, Quinn reflected dryly, it would be the first time he had fired someone for working too hard.

He liked the feeling of Magenta clinging on tight with her head pressed hard against his back, but as they rode through London he could sense her tension. He was in a hurry to see her restored to her fighting best; he had no intention of buying a company and losing its chief asset in the same day, he told himself firmly as he took a short cut through the market district. It wasn't usual for him to take quite such a personal interest in his staff, but Magenta had touched something inside him. The fact that she had worked until she'd quite literally dropped played on his mind. Seeing one of the all-night open-air booths was still serving, he stopped the bike. 'Hot dog—ketchup, mustard?'

'What?' She stared at him with that same bemused expression in her eyes.

'When did you last eat? Never mind,' he said, swinging his leg over the bike. 'Stay here, or come with. Either way, I'm getting you something hot to put inside your stomach.'

She ate like a ravenous child, dripping ketchup down her fingers. She stared at the mess and frowned—it took her back to childhood, maybe. He grabbed a hank of paper tissues and wiped her hands. 'Better?' Dipping his head, he stared into troubled eyes.

She had enough smarts to refocus fast. 'I haven't made the best of starts, have I?' she suggested wryly.

'Drink your tea.'

She did so, blowing on it with attractive full, red lips before gulping it down with relish. 'Sorry. I hadn't realised how hungry I was.'

His lips curved. When he was heavily into a project, eating was the last thing on his mind. 'Work will do that to you.'

'So you're the same?' she guessed.

Her eyes were a clear, deep blue and she was staring at him keenly. 'I'm a little obsessive,' he admitted. 'Come on—let's get you home.'

He got another jolt when he walked into Magenta's house to find it furnished like a sixties stage-set. 'Nice place you have here…' He recognised an Eero Aarnio Bubble Chair, and an iconic Egg Pod swinging seat with a blood-red lining. Did she always live like this, in a fantasy world that mirrored each new campaign she was working on? He hoped not. He'd seen the notes on his desk regarding Magenta's next big campaign. It featured a safari theme. There was hardly room to swing a small cat in here, let alone a big one.

His mood changed, darkened. Was business Magenta's life? Was that all there was? A sense of isolation overwhelmed him—a sense of *déjà vu*. He had thought of little else apart from work on his drive to the top. They weren't so different.

'Is this the kitchen?' He pressed open a door. 'You go and change while I make some coffee. Do you want something more to eat?'

'No!' She laughed.

He was pleased to see it.

'You?' she said.

He felt a jolt when their eyes met. 'Maybe…' He was hungry.

'There are eggs in the fridge.'

'That's good for me. Go.'

He got busy in her neat, attractive kitchen, finding the eggs, a bowl, some cheese and plenty of seasoning. He thought about Magenta as he whisked the eggs. She concerned him on several levels. Her friend Tess had been at pains to tell him how hard she worked. She'd been holding everything together single-handed for months now, apparently, fending off her father's creditors whilst still managing to energise her team and come up with a host of brilliant ideas. She'd drawn him in.

'You're back,' he said, feeling a bolt of something warm and steady when she walked into the room. She was slender but womanly, tall, but not too tall. She was beautiful, quirky and under-appreciated—at least by a man. It was strange where his senses took him—sixth sense, his mother had called it. 'Omelette good for you?' he said on a lighter note.

'You are joking?' she protested with a laugh.

'Well, I've made an extra one. You should eat more.'

'I have eaten.' She held up her squeaky-clean hands to remind him.

'Eat,' he said, taking in the dark circles beneath her eyes.

She perched at the breakfast bar, crossing her silk-clad legs one over the other—slender legs, sexy heels, sheer stockings. He could see the outline of her suspender button beneath the fine wool skirt. 'So you're not coming back with me?' he enquired.

'I've called a cab. I hope you're not offended. It's just that it's hard to arrive on a motorcycle ready for a meeting—apart from the fact that bike-riding sends my heart-rate soaring, I didn't want to be late this time.'

She smiled faintly and he smiled too. 'Good thinking. You should look after yourself better, Magenta,' he said, noticing how in spite of all her protests she was wolfing down the omelette.

'Are you like this with all your employees, Quinn?'

'If you mean do I cook for them? No. Do I want them in peak condition producing their best work for me? That would be yes.'

'And that will be my taxi,' she said, forking up the last mouthful on her plate as the door-bell rang. 'And that was a delicious omelette. Thank you, Quinn.'

'See you back at the office.'

'You can count on it,' she said.

* * *

Magenta Steele was the consummate professional as well as a
good-looking woman—though she was elusive, Quinn thought
as he brought their meeting to a close. He could pin her down
in business—having heard her pitch, he could be fairly certain
they'd win an industry award for her sixties campaign, for
example—but when it came to knowing what made Magenta
the woman tick, that was a whole different ball-game.

'Dinner tonight,' he said as she packed up her briefcase.
'That wasn't a question, Magenta,' he added when she looked
at him with surprise. 'If we're going to take this company
where it needs to go, you and I have to embark on a crash
course of familiarisation so we can do more than work together. We have to be able to read each other's minds.'

'Talking of which,' she said, a faint smile creeping onto
her lips as she busied herself sorting documents, 'is the theme
I suggested for the party okay with you—or do you think it
too predictable?'

'Sixties?'

'Medallions, flares and lots of chest hair?' She looked at
him now, looked him long, hard and straight in the eyes.

'I think I can come up with something.'

'I'm sure you can.'

But it wouldn't wait until the party, Quinn thought as
Magenta left the room.

'You're impossible,' Tess told Magenta when she heard
Magenta had booked a table for supper with Quinn for six
o' clock that evening. 'What sort of dating time is that? And
why a steak house? Haven't you heard of sexy venues and
subdued lighting?'

'Not when I'm holding a business meeting—this isn't a
date. Quinn and I have important things to discuss.'

'Like what? Your place or mine?'

'Like where we're going with the business. I'm only pleased
that he's involving me.'

'Magenta, are you blind? First off, you're the heart of Steele Design—you're the major reason people come to us for ideas. Quinn is never going to get rid of you. And, secondly, perhaps most important of all, Quinn is one hot-looking man.'

'And my employer. I never mix business with pleasure.'

'Never say never—and by the way, you with serious frown lines sprouting like weeds on your face, you're coming with me.'

Shaking her head in bemusement, Magenta allowed Tess to drag her out of the office. It was their lunch hour and she had been neglecting her friends recently. *Calm down—go with the flow for once*, she told herself firmly.

'A hairdresser's?' Magenta said, gazing up at what seemed to be a vaguely familiar door.

'Bed-head to beauty queen,' Tess promised, chivvying her inside. 'I bring you my friend,' she told the young man with floppy hair. 'You'd better look after her, Justin. I hold you personally responsible for the safe return of this woman. She must look refreshed and years younger by the time you've finished with her—like she's never done a day's work in her life.'

'Miracles take a little longer,' Justin opined, studying Magenta critically.

'If I'm a lost cause…' Magenta was already leaving.

'Lost, you may be,' Justin declaimed in stentorian tones. 'But now I have found you all will be well again.'

'Oh, well, that's okay then,' Magenta said uncertainly, noticing Tess was blocking her only escape route to the door.

'And see she gets her nails done, will you?' Tess added in an aside. 'Something Jackie Kennedy—French manicure, perhaps? She might look like she works down a coal mine, but she's actually a creative.'

'I know the type,' Justin assured her in a theatrical whisper.

'Just make sure she's ready to play her role in a very

important sixties party tomorrow night. Oh, and she's got a date tonight, so make it sexy.'

'Got it.'

'You've gone too far this time,' Magenta complained, but Tess was already pulling faces at her from the wrong side of the door.

Magenta caught sight of her reflection in one of the many mirrors on the way out of the salon. Justin had given her a new look all right. Her hair was long, sleek and shiny, as opposed to the notorious bed-head frizz-top, as diagnosed by Tess.

Trust a friend to tell you the truth, Magenta thought wryly, brushing her long fringe out of her eyes. Justin had modelled her on one of his favourite sixties icons, he had explained, a model called Jean Shrimpton who had already appeared on the cover of *Vogue* at the age of eighteen. 'But I'm twenty-eight,' Magenta had protested.

'And don't look a day over forty,' Justin had told her reassuringly. 'That's how you will continue to look unless you allow me to work a little magic.'

It was when Justin talked about magic that the dream started coming back to her—bits and pieces to begin with, and then rushing in on her like a tidal wave she couldn't escape. Not that it had anything to do with real magic; she knew that. Dreams were the work of an over-active mind. All she had to do was slow down a bit and she'd sleep soundly at night again.

Slowing down meant walking through the park instead of powering along the pavements, but slowing down allowed more thoughts to crowd in. There had been a pregnancy, she remembered—yes, a pregnancy in a dream, but the baby had seemed very real to her. It still did…

Silent tears crept down her icy cheeks.

She wanted a baby.

Having a baby had never crossed her mind before. She

hadn't realised there was anything missing in her life. She hadn't had time to realise anything was missing; work took up every minute. Slowing to a halt in front of a park bench, she sank down onto the cold wooden slats. Stretching out her legs in front of her, she gazed across the placid surface of the boating lake. She'd made a baby with Quinn? Well, that should have brought a smile to her face.

It didn't.

Picking up a pebble, she stood up and skimmed it across the surface of the lake. Ripples spread outwards, unstoppable ripples. There was nothing she could do to change the direction of those ripples any more than she could change the direction of her life to match the dream.

There was no baby.

Wrapping her arms around her empty belly, she mourned the dream-child in wistful silence until a spike of cold wind reminded her she should be getting back. She turned reluctantly. Dreams, Magenta reflected as she hurried back to the office—who knew what secret lives people lived in their dreams?

Sometimes dreams weren't just longings, they were premonitions.

And that was crazy thinking. She shouldn't be greedy. She should think about all the things she had instead and be grateful. Wasn't that enough for her?

A hollow *no…*

Magenta had almost walked past the store when she stopped dead and retraced her footsteps. She stood in front of the window staring at the dress in silence. It couldn't be. But it was. It was the same dress—the identical dress. It was the flattering navy-blue shift dress Quinn had bought for her in the dream. She stared at it, hesitating until her heart rate reached danger point, and then she hurried towards the entrance. She had to have it…

They'd sold out of her size.

It wasn't meant to be, Magenta told herself sensibly as the sales assistant tried to persuade her to try on any number of alternatives. 'They're all lovely,' Magenta agreed politely. 'But not quite what I'm looking for.' *Not nearly.*

But she should make some sort of special effort tonight, make a good impression on Quinn for a change. She couldn't go out in the clothes she'd worn all day at the office, so she chose something modest with a twist. Minimal, loosely draped and delicately loose, it was a silk crêpe dress in a shade of ice-blue that brought out the colour of her eyes. Having thanked the woman for helping her choose, she made her way to the exit. She was still short of a costume for the party tomorrow night—and she didn't want to be predictable.

She was tired of predictable, Magenta mused as she hurried along the brightly lit parade of shops. Tess was right, she did take herself too seriously, and the party was everyone's chance to break out. Heading for her favourite vintage shop, she ducked inside.

Well, that was certainly something different, Magenta thought a little later, smiling triumphantly as she hugged the package containing her prize purchase close to her chest. She doubted anyone else would have thought of wearing the outfit she had chosen to a party.

CHAPTER NINETEEN

SHE arrived at the steak house exactly on time. Quinn did too, it turned out. They walked up to each other at the entrance with a laugh. 'Shall we skip the meeting?' Magenta suggested.

'Skip it why?' Quinn said as he held the door for her.

'I thought the purpose of this meeting was to help us to get to know each other better so we read each other's minds—it seems we already do.' Magenta smiled as the *maître d'* came forward to take her coat.

'You look beautiful,' Quinn murmured.

She was glad she had gone to the trouble of buying a special dress. 'And you look…' Was this appropriate chat for a business meeting? But Quinn did look incredible. With his thick, black hair as neatly groomed as it could be, and wearing a crisp white shirt, plain dark trousers with a heavy casual jacket, he looked tanned, vital, dark and amazing. She wasn't the only woman in the restaurant to notice.

He held her arm as he ushered her towards a secluded booth. 'You've loosened up, Magenta.'

'Have I?' She raised an eyebrow as Quinn handed her a menu.

'Your eyes aren't shooting daggers at me.'

'I haven't done that for some time, surely?'

'Since I scared you with the motorbike.'

'You don't scare me—it does.'

'Lucky for you, I brought the car tonight.'

Something looped inside her like a video playing a scene from a film. 'The Aston Martin DB5?'

'You saw me drive up.' Quinn's cheek creased as he grinned at her, and for a moment she was too startled to say a word.

'That's right,' she managed, telling herself the car was just some ridiculous coincidence. 'But who said you were taking me home?'

'Would a gentleman allow a lady to take a cab late at night?'

No. And if she attempted to go anywhere on her own she guessed Quinn would follow her at a discreet distance until he was sure she was safe. 'But it's early,' she pointed out, glancing at her wristwatch. 'Our meeting shouldn't take more than an hour, so I'll be quite safe going home on the bus.'

'You could,' Quinn agreed mildly, appearing to be intent on the menu. 'Steak small, medium or large? Well-cooked or bloody? Sauce, no sauce?'

'Fillet, medium, grilled, with salad, no sauce.'

'We'll take two of those,' he told the waiter. 'And some wine, beer?'

'Water—fizzy.'

'Done.'

It was all so normal suddenly between them, without a hint of mystery or magic to raise a single awkward question in her mind. She had to stop with the imagination. She wasn't at work now, thinking up some far-fetched ad campaign; she should be concentrating on the here and now and forget about what might have been in a dream.

'What's this?' Magenta said half way through her delicious, crunchy pudding of lemon-meringue pie and vanilla ice-cream when the wine waiter produced a bottle of champagne and opened it for them.

'A celebration?' Quinn suggested dryly. 'My guess is you've been too busy working even to think about celebrating the fact that Steele Design has a new lease of life—largely thanks to your efforts.'

'And your money,' she pointed out.

'I hope I have some skills to bring to bear too.'

'That's why I went after you.' Magenta blushed as she had a flashback to her dream. She pushed it aside. They were professionals; of course he meant business skills.

'Are you saying there's a possibility we might make a good team?' Quinn's lips pressed down attractively.

'Why not?' She held his gaze as the waiter served their champagne.

'To the future of Steele Design,' Quinn said, raising his glass.

'I'll drink to that.'

'I'll handle the business side of things, keep all the aggravation out of your hair, while you handle the ideas.'

'Sounds like a dream team to me.'

Realising what she had said, Magenta froze. She felt like a computer stalling when it couldn't handle an input overload, but Quinn didn't miss a beat. 'To the dream team,' he said mildly, chinking glasses with her.

She didn't fight him when Quinn suggested taking her home in his car. It was even colder when they got outside, and there were little flurries of snow in the air. Quinn settled her inside the strangely familiar interior and even helped her to secure her seat belt when he got in. That felt good: twenty-first-century man with old-world manners. It didn't come much better, in fact.

They continued to talk about the business, but there was always something left unsaid between them, Magenta felt, so she said it. 'Quinn, do you dream?'

'Doesn't everyone?' He turned right onto the main road, confidently negotiating the steady buzz of traffic.

'I'm talking about the dreams we have when we're asleep. I know everyone dreams during the day, but you're in control of that.' Quinn glanced at her and she could see she'd got his attention. 'You only have to think of something you want, if you want to dream when you're awake, and before you know it you're weaving a whole fantastic drama round it.'

'Is that right?' Quinn said dryly.

'You know it is,' she said, feeling a throb of warmth as their eyes met briefly. 'What I'm talking about are dreams beyond our control, like the ones we have at night. Dreams that creep up on us and take everything in a new direction—a direction we could never have dreamed of.' She laughed. 'If that makes sense?'

'It makes perfect sense to me.'

Was Quinn teasing her? It was impossible to tell. 'Do you have dreams like that, Quinn? Dreams that make a weird kind of sense even though you know they could never happen?'

'Like a parallel life that seems to be reality?' he suggested, sending a shiver down Magenta's spine. 'Sometimes.'

He drew up outside her door, leaving no more time for questions—unless she invited him inside. The light was glowing in the window. It looked welcoming, and she was glad she had left it on. Prepared for a knock-back, she decided to risk it. 'Coffee?'

Just as she expected, Quinn looked at her and shook his head. 'I only drink Blue Mountain.'

It was as if she had received an electric shock, but she controlled it. 'Lucky for you, that's the only brand I drink.' Her face relaxed into a smile. Everything warmed up inside her—or at least those parts of her that were already overheated, thanks to the Quinn effect, just heated up some more.

'Shall we?'

Quinn released her seat belt. His face was very close and his mouth was just a whisper away. How she wanted him. He could just turn and kiss her—brush her lips...

She'd settle for that, Magenta told herself, only to see Quinn curb a grin. 'You think I'm funny?'

'I think you mentioned coffee.'

'I did,' she agreed.

Coming round to her side of the car, Quinn opened the door for her and helped her out.

I could get used to this, Magenta thought. *This too*, she realised as Quinn put his arm around her shoulders and drew her close to keep her warm.

'Let me,' he said when she took out her key.

He opened the door, stood back to allow her to precede him and then followed, shutting the door behind them.

This wasn't supposed to happen, Magenta thought as Quinn shucked her coat off in one sweeping move. She wasn't supposed to tear his jacket from his shoulders and rip at his shirt buttons like a loved-crazed hussy. And Quinn wasn't supposed to kiss her as if they'd known each other longer than for ever and had been apart for far too long. They grappled with each other as if no amount of kissing or embracing would ever be enough for them and as if any future parting, however short that parting might be, was unthinkable.

'Bed,' she managed to gasp, glancing up the stairs.

'We'll never make it.'

Fighting with Quinn's belt buckle, she was tempted to agree. She'd taken quite a journey in that dream from sexual *ingénue* to sensualist, and she wouldn't be denied now.

Finally, she managed to wrest the belt from Quinn's belt loops and tossed it aside. He kissed her again tenderly, cupping her face in his hands in a way that brought the dreams back full force. She always felt so cherished when Quinn kissed her this way.

But Quinn had never kissed her before—not even close.

So why this heat, this passion? Why was this so familiar?

Then hunger overcame them and she didn't want to work it out. Their clothes lay scattered on the floor, and they found a new use for the stairs: pressing her down on one step, Quinn moved over her.

Adding to her almost unbearable arousal, she now discovered she could see everything they were doing in the hall mirror. Quinn, muscular, male and completely naked without a single imperfection—and Magenta Steele with plenty, but Quinn didn't seem to notice. He was staring deep into her eyes, showing her things that went back a lot longer than a dream.

But right now it was the present that mattered. She had seen the heat in Quinn's eyes and now his hand had found her.

'Tell me what you want, Magenta.'

'All of you.'

'Like this?'

'Yes,' she gasped as Quinn sank deep inside her. *Yes and yes again*. Nothing in the dream had been half as good as this. Lying back against the thickly carpeted staircase, she dug her fingers into his buttocks, driving him hard, while Quinn thrust deeply into her to a rhythm that was both exciting and new, yet wholly familiar.

Release was violent and simultaneous. Quinn roared something hoarsely as Magenta cried out his name. Their grip on each other was ferocious as they bucked and moaned in a paroxysm of pleasure, and when Quinn finally loosened his grip on her she lay against his chest, panting helplessly.

'Was that good for you?' he murmured dryly.

From somewhere she managed to find the strength to ball up one hand into a fist and tap it weakly against his chest.

'I take it that's a yes?'

Raising her head, Magenta stared into Quinn's eyes. Her own eyes would barely focus, but she managed a single word.

'More?' Quinn echoed. 'Bed this time, I think.' Swinging her into his arms, he took the stairs two at a time.

'Front room—big bed—'

Quinn was inside her before her head touched the pillow. It felt so right, so good; rather than abating, her hunger had grown. 'The more you make love to me, the more I want you.' This revelation was no more than the truth. Gripping Quinn's shoulders, she urged him on while Quinn worked steadily and confidently towards the inevitable conclusion.

'My turn,' she told him while she was still gasping for breath.

'Greedy.'

'Who made me that way?' Tracing the line of Quinn's sexy mouth with her fingertip, she straddled him and, taking him deep, she rocked while Quinn worked magic with his hands.

They made love through the night, with no time to dream. Quinn had the energy of a Titan, and, starved of love for so long, she matched him every step of the way. They finally fell asleep in a tangle of exhausted limbs.

When dawn woke them, Magenta's first thought was Quinn. She slumped back on the pillow with relief to find him watching her. This was definitely better than a dream.

And things got better still when Quinn was in no hurry to get away—he didn't mention work once.

'I didn't want to wake you,' he said, stroking her hair. 'You looked so peaceful. Were you dreaming?'

Their faces were close enough on the pillows for Magenta to see the slightest flicker of thought cross Quinn's eyes. 'I didn't need to.' Turning her head, she kissed his hand as he caressed her. 'Did you?'

'I can't remember sleeping so well for quite some time.'

Now she was in his arms again and any discussion about Quinn's dreams would have to wait.

'You look perky,' Tess commented when Magenta arrived in the office on the day of the party.

So much for trying to hide things from your best friend,

Magenta thought wryly as Tess narrowed her eyes to scan her face. 'Good sex? No—don't tell me. I might have to hate you.'

'We could never hate each other, Tess.'

'You're definitely pushing it,' Tess warned. 'Do I take it things are going well for you and the Mighty Quinn?'

'You know I never discuss my private life.'

'Only because you don't have one—or didn't used to,' Tess amended, glancing towards the window where they could see Quinn telling the DJ where to set up.

'Don't you think we should concentrate on getting the right mix for the fruit punch rather than the wrong end of the stick? We don't want everyone falling over after the first drink.'

'Why not?' Tess demanded. 'Last man standing's mine.'

The sixties-style gym suit, which was the outfit Magenta had chosen to wear for the party, was like a navy-blue shirt and bloomers all in one. There was a neat little collar, a breast pocket, buttons down the front and a coloured belt. Highly flattering, it was not.

What had she been thinking? Magenta wondered, turning to look at her rear view in the rest-room mirror. No need to ask if her bum looked big in this—it did. And, having seen what some of the other girls were wearing, she could only imagine Quinn's reaction when he compared her to the young girls in their tight-fitting hot-pants and micro-minis. But she'd bought the kit and now she'd play the game.

She'd been a little late getting ready, as they'd just learned Steele Design had won a major contract to promote a new colour magazine for a national newspaper, so the party was already underway by the time she was ready to join in. She refused to think of the coveted contract as a coincidence. Had she been asked to promote Shiver Shiver Pink lipstick or *Almost* underwear? No.

Magenta gasped as some new arrivals, girls she knew, ran

past her straight off the street complaining about *shivering* without their thermal *underwear*.

Was that a coincidence? Was she going to see a twist of fate behind every door?

'Oh, hi, Quinn.'

'Hi, yourself,' he said, grinning down at her as he held the door. 'You look… For once I'm lost for words,' Quinn admitted, scanning Magenta's fancy-dress outfit with a bemused expression on his face.

'You don't like it?'

'Is that what you're planning to wear for the party?'

'Well, these aren't my new work clothes, if that's what you mean.' She could have predicted Quinn's outfit right down to the red, fuchsia-pink and black-striped socks—and rather wished she couldn't. It made her head reel. 'You don't think this outfit is right, do you?'

'I think you look cute—but maybe cute is wrong tonight? You just landed the biggest contract in Steele Design's history, so maybe elegant-sexy would be better. You can still be cute,' Quinn added hastily, tongue firmly lodged in his cheek.

'That's good to know,' Magenta said dryly. 'I'll go and change.'

'But first.' Drawing her into the shadows, Quinn teased her lips apart and then he kissed her.

Each time Quinn drew her into his arms and she inhaled, touched, experienced him, it was like the first time all over again—and the first time had been more than magic. 'Hmm. I don't feel quite so bad now,' Magenta admitted when Quinn finally released her.

'And you're going to feel even better when you see what I've got for you.'

'Quinn!' Magenta exclaimed, pressing her hand to her chest in pretended outrage.

'A small gift.'

'Small? If it's something small, I can relax.'

'You can,' Quinn confirmed, drawing her with him into his office. 'Well? What do you think?' he said, standing back.

Magenta stared at the dress hanging on a padded hanger from a hook. She had to say something. It was expected of her. Good manners demanded she *must* say something. 'Thank you,' she stuttered, wondering if the world and everyone in it had gone mad.

'There's a pair of shoes I thought you might like too—and some opaque-black tights to finish off the outfit.'

She was the one who was about to be finished off, as her heart banged wildly in her chest. Did she believe in second sight? No. Could dreams predict the future? No again. So, how to explain the figure-flattering dress in navy-blue silk and the pair of red-soled shoes? 'Quinn, these are fabulous— and exactly what I would have chosen myself.' *Given a huge hike in salary*, Magenta thought, giving herself a moment to salivate over the fabulous shoes. 'How did you know what I'd like?'

'An informed guess,' he explained, thumbing his stubble.

But there was something else, something she couldn't read behind Quinn's steady gaze. 'And you're sure you don't dream at night?' she said.

CHAPTER TWENTY

THEY were both lost in their own thoughts on the drive home from the office. The party had been a huge success, with no time for further revelations from Quinn or opportunity for Magenta to dig for clues.

Which was probably just as well, Magenta reflected as she stroked the delicate panels of her new silk dress. Tonight belonged to their colleagues, and their cheers still rang in her ears. She would never have been able to join in the celebrations if she and Quinn had got any deeper into a discussion about dreams. But there was nothing to stop her doing a little probing now. 'What made you buy the dress for me?'

He glanced across. 'Intuition told me it might come in useful.'

And, as his lips curved in a grin, she pressed, 'Intuition? Do you often get presentiments about the future?'

'I get hunches,' he admitted. 'Am I psychic? I wouldn't have taken so long to get where I am today if I were.'

'Thirty-two *is* rather ancient,' Magenta agreed wryly.

'Your place or mine?'

A bolt of arousal hit her. Quinn as always had come right to the point. Reluctantly, she put her sensible head on. 'Wherever we can talk.' Quinn wasn't getting off the hook so easily this time.

'Mine's closer.'

'Sounds good to me.'

This time when they went inside she made the coffee and laid her cards out on the table right away. 'Quinn—discussion first.'

'Hmm, this sounds serious.' He reached past her for the mugs and, while her guard was down, he swung his arm around her waist. 'I'll issue any timetables we have around here.' Quinn stared her in the eyes, leaving Magenta in no doubt as to his agenda.

The click of the coffee machine was Quinn's cue to release her. 'Boy, do I need this,' he said, pouring them both a generous slug.

While he was distracted she led the way into his orangerie where they could see the stars as they talked. She trembled with awareness when Quinn came up behind her. She put her hands over his and rested back against his chest as she gazed up at the waxing moon. 'So, Quinn, do you dream?'

Quinn took the coffee mug out of her hands and put it on a small glass-topped table. 'Maybe,' he admitted. 'I'm usually asleep, so I can't be sure.'

'Quinn.' She turned to face him. 'I'm being serious.'

'Oh, really?' His faint smile was softly mocking. 'How can that be, when all you want is for me to admit that we meet up in our dreams? Crazy woman,' he murmured, drawing her close.

Quinn's eyes were warm and amused and his lips were close. It would be the easiest thing in the world to sink into his embrace and to forget about everything, but she was determined to discover the truth. 'I'm not asking you to believe in magic—and, I can assure you, I'm not crazy.'

Quinn held his gaze. 'What do you want me to say, Magenta?'

'I just want you to admit that there's more to life than what we can see and touch, hear and feel.'

Now he was grinning. 'Do you want me to lose my hard-ass reputation altogether?'

'I didn't think it bothered you what people thought.'

'It does if it impacts on the business.'

For a moment she had a flashback, and that flashback included a baby...

'Magenta?' Seeing the wistfulness in her face, Quinn drew her with him to a chair and sat her down on his knee. 'What's happened?' he murmured, drawing her close. 'Never mind all your questions, don't you think it's time you came clean with me?'

She rested still for a moment, knowing she had to tell him. She *had* to.

'How bad can it be?' Quinn prompted.

The dream? Apart from the baby—if it were possible to leave that aside, which it wasn't—the dream was not bad at all, especially with some careful editing.

So she told him, leaving nothing out—other than the fact that Quinn had told her that he loved her. She concentrated more on the fascinating detail of the sixties, including Quinn's appalling behaviour at the start.

'But you won me round in the end, apparently,' he said wryly.

'I tamed you and trained you.'

'Proves it was a dream.'

'You're impossible.'

'You're repeating yourself.'

Now *she* was smiling. Quinn's humour did it for her every time. Plus, he was intuitive and compassionate—not forgetting hot. She still shook her head at him as if he were an impossible case, before going on to recount all the incredible events from the dream. But when she came to the part about the baby she couldn't go on.

'There's no need to put yourself through this, Magenta. You want a baby—that's not so unusual.'

'But it felt so real.' She dashed tears from her eyes. 'And now I feel like I've lost it.'

'That's an anxiety dream,' Quinn told her, bringing her close to drop a kiss on the top of her head. 'You haven't lost your baby, because you haven't been pregnant—not yet.'

'Not yet?' Magenta shook her head at Quinn. 'You are definitely impossible.'

Quinn's answer was to throw her a sexy smile. 'Who knows what the future holds?'

She tried to pull away. The pang of loss and longing was still too strong to make a joke of it.

'Don't stop me getting close,' Quinn said, pulling her back onto his knee again. 'Don't shut everyone out so the only way you have to experience the things you wish for is in your dreams. Don't do that, Magenta, you'll miss out on so much—too much.'

'Says the expert.'

'My hopes and dreams have all been centred around the business—who knows what I dream about at night? I can only hope it isn't balance sheets.' He grinned.

'How do you explain my dream?'

'Maybe you worry you can't have children—or maybe you think you won't meet someone you'd like to have a baby with.' Quinn's beautiful eyes narrowed consideringly. 'Whatever. It's common knowledge you have the best imagination in the business, Magenta Steele—so am I surprised you have colourful dreams?' Quinn's lips pressed down. 'What do you think?'

Magenta wrapped her arms around her waist and remained silent.

'I'm going to tell you what I think,' he said, making her look at him. 'I think we should get to know each other outside the bedroom.' That caught her attention. 'Starting tomorrow night with a proper date.'

And, when for once she didn't argue, he added, 'I know this really cool jazz club...'

* * *

Life could be even better than a dream you could manipulate, Magenta had discovered, thanks to Quinn. She had no time for daydreaming in the weeks and months that followed; he took up all her time. Winter juddered reluctantly into spring, and then another year passed. With the first warm days of that new year the bulbs began to flower, carpeting the London parks with drifts of sunny, yellow daffodils and spikes of vivid purple, white and yellow crocuses. They took time off from work—lunch hours, coffee breaks—whenever the weather permitted. Muffled up in scarves and heavy jackets, they walked hand in hand, fingers intertwined as they talked business and pleasure, finishing each other's sentences and sparking ideas off each other—whether those ideas related to some new advertising campaign, or to the colour of the sitting room in their new apartment. Magenta always won when it came to colour schemes, though she had to fight Quinn tooth and nail over business—just the way she liked it.

But today was a special day. Today was a day for skimming pebbles across a pool.

'I have something to tell you,' she said, drawing to a halt in front of a familiar bench.

Quinn grimaced. 'Just so long as it has nothing to do with a dream.'

'No, this is real enough.' Picking up the flattest stone she could find, she angled her wrist and sent it skimming across the water.

'One…two…three…four!' Quinn was behind her with his arms looped loosely around her waist, counting the times the stone flipped up in the air as it travelled over the surface of the water. His breath warmed the top of her head.

'Does that mean we're expecting quadruplets?'

'Quinn?' Magenta swung round to face him.

'How did I guess? I can't live with you every day and fill my eyes with you without noticing those secret smiles you've been smiling, and the excitement you've been trying so hard to hide. Also, since we're pretty close,' he added wryly, 'I've noticed that you're late. So, Magenta Steele, I believe you have something to tell me?'

'Gray Quinn, you're a spoiler.' Pressing her hands against his chest, she threatened to push him in the water. Quinn didn't move an inch.

'This isn't what you want?'

'Of course it is!' Magenta exclaimed as Quinn swung her round in the air. 'And you?'

'I thought loving you made my life complete—you just proved me wrong.'

'So I'm second best now?' she teased him, snuggling her head into Quinn's hard chest.

'I think my heart's big enough to hold you and a whole football team of children safe inside it. You should know by now that you're the only woman I'll ever love, Magenta. And now you're the mother of my child,' Quinn murmured, staring straight into her eyes.

'I love you, Gray Quinn.'

'I love you too—and you just reminded me why.'

'What did you say?'

'What I've been saying to you for months now: I love you.'

Grabbing hold of the edges of Quinn's jacket, she shook them imperatively. 'No, not that—I'm talking about the actual words you said, about me being the mother of your child.'

With an indulgent groan, Quinn shook his head. 'Not that dream again.'

'There are some things you can't explain,' Magenta said stubbornly.

'Such as?'

'Words I heard in the dream that you just repeated—explain that away,' she said with a dramatic flourish.

Holding her in front of him, Quinn stared down into her eyes. 'Let's put this to bed once and for all, shall we? Everyone accepts that the subconscious plays on and on while we're sleeping—all those things we can't bring ourselves to think about during the day or don't have time for. We fall asleep and they all come flooding back—whether we want them in our heads or not. And then we embroider them to suit our deepest desires—like you desiring me, for instance.'

'*What?*' Balling her hands into fists, Magenta pummelled Quinn's unyielding chest. 'The world doesn't revolve around you, Gray Quinn.'

'Your world does, apparently.' He had to dodge out of the way this time.

'Okay,' said Magenta, setting her jaw. 'So what about the little things—the coincidences like the dress and shoes you bought me, also in the dream? And the hot-dog stand?' she said excitedly, growing in conviction.

'If they were all in the dream, then that was exactly as you say—coincidence. The dress and shoes I gave you aren't such a mystery. The girls leave their magazines lying about all over the office and, contrary to popular opinion, men do glance at them. I guessed the featured outfit of the month would be pretty high on your wish-list.'

'And the hot-dog stand?'

'We pass it on the way to your old place.' There was a smile in Quinn's voice. 'I don't think you can read too much into that, Magenta. You were hungry, I bought you a hot dog—whoo-hoo.'

Magenta sighed. Didn't everyone want a little magic in their life? But she had Quinn. She should be satisfied, she told herself, feeling warmth consume her as she stared into his face.

'I'm sorry if I burst your bubble, baby.'

'It's not that.'

'Yes, it is. However sceptical people think they are, everyone hopes that a little magic will touch their life. There wouldn't be a game of chance or a dating site in existence otherwise—and that's only the tip of the iceberg.'

'My dream was just that, in your opinion—a projection of my deepest hopes and fears onto my sleeping mind.'

'I'm afraid so.'

'Then I think you're an unromantic killjoy, Gray Quinn.'

'Really?' Quinn murmured, not even slightly ruffled by this opinion. 'So, what do you make of this?'

'What is it?' Magenta asked, staring at the small velvet box.

'Why don't you open it and find out?'

She did as Quinn said, only to feel every bit of blood drain from her face. 'It's fabulous,' she whispered. And it truly was.

'It's no more than you deserve,' Quinn told her, removing the flawless blue-white diamond and placing it on Magenta's wedding finger. 'Think of it as a bonus for landing the magazine account. I saw it in the jeweller's window and couldn't walk past it. For some reason, it called to me.'

'And that's all it is—a bonus for my work?'

'What do you think?' Catching Magenta into his arms, Quinn held her close. 'Do you want the full-on kneeling-in-the-mud routine, or can I ask you standing up?'

'On your knees,' she commanded.

'Heartless woman.'

Heart full, she thought.

'Magenta Steele, will you make me the happiest man in the world by consenting to be my wife? What am I talking about?' Quinn said, breaking off to shake his head. 'I'm already the happiest man in the world.'

'We don't need to get married?'

'To bring up a baby in a household full of love together? No, I don't think we do.' Catching hold of Magenta's hands, Quinn held them to his warm lips for a few intense moments, and when he looked up again his eyes were dancing with the humour she loved. 'But if you want the ring…'

'Stop teasing me, Quinn,' she warned him. And, instead of telling him to get up, she knelt down too. 'I'll take you with or without the ring, as you well know.'

'And I want you whether we get married or not—and that would be for ever,' Quinn added, staring deep into Magenta's eyes. 'Not just for the duration of a dream.'

HER IMPOSSIBLE BOSS

CATHY WILLIAMS

Cathy Williams is originally from Trinidad, but has lived in England for a number of years. She currently has a house in Warwickshire, which she shares with her husband, Richard, her three daughters, Charlotte, Olivia and Emma, and their pet cat, Salem. She adores writing romantic fiction and would love one of her girls to become a writer—although at the moment she is happy enough if they do their homework and agree not to bicker with one another!

CHAPTER ONE

WIDE, sensual mouth compressed, Matt stared down at the makeshift CV sitting in front of him. It was difficult to know where to begin. The colourful list of jobs complemented by the even more impressive lack of duration at each one of them told their own story. As did the brief, uninspiring academic profile. In the normal course of events he would have tossed this application into the bin without even bothering to read the sketchy handwritten personal profile at the end. Unfortunately, this was *not* the normal course of events.

He finally looked across his highly polished mahogany desk at the girl perched nervously on the chair facing him.

'Eight jobs.' He pushed himself away from the desk and allowed the lengthening silence to fill in the blanks of what he wanted to say.

Tess Kelly had come to him via a reference from her sister, and, in no position to be choosy, here he now was, interviewing for a nanny for his daughter. From what he could see, not only was Tess Kelly resoundingly lacking in any relevant experience, she was also flighty and academically challenged.

Huge green eyes looked back at him and he followed

her nervous gesture as she chewed her bottom lip. He might have his hands tied, but that didn't mean that he was going to make this process easy for her.

'I know it sounds like a lot...'

'You're twenty-three years old and you've held down eight jobs. I think it's fair to say that it is a lot.'

Tess looked away from the cool dark eyes resting on her. Under his unflinching, assessing gaze, she was finding it impossible to keep still. Why on earth was she here? She had arrived in New York three weeks previously to stay with her sister, with the proviso that she take some time out to consider her options and get her act together. At least those had been the parting words of her parents as they had waved her off at the airport before she'd disappeared across the Atlantic.

'You're twenty-three years old, Tess,' her mother had said firmly, offering her a plate of homemade biscuits to soften the blow, 'and you still don't seem to have any idea what you want to do with your life. Your dad and I would just like to see you settle down. Find something that you enjoy doing—something you might want to stick with for longer than five minutes... Claire knows all the ins and outs of the business world. She'll be able to give you some helpful advice. It would do you good to spend your summer somewhere else...'

No one had mentioned that part of the process would involve getting a job as a nanny. She had never worked with any child in her life before. She couldn't remember having ever expressed the slightest curiosity about working with one. And yet here she was, sitting in front of a man who chilled her to the bone. The very second she had spun round at the sound of his velvety voice, to see him lounging against the doorframe, inspecting her, she had felt a shiver of apprehension skim down her spine. She had prepared herself for someone portly and middle-aged. He was, after all, her sister's boss. He owned the company, he ran it, and according to Claire he took no prisoners. How could he do all that and still be in his early thirties? But he was—and, contrary to all expectations, not only was he young, he also had killer looks. Drop-dead, truly sensational killer looks.

But his emotional detachment was terrifying, and his perfect bone structure proclaimed a face that never cracked a smile. Tess wondered how her sister could work for him without having a nervous breakdown.

'And your academic history… I'm finding it hard to tally your lack of qualifications with your sister's achievements. Claire has a first class degree and is head of my corporate law department. You have…let's count them…six mediocre GCSE grades and a certificate in Foundation Art…'

'Yes, well, I'm not Claire, Mr Strickland.' Two patches of colour appeared on her cheeks. 'Claire and Mary both excelled at school…'

'Mary being…?'

'My other sister. She's a doctor. They were both high-achievers. Not everyone is built along the same lines.' Cheerful by nature, Tess was finding that she *loathed* this man. From his opening words to her— *'You're half an hour late and I don't tolerate lateness.'* —to his sweeping assumption that she was a failure. He hadn't said it in so many words, but it was there, lurking in the cold, disdainful expression behind those bitter chocolate eyes.

'Okay. Let's do away with the formalities and cut to the chase, shall we?' Matt leaned forward and rested his elbows on the desk. 'You're here because I am not in a position of choice. I don't know what, precisely, Claire has told you, but let me clarify. My ex-wife died some months ago and since than I have had full custody of my ten-year-old daughter. In that period she has seen off almost as many nannies as you have seen off jobs. Consequently, the agency I deal with have effectively closed their doors to me. I have three housekeepers, but they are not suitable for the demands of the job. I could look further afield, but frankly this is a three-month posting—and finding a career nanny who is willing to offer herself for such a short period of time will not be easy. Time, Miss Kelly, is of the essence as far as I am concerned. I work huge hours. I have neither the time nor the ability to cover. Your name cropped up. Your sister sings your praises when it comes to your socia- bility. Ergo, you are here now—despite your glaring shortcomings.'

Not for the first time, Matt considered the train of events that had led to where he was now.

Divorced for eight years, he had been an infrequent spectator to his daughter's life. Catrina, his ex-wife, had removed her to Connecticut a year after their divorce had become final, and had played so many games when it came to making arrangements for him to visit that the years had elapsed without him ever really feeling con- nected to Samantha. And then, six months ago, Catrina had died in a car accident, and the daughter he had never really known had landed on his doorstep—resentful, grieving, and silently, wilfully hostile.

Nannies, a necessity for him, had come and gone, and he now found himself between a rock and a hard place.

'I'm sorry. I'm *so* sorry. Claire didn't mention details… Your poor, poor daughter…' Tears of sympathy were gathering in the corners of Tess's eyes and she blinked them away. 'I'm not surprised she's finding it difficult to settle down.'

Taken aback by such an emotional response, Matt reached into a drawer in his desk and pulled out a box of tissues, which he handed to her.

'So, whilst you're not my idea of the ideal candidate…' He carried on over the subsiding threat of her tears.

'I guess you're worried because I've had so many jobs over the years…' Tess was prepared to give him the benefit of the doubt. He might be harsh and forbidding, but he was in a difficult position and no doubt justifiably anxious that he take on someone who wouldn't let him down.

'Correct. Samantha would not benefit from someone who decides to stick around for a few days and then walks out because she's bored. Even though there have been a lot of nannies, they have all endeavoured to give it their best shot. Are you capable of that?'

'Yes. Yes, I am.' She looked at him. Despite the unforgiving nature of his expression, a little voice whispered, he really was very good-looking—beautiful, almost. Suddenly hot and bothered, she looked away, twisting the tissue between her fingers.

'Convince me.'

'I beg your pardon?'

'I may not be in a position to pick and choose, Miss

Kelly, but I would still like you to persuade me that I am not about to make a mistake with you. Your sister may well sing your praises, and I trust Claire, but...' He shrugged and relaxed back. 'Persuade me...'

'I wouldn't leave anyone in the lurch. I really wouldn't, Mr Strickland.' She leaned forward, her face flushed and sincere. 'I know you think that I'm probably not very good at sticking to anything. Well, actually,' she confessed, 'my family would all probably agree with you. But I've actually been indispensable in many of my past jobs. I've never let anyone *down*—not really. No, not at all, come to think of it. Even when I quit the receptionist's job at Barney and Son, Gillian was there to take over. To be honest, I think they were all a little relieved when I decided to leave. I was forever transferring people to the wrong department...'

'Let's try and stick to the theme.'

'Yes. Well, what I'm trying to say is that you can trust me with your daughter. I won't let you down.'

'Even though you have no experience in the field and might get bored with the company of a ten-year-old child?'

'I don't think kids are boring! Do you?'

Matt flushed darkly. *Was* he bored in Samantha's company? He had precious little experience in that area to provide a qualified answer. His relationship with his daughter was fraught at best. They conversed intermittently, and across a seemingly unbreachable chasm. She was sulky and uncommunicative, and he knew that he was not a feelings person.

Matt dismissed that brief moment of intense introspection.

'So how would you plan on looking after her?' He pushed the conversation forward and focused on her.

She had a fascinatingly transparent face. Right now, giving his question some thought, she was lost in a slight frown, her lips parted, her apple-green eyes distant. Tess Kelly wasn't the sort of woman he had been expecting. Claire was tall, brisk, efficient, and permanently attired in a suit. The girl sitting opposite him was a living, breathing testimony to the power of misconception. She looked as though she had never been anywhere near a suit and her hair...

No fashionably tailored bob, but really, *really* long. Several times he had been tempted to angle himself so that he could see just how long for himself.

'Well...I guess there are the usual sights. Museums, art galleries. And then there's the cinema, the zoo... I love Central Park. We could go there. I'm sure she'll be missing the familiarity of her home and all her friends, so I'll make sure to keep her busy and occupied.'

'And then there's the matter of schoolwork.'

Tess blinked and looked at him in confusion. 'What schoolwork?' she asked, perplexed. 'It's the holidays.'

'Samantha's education was severely disrupted because of Catrina's death, as you can imagine. More so when she came to New York. There seemed little point in registering her for a school here, which she wouldn't be attending on a permanent basis, and the tutors I employed for her came and went as regularly as the nannies. Consequently there are gaps in her learning which will have to be addressed before she sits exams at the beginning of September for her new school.'

'Okaayyy…and where do I fit in?'

Tess continued to look at him blankly and he clicked his tongue with impatience. '*You're* going to have to take charge there.'

'Me?' Tess squeaked in consternation. '*I* can't become a tutor! You've seen my application form! You've *made fun* of my lack of qualifications!'

The thought of trying to teach anything to someone else horrified her. She wasn't academic. She became nervous just thinking about textbooks. The youngest of three girls, she had grown up in the shadow of her clever sisters, and from an early age had dealt with the problem by simply opting out. No one could accuse her of being thick if she simply refused to compete, could they? And she had known that there was no way that she could ever have competed with either Claire or Mary. How on earth could he expect her to suddenly become a *tutor*?

'I'm sorry to have wasted your time, Mr Strickland,' she said, standing up abruptly. 'If teaching is part of the job, then I'm going to have to turn down the position. I…I can't. Claire and Mary are the brainy ones. I'm not. I've never been to university. I never even wanted to go. I did a foundation course in Art when I was sixteen, and that's the extent of my qualifications. You need someone else.'

Matt looked at her narrowly and allowed her to ramble on. Then, very calmly, he told her to sit.

'I'm getting the picture about your academic quali-fications or lack of them. You hated school.'

'I didn't *hate* school.' Having not wanted the job to start with, Tess now realised that she did. His daughter's plight had touched her. The thought of her being so young, and dependent on a father who was obviously a workaholic, tugged at her heartstrings. For the first time she really wanted to get involved. 'I'm just no good when it comes to textbooks.'

'I have no time for people who wave a white flag and concede defeat before they've even given something a fair chance,' Matt said bracingly. 'I'm not asking you to teach to degree level. I'm asking you to tutor Samantha in some of the basics—maths, english, sciences. If you want to persuade me that you're interested in taking on this job, then you're going about it the wrong way.'

'I'm just being honest! If…if you don't want to employ any more tutors for your daughter, then why don't *you* help her with her schoolwork?' She faltered. 'You run a business, so you must be qualified…or maybe you don't need maths and English in what you do…? Some children don't cope well with home-tutoring. Perhaps your daughter is one of those…'

'Samantha could cope very well with home-tutoring,' Matt said shortly, 'if she was prepared to put effort into it. But she's not. She might benefit more from teaching in a less structured manner. And, no, there is no way that I can help out. I barely have time to sleep. I leave this apartment at seven-thirty in the morning, which is an hour later than I used to before Samantha arrived, and I try and make it back by eight in the evening when I'm not away. Which is a push at the best of times.'

Tess was distracted sufficiently from her own agonising to shoot him a look of frank horror. 'You work from seven-thirty in the morning to eight at night? Every day?'

'I cut myself some slack on the weekends.' Matt shrugged. He could think of no one who would find anything out of the ordinary about those working hours. The high-fliers in his company—and there were a lot of them—routinely had punishing schedules and thought nothing of it. They were paid fabulous sums of money and quid pro quo, after all.

'What does that mean?'

'Where are you going with this?' Matt asked irritably. 'You're straying from the topic.'

'I'm sorry,' Tess breathed. 'I just feel so sorry for you.'

'Come again?' Matt could hardly credit what he was hearing. If they haven't been discussing something so important, he would have laughed. Never, but *never*, had anyone *felt sorry* for him. Quite the opposite. Being born into a legacy of wealth, power and influence had opened a thousand doors. Without siblings, the task of taking hold of the family fortunes had fallen onto his shoulders, and not only had he looked after the billions but he had gone several steps further and dramatically increased their worth. He had diversified and invested in areas his father would never have dreamed of, and in so doing had attained a position of impenetrable power. He was virtually untouchable. The economic and financial crises that had seen off so many of his rivals had skirted harmlessly around him. It was a situation he had engineered, and one he enjoyed.

'I can't think of anything more horrible than being slave to a job, but you're right. I'm getting off the subject.

I was just wondering why you didn't cover the school-work with Samantha yourself if you think that the home-tutoring doesn't work, but I can see that you don't have the time.'

Was it his imagination or was there a hint of gentle criticism there?

'Good. I'm glad we agree.'

'Would you mind me asking you something?' Tess ventured, clearing her throat. When he tilted his head to one side she said, tentatively, 'When do you have time for your daughter, if you work such long hours?'

Matt stared at her in disbelief. The directness of the question put him soundly on the back foot—as did the fact that he was seldom in a position of having to field direct questions of a personal nature. Women just *didn't* go there. But she was waiting for an answer.

'I fail to see what this has to do with the job,' he said stiffly.

'Oh, but it has lots to do with the job! I mean, I'm sure you have special times set aside, and I would want to know that so that I didn't intrude. I just don't see where those special times would fit in if you're working from seven-thirty to eight every day, and only taking a bit of time off over the weekends.'

'I don't have a structure for the time I spend with Samantha.' His voice was cold and uninviting. 'We very often go to The Hamptons so that she can see her grand-parents on the weekend.'

'That's lovely.' Tess was unconvinced.

'And now that we've covered that, let's move on to your hours.' He tapped his pen absently on the desk, beating a staccato rhythm that made her feel as though she was being cross-examined rather than interviewed. 'I'll expect you to be here every morning no later than seven-thirty.'

'Seven-thirty?'

'Does that pose a problem?'

Torn between truth and tact, Tess remained silent until he prompted, with raised eyebrows, 'I'm taking that as a *no*. It's a requirement of the job. I could occasionally request one of my housekeepers to cover for you in an emergency, but I would hope that the occasion doesn't arise.'

Tess had always been punctual at all her jobs—the very many she had had over the years—but it had to be said that none of them had required her to wake up at the crack of dawn. She wasn't an early-morning person. Somehow she knew that was a concept he would never be able to understand. She wondered whether he ever slept.

'Do all your employees work long hours?' she asked faintly, and for some reason Matt had the strongest in-clination to burst out laughing. Her appalled look said it all.

'They don't get paid the earth to clock-watch,' he said seriously. 'Are you telling me that you've never worked overtime in your life before?'

'I've never had to,' Tess told him earnestly. 'But then again, I've never been paid the earth for anything I've done. Not that I mind. I've never been that interested in money.'

Matt was intrigued, against his will. Was this woman from the same planet as he was? He should stick to the programme, but he found himself strangely willing to digress.

'Really?' he said with scepticism. 'In that case, I applaud you. You're one of a kind.'

Tess wondered whether he was being sarcastic, but then, looking around her at the luxurious surroundings of his penthouse, where the old sat comfortably with the new and every hanging on the walls and rug strewn on the floor screamed wealth, she realised that he would be genuinely mystified at her indifference to money.

It had very quickly struck her, the second she had walked through the front door of his apartment, that Matt Strickland was a man who moved in circles so far removed from her own that they barely occupied the same stratosphere. The people he mixed with would share the same exalted lifestyle, and it was a lifestyle that could not be achieved without an unswerving dedication to the art of making money.

But Tess had been telling the absolute truth when she had told him that money didn't interest her. If it had, she might have been a little more driven when it came to a career.

Nor did she have a great deal of respect for someone who put money at the top of their list. Someone, in short, like Matt Strickland. Even though she could appreciate that he was clever and ambitious, there was a hard, cutting edge to him that left her cold.

She sneaked a quick look at that striking face, and her heart beat a little faster and a little harder in her chest.

'You're not saying anything. I take it that you disapprove of all of this?' He gestured sweepingly with one hand. This was a woman, he realised, whose silences

were as revealing as the things she said. It was a refresh-
ing trait.

'It's all very comfortable.' Tess tiptoed around telling
him the absolute truth—which was that expensive fur-
nishings and investment paintings all came at a price.

'But…?'

'I prefer small and cosy,' she admitted. 'My parents'
house is small and cosy. Obviously, not *that* small. There
were five of us growing up. But I think that their entire
house would fit into just a bit of this apartment.'

'You still live at home with them?' His sharp ears had
picked up on the intonation in her voice and his curiosity
was instantly roused. What was a twenty-three-year-old
woman still doing living at home? And, he noted distractedly, a strikingly pretty twenty-three-year-old girl?
Huge green eyes dominated a heart-shaped face that
even in moments of thought carried an air of animation.
Her long hair was the colour of caramel, and…

His eyes drifted lazily downwards to the full breasts
pushing lushly against a small cropped vest, the silver of
flat stomach just visible between the vest and the faded
jeans that moulded slim legs.

Annoyed at being distracted, Matt stood up and
began to prowl through his office. Originally a library,
it was still dominated by the hand-made wooden bookcase that stretched along the entire length of the back
wall. A rich Oriental rug, handed down through the
generations, covered most of the wooden floor. The only
modern introductions were the paintings on the walls
and, of course, the high-tech paraphernalia essential to
his work.

'I…at the moment I do,' Tess mumbled, with sudden awkward embarrassment.

'And you've *never* lived on your own?'

The incredulity in his voice made her spin round to glare at him defensively. She decided that he really was truly hateful. Hateful and judgemental.

'There was never a need for me to live on my own!' she said in a high pitched voice. 'I didn't go to university, and there was no point looking for somewhere to rent when it was just as convenient for me to carry on living at home.' As if it were spelt out in bold neon lettering, she was appalled to hear with her own ears just how hopeless that made her sound. Twenty-three and still living with Mum and Dad. Angry tears threatened to push their way to the surface and she blinked rapidly, forcing them back.

'Remarkable.'

'Most of my friends still live at home. It's not that remarkable.'

'And you never felt the need to spread your wings and do something different? Or did you give up and wave the white flag before you could get around to challenging yourself?'

Tess was shocked at the strength of her reaction. She had never shown any inclination towards violence before, but she could easily have leapt out of her chair and thrown something at him. Instead, she subsided into angry silence. Her entire nervous system picked up pace as he circled her and then leant down, arms on either side of her chair, effectively caging her in.

'I don't see what my home life has to do with this

job,' she breathed jerkily, looking anywhere but at the brown muscular forearms on either side of her.

'I'm trying to get a measure of you as a person. You're going to be responsible for the welfare of my daughter. You come with no references from a professional agency. I need to find out that you're not going to prove a liability. Shall I tell you what I've concluded so far?'

Tess wondered whether she had a choice. Had her tongue been able to unglue itself from the roof of her mouth, she might have summoned up the courage to say something along those lines, but sarcastic rejoinders weren't her forte and his proximity was wreaking havoc with her composure. Her skin was tingling, and she felt as though she was having to drag the oxygen into her lungs in order to breathe.

It was a relief when he pushed himself away from her chair and resumed his place behind the desk.

'You're lazy. You're unfocused. You're lacking in self-confidence and you've been perfectly happy to carry on being that way.' He enunciated each derogatory bullet point with the cold precision of a judge passing sentence on a criminal. 'You still live at home and it doesn't seem to have occurred to you somewhere along the way that your parents might not be as happy with that situation as you are. You pick jobs up and you put them down again because you don't want to be stretched. I'm no psychologist, but I'm guessing that it's because you think you can't fail at anything if you never bother to give your all to it.'

'That's horrible.' Unfortunately there were elements of truth in some of what he had said, and for that she hated him. 'Why are you interviewing me for this job if you have such a low opinion of me?' she asked on a whisper. 'Or has the interview ended? Is this your way of telling me that I haven't got the job? Yes, it is. And, that being the case—' Tess inhaled one deep breath that steadied her fraying nerves '—then I can tell you what I think of you too!' She looked at him with stormy green eyes and drew herself upright in her chair. 'I think that you're arrogant and rude. You think that just because you…you make a lot of money and grew up with a lot of money you can treat people any way you want to and be as offensive as you want to be. I think that it's awful that you obviously work so hard that you have no time left over to give your daughter—who *needs* you! Or maybe you just don't know *how* to give yourself to anyone else!'

Her breathing was jerky from the effort of pouring emotions she'd never known she possessed into what was, for her, an all-out shouting match. The worst of it was that she didn't feel good about herself—even though she had spoken her mind, and even though speaking her mind should have achieved some sort of healthy cleansing.

'And I'm *not* lazy,' she concluded, deflating like a balloon with its air suddenly released. 'If that's all.' She stood up and tried to gather some shreds of dignity. 'I'll be on my way.'

Matt smiled, and Tess was so flustered by that smile that she remained rooted to the spot, dithering as though her legs had forgotten how to work.

'You have fire. I like that. You're going to need some of it when it comes to handling my daughter.'

'Wha—at?'

He waved her down into the chair and leaned back. 'It's healthy to hear a little criticism now and again. I can't remember the last time anyone raised their voice in my presence.' Particularly, he could have added, when it came to women. As if a switch had been turned on in his head, he suddenly keenly noted the fading pinkness in her cheeks. Her hair had fallen forward and was now spread over her shoulders, falling like spun silk over her breasts, almost down to her waist. She was regaining some of her lost composure but her breasts were still heaving.

He was shocked by the sudden responsive stirring in his loins. God, he had a girlfriend! An extremely clever, very high-powered girlfriend. One who understood completely the constraints of his job because they mirrored her own! They were on the same wavelength. She was diametrically, radically and dramatically the opposite to the elfin creature with the big green eyes sitting opposite him. Vicky Burns was focused, driven, and university-educated to the highest possible level.

So why the hell was he wondering what Tess Kelly looked like with her clothes off and only her long, long hair to cover her modesty?

He wrote a figure on a piece of paper and slid it across the desk to her.

Tess leant forward, and of their own accord his eyes strayed to the cleavage she revealed as she reached for the paper.

With a sigh of pure frustration Matt rubbed his eyes and half swivelled his chair, so that he was facing the vast windows of the library, framed with their heavy velvet curtains. It was a safer sight than the one his rebellious eyes had been absorbing.

'This is too much, Mr Strickland. I couldn't possibly accept.'

'Don't be ridiculous!' Annoyed with himself for his uncustomary lapse of self-control, Matt made his voice sharper than intended. He reluctantly turned to look at her. 'It's perfectly reasonable. You're being asked to do a hugely important job, and for that money...well, consider yourself on a learning curve as far as overtime goes. There's just one more thing. You'll have to dress the part.' He flushed darkly at the confusion on her face. 'Looser clothing. It's more practical in this heat. Particularly if you intend on doing...er...outdoor activities...'

'But I don't have any loose clothing.'

'Then you'll have to buy some. It's not an insurmountable problem, Tess. You will have access to an account for all expenses to do with the job. Make use of it.' He stood up, back in control of his wayward body, and waited as she scrambled to her feet, gathering her satchel which she slung over her shoulder.

'Now it's time for you to meet my daughter. She's upstairs in her bedroom. I'll show you to the kitchen. You can familiarise yourself with it. Make yourself a cup of coffee. I'll bring her down.'

Tess nodded. After her gruelling interview, from which she was still reeling, the prospect of meeting Samantha wasn't as daunting as she would have expected. What could be more full-on than her father had been?

The apartment, sprawling in all directions, occupied

the entire top two floors of the building. Matt showed her into a kitchen which was as stunningly modern as the rest of the apartment was shamelessly and opulently old. Granite surfaces positively gleamed, and were completely bare of any of the normal clutter associated with day-to-day life. Tess foresaw problems should she attempt to do any cooking with her charge. She would be terrified of ruining the show home look.

'Make yourself at home,' he insisted, while she continued to look around her with the lost expression of someone suddenly transported to foreign territory.

For a few seconds Matt watched her with rare amusement. 'It doesn't bite,' he said, and Tess flushed. 'There's tea and coffee in one of the cupboards, and in the fridge…' he indicated something sleek that was camouflaged to look like the rest of the kitchen '…there should be milk. My housekeepers make sure that the kitchen is stocked, especially now that Samantha's around. If you're lucky, you might even locate some biscuits somewhere.'

'You mean you don't *know* where things are in your own kitchen?'

Matt grinned, and Tess had a disconcerting window into what this man would look like shorn of his arrogance. Not just beautiful, but dangerously, horribly sexy.

She lowered her eyes as a new, prickly feeling undermined her still shaky composure.

'Terrible, isn't it?' He was still grinning and moving towards the door. He raised his eyebrows. 'Maybe you could work that one into the next speech you give me about my shortcomings.'

Tess smiled weakly back, but somewhere in a part of her she hardly recognised warning bells were beginning to ring—although what that meant she had no idea.

CHAPTER TWO

'WELL? *Well?* What did you think? Have you got the job?'

Claire was waiting for her. Tess had barely had time to insert her key into the front door and there she was, pulling open the door, her face alight with curiosity.

What did she think of Matt Strickland? Tess tried her best to sum up a guy who represented everything she so studiously avoided. Too rich, too arrogant, too stuffy. When her mind strayed to the peculiar way he had made her feel, she reined it back in.

'Can you believe he didn't want me showing up in tight clothing?'

'He's your boss. He can dictate your wardrobe. Do you think *we're* allowed to show up to work in ripped jeans?' Claire pointed out reasonably. 'Move on. Impressions of the apartment?'

'Barely had time to notice.' Tess sighed. 'I've never had such a long interview. I could tell you all about his office, but that's about it. Oh—and the kitchen. I *did* notice that his apartment is the size of a ship, though, and I'm not sure about his taste in art. There were lots of paintings of landscapes and random strangers.'

'That would be his family,' Claire surmised thought-fully. 'Classy.'

'Really? You think?'

'And finally impressions of the daughter?'

No one had known that he even *had* a daughter, so private was Matt Strickland, and so far he hadn't brought her into the office once!

Tess wondered what there was to tell—considering she hadn't actually met the child. She had waited in the kitchen for what had seemed an unreasonable length of time, and Matt had finally returned in a foul temper and informed her that Samantha had locked herself in her bedroom and was refusing to leave it.

Tess had sipped her tea, distractedly helped herself to her fifth biscuit, absentmindedly gazed at her feet, which had been propped up on a kitchen chair in front of her and pondered the fact that, however powerful, self-assured and downright arrogant Matt Strickland was, there was still at least one person on the face of the earth who was willing to ignore him completely.

'You shouldn't have locks on the doors,' she had in-formed him thoughtfully. 'We were never allowed to when we were growing up. Mum was always petrified that there would be a fire and she would have no way of getting in.'

He had looked at her as though she had been speaking another language, and only later had she realised that he would have had no real experience of all the small details involved in raising a child.

'So, Monday looks as though it's going to be fun,' she finally concluded now. 'Samantha doesn't want to know, plus I have to be there by seven-thirty. You know how hopeless I am at waking up early...'

Which earned her a look of such filthy warning from Claire that she decided to back off from further complaints on the subject. Of course she would do her very best to wake at the crack of dawn. She would set her alarm, and she would set her phone—but she knew that she might easily sleep through both. What if she did?

She still remembered all the choice words he had used to describe her, and her fact was still worrying at the problem when, the following evening, she answered the landline to hear Matt's dark, smooth voice at the other end of the phone.

Immediately Tess was hurled back to his apartment and that first sight of him, lounging against the doorframe, looking at her.

'You've probably got the wrong sister,' Tess said as soon as he had identified himself—as though there had been *any* chance of her not recognising that voice of his. 'Claire's having a bath, but I'll tell her you called.'

'I called to speak to you,' Matt informed her smoothly. 'Just to remind you that I'll be expecting you at seven-thirty sharp tomorrow morning.'

'Of course I'm going to be there! You can count on me. I'm going to be setting a number of gadgets to make sure I don't oversleep.'

At the other end of the line Matt felt his lips twitch, but he wasn't about to humour her. He got the distinct impression that most people humoured Tess Kelly. There was something infectious about her warmth. However, when it came to his daughter, a stern angle was essential.

'Hello? Are you still there?'

'I am, and to help ease you into punctuality I'll be sending a car for you. It'll be there at seven. You forgot to leave me your mobile number.'

'My mobile number?'

'I need to be able to contact you at all times. Remember, you'll be in charge of my daughter.'

Unaccustomed to being reined in, Tess immediately softened. Of *course* he would want to have her mobile number! He might not be demonstrative when it came to his daughter—not in the way that her parents had always been demonstrative with *her*—but keeping tabs on the nanny showed just how important it was for him to know the whereabouts of Samantha at all times.

She rattled it off, and turned to find Claire looking at her with a grin.

'Step one in being a responsible adult! Be prepared to be answerable to someone else! Matt's a fair guy. He expects a lot from the people who work for him, but he gives a lot back in return.'

'I don't like bossy people,' Tess objected automatically.

'You mean you like people who don't lay down any rules to speak of and just allow you to do whatever you want. The joys of being the baby of the family!'

Tess had always been perfectly happy with that description in the past. Now she frowned. Wasn't the unspoken rider to that description *irresponsible*? Her parents had shipped her out to New York so that she could learn some lessons about growing up from her sister. Was it their way of easing her out of the family nest? Had Matt been unknowingly right with his observations? Taking on the job of looking after someone else's child—a child who had already been through a lot and clearly had issues with her father—was not the job for someone who refused to be responsible. Matt Strickland was prepared to give her a chance in the face of some pretty strong evidence that she wasn't up to the task. Being labelled *the baby of the family* no longer seemed to sit quite right.

She had half expected to arrive the following morning and find herself taking orders from one of those mysterious people he had mentioned who would be there to pick up the slack, but in fact, after her luxurious chauffeured drive, during which she'd taken the opportunity to play tourist and really look at some of the sights from air-conditioned comfort, she found herself being greeted by Matt himself.

The weekend had done nothing to diminish his impact. This time he was dressed for work. A dark suit, white shirt and some hand-tailored shoes—a combination that should have been a complete turn off, but which instead just seemed to elevate his sexiness to ridiculous levels.

'I wasn't expecting you to be here,' Tess said, immediately taken aback.

'I live here—or had you forgotten?' He stood aside and she scuttled past him, weirdly conscious of her body in a way that was alien to her.

Under slightly less pressure now, she had her first opportunity to really appreciate her surroundings. It was much more impressive than she could ever have dreamt. Yes, the place was vast, and, yes, the paintings were uniformly drab—even if the portraits *were* of his family members—but the décor was exquisite. Where she might have expected him to err in favour of minimalism, with maybe just the odd leather sofa here and there and lots of chrome, his apartment was opulent. The patina of the wooden floor was rich and deep, and the rugs were old and elaborate. A galleried landing looked down on the immense space below, and stretching the full height of the walls were two windows which, she could now see, offered a tantalising view of Manhattan. The sort of view to which most normal mortals could only aspire via the tourist route.

'Wow! I didn't really take much notice of your apartment the last time I was here. Well, office and kitchen aside.' She stood in one spot, circling slowly. 'Sorry,' she offered to no one in particular, 'I know it's rude to stare, but I can't help myself.' Her eyes were round like saucers, and for the first time in a long time he fully appreciated the privileges to which he had been born.

'Most of the things in here have been handed down to me,' he said, when she had eventually completed her visual tour and was looking at him. 'In fact, I could trace the provenance of nearly everything here. How was the drive over?'

'Brilliant. Thank you.'

'And you're ready to meet Samantha?'

'I'm sorry I didn't get to meet her last time,' Tess said with a rush of sympathy.

Matt, eager to get the day under way, because he had back-to-back meetings, paused. 'Like I said, she's been through a very rough time. It can be difficult to get through to her sometimes.'

'How awful for you. I would have thought that she would have clung to you after her mother's death.'

'Some situations are not always straightforward,' Matt informed her stiffly. 'I don't see you with any books.'

'Books?' Tess was still trying to figure out what *'not always straightforward'* might mean.

'Schoolbooks,' he said patiently. 'I hope you haven't forgotten that teaching is going to be part of your duties with Samantha?'

'Not on day one, surely?'

'I'm not a believer in putting off for tomorrow what can be done today.'

'Yes, well… I thought that I would get to know her first, before I start trying to teach her the importance of fractions and decimals…'

'Ah. I'm glad to see that you've dropped your defeatist approach and got with the programme!'

'I don't have a defeatist approach! Really I don't.' She had thought a lot about what he had said to her, about her waving a white flag, and decided that he had been way off target. She had always firmly believed herself capable of doing anything. Why else would she have attempted so many varied jobs in the past?

Matt held up his hand to silence her. 'No matter. Samantha's collection of tutors have left a number of books over the course of the past few months. You'll find them in the study. Most are untouched,' he added, his mouth tightening. 'I'm hoping that you prove the exception to the rule.'

'I *did* warn you that I'm not academic…'

'I've tried the academics,' Matt pointed out. 'None

of them worked out. Why do you keep running yourself down?'

'I don't.'

'If you insist on labelling yourself as stupid then don't be surprised when the world decides to agree with you.'

'Wait just a minute!'

He had spun around to lead the way, but now he turned slowly on his heels and looked at her with mild curiosity.

'I'm not *stupid*.' Tess had had time to realise that she couldn't cave in to his much stronger, more dominant personality. It wasn't in her nature to make a fuss, but she would have to stand firm on what she believed or let him ride roughshod over her. 'I could have got very good grades, as it happens.'

'Then why didn't you? Was it easier to fail for lack of trying rather than risk trying to compete with your brilliant sisters and not do quite as well? Okay, I withdraw my remark about your being lazy, but if you want to prove your abilities to me then you've got to step up to the plate. Stop apologising for your lack of academic success and start realising the only thing I care about is that you drop the assumption that you can't teach my daughter. She's in the kitchen, by the way.'

Behind him, Tess quietly bristled. While he explained the working hours of his various housekeepers, who took it in turns to come in during the week to ensure that his apartment was never allowed to accumulate a speck of dust, Tess mulled over what he had said like a dog with a bone. She had blithely gone through life doing as she liked, only half listening to her parents' urgings that she settle down and focus. Claire and Mary were focused. In her own good-natured way she had stubbornly refused to be pushed into a way of life which she thought she couldn't handle. No one had ever bluntly said the things that Matt had said to her, or implied that she was a coward, scared of looking like a failure next to her sisters. She told herself that he knew nothing about her—but his words reverberated in her head like a nest of angry wasps.

She nearly bumped into him when he stopped at the kitchen door. She stepped past him to see her charge sitting at the kitchen table, hunched over a bowl of cereal which she was playing with—filling the spoon with milk, raising it high above the bowl and then slowly tilting the milk back in, unconcerned that half of it was splashing onto the fine grainy wood of the table.

Tess didn't know what she had expected. One thing she really *hadn't* expected was, glancing sideways, to see the shuttered look of pained confusion on Matt's face, and for a few powerful seconds she was taken aback by the burst of sympathy she felt for him.

He was tough and uncompromising and, yes, judgemental of her in a way that left her trembling with anger—yet in the face of his daughter he literally didn't know what to do.

Frankly, nor did she. Stubborn, sulky ten year olds had never featured even on her horizon.

'Samantha. Look at me!' He shoved his hands in his pockets and frowned. 'This is Tess. I told you about her. She's going to be your new nanny.'

Samantha greeted this by propping her chin in her hands and yawning widely. She was probably wearing the most expensive clothes money could buy, but Tess had never seen a child dressed with such old-fashioned lack of taste. Clumpy brown sandals and a flowered sleeveless frock. Silk, from the look of it. What ten-year-old ever wore silk? Her long hair was braided into two plaits with, of all things, ribbons neatly tied into bows at the ends. She was dark-haired, like her father, with the same stubborn, aristocratic set to her features. She would doubtless be a beauty in time, but just at the moment her face was sullen and set.

Tess cleared her throat and took a couple of steps forward. 'Samantha! Hi! Okay, you really don't have to look at me if you don't want to…' She giggled nervously, which earned her a sneaky glance, although the spoon and milk routine was still in full force. 'But I'm new to this place so…' She frantically thought of the one thing she and a ten-year-old girl might have in common. 'Do you fancy exploring the shops with me? My sister doesn't wear the same stuff that I do, and I'm far too scared to venture into some of those department stores without someone to hold my hand…'

'Well, it went okay.'

This was the debriefing. When Matt had called her on her mobile, to tell her that he would expect daily reports of progress, she had been at a loss for words. But expect it he did. In his office. Six sharp, after she had handed over her charge to Betsy, the girl who came in to prepare the evening meal.

The very same car that had collected her in the morning had duly collected her from his apartment and delivered her, like a parcel, to his offices, which occupied some prime real estate in downtown Manhattan.

Having seen where he lived, Tess had been more blasé about where he worked. She'd been swept up twenty-eight storeys and hadn't been surprised to find that his office occupied half of the entire floor, with its own sitting room, meeting room, and a massive outer office with chairs and plants, where a middle-aged woman had been busy packing up to go home.

'Define *okay*.' He leaned back into his leather chair and folded his hands behind his head. 'Take a seat.'

He could hardly believe how easily and effortlessly she had managed to break the ice with Samantha. Compared to the other nannies he had hired, who had smiled stiffly and tried to shake hands and had thereby seemed to seal their fate.

Tess shrugged. 'We're still a long way from being pals, but at least she didn't give me my marching orders.'

'She spoke to you?'

'I asked her questions. She answered some of them.' His low opinion of her still rankled, but she would rise above that if only to prove to herself that she could. 'She hates her wardrobe. I think we bonded there. I'm sorry but I'm going to have to turn down your request to purchase "loose" clothing. I can't take your daughter shopping for young, trendy stuff and then buy drab, tired stuff for myself...'

'Young, trendy stuff?'

'Do you know that she's never owned a pair of ripped jeans?'

'Ripped jeans?'

'Or trainers. I mean proper trainers—not the sort you get for school sports.'

'What *are* proper trainers?'

Matt looked at her. She was flushed, her skin rosy and dewy from walking in the heat, and her hair was up in a high ponytail with long caramel strands escaping around her face. In every conceivable way she was the complete antithesis of any woman he had ever gone out with—including his ex-wife. Vicky, his girlfriend, was striking, but in a controlled, intelligent, vaguely *handsome* way, with short brown hair and high cheekbones, and a dress code that consisted almost entirely of smart suits and high heels. And Catrina, while not a career woman, had descended from old money and had always dressed with subtle, refined, understated glamour. Cashmere and pearls, and elegant knee-length skirts.

He could easily believe that Samantha had never owned a pair of ripped jeans, or faded jeans, or possibly even *any* jeans. As far as he could remember neither had his ex-wife.

He felt his imagination do the unthinkable and begin to break its leash once more, throwing up all sorts of crazy images of the fresh faced girl in front of him.

She was telling him about *'proper trainers'* and he was appalled to discover that he was barely taking in a word she was saying. Instead, he was fighting to dismiss thoughts of what she looked like out of those tight jeans and that small green vest with its indistinct logo of a rock band. It was a primitive urge that had no place in his rigidly controlled world.

'Anyway, I hope you don't mind, but I bought her

one or two things. Trainers, jeans, a few tops from the market…'

'You bought her stuff *from a market*?'

'A lot trendier. Oh, gosh, I can tell from your expression that you don't approve. Don't you ever go to a market to shop?' It was an innocuous question, but for some reason it shifted the atmosphere between them. Just a small, barely noticeable shift, but she was suddenly and uncomfortably aware of his almost black eyes resting on her, and the way her body was responding to his stare.

'I've never been to a market in my life.'

'Well, you don't know what you're missing. One of my friends used to work at a market on the weekends, before she went to college to do a course in jewellery-making. I know a lot about them. Quite a bit of what gets sold is imported rubbish, but some of it's really, really good. Handmade. In fact, I thought at one point that *I* could go into that line of business…' Her cheeks were bright with enthusiasm.

'Never mind. You're here now,' Matt said briskly. 'Tell me what your plans are for the rest of the week. Have you had a chance to discuss the business of school-work with her?'

'Not yet…it's only been one day! I *did* glance at those books you mentioned, though…when we got back to the apartment and Samantha was having a bath…'

'And?'

Tess opened her mouth to let him know in advance that she had never been that good at the sciences, and then thought better of it. 'And I suppose I can handle some of it.'

'That's the spirit! Now all we have to do is devise a curriculum...'

'She's nervous about going to school here,' Tess blurted out. 'Has she told you that?'

Matt shifted uncomfortably in his chair. 'I hope you reassured her that there is nothing to worry about.' He papered over the fact that he and Samantha had barely had *any* meaningful conversations since she had arrived in Manhattan.

'It's *your* job to reassure her of that.' Tess looked at him squarely in the eyes. Confrontation had always been something she had studiously avoided. She could remember many an argument between her sisters, both intent on emerging the winner, and had long ago reached the conclusion that nothing was worth the raised voices and the heated exchanges—except she wasn't going to duck under the radar now and assume responsibility for something she knew wasn't hers.

'I've been thinking...' she ventured tentatively.

'Should I be alarmed?'

'You have all these rules that I'm supposed to follow...'

Matt threw back his head and laughed, and then, when he had sobered up, directed a grim look at her. 'That's what normally happens when you do a job for someone else. I've taken a big risk on you, and you're being richly rewarded, so don't imagine for a second that you can start trying to negotiate on some of the things you're supposed to do.'

'I'm not trying to negotiate anything!' Tess said heatedly. 'I just think that if there are all these rules for me, then there should be some rules for you.'

Matt looked at her incredulously, and then he burst out laughing again.

'What's so funny?'

'What *you* seem to consider rules most people would consider their job description. Is that how you approached all those jobs you had? With the attitude that you weren't prepared to work for anyone unless they were prepared to bend their rules to accommodate *you*?'

'Of course not.' When things had become too tedious she had simply given up, she thought uncomfortably. 'And I'm not trying to bend any rules.' What *was* it about this man that fired her up and made her argumentative?

'Okay. Spit it out, then.'

'I made a little list.' She had scribbled it in the car on the way over. Several times she had ever asked Stanton, the driver, what he remembered about his childhood—what stood out in his head about the things he had done with his parents that he had really enjoyed.

Matt took the list and read it through. Then he read it again, his expression of disbelief growing by the minute.

'"Monday night,"' he read aloud. '"Monopoly or Scrabble or some sort of board game as agreed upon. Tuesday night, cookery night."' He looked at her flushed, defiant face. '"Cookery night"? What the hell is *cookery night*?'

'Cookery night is an evening when you and Samantha prepare something together. It could be anything. A cake, perhaps, or some cookies. Or you could be even more adventurous and go for something hot. A casserole.'

'Cakes? Cookies? Casseroles?' His voice implied that she had asked him to fly to the moon and back. 'Isn't that *your* job?' he asked with heavy sarcasm. 'Correction. It shouldn't be a question. It's a statement of fact. Everything on this list consists of things *you* should be doing. In case you'd forgotten, my work keeps me out of the house for long periods of time.'

'I understand that you're a workaholic—'

'I'm not a workaholic.' He considered crumpling the list and chucking it into the bin, but was tempted to carry on reading. 'I run a company. Various companies. Believe it or not, it all takes time.'

'DVD night' was scheduled for Wednesday. He couldn't remember the last time he had watched a DVD. Who had time to sit in front of the television for hours on end? How productive was *that*?

'You have to make time for Samantha,' Tess told him stubbornly. 'I don't think you even know how scared she is of joining a new school. All her friends were at her school in Connecticut. She's terrified of making new ones!'

'Understandable, but kids adapt easily. It's a known fact.'

'That's easy for you to say,' Tess retorted, digging her heels in and refusing to budge. 'I can remember how scary it was going to secondary school! And I *knew* people who would be going with me. Just the thought of new teachers and new schoolbooks…'

'You didn't see it as a challenge you could rise to? No, maybe not, if you refused to settle down and do the work. But this isn't about you, and you're not Samantha. Granted, things haven't been easy for her, but being surrounded by new kids her own age will be a good thing. I'm *not*,' he said heavily, 'asking her to forget all the people she knew in Connecticut…'

'Maybe it feels that way to her.' Tess despaired of getting through to him. Where she had always seen the world in shades of grey, he seemed to see it entirely in black and white. Which, she wondered, was worse? The shades of grey that had prevented her from ever focusing on any one thing, or the black and white that seemed to prevent *him* from letting go of the reins for a second?

'What,' he asked, looking down at the list, 'is a "talking evening…"?'

'Ah. That one. I *was* going to slot in a games night…'

'I thought we had a Games night—where we play "Monopoly or Scrabble or some sort of other board game as agreed upon…"'

'I mean perhaps, take her to a rugby game. Maybe not rugby. Not in America, anyway. A soccer game. Or basketball. Or baseball. But then I really can't see you getting into any of that stuff.'

'Ah, *those* games. For guys who aren't workaholics…'

'You're not taking any of this seriously, are you?'

Matt looked at her speculatively. *Was* he taking any of it seriously? None of the previous nannies had presented him with lists before. He didn't think that any of them would have had the nerve. In fact he couldn't think, offhand, of anyone working for him who would have had the nerve to tell him what he should and shouldn't do.

On the other hand, none of the other nannies had had the success rate that she had—even after one day.

'Okay—here's the deal.' He sat back and folded his hands behind his head, the very picture of the dominant male. 'I'll consider some of your suggestions, but you'll have to be present.'

'Sorry?'

'Baking cookies and cakes... What do I know about that? My housekeeper looks after that side of things, or else I ensure food of the highest standard is delivered.'

'You just have to follow a recipe,' Tess pointed out. Did he even possess a recipe book? She hadn't seen any in the kitchen. Maybe he had a stash of them in his library—although she doubted that.

Matt stood up abruptly and walked towards the window, looking down at the matchstick figures scurrying along the pavements and the small yellow taxis like a toddler's play-cars.

'Have you shown this list to my daughter?' he asked, turning around to look at her.

In return she frowned at him. 'Not yet. I did it in the car on the way over. I mean, I *would* have had it typed out, but I...I didn't have time.'

'Then how do you know that she's going to go along with any of these schemes?'

'They're not *schemes*.'

'Okay. Ideas. Suggestions. Brainwaves. Call them what you want. How do you know that she's going to be keen to...let's say...play a board game for two hours?'

'Oh. Right. I see what you mean.'

'I very much doubt that,' Matt said irritably. 'Kids

these days prefer to sit in front of their computers. It's how they connect with their friends. Samantha has a very advanced computer. It was one of the first things I bought for her when she came here to live with me.'

'I'll do it,' Tess decided. 'If you need me around, then I'll do it.'

Need was a word that didn't feature heavily in his vocabulary—not insofar as it applied to him, at any rate. He opened his mouth to point that out, and then realised that, like it or not, the prospect of trying to coax a positive reaction from his daughter whilst trying to appear relaxed in front of a game of Scrabble was the equivalent of looking up at an insurmountable precipice and trying to work out how to scale it in a pair of flip-flops.

'It's hardly a question of need,' he stated, frowning.

'Some men find it difficult to take time out for quality family time…'

'Spare me the psychobabble, Tess.'

He met her eyes and for a split second she felt almost dizzy. She wondered whether it was because she was just so unused to any of this. Standing up for something and refusing to back down. Telling a man like Matt Strickland—who was her sister's *boss*, for goodness' sake—that he *should* be doing stuff, when it was obvious that no one *ever* told him what he should be doing. Getting involved enough to go beyond the call of duty for a job she had been reluctant to accept in the first place.

Her mouth went dry and she found that she was sitting on her hands, leaning forward in her chair. Crazy!

'It's not psychobabble,' she said faintly. 'It's the

truth! What activity would you…would you like to start with?'

'Ah. A choice?' Matt looked at the list. 'You do realise that choosing to participate in these activities will curtail your free time in the evenings?'

'That's okay.'

'I'll make sure that you're paid overtime, of course.'

'I don't care about the money,' Tess muttered, looking in fascination at his downbent head as he continued to frown over the list, as though trying to work out which was the most acceptable of the options on the table.

'But you might,' he murmured, not looking at her, 'regret committing to something that's going to involve time you might otherwise spend seeing New York…going out and having fun. Isn't that going to be a problem?'

Quite suddenly he raised his eyes to hers, and there it was again—that giddy feeling as though she was free-falling through space.

'Why should it be a problem?' she asked breathlessly.

'Because,' Matt murmured, 'you're young, and I've gathered that you came here to have fun. Since when has your definition of *fun* been spending time with your employer and his daughter, playing a game of Scrabble?'

Never, Tess thought, confused.

'Right.' He stood up, and she hastily followed suit. Her allotted time was over. 'First of all, you will be reimbursed—whether you like it or not. And as for which activity takes my fancy…having done none of them for longer than I can remember…'

He grinned. A smile of genuine amusement. And

for a few heart-stopping seconds he ceased to be Matt
Strickland, the man who was employing her, the man
who represented just the sort of staid workaholic that she
privately abhorred, and was just a man. A suffocatingly
sexy man who made her head spin.

'Your choice. I'll be home tomorrow by six.'

CHAPTER THREE

'OKAY. So let me get this straight. You've now got yourself a clothes allowance, no limits, and *you're going on
a date with my boss.*'

'It's not a date,' Tess said irritably, but she was only
half concentrating on Claire who was lounging fully
clothed in a tight green dress with high heels—also
green. Claire was killing time before going out with the
guy she had been seeing for the past eighteen months—
an investment banker whom Tess had met several times
and liked very much, despite the fact that the second he
left the room she could never seem to quite remember
what he looked like.

'No? What is it, then? Cosy restaurant? Bottle of
Chablis? Candlelight? No one's ever had a clue as
to what Matt Strickland does in his private life, and
here you are, less than three weeks in, and *you're on a
date.*'

Small and black or small and red? Tess was thinking,
looking at the selection of outfits she had bought earlier
that day. Five seconds of tussling with her moral conscience and she had shamelessly capitulated once inside
the fashionable department store to which she had been
directed—because, he had told her, he would be taking

her to dinner to get her feedback, and she would need something fairly dressy to wear. Were it not for him, she'd reasoned to herself, she wouldn't have to spend money on clothes for restaurants she wouldn't be going to. So if he wanted to foot the bill, then why not?

Besides, Samantha had been having fun. They had made a deal. Tess would pretend to yawn inside the toy shops and Samantha would tap the over-sized face of her newly acquired Disney watch in boredom inside the grown-up clothes shops, and then they would break for lunch at a place upon which they had both agreed, and which was based on a menu of pizzas and burgers. Good, fortifying food before they dutifully visited some place of culture in the name of education.

Tess had discovered that in New York there was a cultural destination for every day of the week for at least a year. Having always considered places of culture as unutterably boring, she was slowly discovering that they weren't half bad—especially when being explored with someone with an equal lack of knowledge. Even if that particular someone happened to be a ten-and-nine tenths-of-a-year-old child. They would learn together along the way, and it had to be said that Samantha was as sharp as a tack. Indeed, Tess had delegated most of the guidebooks to her, and her job was to describe what they were looking at, including its history.

'I think I'll go red.'

'Why do you care if it's not a date?' Claire smirked, easing herself off the bed and dusting herself down. 'And please don't tell me again that it's not a date. For the past three weeks I've hardly seen you, and now you're off to a restaurant with him. Surely you've said everything there is to say over your games of Monopoly and your cinema evenings?'

'Has it been three weeks?' Yes. Yes, it had. Time seemed to be moving at the speed of sound. After her initial hesitation about getting involved with Matt and the tense relationship he had with his daughter, she seemed to have dived in—headlong. Games night—their first night—had been a muted success, and since then things had picked up because he had been making an effort. He was getting back to the apartment before seven without fail, and throwing himself into every activity with such enthusiasm that it was difficult not to be swept away along with him. Samantha, wary at first, was slowly beginning to thaw, beginning to really enjoy herself, and it was hard not to be caught up in the changing tide.

'It's a *debriefing*,' Tess concluded. 'And I only wish I didn't have to go. I'd much rather be living it up in Manhattan on a Friday night out with you and Tom. Okay, maybe not you and Tom, but with other people. Young, exciting people. Artists and writers and poets.' The sort of people she thought she *should* be thrilled to hang out with, in other words. 'I haven't really had a chance to report back to Matt on how things are going with Samantha. This is purely about my job. I think I've put on weight. Have I put on weight? This dress feels a bit snug.'

'Tess…' Claire said hesitantly. 'You're not going to do anything stupid, are you?'

'Anything stupid? Like what?'

'I don't know what Matt Strickland gets up to in his

personal life, but there's a reason why he is where he is today. He's tough and he's pretty ruthless…'

'What are you trying to say?'

'Don't fall for the guy.'

'I wouldn't!' Tess turned to her sister. 'My dream guy isn't a high-flier who wants to make money. You know that. My dream guy is down to earth and sensitive, and when I find him I'll recognise him.'

'That's not how life works.'

'I'm just doing my job, and for the first time in my life I'm actually enjoying what I'm doing. You have no idea what it's like to see Matt and Samantha together. Okay, it's not perfect, but it's beginning to work, and I'd like to think that I've had something to do with that. It seems to me that the whole world wants me to settle down and find something I wants to stick with. I think I've found it. I like children and I like working with them. It's something positive that I'm going to take away from this whole experience and please don't confuse that with anything else!'

It was the first time she had come even close to being at odds with her sister, and she relented as soon as she saw Claire's shocked expression.

'I can take care of myself, so don't worry about me. I'm not falling for Matt Strickland! I'm getting to know him. And the only reason I'm getting to know him is because I need to for the sake of his daughter.'

She could have added that Matt Strickland had become three-dimensional, and that her head was slowly becoming crowded with images of him. Matt frowning in concentration in front of a recipe book for beginners she and Samantha had bought three days ago. Matt exultant when he managed to buy a hotel and charge exorbitant rent in a game of Monopoly. Matt teasing but tentative as his daughter brought him hesitantly into her life in Connecticut over the images of her friends on her computer.

This dinner, she knew, was purely about business. He would point out any areas of concern he had with her. He would see room for improvement. No need for nerves, and no need to be unsettled by anything Claire had said.

For the first time Tess was beginning to get a handle on just how much she had been protected through the years by her parents and by her sisters. They had allowed her to retreat from the competitive race academically. Claire and Mary had indulged her when she had turned her back on schoolwork. Had they felt sorry for her because they'd known how impossible it would be to live up to the standards they had set? Or had they enjoyed vicariously living a different kind of life through her? A life without responsibilities? And her parents had been almost as bad. No wonder Claire now thought that she was incapable of protecting herself when it came to the big, bad world! The fact was that she was finally growing up. She was taking on responsibilities. She was more equipped now that she had ever been to deal with whatever life threw at her.

Self-confidence restored, she slipped on the red dress, stuck on high, wedge-heeled sandals with delicate straps, and then stood back and examined her reflection in the mirror.

She didn't often do this—stare critically at herself in the mirror—but doing it now, really taking time to see how she looked, she wasn't disappointed. She would never be tall and spindly, but she looked okay. Her hair was loose and it shone, and she was already acquiring a healthy glow from the baking summer sun. Claire and Mary both had a typically Irish complexion: dark hair, pale skin with a hint of freckles, and of course the family trademark—bright green eyes. Tess, however, was warmer in colour, and it showed. The sun had also lightened her hair. She wasn't blonde, but lighter, with more varied shades of caramel.

With Claire loitering somewhere outside, ready to resume their conversation, Tess waited until Matt's driver paged her on her cell phone and then hurried out of the apartment, stopping to peep into the kitchen only to announce that she was off.

After three weeks she had become accustomed to being driven around New York. She no longer felt like royalty inside the limo, and she was hardly aware of the streets slipping by until the car finally stopped outside an elegant restaurant—just the sort of restaurant that would have chucked her out had she turned up in her normal gear of jeans and a tee shirt.

Stanton, Matt's driver, swooped round to open the car door for her.

Inside, a small foyer opened to an expanse of gleaming wooden floors and circular tables with starched white linen tablecloths and comfortable brown leather chairs. Every table seemed to be full of people chattering and, frankly, looking unashamedly glamorous. It was almost as though a Hollywood director had decided to film a movie inside a restaurant and supplied his own cast.

Two impressive wooden tables were home to the most towering vases of flowers Tess had ever seen. White lilies intricately laced around a honeycomb of twisted driftwood neatly partitioned the restaurant, so that there was at once an atmosphere of pleasant busyness that was yet strangely intimate.

Even by the impossibly high standards of opulence to which she had been exposed, this was in a league of its own, and Matt, sipping a drink and waiting for her in the most private corner of the restaurant, looked perfectly at ease in the surroundings.

Nervous tension beaded her upper lip, and suddenly, unexpectedly, her body was doing strange things. For a few seconds her breathing seemed to stop, and—perversely—her heart began beating so fast that it felt as though it would burst out of her chest. Her mind had shut down. There was not a thought in her head. Even the sound of the diners and the clatter of cutlery faded to a background blur.

He was wearing a black jacket that fitted him like a glove, and the white of his shirt threw the aristocratic harsh angles of his face into stunning prominence. He looked vibrant and drop-dead gorgeous, and she almost faltered in her high heels as she walked towards him.

In the act of lifting his glass to his lips, he seemed to still too.

Suddenly self-conscious, and embarrassed at being caught red-handed in the act of staring, Tess plastered a brilliant smile on her lips as she weaved her way towards him.

'I didn't realise that we would be having a meeting in such grand surroundings,' she carolled gaily, making sure to get the conversation onto neutral work-orientated territory as soon as possible. If nothing else, it did wonders to distract her from the glimpse of hard-muscled chest just visible where the top two buttons of his shirt were undone, and the way his fine dark hair curled alluringly around the dull silver strap of his watch.

Matt tore his eyes away from her and glanced round at the sumptuous décor which he casually took for granted. 'The food's good. It's the reason I keep coming back here. French food always makes a change from steak.'

'Not nearly as good as the spaghetti Bolognese your daughter cooked for you a few days ago, though. You have no idea how long it took us to stockpile all the ingredients. Everything had to be just right. The mushrooms. The shallots. The quality of the mince.'

Tess was babbling. Where had this sudden attack of nerves come from, she wondered. She had seen enough of Matt Strickland in the past few weeks to have killed any nerves she might have around him, surely? But her pulses were still racing and her mouth still felt dry, even after the two hefty sips of wine she'd gulped down from the crystal wine glass in front of her.

'And let's not go into the length of time it took us to find just the right recipe book,' she confided. 'I think Samantha looked at every single one at three separate bookshops. I had to stop her from trying to wheedle me into buying her a pasta machine. Can you believe it? I told her that it might be better to start simple and then move on to the complicated stuff. You…er…have an incredibly well-equipped kitchen. Everything new and shiny…' She trailed off in the face of his unnerving silence. 'Why aren't you saying anything?' she asked awkwardly. 'I thought you wanted me here to talk about how things were coming along with Samantha.'

'You have a way of running away with the conversation,' Matt murmured. 'It's always interesting to see where it's going to lead.'

Tess tried and failed to take that as a compliment. The smile she directed at him was a little wobbly at the edges. 'You make me sound like a kid,' she said in a forced voice, and he tilted his head to one side, as though giving that observation some thought.

'Maybe that's why you've worked out so well as her nanny.' He flashed her a veiled amused look, but for some reason Tess was finding it hard to see the funny side. 'The other nannies the agency supplied were nothing like you. They were far more regimented. Samantha refused to be told what to do, ran circles around them, and they eventually ended up handing in their notice. The more she had, the more I gave instructions to the agency that the next one should be stricter. I can see now that it was completely the wrong ploy. I should have been trying to find someone who was more on her level.'

'How many did she have?'

'Five—although one only lasted three days. They did their best to discipline her. In nine times out of ten they might have had success with that approach...'

'*I* discipline her,' Tess interrupted defensively.

'Do you? How?'

'If you don't like the way I do things...'

'Don't be ridiculous, Tess. Haven't I just told you how well I think you're doing? You've achieved wonders in a matter of weeks!'

'But I don't want you to think that the only reason

I've succeeded is because I let her do exactly what she wants! You gave me permission to get her a new wardrobe of clothes. Do you remember I discussed this with you? Do you remember I told you to look around at the other kids her age in New York and see what they were wearing? When she goes to her new school she might find it easier if she shows up in the same sort of clothes as everyone else. I said all this to you and you agreed! So we went shopping and, yes, some of her things *did* come from markets, but she'd never been to a market before. She enjoyed the experience!'

'How have we landed up here?'

'We've landed up here because…because…' What should have been a cool, businesslike conversation in relaxed surroundings was falling apart at the seams—and it was *her* fault. Was it any wonder that he was staring at her as though she had taken leave of her senses? He had complimented her on her progress and she had responded by snapping. She was miserably aware that she had snapped because she didn't want him implying that she was somehow immature, and she wasn't sure why she cared.

'Because it hasn't all been about Samantha having fun. I've had to really coax her out of her shell, and I admit it's easier to coax a child when you dangle something in front of her that she wants. But I've also been doing schoolwork with her…'

'Yes. I know.'

'You do?'

'She's told me.'

Tess didn't miss the flash of quiet satisfaction that crossed his face, and she made a big effort to remind herself that *this* was why she so enjoyed the job. Because she had been instrumental in helping to heal some of the rifts between Matt and his daughter. And if Matt patted her on the back and patronisingly complimented her on getting the job done because she was immature enough to win over her charge, then so be it.

'You've proved yourself wrong.' He leaned back in the chair as menus were placed in front of them and more wine was poured into glasses. 'How does that feel?'

'I've only gone through the basic stuff with her,' Tess mumbled, blushing.

'It's a mountain when your starting point was insisting that you were incapable of doing simple maths and science.'

A slow, palpable sense of pleasure radiated through her, made her feel hot and flustered, and although she knew that his dark, lazy eyes were on her, she couldn't bring herself to meet them.

'Well, I won't be taking a degree course in them any time soon.' Tess laughed breathlessly.

Claire might have given her long lectures about his ruthlessness, but this was a side of him to which she had been not privy. Claire hadn't seen the complete human being. She had just seen the guy who issued orders and expected obedience.

'But doing something of which you didn't think yourself capable must have gone some distance to bolstering your self-confidence...'

Her eyes flew to his, and she had a few giddy seconds of imagining that those dark, deep, brooding eyes of his could see right down to the very heart of her. Her voice was shaky as she gave her order to the waiter, and when she thought that the conversation might move on she was greeted with a mildly expectant silence.

'I've always had bags of self-confidence,' she muttered eventually. 'You can ask either of my sisters. While they were buried under heaps of books, I was always out having a great time with my friends.' Why did she get the feeling that he didn't believe her? And his disbelief had to be infectious, because she was almost failing to believe herself. 'I may not be going out a great deal in the evenings now, because of my working hours,' she said, relentlessly pursuing the point even though he hadn't contradicted a word she had said, 'but I'm normally the kind of girl who always had lots of invitations.'

'And you miss that?'

'We're not here to talk about me.'

'But in a way we are,' Matt pointed out smoothly. 'You spend more time with my daughter than I do. It's important for me to know your frame of mind. I wouldn't want to think that you might be storing up resentments. So…you've spent most of your evenings over the past few weeks at my apartment. Does that bother you? When you're accustomed to spending your time going out with friends?'

He watched her fiddle with the stem of her wine glass. Her cheeks were flushed. Her thick, straight, toffee-coloured hair hung like a silky curtain over her shoulders, halfway down her back. Amidst the plush, formal surroundings she looked very, very young, and suddenly he felt very, very old. A quick glance around him confirmed that there was almost no one in the restaurant under the age of fifty. The fabulously high prices excluded all but the very rich, and he was an exception when it came to being very rich and the right side of forty. He had grown up in an ivory tower and had never had cause to leave it. It discomfited him to think that curiosity, if nothing else, should have driven him out at least for a brief period of time.

Annoyed to find himself succumbing, even temporarily, to an unusual bout of passing introspection, Matt frowned, and Tess, seeing the change of expression, was instantly on her guard.

Was he going to tell her that she needed to stop spending her evenings at his home? Did he *disapprove*? Maybe he hankered after more one-to-one time with Samantha and she, blithely unconcerned, was in the process of just *getting in the way*.

Maybe she should suggest reverting to normal working hours...

Dismayed, Tess realised that she didn't want to do that. How had that happened? How had Matt Strickland and his daughter and their complicated family life suddenly become so integral to her day-to-day existence?

Her thoughts were in a whirl as food was placed in front of them—exquisite arrangements of shellfish and potatoes that Tess would have dived into with gusto were it not for the feverish whirring of her mind.

'I'll curtail my hours if you want me to,' she heard herself say in a small voice.

'I don't believe that's what I was asking you,' Matt told her impatiently. He had become accustomed to her never ending cheerfulness, and the despondent droop of her shoulders made him feel like the Grinch who stole

Christmas. 'You're my employee,' he said tightly. 'And I have certain obligations as your employer.'

Tess hated that professional appraisal. She realised that she didn't *want* him to have any obligations as the guy who had hired her, but when she started to think about what she *did* want her thoughts did that crazy thing again and became tangled and confusing.

'I wouldn't want you to turn around at some later date and accuse me of taking advantage of you.'

'I would never do that!' Tess was horrified and offended.

'You've insisted on forgoing any overtime payments...'

'You pay me enough as it is! I *like* sticking around in the evenings and helping out with Samantha.'

'Doesn't do much good for a social life for you, though, does it?'

'I didn't come over here to cultivate a social life,' Tess said firmly. Well, she admitted to herself, that *was* a bit of an exaggeration, thinking back to the dismay with which she had greeted the suggestion of a job, but that was in the past so it didn't count. 'I came here to try and get my act together and I have.' Her natural warmth was returning and she smiled at him. 'I feel like I've finally found something I really enjoy doing. I mean, I think I have an affinity with kids. I don't get bored with them. You'd be surprised how clever and insightful Samantha can be without even realising it. I can get all the socialising that I want when I get back home.' Which was something she wasn't going to start thinking about just yet.

'And do you socialise with anyone in particular there?'

'What do you mean?'

'You're an attractive young woman.' Matt shrugged and pushed aside his plate, which was swept up by a waiter seconds later. 'Left any broken hearts behind?'

'Oh, hundreds!' Tess said gaily. If he thought that she was immature and green around the ears, how much more cemented would that impression be if he knew that being 'one of the lads' and having loads of friends who happened to be boys was a far cry from having a solid relationship with one in particular.

'So was that part of the reason you came over here?'

'No!' Tess protested uncomfortably.

'Because no boy is worth it. Not at your age.'

'I'm twenty-three. Not thirteen.' Just in case he had missed that, which she suspected he had. Because she had never, not once, caught him looking at her with male interest. While she...Tess flushed and felt something scary and powerful stir in her, as though finally being allowed to take shape. *She* had looked at *him*. Released from their Pandora's Box, little snapshots of him began swirling in her head. The way he looked when he was laughing, the way he raised his eyebrows in lazy amuse-ment, that half-smile that could send shivers down her spine—except it hadn't. Not until now.

Uncomfortable in her own skin, Tess struggled to get her thoughts in order while her innocuous remark hovered in the air between them, challenging him to assess her in a different way altogether.

As though the reins of his rigid self-control had

suddenly been snapped, Matt was assailed by a series of powerful, destabilising images. She might look young, with the stunning attraction of dewy skin and an open, expressive face that was a rare commodity in the hard-bitten world in which he lived, but she wasn't thirteen. She especially didn't look like a teenager in that dress she was wearing, which left just enough to get the imagination doing all sorts of interesting things. It took massive will-power to pull himself back from the brink of plunging headlong into the tempting notion of taking her to his bed.

She was his daughter's nanny! What the hell was going on in his head? It grated on him to know that this wasn't the first time he had played with the idea. He should know better. Work and play mixed as success-fully as oil and water. He had never brought his private life to work and he wasn't about to start now. Tess Kelly might not hold down a job within the physical walls of his offices, but she was as much his employee as any one of the hundreds who worked for him.

And, even taking that small but vital technicality out of the equation, Tess Kelly didn't conform to anything he required from a woman. Having lived through the horror that had been his marriage, wedded in unhappy matrimony to a woman who had fulfilled all the require-ments on paper and none in practice, as it turned out, his checklist when it came to women was stringent.

It was essential that they were as focused as he was. Focused and independent, with careers that were de-manding enough to stave off any need for them to rely on him to define their lives. Like him, Catrina had come from old money, and her life had consisted of fundraisers and charity balls and lunches and all those other little things that had left her with plenty of time to decide that his duty was to provide a never-ending diet of excitement. There had been no need for her to work, and she had, in any case, never been programmed for it. And into the void of all those empty hours when he had been working had crept the seeds of bitterness and disenchantment. She had wanted a rich partner who wanted to play, and he had failed to fulfil the specification. In the aftermath of that experience, and the consequences it came to entail, Matt was diligent in never straying beyond his own self-imposed boundaries.

Belatedly, because she had been away and contact between them had been sporadic and via e-mail, he remembered Vicky. She was in Hong Kong, getting a taste for the Eastern markets. She was due back in a couple of days' time. He tried to pull up a memory of what she looked like, but the second he thought of her dark tailored bob and the neat precision of her personality another image of a bubbly, golden-haired girl with a dusting of freckles on her nose and a personality that was all over the place superimposed itself on the woman who claimed to be dying to catch up with him.

Irritated, he frowned. Then his face cleared and that vague feeling of being out of sorts began to ebb away.

'Tell me your plans for the next few days.' He pushed himself away from the table and signalled to the waiter for some coffees.

'Plans?' Still fretting over her tumultuous thoughts, it took Tess a few seconds to register that he had completely changed the subject. 'A museum, and then a quiet day just relaxing with Samantha tomorrow. Maybe I'll grab an early evening and catch up with my social life, now that you've put that idea into my head.'

'And then on Friday perhaps we might visit the zoo…' said Matt.

This was a breakthrough. Instead of just following the tide, he was actually generating an idea of his own! Pure delight was all over her face as she nodded approvingly. She would take a back seat, watch father and daughter together, remind herself that her involvement with them both began and ended as a job.

And Matt, watching her carefully from under lowered lashes, calculated on Vicky's presence. The two of them, side by side, would squash uninvited rebellious thoughts for which he had no use. He and Vicky might not be destined for the long haul, but she would be a timely reminder of what he was looking for in the opposite sex.

Matters sorted satisfactorily, and feeling back in control, he signalled for the bill.

CHAPTER FOUR

OVER the next two days Tess had ample opportunity to think about herself. Matt had asked some very relevant questions, and had kick-started a chain of thoughts that made her uneasily aware that the things about herself she had always taken for granted might just be built on a certain amount of delusion.

She had always considered herself a free spirit. Her sisters had been the unfortunate recipients of their parents' ambitions. Neither of their parents had gone to university. Their mother had worked as a dinner lady at the local school, and their father had held down a job in the accounts department at an electrical company. But, they were both really clever, and in another time and another place would have gone to university and fulfilled all sorts of dreams. They hadn't, though, and consequently had taken an inordinate interest and delight in Claire and Mary's superhuman academic achievements.

Tess had set her own agenda from an early age and had never deviated. Just in case her parents got it into their heads that she was destined to follow the same path, she had firmly set her own benchmark.

She had always thought that she loved *living* too much to waste time hiding away in a room in front of a pile of books. She liked *sampling* things, getting a taste for different experiences. She refused to be tied down and she had always been proud of her thirst for freedom.

Matt's take on things had badly damaged that glib acceptance. She wondered whether her happy-go-lucky attitude stemmed from a deep-rooted fear of competition. If you didn't try, then you weren't going to fail—as he had said to her on day one—and she had never tried and so had never set herself up for a fall. She had been offended and resentful at his implication that she lacked self-confidence, and yet she knew that she had never made the most of her talents. Underneath the pretty, popular, happy-go-lucky girl, had there always been an anxious, scared one, covering up her insecurities by wanting to be seen as the antidote to her sisters? Had she cultivated her social life—always being there for other people, always willing to lend a hand and always in demand—because that had helped her prove to herself that she was every bit as valuable as her two clever sisters?

Tess didn't like this train of thought, but, having started, she was finding it impossible to stop. One thought seemed to generate another. It was as though a locked door had suddenly been flung open and out had spilled all manner of lost, forgotten and deliberately misplaced things from her childhood.

For the first time she had no inclination to share her thoughts with her sister, indeed, was relieved that Claire had taken herself off for a week's break with Tom and wouldn't be returning until the middle of the following week.

As she was getting ready on Friday morning for their

expedition to the zoo, Tess made herself address the other discomforting issue that had been nagging the back of her mind—the other loaded pistol that Matt had pointed at her head and forced her to acknowledge. *Why* had she suddenly jettisoned her social life? Why? She had arrived in Manhattan a carefree, fun-loving girl, with no thoughts beyond enjoying a lovely break from Ireland and perhaps trying to figure out what job to apply for when she returned. So how had she suddenly found herself in the position of willingly sacrificing her social life for the sake of a job? Why did the thought of going out and having a good time with young people her own age leave her cold? Of course she enjoyed Samantha, and loved the small changes in her personality she could detect as the days passed. It was rewarding to watch the person emerge from the protective, wary shell—like watching a butterfly emerge from its cocoon—but beyond that she just really liked being in Matt's company because she fancied him.

Tess hadn't recognised that for what it was because she didn't think she had ever truly fancied anyone before. She had never questioned all those stolen glances and the way her body responded when he was around. Even now, as she wriggled into a navy and white striped vest and brushed out her hair before tying it up into a ponytail, she could feel her body tingling at the thought of seeing him. *That* was why she had thought nothing of putting her social life on hold. *That* was why she was happy to spend evenings at his apartment, sometimes just sitting cross-legged on the sofa with Samantha, watching something on the telly, while on the chair close by Matt

pretended to watch with the newspaper in front of him
and a drink at his side.

Tess felt a little thrill of excitement race through her.
She was in lust, and it felt good even if nothing would
come of it. Because she certainly hadn't caught him
stealing any glances at *her*, and she couldn't imagine
him thinking about her in some way—not the way she
realised she thought about him.

Tess could only assume that the very sheltered life she
had led was the reason why she was only now feeling
things that most women her age would have felt long
ago. Where her sisters had flown the nest and pursued
university degrees, then moved to new, exciting cities
to begin their illustrious careers, she had remained at
home, circulating with more or less the same crowd
she had grown up with—a protective little circle that
had, she could see now, been comforting and restric-
tive in equal measure. She felt as though she was finally emerging from cold storage. It was exciting. And
who knew what lay round the corner? she thought, with
the optimism with which she had always greeted most
situations.

The journey to Pelham Parkway was baking hot, but she
had dressed for the heat in a pair of cool linen trousers
and flip-flops. It was going to be a long day. The zoo
was enormous—one of the largest urban zoos. She had
agreed with Matt that she would contact him by text as
soon as she arrived, so that they could agree a meeting
point, but with this new awareness of him burning a
hole in her she found herself texting Samantha instead,
and then making her way to a convenient spot where she

could wait for them to finish their animal sightseeing on the monorail.

On the way, her stomach rumbling, she bought herself a giant hot dog, and was sinking her teeth gratefully into the eight-inch sausage, onion, ketchup and mustard indulgence when she spotted Samantha running towards her.

Samantha was no longer the primly dressed ten-year-old of a few weeks ago. She was in a pair of trendy cut-off denims, some flat espadrilles and a tee shirt that advertised a teenage musical.

'Have a bite.' Tess offered the hot dog to her and stood up. 'I'm never going to finish this.' She was driven to search out Matt, but resisted the impulse.

'I thought you were giving up junk food.' Samantha took the hot dog and smiled up at her. 'Because you were piling on the pounds.'

'Next Monday. I have it pencilled in my diary.'

'Anyway, they're waiting for us, so we'd better go.'

'*They…?*'

'Vicky was tired and had to rest, even though she's been sitting on the monorail for twenty minutes.' Samantha made a face while Tess confusedly tried to compute a name that meant nothing to her and had never been mentioned before. Was Vicky a relative?

She hurried after Samantha, and after a few minutes came to a shuddering halt by a café—one of the many that were dotted around the zoo. It was packed. Kids were eating ice cream, infants with more common sense than the adults were howling in pushchairs because they were hot and sticky and wanted to leave. She could easily have missed the couple sitting at the back, because they were surrounded by families trying to find somewhere to sit and children being called back to tables by anxious parents. But her eyes were automatically drawn to Matt and she grinned, because he looked just as she would have expected him to look away from the comforts to which he was accustomed. He was a man who took for granted the bliss of air-conditioning in summer and the luxury of personal shoppers who did everything for him and spared him the inconvenience of having to do battle with crowds. It was a real indication of how determined he was to involve himself with his daughter that he would ever have suggested a zoo expedition and accepted this less than luxurious experience as a necessary consequence.

For a few seconds she found it hard to tear her eyes away from him. In a pair of light tan trousers and a navy blue polo shirt, he looked dark and sexy and dangerous. He was wearing dark sunglasses, which he proceeded to remove, and the thought of his eyes on her as she tried to manoeuvre a path through the crowds sent a little shiver down her spine.

She could fully understand how he had managed to turn her notion of sexual attraction on its head. She had foolishly assumed that because he represented the sort of man she didn't find attractive personality wise her body would just fall in line and likewise fail to respond. She hadn't bargained on the fact that her body would have a will of its own and would go haring off in the opposite direction.

Samantha had made it to him, and it was only when they were both looking at her that Tess took in the woman sitting next to him at the small, circular metal table. For a few seconds her steps faltered, because if this was a relative then she certainly wasn't a relative of the comfortable variety.

Holding a cup primly between her fingers, and with dark shades concealing all expression, was a strikingly attractive woman with an expertly tailored bob that was sharply cut to chin level. A pale lemon silk cardigan was casually draped over her shoulders.

Matt half stood as she reached the table but his companion remained seated, although she pushed the shades onto her head revealing cool brown eyes.

'Tess…I'd like you to meet Vicky.'

The expected return of his common sense was failing to materialise. It had been a trying morning. Samantha had been disappointed that their cosy party of three had expanded to include Vicky, and although Matt told himself that it was healthy for her to deal with the fact that Tess was not a member of the family he had still felt as though some of the progress he had made with his daughter had been somehow undermined by the inclusion of Vicky in their day out.

And then had come his disappointing reaction to seeing Vicky. His interest had not been re-ignited, and indeed he had been irritated by her.

She had had precious little contact with Samantha before her three week visit to Hong Kong, but had immediately seen fit to try and establish a relationship. He had been all too aware that his daughter had retreated into herself and had blamed him for this unwelcome development.

All in all, a bit of a nightmare, and now, seeing Tess

next to Vicky, he was already beginning to draw unwelcome comparisons.

'You're the nanny!' Vicky offered a cool smile. 'Matt's told me about you in his e-mails. What a blessing that you turned up when you did! This little thing has been super-naughty with her nannies—haven't you, sweetie? You're very young, aren't you?'

E-mails? Tess didn't like the thought of being discussed behind her back, and it was dawning on her that this was Matt's girlfriend. The fact that he even had one came as a shock, but as the reality of it began to sink in she wondered how on earth she could ever have expected otherwise. Men like Matt Stickland were never short of women throwing themselves at him. He was as rich as Croesus and sinfully good-looking. Now, in light of this, her silly infatuation with him—if it could even be called that—struck her as tellingly naïve.

This woman was far more the type he would go for, even if his body language was saying otherwise. She was clever and accomplished, and, as the day progressed, Tess was left in very little doubt that there was absolutely nothing the woman hadn't already achieved or else was about to.

Vicky talked non-stop. She tried to make jokes with Matt, who smiled stiffly and contributed very little to the conversation. She gave long, educational lectures to Samantha about every animal they passed and was undeterred by the silent, faintly hostile response. She confided in Tess every qualification she had ever gained and her progress in her career step by step, starting with when she was a lowly junior manager and culminating in her exalted position now, as CEO of one of the largest listed companies in America. She was smart and she was self-confident, and she had scaled heights in her career that most women might only ever dream of.

Matt wouldn't raise his eyebrows and make some dry, amused remark about *her* taste in television programmes. He would have informed discussions with her and talk about everything from the state of the economy to world politics.

Tess waited two and a half hours before she felt it polite to tell them that she would be on her way. Samantha, like her, was drooping, and had been for a while. A small, quiet bundle, shorn of the tentative beginnings of exuberance that had marked the past week or so.

What a hellish disaster, Matt thought in raging frustration. What the *hell* was Vicky's agenda? She had monopolised the conversation, glorified herself, done her level best to ingratiate herself with Samantha.

'You've hardly been here two minutes.' He frowned at Tess, who was fidgeting apologetically, playing with the clasp on the leather satchel slung over her shoulder. 'What do you mean *you're going*?'

'I have some stuff to do.'

'Your working day hasn't come to an end. It's not yet five-thirty.'

He felt, with considerable irritation, Vicky's arm link through his and the weight of her as she leant against him.

'We could go off and do something,' Samantha interjected in a cool, childish voice. 'Tess could drop me home. Couldn't you, Tess? We could even stop off and have something to eat on the way. Burgers and fries,' she added, because somewhere along the line there had been a long lecture from Vicky on the dangers of the wrong diet. At the time she had been focusing on the last of the hot dog disappearing into Samantha's mouth.

'You'll leave with us,' Matt rasped, sliding his eyes down to where his daughter was staring at him, sullen and tight-lipped. 'And I don't want any arguments, Samantha. I'm your father and you'll do as I say.'

In the sweltering heat, tempers were frayed. Tess miserably wondered whether Matt would rather have stayed at home with his girlfriend. Did his foul mood stem from the fact that he could think of better things to be doing with his time? Didn't he know that his relationship with Samantha was still so fragile that coming down heavy on her now was going to jeopardise everything they had begun building together?

She felt as though she had failed them both. She told herself stoutly that their relationship wasn't her concern, that she was just a ship in the night, passing through their lives, but right here, with people bustling around them and Samantha looking to be on the verge of tears, Tess suddenly felt miserable and depressed.

'I'll be at work bright and early on Monday morning,' Tess said brightly. 'Or we could even do something tomorrow, if you like…?' This was to Samantha, but Vicky was quick to step in, smiling and giving Matt's arm a gentle squeeze.

'We'll be fine.' Her voice was hard as nails. 'I just got back from the Far East. I'd quite like to have my little unit to myself over the weekend. Besides, don't you have anything better to do than spend your Saturday with a ten-year-old child?'

Those ringing words were a timely reminder to Tess that she needed to get her act together. Hadn't Matt mentioned something along those lines to her himself? Had he and his girlfriend been exchanging jokey e-mails about her? The sad little nanny with no life to speak of in one of the most exciting cities in the world?

The journey back to her sister's apartment was long and hot and tedious. The upside was that there would be no one around to question her tearful mood. The downside was that she did, actually, feel as though she needed a sympathetic shoulder to cry on.

Nothing could distract her from the sobering realisation that she had made a complete fool of herself by lusting after a man who wasn't interested in her. It was a sign of her own vanity—which was something she had never even known she *possessed*—that she hadn't once stopped to ask herself whether he was involved with a woman. There had seemed to be none on the scene, and he had mentioned no names, and so she had made her own incorrect conclusions.

It was a little after eight when the buzzer sounded. Claire had an intercom system in her flat. It was an excellent way of avoiding unwanted visitors. You could see them on the little television-style screen and then just duck low until they got the message and disappeared.

Her heart flipped when she made out Matt's face. He looked impatient and at the end of his tether, and she was determined to ignore him, but instead found herself picking up the phone to ask him what he wanted.

'You. I need to talk to you.'

'What about? I thought you were going to be spending

the weekend playing house with your girlfriend.' She clapped her hand to her mouth. 'I'm sorry I said that. I'm tired. Can it wait until Monday?'

'No. It can't. Buzz me up.'

'What's so important?' Tess persisted. 'I'm about ready to go to bed.'

'It's not even nine. It's a Friday evening. You're not ready to go to bed. Buzz me up.'

'What do you want!' was the first thing she asked when he was standing in the doorway, filling it out and sending her nervous system into frantic disarray. He was still in the clothes he had worn to the zoo. She, however, had changed, and was now wearing a pair of black pyjama bottoms and a small vest. No bra. She folded her arms and backed away, following him with her eyes as he strode into the apartment and headed directly to the kitchen.

'I think,' he said, opening the fridge and extracting a bottle of beer, which he proceeded to flick open after he had hunted down a bottle opener in one of the drawers, 'I need a drink.'

'Look, you can't just barge in here—'

'Your sister's away, isn't she? Visiting the boyfriend's parents, if I remember correctly?'

'Who is with Samantha? Is…is your girlfriend with her?'

Matt drained a quarter of the bottle in one long, thirsty gulp while looking at her as she hovered to the side, ill at ease and wary. Tension was climbing its way up her spine. What did he want? When she thought about the excitement that had infused her at the start of the day, when she had dressed with thoughts of him in her head, she felt humiliation washing over her all over again.

'Today didn't go as planned.' Matt finished the beer, wondered whether to have another. But he had already drunk too much for his own good—had had to get his driver to ferry him across to Tess's apartment. Hell, what else was alcohol for, if not to smooth away the rough edges of uncomfortable situations? He had made an appalling mistake in asking Vicky to accompany them. It had been a massive error of judgement. And for a man who could count his errors of judgement on the fingers of one hand, it tasted like poison. He helped himself to another beer and angled her a challenging look as she mutely stared at him, her mouth half open in surprise.

'No,' Tess agreed stiffly. Now that she was looking at the detail, she could see that his hair was rumpled and he looked a bit *askew*—a bit like a guy who wasn't completely in control of everything around him. Vulnerable, it struck her. 'If you'd wanted to spend time with your girlfriend, then a group outing might not have been the best idea. Or did you think that I would be a good buffer between your girlfriend and your daughter?'

Matt tilted his head back to swallow some beer and continued to stare at her.

Held reluctant captive by those dark, brooding eyes, Tess felt her skin begin to tingle—and she hated the feeling. It reminded her of how weak she had been to allow this man to climb under her skin. She hated the intensity of his silence. It felt as if he was sifting through her thoughts, turning her inside out and exposing all her doubts and weaknesses. He already seemed too capable of forcing her to face up to failings she hadn't known existed.

'Well?' She angled away from him and sank into one of the kitchen chairs. 'I got the impression that Vicky hadn't had a lot of contact with Samantha.'

'Almost none,' Matt agreed.

'So what was the grand plan, Matt? To get the nanny to pave the way for a happy family unit? Take some of the heat off your girlfriend?'

'Vicky was never a contender for a happy family unit.' He had been leaning against the wall. Now he pushed himself away, dumping the empty beer bottle on the counter *en route* to a chair, which he sat on, his big body indolent and relaxed under the influence of drink. Not too much, but certainly enough to paper over the sharp edges of his mood.

'Well, that's none of my business,' Tess muttered. Of their own volition, her eyes flicked towards him, taking in all the details of his body, and she realised that there was a familiarity to what she was seeing that was scary.

'Turns out—' he laughed shortly, stretched out his legs and stuck his hand in his trouser pocket '—that I was on my own when it came to that misconception.'

'I don't know what you're talking about. Have you been drinking?'

'Now, what would give you that idea?' His eyes locked with hers and there was a lazy amusement there that made her go hot and cold. Even when she hurriedly looked away, she could feel him *looking* at her in a way that he hadn't looked at her before—looking at her in a slow, leisurely way that made her want to fidget. 'I let that relationship get out of hand,' Matt mused. 'I took my eye off the ball. While I was under the impression that we were having a casual fling, it turns out that Vicky was making all sorts of plans.'

'What sort of plans?' Tess was fascinated to hear more. Matt had never breathed a word about his personal life, but she wasn't looking at the Matt she knew. She was tiptoeing on the very edge of seeing a side to him that hadn't been in evidence before, and she was eaten up with curiosity.

'Are you having fun?' He laughed softly under his breath and Tess flushed.

'Of course not! *You* came here, don't forget! And if you want to talk, then that's fine by me.'

'I actually didn't come here to talk about Vicky,' he murmured. He shifted in the chair, leaned back into it. 'You distract me.' He enjoyed the way she blushed madly when he said that, and leaned forward as though not quite believing her ears. 'You make me lose track of what I want to say.'

'*I'm* not making you lose track of anything,' Tess said briskly, but there was slow burn inside her that felt good.

'Oh, right. It's the demon drink. I'll stick to the agenda, in that case. My daughter has reverted to her old ways.' He leaned forward abruptly, elbows on thighs, and pressed his thumbs against his eyes.

His body language spoke a thousand words and Tess automatically moved towards him, hovered for a while, not quite knowing what to do, and eventually pulled her chair so that she was sitting right alongside him. Should she reach out and try to comfort him? Confused and addled, she opted for sitting on her hands.

'What do you mean?'

'I mean…' Matt looked directly at her and raked his hand through his hair. 'We got back to the apartment and she promptly proceeded to shut herself in the bedroom.'

'But didn't you go in to try and talk to her?'

'Of course I went in! She lay there with her back to me and her headphones stuck in her ears—and, *hell*, I can't *force* her to have a conversation with me, can I?'

'So what did you do?'

'I had a couple of whiskies in rapid succession. It seemed like a good idea at the time.'

'And Vicky…?'

'Dispatched. The point is, I'm back to square one.' His smile was tight and bitter. 'It seems that the ground I believed I'd covered was just a bit of wishful thinking.'

'That's not true!'

'No? Then perhaps you'd like to explain my daughter's lack of response?'

'She's ten years old! She's not capable of thinking things through in an adult way. She's had a disappointing day. I suppose she thought that she would have you to herself…'

'You mean have *both of us*…'

'No,' Tess said firmly. '*You*. She didn't bank on your girlfriend showing up, and she really didn't bank on her—I don't know—being so proprietorial…'

'Nor did I,' Matt muttered under his breath. Vicky had made *plans*! A stint in the Far East together, his daughter conveniently dispatched to a boarding school somewhere... She had even checked out possible acquisitions he could make once they were living in Hong Kong! He had been furious and appalled, and then had turned his wrath against himself—because, as he had told Tess, he had taken his eye off the ball and had reaped his just rewards. But his relationship with his daughter was the biggest casualty of his slip-up, and damn if he knew how he was going to rescue the situation.

'Samantha's not...'

'Not *what*?' he gritted into the developing silence. 'No need to tread on eggshells, Tess. I've already blown it. I think it's fair to say I can withstand whatever you have to say.'

'You haven't blown it! It's just that Samantha... Well, I don't think she ever really understood why she saw so little of you over the years.'

'She's told you this?'

'In bits and pieces. I mean, please don't think that we sat down one day and had a heart-to-heart, because we didn't. I don't think children of that age ever do. I don't think they know *how to*. But I've gleaned it over time.'

'You've *gleaned* it? And how did you respond?'

'What could I say? You've never spoken to me about your marriage...and, anyway, it wouldn't be my place to have that conversation with your daughter. That's something you would have to do. I thought, I guess, that you would. In time.'

'God. What an unholy mess.'

He looked wiped out, and she reached out and tentatively put her hand on his shoulder. When he responded by taking hold of it, she assumed it would be to politely dismiss her gesture of sympathy, but instead he kept hold of it, playing idly with her fingers with frowning concentration.

'Catrina and I were the perfect couple on paper.' Matt glanced at her, but Tess wasn't sure that he was seeing *her*. 'Our families knew each other. We moved in the same circles and came from the same background. I suppose you could say that there was an understanding—and the understanding was hastened along when Catrina fell pregnant. I wasn't gutted. Yes, I was young, but I was content to marry, and marry we did. With all the pomp and ceremony that vast wealth can buy. The cracks opened up almost immediately. Catrina was a socialite. I was an ingrained workaholic. She saw no reason why I should put time and effort into making money. As far as she was concerned my job should have been to lead the life of a playboy. Go skiing in winter for a couple of months. Take long summer holidays at her parents' house in the Bahamas. Take up golf. Lead a life that would complement hers.'

Tess tried and failed to picture Matt taking up golf and having long holidays. He was still playing with her hand, and it was doing all sorts of strange things to her body. Whilst she was desperate to concentrate one hundred percent on what he was saying, part of her was wrapped up with the tingling in her breasts, the dampness spreading between her thighs, the warm feeling in her belly that made her want to sigh and close her eyes.

'The more she nagged, the faster I withdrew into the

safety of work. We were a divorce waiting to happen, but I'm not sure it would have if I hadn't found out that my best man at the wedding had stepped in to carry out the duties she felt I was failing to do.'

Tess couldn't imagine what that would have done to a man as proud as Matt.

'My divorce was what dictated the relationship I developed with my daughter, and so here we are.' He gave her a crooked smile. 'Any thoughts?'

CHAPTER FIVE

'I DON'T understand. Surely the court would have awarded you joint custody, Matt?'

'A vengeful wife has a lot of tools at her disposal when it comes to making free and easy with court judgements,' Matt told her drily. 'Weekends were cancelled on a whim. I lost count of the number of times I travelled to Connecticut only to find that Catrina had taken Samantha off on a trip, destination unknown, leaving a bewildered maid to try and explain in broken English that there would be no visit that weekend. Toys were routinely left at an empty house. I never knew whether Samantha got them or not.'

Matt's eyes glittered with open pain and bitter regret. This was a man who opened up to no one, and Tess wasn't sure whether this flood of confidence and self-recrimination was something he would live to rue, but she stroked his face with a trembling hand while her mind frantically spun off at another devastating angle.

While she had been busily telling herself that what she felt for Matt was an understandable case of lust, she had failed to recognise that it ran much deeper than that. She had long stopped being a concerned spectator to someone else's problems. She hadn't forsaken her social life because she lusted after Matt Strickland and was driven to spend as much time in his company as she could, like a lovelorn teenager. She had forsaken her life because she had unwittingly become sucked into his. It had been easy, at first, to dismiss him as the sort of man who took advantage of everything and everyone around him, but slowly but surely she had begun glimpsing other sides of his complex, absorbing personality.

She had watched him subdue his natural inclination to dominate so that he could make strides in getting to know his daughter. She had been ensnared by a wit and intelligence that was far greater than she had originally imagined. She had been seduced by those snatches of humanity she saw in his less guarded moments.

She had fallen in love with the whole man, and the time she had spent ignoring that reality hadn't served to protect her—it had just rendered her horribly defenceless.

Looking back now, Tess could see that love had just been waiting round the corner, ready to ambush her and turn her world on its head. Matt Strickland had overwhelmed her. She had been waiting for something gentle and careful, and had been unprepared for the chaos and power of real love, gutsy and demanding, when it finally came. She had expected that the guy who won her heart would be kind and sensitive. She had been utterly unprotected against a man who'd broken through to her heart like a battering ram and grabbed it when she hadn't even been looking—when she hadn't even taken the time to steel herself.

Her heart was racing. Inexperience left her unsure as to what to do. She had never considered herself extraordinary because she hadn't fallen into bed with any man. It just had never happened, and she had accepted that with a shrug of her shoulders.

'My relationship with Samantha became distant,' he said heavily. 'Stilted. Nothing I did, when I *did* manage to see her, could reverse the effects of the separation, and God only knows what Catrina had been telling her when I wasn't around. And just when I thought that some progress was being made...*this*...!'

'You came here,' Tess murmured.

'Where else? You know the situation better than anyone.'

He gazed at her with those stunning eyes and her breathing became laboured. Without warning, the atmosphere shifted. She could sense him grow still. It was impossible to think straight and nor could she tear her eyes away from his dark, outrageously sexy face. She wanted him so badly that it was a physical pain inside her, and her craving was made all the more irresistible because of the intensity of the emotion underlying it. She leaned forward and kissed him very chastely on his cheek, and the shock of contact almost had her reeling back.

'It'll be all right,' she whispered huskily. 'Samantha may have been disappointed at the way today turned out, but you've already started building the blocks of a relationship with her and she'll have that to fall back on.'

She was losing herself in the intensity of his gaze, and with a soft moan she did the unthinkable. She placed the palm of her hand on his chest and leaned into him once again. This time her kiss—not on his cheek, but daringly, recklessly, on his lips—was sweetly lingering, and an exquisite rush of pleasure crowded her mind, driving coherent thought away, taking away the ability to analyse what she was doing. She felt that if she stopped breathing just for a second she would be able to hear the frantic beating of her heart.

It didn't occur to her that she might be making a complete fool of herself. She had acted on impulse and she didn't regret it.

When he curved his hand at the nape of her neck and pulled her towards him she melted into the embrace as though this was the moment she had been born to savour.

This wasn't why he had come. Was it? He knew that she had been the first person he thought of in his frustration. He had called his housekeeper and had been waiting by the door for her to arrive so that he could come here and do...*what*?

What had he been expecting? At the back of his mind, had he already succumbed to the desire to take her to bed? From every angle, seeing Vicky had been a disaster. Not just from the point of view of his daughter. He had looked at her standing next to Tess and suddenly he hadn't been able to remember what he had ever seen in the woman.

Her statuesque beauty now seemed angular and unappealing. Where Tess was soft, her face open and transparent, Vicky was a hard-bitten career woman. He had been bored by her monotonous monologues about the Hong Kong market, impatient with her informed conversation.

Had he come here because he had been driven by something more than just an urge to offload?

The fact that he had even felt the need to offload was, in itself, cause for wonder.

The honeyed moistness of Tess's mouth was driving him crazy, but he still managed a final last-ditch attempt to control the situation.

'What's happening here?' He pushed her away and his resolution was immediately floored when he felt her tremble against him. 'We...shouldn't be doing this.' His voice was rough and uneven.

'Why not?'

'Hell, I can think of a hundred reasons!'

'You're not attracted to me...?'

'That's not one of them.' His mouth hit hers with a hunger that detonated an explosive pleasure inside her that she had never known existed. Her whole body was suddenly on fire and she could hardly sit still. She needed to wriggle just to try and assuage the burning restlessness blazing a trail through her.

'I'm not about to make love to you in a kitchen!' Matt growled, and Tess whimpered, her eyes fluttering closed, as he lifted her off the chair and began heading towards a bedroom—mistakenly kicking open the door to Claire's room first and then, two seconds later, getting it right.

He deposited her on the bed and she lay there in a state of heightened excitement, watching as he closed the curtains and then fumbled with his belt, finally whipping it off in one swift pull.

Released from the mindless intoxication of his body

being in contact with hers, she felt the reality of her virginity penetrate through to her fuddled brain.

This was a situation she had never envisaged, and there was no ready process she could think of for dealing with it. She just knew that she was beyond the point of walking away. And it felt *right*, she told herself fiercely. She was in love with him! She wasn't going to listen to any little voices in her head trying to push their way to the surface and preach to her about consequences. She wasn't—because there were always consequences to everything. If she didn't do this—if she turned her back on this one moment in time—then she would forever live with the consequence of that. Would forever wonder what it would have been like to surrender to this big, powerful man who had stolen her heart.

Optimistic by nature, she pleasurably played with the thought that this could lead anywhere. Who was to say?

He had stripped off his shirt. Her breath caught in her throat and she drank in the muscular beauty of his body. When he moved, she could see the rippling of sinew and the raw definition of his torso. He reached for his zip and she nearly fainted in anticipation. Her clothes were an irritating encumbrance, but she lacked the courage to divest herself of them.

He walked slowly towards her and she squirmed. Her eyes flickered away as he tugged down the zip and she heard the soft drop of his trousers, the sound of him stepping out of them, and then she was looking at him, shyly at first, and then mesmerised by the massive surge of his powerful erection.

With small, squirming movements, she edged up

into a sitting position and hooked her fingers under her vest.

'I've thought about this,' Matt muttered in a driven undertone, and her eyes widened in surprise.

'You have?'

'Why so shocked? You're sexy as hell. You must know the effect you have on a man... No, don't lift a finger. I want to take off your clothes piece by gradual piece.' He gave her a slow, curling smile that made her bones melt, and then he straddled her.

She fascinated him, and suddenly he could barely wait a second longer. Like a horny teenager, he covered her body with his own and kissed her with bruising ruthlessness, his hand moving along her thigh and easily slipping underneath the silky trousers. She was as soft and as smooth as satin. Just the feel of her was enough to wreak havoc with his control, and he had to slam the door shut on his raging libido or else risk making a fool of himself.

She wasn't wearing a bra. He had spotted that the second he had walked through the door. He caressed her full breasts through the thin, stretchy fabric of her vest, felt the way they moulded into his big hands and the way her nipples were tight and stiff under his fingers. He wanted to do this slowly, to take his time, and was disconcerted to realise that he had been fantasising about this for weeks. It had never risen to the surface of his consciousness but it must have been nagging at the back of his mind, and touching her now had released the nebulous, intangible notion. His hand shook as he heaved himself up so that he could pull off the vest with one hand.

'God, you're so damned beautiful,' he rasped, bending to nuzzle one breast, teasing her nipple with the tip of his tongue while she panted and moaned.

Having thought that he had barely noticed her as belonging to the female sex, Tess allowed herself to fully occupy Cloud Nine. He wanted her. He thought that she was beautiful. For the moment it was enough, and as she squirmed underneath him, desperate to get rid of her clothes, she felt herself letting go.

She pushed her fingers into his hair and urged his head down so that he could fiercely suckle her pouting nipple. He grappled with her trousers, levering himself up so that she could wriggle herself free of them.

His effect on her was electrifying. She felt as though this was what her body had been designed for—to be touched by this man. She arched upwards and cried out helplessly as he continued to move his mouth over her breasts. She ran her hands across his shoulders and felt the bunched muscles. She couldn't seem to remain still. When she angled her body up her nakedness touched his, and his stiff erection against her was explosive.

Tess had had boyfriends in the past, but none of them had ever affected her like this. Indeed, she'd had no desire to submit her body to theirs the way she wanted to submit her body to this man. She had enjoyed kissing, and there had been a bit of amateurish fondling, but this was in a league of its own, and her body sang under his expert touch.

He parted her legs with one hand, and as he continued to lavish attention on her breasts he began to move his hardness between her thighs, driving her into a frenzy.

'Talk to me,' he commanded hungrily, and Tess looked at him, confused.

'About what?'

'About how much you want me. I want you to tell me…' He laughed softly, and then demonstrated exactly what he meant by talking to *her*, telling her how much he wanted her and what he wanted to do to her. All the time his hard, pulsing erection pushed between her parted legs. Tess was going out of her mind.

'I want you…*now*…' she groaned, when she thought that she wouldn't be able to take any more.

'I'm not finished enjoying you yet.' He gradually began trailing an erotic path down the length of her body, relishing the salty taste of her perspiration on his tongue. Her uncontrolled passion matched his own and he liked it. As with everything she did, she was generous in her lovemaking. He realised that it was what he had expected. She didn't hold back. Her personality was forthright, open, giving. Her lovemaking was the same, and it unlocked a barrage of mindless desire he hadn't been aware he possessed.

He paused as he neared her thighs, and reared up to support himself on his hands so that he was looking down at her, appreciating her soft, feminine mound which was slick with moisture. The sweet, honeyed, musky smell of her threatened to tip him over the edge— and that was before he even touched her. Which he fully intended to do. With his hands, with his fingers, with his mouth, until she was begging for release.

He blew softly against her and Tess gasped. She was discovering a whole new side to herself, and she wouldn't have been able to stop herself now even if she had wanted to. She didn't think that she had ever known what it was like to have a man turn her on—but then she had never *met* a man like Matt.

She froze as he gently parted the delicate folds of her femininity, and sank back with a soft sigh of pleasure as he darted his tongue between and tasted her. She covered her face with one arm and her mouth fell open. The sensation was so exquisite that she could hardly breathe. All the muscles in her body seemed to go limp and she gave herself over to his gentle, persistent mouth which continued savouring her.

His dark head between her legs was the most erotic thing she had ever seen in her whole life. His exploring mouth became more demanding, and she could no longer keep still. Her body was spiralling out of control.

But before she could climax right there, Matt heaved himself up.

'I need,' he muttered shakily, 'to get some contraception.'

'Please,' Tess whimpered, digging her fingers into his shoulder, because he just couldn't leave her *now* to start fumbling for a condom. Her periods had always been as regular as clockwork. She was as safe as houses and she needed him inside her *right now*. Her body was screaming out for it.

'I'm safe,' she gasped.

Matt needed no further encouragement. He really wasn't sure whether he had any contraception on him anyway. He was ultra-careful, always made sure to carry his own protection, but his sex-life with Vicky had been sporadic, and she had, anyway, been on the pill. He was uneasily aware that even if he hadn't had any, if she hadn't given him the green light, he might just have chanced it—because his body was on fire and the only way he could douse it was by taking her. He had never been so out of control in his entire life. For someone who had imposed stringent discipline in all areas of his life, because there was no such thing as a happy surprise, it was weirdly exhilarating to be suddenly and temporarily freed from the shackles.

He thrust into her with an intensity that made her wince and cry out in pain. Confused, Matt eased himself back. He was big. He knew that. And she felt tight—so tight that he might almost think...

'Are you a *virgin*?' he asked with dumbstruck incredulity, and Tess turned her head away.

After the initial discomfort the pain was receding fast, being replaced by a driving, burning need to feel him push into her again.

'Just carry on, Matt...please...I need you...'

'Look at me,' he growled. 'I'll be gentle...' His eyes held hers as he moved slowly and surely, building into a rhythm that took her breath away. However much he had teased her and touched her, in unimaginable places, to have him inside her was the greatest intimacy of all. Tess wrapped her arms around his waist and her body bucked as he moved faster and deeper. She felt his physical release just as her own body spiralled out of control, causing her to cry out and dig her fingernails into his back. His spasms as he ejaculated into her were the most wonderful things she had ever experienced.

She loved this man, and she had to resist the urge to tell him. She held that warm knowledge to herself, and there was a smile of pleasure and fulfilment on her lips when she finally shuddered one last time and then lay, spent.

Matt rolled off her and propped himself on his side to look at her.

'So…tell me about that…'

'Tell you about what?' Tess murmured sleepily. 'That was amazing. Was it…' She looked at him, suddenly anxious. 'Was it okay for you?'

'It was…pretty amazing. I was your first.'

'I'm sorry.'

'Don't apologise.' He smiled and stroked the side of her face. A *virgin*. A twenty-three-year-old virgin. He hadn't known they existed. 'I liked it. Why me?'

Tess drew her breath in sharply. 'I guess,' she said, reaching to hook her hand around his neck and nuzzle the dewy moisture there with her lips, 'you just really turn me on. I don't understand it, because you're not the type of guy I ever imagined myself going for, but when I'm near you I just seem to fall apart.'

'You might have guessed that it's the same with me,' Matt confessed a little unsteadily. He could feel his body confirming that admission, hardening again in record time. 'I should have been able to restrain myself, but…'

Tess felt him stir against her naked thigh and a heady sense of power filled her. But nudging its way through to her fuddled brain were snatches of uneasy recollection of how, exactly, they had ended up in bed together. He had come to talk about Samantha. Had he been drinking? He certainly hadn't been as composed as he usually was. It had been the first time she had seen him with all his barriers down, and his unexpected vulnerability combined with her fledging acknowledgement of how she felt about him had been an intoxicating mix. From being the girl who had stayed on the sidelines as her friends had all fallen into bed with guys they'd later avoided, or succumbed to languishing by telephones waiting for calls, she had gone to being a girl who had flung herself at a man because she just hadn't been able *not* to.

'Why should you have been able to restrain yourself?' she asked anxiously. 'Did I take advantage of you?'

Matt shot her a gleaming look of surprise. 'When you say things like that I feel about a hundred years old.' He laughed softly. 'Don't worry. I'm wonderfully adept when it comes to women cruelly trying to take advantage of me. I find it pays to just relax and go along for the ride.'

'You're teasing me.'

'I'm enjoying your lack of cynicism. When I came here, I was at the end of my tether. You relax me, and I like that.'

Tess wasn't sure if that was strictly accurate. It could be said that simply lovemaking had relaxed him. But she wasn't going to analyse the finer points of his remark. She was going to take it at face value because she had never felt so wonderfully, gloriously *complete* in her whole life.

She guided his hand to her breast, and he grinned wickedly and pushed her back against the bed, slung his thigh over hers. She felt the weight of it with a feeling of bliss.

'You're a fast learner.' His voice was thick with satisfaction.

This time their lovemaking was fast and hard. Matt liked giving pleasure. He knew just where to touch her and how to make her body respond. Shorn of inhibitions, Tess was his willing student. She wanted to be guided. She wanted to give him as much pleasure as he gave her. She was guiltily, horribly aware that she wanted a great deal more than he probably suspected, but for the moment she was greedy enough to take what was on offer.

Their bodies were slick when they were sated. In a minute Matt would have to leave. He would talk to Samantha in the morning. He told her this as she lay against him, her body naturally curving against his as though it had been fashioned just for that purpose. His admission that it would be an uphill task made her smile.

'Talking's not that difficult,' she breathed with drowsy contentment. 'Communication is the key thing when it comes to all relationships. I know that sounds like a cliché, but I think it happens to be true. Maybe...' she tested the water '...that's why your relationship with Vicky didn't work out...'

Matt shrugged. 'It doesn't matter why my relationship with Vicky didn't work out.'

Tess thought that it mattered to *her*. He had married the perfect person and it hadn't worked out. He had gone out with the perfect replacement and that hadn't worked out. Amongst her tangled thoughts she figured that if only she could pinpoint *why* the perfect exes hadn't worked out, then maybe—just maybe—she could avoid the mistakes her predecessors had unwittingly made.

She refused to accept that the most wonderful physical and emotional connection she had ever made with another human being was destined to be short-lived.

'She seemed very nice…' Tess persisted. 'And you must have had a lot in common.'

'Look.' Matt propped himself up and turned on his side to face her. 'Drop it, Tess. It's of no importance. Like I told you, I took my eye off the ball with Vicky. She started getting ideas.'

His face was shuttered. He was locking her out of this conversation.

'I guess it's understandable.' Tess tried to laugh. She was no good when it came to playing underhand games. She would have been hopeless at persuading a confession out of anyone, and it showed in the shaky tremor of her voice when she spoke.

Matt looked at her narrowly. Her upturned face was sweetly, delectably soft and vulnerable, and a prickle of unease curled in him. But the touch of her was so heady, and the feel of her was like a shot of adrenaline to his jaded palate…

In short, she was irresistible. But just in case…

'Vicky wanted a happy ending,' he said bluntly. 'It wasn't going to happen. I've been married once and I lived to rue the day. The only good thing to emerge from that disaster was my daughter. I'm not a candidate for a repeat performance. I'm telling you this because I don't want *you* to get any ideas.'

'You mean crazy ideas like Vicky got?' It was like being sliced in two. The path was forked and she was being given a choice. Follow the road he indicated or else walk the other way. If she had thought that a fleeting glimpse of his vulnerability indicated hint of softness, then she had been mistaken. The dark, fathomless eyes locked onto hers were deadly serious, and Tess very quickly made her decision.

Take what he was offering. She had fallen in love with him and she couldn't walk away. When had she ever been able to do anything by halves? She had given herself to him completely, and if it made no sense then that was something she would have to learn to deal with.

'I guess…well…she's in her thirties. Maybe she could hear her biological clock ticking away. But not me! At twenty-three, life is still a grand adventure, and I don't want you to think that I'm going to start demanding anything of you—because I'm not.'

It would be a disaster if he found out what she felt about him. One night of passion and a woman confessing undying love would be his nightmare. He would run a mile and he wouldn't look back. She would cease being the girl who could make him relax and would turn into a needy, clinging harridan who wanted more out of him than he was willing to give. Having never had much of a head for numbers, Tess could do the maths pretty quickly when it came to *this* particular scenario.

'In fact, like I said, you're not the type of man I would ever fall for,' she confided.

'I'm not…?'

'No! I may not be experienced, but I'm not foolish enough to think that lust has anything to do with love.'

'You just gave your virginity to me because…?'

'Because I wanted to. No one's really ever turned me on like...'

'Like me?' Matt interjected smoothly. 'I believe you. Lust can be powerful. Overwhelming. And maybe you came to New York looking for an adventure. Why else would you be using contraception? You're young, you're beautiful... Did you get bored where you lived?'

Tess was still lagging behind, wondering whether she should own up to the fact that she wasn't actually using any contraception at all but was perfectly safe anyway. Matt's low, seductive murmur seemed to be coming from a long way away. His clever mind was leapfrogging through what she had said and making its own deductions. She had come to Manhattan seeking adventure. She had been bored and restless. She had taken the necessary precautions not because she was desperate to lose her virginity but because she wanted to be prepared in case the situation arose. Perhaps she had been dazzled at the thought of Manhattan and everything and everyone it could offer. That would make perfect sense to him. He was a man with a healthy sexual appetite. He would fully understand how, at the age of twenty-three, her virginity might have become an albatross around her neck rather than a treasure to be hugged until the perfect man came along. Hell, there was no such thing as a perfect soul mate anyway!

Tess half listened and made vague appropriate noises. For a man with a brilliant mind he seemed very good at arriving at all the wrong conclusions, but she knew that he had to. He had to make sense of her and slot her into a category that didn't threaten the pattern of his orderly life because he wanted her. He wasn't at all surprised that she had chosen to lose her virginity with *him*. He was supremely confident of his own sexual magnetism. His misguided conclusions and freewheeling assumptions even made sense in a weird, convoluted way.

She wasn't sure she recognised herself as this woman who knew what she wanted, was in search of sexual adventure, and had the good sense to go on the pill, throwing caution to the winds so that she could have a no-strings-attached relationship with him.

It would have been so much easier if she *had* been that person, she thought ruefully. Instead, here she was—not too sure what she was doing or what she had got herself mixed up in.

'So on Monday…' He kissed her with such leisurely, thorough expertise that she forgot how precarious her life had suddenly become. 'I'll make sure that I'm back by six. We'll take Samantha out for a meal somewhere. I'm hoping conversation might be back on the agenda with her. And afterwards…'

Tess felt the thrill of excitement. It flooded her veins like a toxin. It closed her mind to any question that she might be doing the wrong thing.

CHAPTER SIX

Tess stared in the mirror at the woman she had become in the space of four glorious weeks. The changes were slight, but *she* had no difficulty in noticing them. Matt Strickland had turned her into a woman. In a series of barely recognisable stages she had grown up. She dressed differently now. The trainers had been replaced with flats. The vests were a little less clinging.

'I don't want other men looking at you,' he had told her, with a possessiveness that had thrilled her to the bone. 'Is that a crime? When you wear those tight vests men look, and when they look I want to kill them. And don't even *think* of going anywhere without a bra. That is a sight to be afforded only to me.'

The vests had been replaced with looser silk tops that made her look sophisticated and glamorous, and she liked her new image. He claimed not to have an ounce of jealousy in his body, but when she had idly watched a man walk past a week ago, her mind a thousand miles away, he had tilted her face to his and told her, with a forced laugh, that he wanted her to only have eyes for *him*.

Tess stored and treasured all those passing moments. They had to mean *something*! He made no effort to conceal the fact that he wanted her. Sometimes, with Samantha between them as they ate dinner, she would glance up and find his eyes on her, and she would see naked hunger there. Her breasts might ache just at the sight of him, and she might feel that telltale dampness between her thighs, but she knew that her effect on him was just as powerful. He had told her that business meetings had become a minefield because just the thought of her could give him an instant erection.

Tess loved hearing things like that, because they seemed to indicate that something would come of their relationship—although she was smart enough never to let any mention of that leave her lips.

She had also made sure not to breathe a word to Claire. Nor had she mentioned it to her parents or any of her friends, whose lives seemed so distant now anyway.

At first she had worried that keeping it secret might be difficult. Claire had always been able to read her like a book, and she would have been able to chivvy it out of her without any trouble at all if she had smelled a rat, but in all events it had been much easier than expected. Tom had proposed, and Claire was residing in a parallel universe. She spent most of her time at his place, and disappeared on weekends to his parents' house in Boston, where a wedding planner was feverishly working to produce a magical wedding in six months' time. Even her parents skirted over what was happening in her life because they, too, were wrapped up in their contribution to the Big Day.

Menus were discussed and seating plans were debated and bridal magazines were pored over until Tess wanted to scream—because where was *she* going with her clandestine relationship with Matt?

Time was moving on. Her ticket to return to Ireland was booked for the beginning of September. But she could easily alter that. Her parents had lived for years in America before they'd moved back to Ireland. All three children had been born in America. Tess had dual nationality and she could have produced that, like a rabbit from a hat, at any given moment in time—but that moment had not arrived. Matt didn't talk about the future and nor did she.

But she would *have* to talk about it. She had spent weeks ducking below the radar and enjoying each day as it came. She could hardly believe that once she had been a girl who *had* lived her life like that, content never to dip her toes in the water.

Hence she was dressing with particular care tonight. Samantha was with her grandparents in the Hamptons for the weekend, and she and Matt would have the apartment all to themselves. It would be the perfect opportunity to discuss this *thing* they had, which had no name. She would use all the feminine wiles at her disposal. Wasn't all fair in love and war?

Her dress was a wonderful long affair in shimmering pale yellow. It fell softly to the ground and left her brown shoulders bare. Her shoes were delicate sandals with yellow straps.

The drive over gave her twenty-five minutes to plan what she was going to say and when. Just thinking about it made her nervous. She wondered whether he was still as allergic to commitment as he had once said he was, then told herself that that wasn't the most important thing, because she could stay on in Manhattan with him, looking after Samantha. She wouldn't actually be demanding anything. The words *a stay of execution* uncomfortably sprang to mind, but as quickly as they had taken shape they were dismissed, because she couldn't afford to let herself start being pessimistic.

Scrape the surface, though, and she was a bag of nerves by the time they reached his block of apartments and the elevator was silently transporting her to the top floor.

Matt had had a key to his penthouse cut for her, and occasionally she used it, but it had never felt right. She had been given a key to facilitate her job as Samantha's nanny. She wanted a key because Matt saw her as the other half of a couple and trusted her enough to come and go as she pleased. So now, as always, she rang the doorbell and waited in restless tension, clutching her little handbag in front of her.

When he pulled open the door her heart flipped over, as it always did, and for a few seconds she was completely lost for words.

He never failed to render her speechless. She saw him almost every day, had made love to him countless times, had watched, fascinated, the lithe suppleness and latent power of his naked body, and yet every time she laid eyes on him it was as if she were seeing him for the first time. He took her breath away, and however much he assured her that she had the same devastating effect on him she didn't believe him. Compared to the women he could have at the click of his fingers, she was just an averagely pretty face.

But she wasn't going to think like that. Not tonight, when she wanted to think positive.

The long look he gave her thrilled her from the crown of her head to the tips of her toes and she smiled shyly.

'Do you like it?' She stepped into his luxurious apartment and gave a little twirl. The dress followed her, as soft and tantalising as a whisper.

He caught his fingers in her hair and pulled her towards him.

'You look like a goddess,' he murmured. 'Some kind of exquisite, ethereal creature.' His finger was now tracing her bare shoulder and her body reacted with mindless excitement. She could already feel her nipples tightening, and her breasts were heavy and sensitive, in expectation of being touched by him. She felt faint thinking about his mouth circling her nipples and licking them until she could scarcely breathe.

But she pushed him gently away and walked towards the kitchen, from which was wafting a delicious smell.

'Have you surprised me by cooking?' she teased, putting some necessary distance between them because she didn't want the evening to start with them in bed.

'You know I don't do that.' She looked so damned edible standing there, delicate and fragile and breathtakingly pretty—an exotic counterpoint to the hard masculinity of his kitchen. He would have pinned her against the wall and taken her without preamble, but she had dressed to impress and he would savour the anticipation of getting her out of her clothes. 'My dependable caterers have done justice to some fillet steak and…' he came close, close enough for her to breathe him in, and lifted the lid of a saucepan '...some kind of sauce.' He remained where he was, dipped his finger into the sauce and held it to her mouth. 'Taste it and enlighten me,' he murmured, already so hot for her that it was beginning to get painful.

He lounged against the counter, his feet loosely crossed at the ankles, and gave her a look of burning satisfaction as the pink tip of her tongue licked the sauce from his upheld finger. Like a cat finishing the last remains of the cream.

'Brandy and peppercorn, I think. And I don't see why you *can't* cook for me now and again.' She gave a mock sigh of wistfulness. 'You're a perfectly good cook. I know. You've done lots of wonderful things with Samantha. Remember that risotto?'

'Correction,' Matt told her wryly, 'Samantha has done lots of wonderful things with me. My role is solely to do as I'm told.'

'Since when do you *ever* do as you're told?' She relaxed enough to smile, but tension was still blazing inside her.

'You can always put that to the test.' He leant against the counter, hemming her in. 'Command me, my beautiful little witch,' he breathed into her ear, before nibbling the side of her neck and sending a flurry of piercing, pleasurable sensations rippling through her. 'Would you like me to get down on my knees and push that sexy dress up so that I can drive you wild with my mouth? Hmm? Or we can always go for something a little more kinky.... It would appear that dessert comes with custard...'

'Stop it!' Tess laughed, hot and flustered, and feebly pushed him away—but he had set up a very evocative image in her head that she was finding difficult to dispel. 'We're not going to do any such thing.'

'Sure? Because I saw a flash of temptation in your eyes just then... Now, let me just see how much you dislike the idea...' To hell with not moving too fast and giving the dress time to have its moment of glory. Still supporting himself with one hand flat against the edge of the granite counter, he reached down and inched the silky fabric upwards. His eyes didn't leave her face.

'You have no self-control, Matt Strickland,' Tess protested weakly.

'Tell me about it. And what about you? I'd say we're even on that score.' He felt the softness of her thighs. The cloth was bunched around his hand and he shrugged it away as he dipped his fingers beneath the lacy band of her thong and slipped them into her.

Tess melted. Her eyelids fluttered shut. This wasn't playing fair! She blindly searched for his mouth with hers, but after just a fleeting kiss he pulled back and whispered, in a sexy, velvety voice, 'No chance. I want to see your face when you come...'

'Okay. You win,' she groaned jerkily. 'But let's go to the bedroom...make love...ah...' She couldn't finish the sentence. Her body was moving of its own accord. Her head was flung back and her eyes were shut as his fingers continued to plunder her, moving fast and hard, then slowly and gently, teasing every ounce of sensation out of a body that felt as limp as a rag doll.

Colour climbed into her cheeks and her breathing became laboured, and then she was falling over the edge, shuddering with the power of her orgasm and crying out, at which point Matt brought his mouth against her so that he could breathe in the wildness of her groaning.

'That,' he murmured when she had climbed down from the mindless heights of pleasure, 'is an excellent way to start any evening.'

Under normal circumstances Tess would have been in enthusiastic agreement with that statement. Matt knew just how to excite her in unimaginable ways. But to-night she had another purpose, and as soon as she had smoothed down her dress she was back to feeling as nervous as a kitten.

Without looking for ways to be critical, she realised that he was utterly oblivious to her mood—but then thoughts of her leaving would probably not have crossed his mind. For weeks Tess had nurtured the hope that what they had would leave him wanting more. They shared a lot together. He might be ruthless and driven in the work place, but with her he had been tender and thoughtful, and with Samantha he had shown boundless patience and a resilient ability to take the knocks and somehow find a way of turning them around. Would he be able to give her up without a backward glance? She had subconsciously chosen to think that he wouldn't, but now, as he whistled softly and made a great show of doing things with the pots and pans, she wasn't sure.

If he was that tuned in to her feelings then surely he would have picked up on the fact that she was more subdued than usual?

Now he was chatting to her about work. He sometimes did that, even though he had once commented wryly that he really didn't know why he bothered, because the second he started he could see her eyes glazing over.

She accepted the drink that was proffered and settled on one of the leather dining chairs at the kitchen table. He was fairly useless in the kitchen. A tea towel was slung over one shoulder and every cooking utensil seemed to be out, even though he was really just heating up a variety of dishes. In between stirring things and peering under lids he chatted and sipped his wine, occasionally glancing round at her, and even in the midst of her anxious thoughts she still warmed at the hot possessiveness in his eyes.

'But do you miss it?' Tess asked abruptly, as a plate of food was placed in front of her with exaggerated flourish. 'The long hours, I mean? For weeks you've managed to be pretty sensible about getting back here in time, to see something of Samantha, so do you miss the work you would have been putting in otherwise at the office?'

In the middle of topping up their glasses, Matt paused and looked at her. Something uneasy stirred in him, but he quickly put that to rest by telling himself that nothing was amiss. She might be a little quieter than she normally was, but she had melted at his touch the way she always did. He never seemed to tire of her helpless excitement whenever he touched her. It turned him on in ways that he no longer bothered to question.

'That's a strange question. I work for several hours after Samantha has gone to sleep. It's satisfactory.'

'So…does that mean that you've restructured your life?'

'Where are we going with this conversation?' Matt

tried to keep the irritation out of his voice. He had become accustomed to her undemanding nature. It suited him. She was always happy to fall in with whatever he wanted, and over the weeks he had discovered that her lack of complication suited him in ways nothing else seemed to have suited him in the past, but there was something insistent about her at the moment that seriously threatened to ruin the atmosphere.

'It doesn't have to go anywhere,' Tess told him, picking at her fillet steak. Her appetite was fading fast. 'I'm just asking.'

Matt pushed back his chair and tossed his napkin on a plate of food that was only half eaten. 'I haven't restructured my life.' He linked his fingers behind his head and looked steadily at her flushed face. 'I'm in the process of trying to find a balance.'

'Does that mean you thought it was out of sync before?'

'It means that Samantha is a reality I have to deal with. Originally I thought that I would more or less be able to carry on as normal, with a great deal of help to cover for my absences. It wasn't a viable option. It's a necessary sacrifice and it's been worth it. Whether I'll be able to carry on being consistent remains to be seen. There will be instances when I have to go abroad, and I'll have to get overnight cover when that arises. My mother would be happy enough to come here for a few days, so I don't foresee any problems that won't be surmountable. Now, does that satisfy your curiosity?'

'I wish you wouldn't act as though I'm being a nuisance just by trying to have a conversation with you!' Tess heard herself snap, shocking herself by daring to rock a boat which she had steadfastly tried to keep level for the past two months. But she could no longer help the build-up of anxiety inside her. Once upon a time she had never had a problem in saying what she thought. This was like walking on eggshells. One false move and she sensed that the structure she had built around herself, the little fortress in which she had placed Matt and Samantha, would be shown for the house of cards that it really was.

She was finding it hard to hold on to her sunny optimism.

'What's going on, Tess?'

'Sometimes I like to think that there's a little more to us than just sex…'

The silence stretched endlessly between them, straining until it was so close to breaking point that she could hardly breathe. She certainly couldn't look at him. Instead she fiddled with the fork on her plate, making swirly patterns into the fast cooling brandy sauce which she had hardly tasted.

She looked up when he began clearing the table, and had to resist the temptation to fling herself at him and tell him that she was just kidding. She knew that she had embarked on this relationship with the understanding that she would demand nothing, and she had been good to her word, but she had fallen deeper and deeper and deeper in love with him. She realised now that she had vaguely assumed that time would sort them both out and provide a way forward for their relationship.

When she stood up to help him, her legs felt wobbly. She was relieved when he told her to wait for him in the living room.

She was so absorbed in her thoughts that she wasn't aware of him framed in the doorway until he spoke. She twisted round to look at him.

'You were saying…?' Matt prompted, strolling into the living room to join her on the sofa.

Tess was finding it difficult to reconcile the man looking at her now with a closed, shuttered expression with the man earlier, who had laughed into her mouth and caressed her with such gentleness that she had felt as though they were two halves of the same person.

'I was saying that I'd like to think that what we have is more than just sex.' She smoothed her hands nervously along her dress. 'Do you care about me at all? I guess that's what I'm asking.'

'What kind of a question is that? If I didn't care about you I wouldn't be having a relationship with you.'

'So I'm on a par with Vicky? Is that what you're saying? You care about me the way you cared about her?'

'I prefer not to make comparisons between the women that I sleep with.'

'What's the difference between us?' Tess persisted doggedly.

Matt glared at her. He didn't like being hemmed in, and as someone who had never made a habit of giving an account for his actions he was infuriated that she was persisting with this line of questioning.

'For a start, Vicky never had a relationship with my daughter.'

'But if you take Samantha out of the equation…'

'How *can* I take her out of the equation? She's part of my life.'

'You know what I'm saying,' Tess insisted stubbornly. Having come this far, she was committed to this course of action whatever the outcome.

'No. I don't.' Matt couldn't believe that the evening to which he had been looking forward with impatience and anticipation was collapsing into a mess of awkward questions and unreasonable demands. They should have eaten a very good dinner, drunk some excellent wine, chatted with the ease with which they always chatted, and then progressed into bed where he would have lost himself in her. The fact that she had seen fit to scupper his plans ratcheted up his foul temper by a couple of notches.

'Okay, then I guess I'd better spell it out for you. I know you don't like the thought of planning ahead. *I know that.* The only stuff you ever seem to think about long-term is stuff to do with your work. You can think fifty years in advance when it comes to arranging your work life!'

'There's nothing wrong with that,' Matt gritted, avoiding the unwelcome topic of conversation that was staring him in the face. 'Businesses don't function on a let's-see-what-happens-next basis! Foundations have to be laid and plans have to be followed through.'

'I understand that. But I just want to know where your personal life features in all that foundation-laying and following through. Where do *we* feature in all that? I need to know, Matt, because I'm due to leave America in a couple of weeks...'

Pinned to the spot, Matt refused to be told which direction he should take. He had embarked on a fling with her and had spared little thought for the temporary nature of what they had. She was due to leave the country and, since he wasn't into long term situations, the nebulous matter of her departure didn't impinge at all on his conscience.

He had been clear as to what he wanted and she had readily agreed.

Hell, hadn't she come to America to sort herself out? Hadn't she gone on the pill because she had been willing for an adventure?

He uneasily cast his mind back to her shyness—that tentative, easygoing, sunny disposition that he still found endearing. His notions of her being a wild girl let loose in a big city had been crazily misplaced. Suddenly, like a jigsaw puzzle coming together with the final piece, Matt faced the truth that he had effectively spent the past few weeks subconsciously dodging, and he blanched at it. He had wanted her, and he had therefore talked himself into getting what he wanted by closing his eyes to the obvious.

'What do you want me to say?'

'I…I can stay on if you want me to. I've been giving it a bit of thought. It's not as though I have a job to go back for, and I love working here—working with Samantha. I know when she starts school she won't need me to be around during the day, but that doesn't matter. I could look around for something to do here. You see, I have dual nationality, so that wouldn't be a problem…' Her voice trailed off and she sifted her fingers through her hair and looked at him. 'It's not as though I would *live* here or anything…' The sound of her pride being washed down the drain was as loud as a fog horn in her ears. 'Claire would be happy to have me continue to stay with her. She's hardly ever around, anyway…she spends so much time with Tom. In fact, I would probably be doing her a favour…looking after her place when she's not there…'

'This isn't what we signed up for, Tess.'

The gentleness of his voice brought a lump to the back of her throat. He was letting her down and making sure not to be brutal about it. But at the end of the day being let down remained the same, whether it was done brutally or not. She sat on her hands, not trusting herself to speak for a few fraught seconds.

'I know. I never wanted to get involved with you…'

'Because I'm not the type of guy you ever saw yourself getting involved with.'

'Right. But…' She lifted her eyes bravely to his face and swallowed hard. 'I did. I let myself get involved with you and I just need to know if there's any chance for us.' She couldn't bring herself to tell him that she had fallen in love with him. He didn't want to hear anything she was saying. It was written all over his face. 'Even though,' she qualified gamely, 'it isn't what either of us signed up for.'

Matt was still. A series of flashbacks was playing in his head like a very rapid slideshow. His wife, his marriage, his resolve never to put himself in such a position again. The women he had dated since then had been ships in the night, and he had enjoyed having it that way. He had determined not to take on commitments he knew he would eventually dislike and resent. However ideal the woman in question might seem, it would only be a matter of time before she was shorn of her halo and revealed to have all the needs and expectations that would be guaranteed to drag him under.

And was Tess the ideal woman anyway?

She had never held down a job aside from this one. She had spent her life cheerfully drifting, content to live in the shadow of her sisters. She wasn't independent. She was hopeless when it came to most things of a practical nature. Her personality was so diametrically the opposite of his that he sometimes had to take a step back and marvel.

Yes, those differences were charming at the moment, but they would irritate him on a long-term basis. He was sure of it. Nor, he admitted to himself, did he care for the fact that she was, in effect, offering him an ultimatum. Ask her to stay or else watch her walk away. Matt didn't like ultimatums. He especially didn't like them insofar as they applied to his private life.

'You have some time remaining here,' he heard himself say brusquely. 'Why start asking about the future? Why not just enjoy what we have?' In his way, it was as close as he could come to expressing his feelings. He could promise her nothing.

'What would be the point?' Tess cried out with anguished feeling.

'So in other words,' Matt filled in, his voice unyielding, 'unless I can promise you marriage, you see no reason to stick around?'

'I told you…I don't *want* marriage…'

'Come off it, Tess! Are you going to tell me that you would be happy to get a part-time job over here and shack up in your sister's apartment just so that you could be at my beck and call?'

'I wouldn't see it that way,' she muttered inaudibly.

'I'm honest enough to tell you that you would be making a big mistake.' Feeling suddenly restricted, Matt stood up and paced through the room. She had effected small changes in the time she had been coming to the apartment. There was a little frame of some pressed flowers she had done with Samantha. Some of her CDs had found their way over and were sitting on his antique sideboard. A handful of pictures had been developed, and she had framed those and arranged them on the windowsill. He glared at all those intimate touches, which he had never asked for but to which, he thought bad-temperedly, he had become accustomed.

'We've had fun together. I would like us to continue having fun together until you leave. But if you don't want to then that's your choice.'

He hardened himself to the sound of her silence. He wasn't ending this because he was cruel. He was ending this because he was a hell of a lot more experienced than she was and he could foretell the mistake it would be even if she was wilfully choosing to close her eyes to it.

He needed to lead by example, and he would. It was what he had always done. It didn't feel good, but he couldn't allow himself to give her false hope. *More* false hope. Because it was obvious that she had been mulling over their situation longer than she had let on.

Mind made up, he turned to look at her. He brushed aside a momentary feeling of panic and clenched his jaw.

'You're going to have to be strong to take what I'm going to say now, Tess. We're not suited for one another.

You're right when you say that your choice of ideal man would be the opposite of someone like me. I have a hell of a lot more experience than you, and trust me when I say that I would drive you round the bend.'

'What you're saying is that *I* would drive *you* round the bend.' She breathed in deeply, angry with herself for having revealed so much, and angry with him for his patronising tone of voice. 'You don't mind sleeping with me, but I'm just not good enough for you to have a proper relationship with!'

Dark colour accented his high cheekbones. 'This has nothing to do with whether you're *good enough* for me or not!' he roared, losing control.

She was searching around for her bag, which she located in the kitchen. 'I still have a couple of weeks left working for you.' She held her head up high. 'I'd really appreciate it if I could see as little of you as possible.'

'That,' Matt said tightly, 'can be arranged. Consider yourself relieved of your duties.' Angry frustration ripped through him. He could barely look at her, and yet at the same time was driven to watch in glowering, hostile outrage as she headed towards the door, only pausing when her fingers were curled around the doorknob.

'Would you mind if I at least said goodbye to Samantha?' she asked jerkily, and Matt nodded an affirmation.

Which meant that there was nothing left to be said. It had all gone horribly, catastrophically wrong, but indecision pinned her to the spot until she told herself that it was pointless.

She closed the door quietly and firmly behind her.

CHAPTER SEVEN

DESPERATE to convince Claire that she was on the mend, Tess lay in bed trying to think happy thoughts.

For the first time in two months, she was rudderless. She literally felt like one of the walking wounded. She had told Claire that she felt she might be coming down with something. Actually, she *did* feel she might be coming down with something. She had woken up every morning—every morning for five interminable days, during which time she had heard nothing from him, not a text, not a phone call—with a vague feeling of nausea.

She no longer knew how to plan her days, and no longer had any interest in doing anything, anyway. She would be leaving the country in just over a week, and all she really wanted to do was hibernate. She wanted to scuttle somewhere dark and safe and warm, like a mole, and sleep until the memory of Matt had faded from her consciousness, allowing her to pick herself up and carry on.

She finally understood how much she had allowed him to become the axis of her entire universe. In a matter of just a couple of months she had given away all of her carefree independence, and now that the umbilical cord had been slashed she was floundering like someone deprived of oxygen. She missed him. She missed Samantha, with whom she spoke daily. She had seen her two days previously, and had obviously looked so dreadful that her mumbling something about *being a bit under the weather* had been one hundred percent convincing.

Claire had been sympathetic to start with, and had made a production of keeping her distance.

'I can't afford to catch anything,' she had apologised. 'Life's too hectic at the moment for me to take time out with an infection.'

Tess was beginning to think that she might actually be *willing* herself into a state of ill health. She could barely keep a thing down. If things continued in this manner she would have to be ferried back to Ireland in an air ambulance.

However, now, after five days, Claire was running out of patience.

Tess still lay with her eyes closed, telling herself that her nausea was all in her mind, when the bedroom door was flung open.

'It's nearly ten-thirty!' Claire was dressed to go shopping in one of her signature summer outfits—a silky short dress which would have cost the earth and a pair of complicated gladiator-style sandals—and was munching on a sandwich the size of a brick.

Tess tried to duck under the duvet.

'You can't *still* be under the weather, Tess!'

'You know I've never been a morning person.' She averted her eyes from the sandwich because it was making her stomach lurch.

'Well, it's Saturday, and you're coming shopping with me. You can't spend the rest of your time here feeling sorry for yourself because you have a bit of a stomach bug! You'll get back to Ireland and you'll kick yourself because you wasted your last week and a half. Might I remind you that there's *nothing to do* back home?'

'I'm going to do that teaching course. I told you!' After years of never settling down to anything, one good thing, at least, had come of her stay in Manhattan. She had been pushed into coming to New York so that she could find direction, and she had.

'Well, whatever,' Claire dismissed bracingly, 'you're still going to get out of that bed and come shopping with me—because tonight you're coming to a party! And I've already got a ticket for you so don't even *think* of telling me that you can't go because your tummy hurts! We're going to get you something glamorous and wonderful and you're going to *have a brilliant time*!'

That was Claire-speak for *do-as-you're-told-or-you-won't-hear-the-end-of-it*.

'I'll give you half an hour, Tess, and then I'll expect to see you up and ready to take on Manhattan!'

Tess had no idea where they would be going that night. She obediently spent the day traipsing behind Claire, making a heroic effort to show enthusiasm over the clothes that were paraded in front of her and being compelled to try on. At five-thirty they returned to the apartment and she was instructed to 'get your act together and change as quickly as possible because the taxi's booked for seven.' She was also instructed to *look happy*, because there was nothing worse than a party-pooper.

Tess did as she was told because she knew that her sister had a point. She really would have to start moving on. She couldn't continue to feel sorry for herself indefinitely. Matt had never promised her anything. He had never, ever given any indication that what they had would extend beyond her stay in America. *She* had been the one guilty of misinterpreting their relationship. She had flung herself headlong into something that defied all common sense and had started building castles in the air because she had been naïve.

When she thought logically about it, she and Matt stood on opposite sides of a great divide. He was the sophisticated, accomplished and confident product of a birthright of wealth and power. Not only had he grown up within the cocoon of a privileged background, but he had expanded a thousandfold on his fabulous inheritance. He had taken over his father's massive business concerns and diversified and branched out because it was in his nature. He was too clever to stand still and so he hadn't.

Compared to him, she was the equivalent of a minnow swimming next to a Great White. In her calmer moments she grudgingly conceded that there had never been a chance for them—not in any real sense of the word. Even if he had loved her madly—which he hadn't—it would still have been a big deal for him to have committed to someone so far removed from his own social background.

So moving on was her only option.

When she was fully dressed she could almost feel confident that she was beginning to. At least she *looked*

the part—which was some of the battle won, if nothing else.

Claire rapped on the bedroom door at six-thirty and
after twenty minutes of clinical inspection pronounced
herself satisfied.

She had ended up buying an off-the-shoulder long
dress, deep green in colour, which was gathered at the
bust and then fell to the ground. It should have made
her look shapeless, but it didn't.

'You have the boobs for it,' Claire had said approvingly, when Tess had emerged from the changing room.
'And the colour goes with you complexion.'

It was a style that couldn't be worn with a bra, and
Tess found herself thinking back to Matt's possessive
reaction to any thought of her going braless in public.
She had found it so intoxicating at the time, and had
read too much into it.

Now, she felt a welcome spurt of rebellion as she
followed Claire out to the taxi.

It was a forty minute drive to a building which, she
was told, was actually a very well known art gallery that
rented out its premises for a select few. Outside a crowd
of people, dressed to kill, were entering in an orderly
line, showing tickets to two doormen.

Inside, the party was in full swing. The art gallery
was über-modern. A large, brilliantly white reception
area branched out on either side to two massive rooms.
In one, a quartet played melodious jazz music. In the
other, people networked. There was the feel of a very expensive warehouse about the place. The walls in both the
rooms adjoining the reception area were painted a pale
slate-grey and adorned with large modernistic works

of art. The lighting comprised thousands of spotlights which, to Tess' relief, were dimmed to a mellow glow. It was like nothing she had ever seen before, and for a while she actually forgot her misery.

Tom was waiting for them, and he and Claire both made a big effort to introduce her to people, but after fifteen minutes Tess could see that her sister was becoming bored with playing babysitter. She shooed her away because, actually, she was quite happy to wander around looking at the art work, and after a while she slunk into the room with the jazz band, so that she could sit and listen to the music.

She had tucked herself at a table at the back of the room, with a glass of champagne in front of her, and was listening to a very perceptive song about unrequited love when a low, familiar voice behind her made her freeze in the act of raising the glass to her lips.

She spun round and half stood. Just one look, one second, told her that she had not even begun to put Matt behind her. He was formally dressed and was wearing a red bow tie—the only splash of colour against the blackness of his suit and the crisp whiteness of his shirt.

'What are you doing here?' Tess asked, in a daze.

'I could ask *you* the same question.' He had seen her from behind, walking into the room with the jazz musicians. There must be at least three hundred people at the do. Not only were the rooms on the ground floor crowded, but upstairs several more rooms were filled with employees and important clients. It had been pure coincidence that he had seen her, because he had spent most of his time upstairs, preferring the arrangement of comfortable leather sofas and chairs to the cocktail party atmosphere of the rooms on the ground floor. However, there had been no mistaking that caramel hair falling down her slender back as she weaved a path through the crowds. For a second he had been shocked enough to lose track of what was being said to him by one of the directors at his Boston office. Then he had made his excuses and followed her.

It irked him that he had not been able to get her out of his head. Everything he had said to her had made perfect sense, and yet she was still managing to infiltrate his waking moments with irritating consistency—like a high-frequency noise that had managed to lodge itself in his head, disrupting his thought patterns and making him lose concentration at inconvenient times.

Of course it had only been a few days, and her absence had been made doubly worse by the fact that Samantha was constantly talking about her. She had accepted the fact that Tess had left. She had known that her stay in America would come to a close, and it was a source of unending relief to Matt that his daughter was in a much better place than she had been a few months ago and so had found it easier to adapt to the young student who had replaced Tess for a few weeks. But she still mentioned Tess daily. Matt had been forced to make noises about plans for Tess returning for a visit, perhaps the following Easter. Maybe sooner! He had been obliged to grit his teeth as he was shown all the photographs they had taken together. He had listened, nodding in agreement, as he was told how much Grandma and Grandpa would have loved her.

He hadn't been allowed to forget the woman! Little wonder that he had found himself following her into this room, standing for a while to watch as she leant forward at a table, one hand idly curled around the stem of a champagne flute, the other cupping her chin as she tapped her feet to the quartet.

If he had been stupid enough to worry about her, he now scowled as any questions on that front were answered. She looked on top of the world. In fact she looked a knockout. And it was clear that she had come to pick up a guy. Why else would she be wearing something that left her shoulders bare and moulded the fullness of her breasts with such loving perfection?

Tess was completely and utterly thrown by the sudden appearance of Matt. It was as if her feverish mind had summoned him up.

'I...I came with Claire,' she stammered, before remembering that she was in the process of *moving on* and therefore letting herself go weak at the knees at the sight of him just wasn't going to do. But he looked so *sexy*. Had he come with someone? Even if he hadn't, he would surely be *leaving* with someone. All eyes were on him, sidelong glances, but then he *was* head and shoulders above every other man at the party.

He was also in a bad mood, and her spirits deflated because she knew why. He had come to a party and the last person he wanted to bump into would be *her*, when he thought that he was well and truly rid of her.

'I never expected to see *you*!' Tess forced herself to laugh. 'What a coincidence! But I guess Manhattan is smaller than you think! Mary says that London is like that! She'll be out having a drink somewhere, and before she knows it she recognises someone!'

'Pull the other one, Tess. You must have known that

I was going to be here.' Matt swallowed the contents of his whisky in one, and dumped the empty glass on the table at which she was sitting. He shoved his hands in his pockets. Did she think that he was going to stand here and make nice with a lot of polite conversation? Well, he wasn't in the mood.

'Why would I know that?'

'Because this is a company do. *My* company do, not to put too fine a point on it. So telling me that you had no idea that I might possibly attend my own party doesn't really wash.'

'*Your* party...' Claire hadn't mentioned it. She didn't know the circumstances of her departure from Matt's employment. Tess had told her that she had contracted a bug, and that with only a short period of time left had been given leave to get well and then enjoy some time out by herself rather than spend her remaining days working once she recovered. Claire would have expected her to have known about the party, and as Tess had asked no questions Claire had offered no information beyond the fact that it was a very dressy affair.

Matt's lips curled as he looked down at her generous breasts, pushing against the soft dark green fabric. 'Is that why you made a point of coming?' he rasped. 'You knew that I was going to be here and you thought that it would be a good opportunity to show me what I was missing? Well, it won't work.' All of a sudden he needed another drink. He glanced around, frowning, and like magic a waiter bearing drinks on a large circular tray appeared. Matt took a glass of wine, though he would rather have had a whisky, and drank half.

Tess had got lost trying to work out what he was attempting to say to her.

'I *didn't* know you were going to be here,' she protested truthfully. 'Claire never mentioned that it was a company do!' She was adding up the implications behind his remark, which had been delivered in a derisive tone of voice targeted to offend, and she was suddenly shaking with anger. 'And even if I *had* known that you were going to be here—*which I didn't*—I would *never* have come here to…to show you what you were missing!'

'No? Then why the over-the-top sexy dress? Not to mention the fact that you're not wearing a bra!'

The mere mention of that did horrible things to her body, reminding her of how easy it was to respond to him even when he wasn't touching her. Even, it would seem, when he was being rude and arrogant and insulting.

'This isn't for *your* benefit!' Her nipples were throbbing and she was mortified at her reaction. She felt that he must be able to see what he was doing to her with those laser-sharp, all-seeing black eyes of his.

'No? Because, like I said, it won't work. I've seen that ploy too many times. It's lost its effect over the years. We're no longer involved, and the best thing you could do for yourself is to move on.'

'I can't believe how arrogant you are, Matt Strickland! I…I can't believe what I ever saw in you!'

'I would bet that it wouldn't take much to remind you.'

The look in his eyes had changed suddenly. Tess's breath caught sharply in her throat. That simmering, *hot* gaze was not what she needed—not now! Did it give him a kick to put her meagre will-power to the test? To prove how much of a hold he still had over her? She wanted to weep in frustration.

Perversely, Matt was relishing this hostile clash of words. He had been chatting and socialising like a man on a tour of duty—looking covertly at his watch, mentally bemoaning the fact that the party still had hours to run. Now he was having fun, in a grim, highly charged sort of way. And he couldn't peel his eyes away from her delectable body. If there hadn't been a roomful of people watching, he would have been sorely tempted to remind her of just what she had seen in him! He pictured himself yanking down that flimsy piece of nothing shielding her glorious breasts, cupping their fullness in his big hands, teasing her nipples with the abrasive pads of his fingers.

From where the memory had been lying, close to the surface, he recalled their last evening together, when he had brought her to a shuddering orgasm in the kitchen of his apartment. He had a graphic flashback to the feel of her body writhing against his fingers. He could even recall the soft fall of that yellow dress she had been wearing.

'Has it occurred to you that I *am* moving on?' Tess lied, tossing her head and trying hard to remember the name of the guy who had badgered her for a while and slipped her his business card.

No. Quite frankly, it hadn't. Nor was he having a good time assimilating the concept.

'Maybe,' she threw at him defiantly, 'you're really not the reason I wore this dress—considering I didn't know that you were going to be here anyway! In fact, for your information, I've already been asked out on a date!'

That was a red rag to a bull. Having just told her that she should move on with her life, Matt underwent a rapid turnaround and was outraged that she should be out on the prowl within *seconds* of their split.

'Who by?' he demanded, keeping his voice well modulated, although inside he was seething with what could only be termed *jealousy*. His weakness infuriated him.

'Tony!' The name came back to her in the nick of time. 'Tony Grayson.'

Sales manager. His career now looked perilously short-lived. Matt drained his glass, flicked back the sleeve of his shirt to look at his watch. 'Well,' he drawled with lazy indifference, 'good luck with that one. I should be careful if I were you, though. New York isn't a small village in Ireland. Give off too many obvious signals and you'll have to be prepared to take the consequences. In other words, don't go near the fire unless you're happy to get burnt.'

He turned on his heel and walked away. Like a punctured balloon, Tess felt herself deflate. She could no longer put on a show of having fun. She just wanted to leave, to get back to the apartment. Like a patient suffering a severe relapse, she needed immediate time and space to recover, because seeing Matt again had knocked her for six.

Knowing that Claire would feel obliged to try and persuade her to stay, she didn't bother to look for her. Instead, she took the coward's way out and texted her a message. By the time she checked her mobile phone Tess would be at the apartment, in her pyjamas.

Three days later, Tess emerged from the doctor's surgery on wobbly legs. At Claire's insistence, she had finally gone.

'You can't climb on a plane feeling under the weather!' Claire had announced, in that voice of hers that permitted no argument. 'The flight back is a nightmare—it's so long, and if you start feeling really poorly on the plane it's going to be awful. You obviously have some kind of persistent stomach bug and you *have* to go to my doctor and get it sorted. If you like, I can come with you.'

Now Tess was weak with relief that she had turned down her sister's offer to accompany her. What would she have said if she had been confronted with the news that Tess was pregnant?

In a daze, she went to the nearest coffee shop and sat down, unseeing, in front of a cappuccino which, having ordered, she no longer wanted.

Her initial reaction—one of sickening disbelief— had ebbed. Now it was replaced by a recognition that all the signs had been there. She had just missed them. After their first time together, when she had been so convinced that there had been no danger of her falling pregnant because she was as regular as clockwork, she had gone to Claire's doctor—the very same doctor who had broken the news to her twenty minutes ago—to have a contraceptive device inserted. The pill would have been easier, but Tess had an aversion to tablets.

'You must be very fertile,' the doctor had said, while Tess had sat here like a statue, trying to absorb what had just been said to her. She had been thinking that it certainly explained her dodgy stomach. A quick look in her diary had confirmed that her period had been late— something she hadn't even noticed because between being on Cloud Nine and then catapulted back down to Planet Earth she just hadn't been thinking straight. In fact, she hadn't been thinking at all.

Across from her, a woman leaned over and asked if she was all right and Tess returned a wan smile.

'I've just had a bit of a shock,' she said politely. 'I'll be fine once I drink this cup of coffee.'

Of course she would have to tell Matt. He deserved to know. But just thinking about that brought her out in a cold sweat of nervous perspiration.

Their last bruising encounter had left her in no doubt that he was over her. He had given her her walking papers and instructed her to move on—because he had. He had spoken to her in the patronising tone of someone dealing with a nuisance who showed promise of becoming a stalker. He had accused her of dressing to attract him, and she knew, deep down, that he hadn't believed a word she had said about not knowing that he would be at the party. He wanted nothing further to do with her and what was he about to get? A lifelong connection that he hadn't engineered. He had trusted her because she had told him that she had taken care of contraception, and in return for his trust he would find himself a father in a few months' time.

But to keep the truth from him would be immoral.

Without giving herself the opportunity to dwell on what she knew she had to do, Tess stood up and hailed the first cab to his offices. If she thought too much about it she would think herself into a change of mind. She was having his baby.

The traffic, as usual, was gridlocked, and Tess was a bag of nerves by the time she paid the cab driver and looked up at the offices that commanded one of New York's prime locations in the heart of the financial sector.

She had been to his office several times before— little visits with Samantha—so she was recognised at the vast reception desk and waved across to the bank of elevators, one of which would take her to the top floor of the thirty-four-storeyed building.

His offices were the working equivalent of his apartment. Luxurious, plush, silent, industrious. His own office, perched at the end of the thickly carpeted corridor, was as big as some people's flats, with one section partitioned for his personal assistant and another, larger one, comprising a comfortable sitting area with leather chairs and plants and little tables. She knew that there was even a bathroom adjoining his office, for those times when he came in very early or was obliged to leave very late.

It struck her forcibly that the size and the opulence of it was a glaring reminder of just one of the many differences between them.

Thinking like that made her feel even more nervous, and she tried to project a composed demeanour as she stopped to chat to his secretary.

He wouldn't be aware that she was even there, and Tess was tempted to give him just a little bit longer to enjoy his carefree life before she blew it to smithereens.

Matt, buzzed eventually by his secretary, felt a kick

of satisfaction knowing that Tess was waiting to see him. She had been on his mind even more, having seen her at that party. He didn't know what she wanted, but when he thought that she might actually be reconsidering her options he felt like a predator in full and final control of its elusive prey. Maybe she had gone to the party to meet a man, but he had thought about that and eventually dismissed the notion. It really didn't tally with what he had come to know about her. At any rate, he liked to think that seeing him had made her realise what she really missed. She would only be around for a few more days, but he was more than willing to reluctantly set aside his pride and take her back to his bed. In fact—and he barely acknowledged this—it was a shame that she had made the fatal mistake of trying to tie him down, because who knew what might have been the next natural step for them…? He might just have offered her the very thing she had so obviously craved…

He didn't immediately look up when she quietly entered, although his senses went on sudden red alert. When she cleared her throat he finally raised his eyes, and then sat back in his chair without saying a word.

'I'm sorry if I'm disturbing you…' she began, painfully aware of his lack of welcome. He might just as well have set a timer on his desk and told her that she had one minute to state her case.

'You're lucky to find me here,' Matt told her politely. 'I have a meeting in a matter of minutes, so whatever you've come to say, you need to say it quickly.'

Faced with such bluntness, Tess dithered in an agony of uncertainty. She had vaguely rehearsed what she might say, but now she was looking at him every single

thought vanished from her head. She felt possessed
of roughly the same amount of confidence as a rabbit
staring at two headlights bearing down on it at great
speed.

'Well?' Matt said impatiently. 'What is it? I haven't
got all day.'

'Even if you had, I still don't think I'd find this easy
to say,' Tess told him shakily.

Something in the tone of her voice infused him with
ominous foreboding. He went completely still and
waited.

'You're going to be mad, but...I'm pregnant...'

CHAPTER EIGHT

MATT froze. He wondered if he had misheard her, but then immediately revised that notion as he looked at her face. She was white as a sheet and leaning forward in the chair, body as rigid as a piece of wood. *Mad?* She thought that he might be *mad*? That seemed to be the understatement of the century.

'You can't be,' he asserted bluntly, and Tess flinched.

'You mean you don't want me to be—but I am. I did a test this morning. In fact, I did more than one test.'

His usually sharp brain seemed to have shut down. Nothing had prepared him for this.

'You were protected,' he told her flatly.

With an abrupt movement that took her by surprise, he propelled himself out of his chair and walked towards the window. For once, his natural grace had deserted him.

'If this is some kind of ruse to get money out of me, then you can forget it!' He leant against the window and then restlessly began to prowl the office. He couldn't keep still. Running through his head was the thought that this just couldn't be happening.

'Why would I be using a ruse to get money out of you?'

'You can't accept that we're finished. You want to walk away with more than just a few memories. You *know* how much I'm worth!'

'I don't know how you can say that!' Tess exclaimed, dismayed. 'Since when do you know me to *ever* think about money? And I wouldn't make something like this up!'

No, she wouldn't. Painful sincerity was etched on her face. Whether he liked it or not, she wasn't lying. She was carrying his baby, and that was a fact with which he would have to deal whether he liked it or not. While he tried to scramble for some other explanation, he was already accepting the truth that had been forced upon him.

But beyond that there were still a lot of questions to be answered, a lot of perfectly reasonable suspicions to be dispelled—if, indeed, they could be. Surfacing through the fog of his confused thoughts, a line of pure logic crystallised, and in the face of that every natural instinct he possessed took second place.

She had bewitched him, made him behave in all sorts of ways that had been alien to him. Yes, he had had a good time with her. She had known how to make him laugh and she had relaxed him in a way no other woman had. But in the bigger picture how much did that really count for?

He had known her for a couple of months! And lo and behold, having assured him that she was fully protected, here she was—pregnant and knowing full well that her future would now be a gold-plated one. Did that make sense? Wasn't there something strangely suspicious about the circumstances?

Matt slammed the door shut on any shady areas in this scenario. He was conditioned to be suspicious. It was his protection. He wasn't about to abandon it now, even if he could see the glisten of tears in her eyes. He reached for the box of tissues he kept in his drawer and handed them to her, but there was a cold cast to his features that sent a chill to her heart.

'So. Explain.'

'That first time…'

Matt cast his mind back with a frown. 'If I recall, you assured me that—'

'Yes, I know what I said!' Tess interrupted fiercely. 'Okay. I lied.' Her eyes skittered helplessly from his dark, incredulous face.

She was aware of him picking up his phone, talking in low tones to his secretary, knew that he was telling her that he didn't wish to be disturbed. While he spoke, she did her best to get her tangled thoughts in order.

'That didn't come out right,' she said, as soon as he was off the line. Nervously, she plucked a tissue from the box on her lap and began shredding it with shaking fingers. 'It wasn't so much a lie as…I economised a bit with the truth. When you asked me whether I was taking any contraception, I was so…so turned on that I didn't want us to stop…'

Without warning Matt's mind did an abrupt detour and swerved off back to that night when they had made love for the first time. He had never been so turned on in his life before. Even thinking about it now… But, no, there was no way that he was going to let his body dictate his handling of this situation. He didn't care how turned on she had been. She had deliberately lied—taken a chance with life-altering consequences attached.

'So you decided to let me go ahead. You *risked a pregnancy* for a moment of passion. You threw away your virginity and played fast and loose with both our lives because you *just couldn't help yourself...*'

'I didn't *throw away* my virginity. I gave it away. I gave it to you because I wanted to—because you were the first man to make me feel like that. I've always had a very regular cycle. I honestly thought that there would be no consequences.'

'I'm flattered that you were so overwhelmed by me that you just couldn't help yourself, but excuse me for thinking of a more prosaic reason that you hopped into bed with me.'

Tess looked at him in confusion. Everything about him was designed to threaten, and she didn't know whether he was aware of that. She had to twist in the chair to follow his movements, and her neck was beginning to ache from having to look up as he towered over her—a cold, distant stranger who had sliced through the fragile bridge that had once connected them. Her heart was breaking in two.

'Yes, I concede that you were turned on. But maybe it occurred to you that if you had to lose your virginity with anyone, why not lose it to someone who was a damn good financial bet? If I recall, I gave you every opportunity to take a step back, but maybe you didn't want to lose the chance. Maybe, subconsciously, you didn't mind playing with fate, because if you did get pregnant then it would be a very profitable venture for you...'

Anger brought a rush of colour to her cheeks. 'A

profitable venture? You think I *wanted* to get pregnant? You think I *want* to have a child at the age of twenty-three, when I'm just finally beginning to see a way ahead for myself? I was actually thinking about going into teaching! I was going to work with children because I got so much pleasure from working with Sam. I was going to go back to school and try and get the qualifications I should have got years ago! Do you really think that I *want* to ditch all of that?'

She stood up, trembling. She shouldn't have come. She had messed up his wonderful life. She should have just returned to Ireland. He would never have known about the pregnancy. In fact, she should never have got involved with him in the first place. She should have taken one look at the fabulous trappings surrounding him and realised that he was not in her league and never would be.

'I'm going to leave now,' she mumbled, frantically trying to hold on to her composure. 'I just thought that you needed to know...and now you do.'

She began walking towards the door. She didn't get very far. In fact two steps. Then Matt was standing in front of her—six feet two inches of menacing male.

'*Going to leave?* Tell me that was a joke.'

'What else is there to say?'

Matt stared at her as though she had taken leave of her senses—maybe started speaking in tongues.

'You've dropped a bomb on me and you *don't think that there's anything more to say?* Am I dealing with someone from the same planet?'

'There's no need to be cruel and sarcastic. It's...I'm dealing with the same shock as you...'

Matt raked his fingers through his hair and shook his head, as though trying to will himself into greater self control.

He was shaken to his very foundations. Had he felt the same way when Catrina had declared herself pregnant with Samantha? He had been so much younger then, and willing to drift into doing the right thing. Since those youthful days a lot of lessons had been learnt. He had erected barriers around himself and they had served him well.

Now he was staring at a problem, and whether he liked it or not it was a problem that would have to be dealt with. But all problems had solutions, and flinging accusations at the woman who was going to be the mother of his child would get neither of them anywhere.

And how clever had he been to accuse her of ulterior motives? Now she was staring at him with big, tear-filled green eyes, as if he had morphed into a monster, when in fact he had just reacted in the way every single man in his position would have reacted under similar circumstances.

That didn't alleviate the niggle of guilt, but he firmly squashed that momentary weakness.

'I don't feel comfortable having this conversation here,' he told her shortly.

'What difference does it make where we have the conversation?' Tess looked down at her feet, stubbornly digging her heels in. She didn't want to go to his apartment. Nor did she want to go to Claire's apartment. For starters, Claire knew nothing of what was going on. Right now she was on a job in Brooklyn, but what if she and Matt went to the apartment to continue their conversation and Claire unexpectedly showed up?

Tess knew that sooner or later everything would have to come out in the wash, but right now she felt equipped to deal with only one horrendous situation at a time. Her mind just wouldn't stretch further ahead.

In truth, she wanted to be somewhere as public and as impersonal as possible. It seemed to make things easier to handle.

'This is my place of work,' Matt intoned, already taking it as a foregone conclusion that she would follow his lead by heading towards the jacket which was slung over the back of one of the leather chairs. 'I've instructed my secretary not to disturb me, but a lot of meetings will be cancelled. Sooner or later she will come in and expect some kind of explanation from me, and when she doesn't get a satisfactory one she'll be curious. Frankly, I would rather not generate public curiosity in my private life.'

'What will you tell her?' Tess reluctantly conceded his point. He was an intensely private man. 'I'm not going to Claire's apartment and I won't go to yours.'

'Why not?' Matt paused and looked at her through narrowed eyes.

Heat shimmered through her. Alone with him... She didn't want her strength to be put to the test. She knew how weak she could be when she was around him. She had to build up an immunity, and enclosed spaces would be the worst possible start to doing that. If he could be considered an illness, and falling in love with him some kind of terrible virus that had flooded her entire system, then detachment was the first step to a possible cure.

'Are you suddenly scared of me?' he asked softly. 'What do you think I'm going to do?'

Tess shamefully thought that the danger would be *wanting* him to do things that he shouldn't do and she definitely shouldn't want. Given a lifebelt, she clutched it with both hands. Hadn't he accused her of the most horrible things? That being the case, why shouldn't she accuse *him* of a few?

'I don't know!' she flung back in a shaky voice. 'You've insulted me. You've as good as told me that I set everything up—that I took risks because I wanted to trap you. You've been a bully. Of course I don't want to be anywhere with you, unless there are lots of people around.'

'Are you saying that you're afraid that I might be physically threatening?'

'No, of course I'm not…'

A dark flush had accentuated his high cheekbones. 'I have never laid a finger on a woman before, whatever the provocation. The thought of it alone is anathema to me!'

'I'm tired,' Tess muttered wearily. 'I don't want to be badgered. Maybe you should just think about things overnight and then we can speak tomorrow. Or the day after, even.'

Matt didn't bother to dignify such delaying tactics with a response. He had never been a believer in putting off for tomorrow what could be done today. Problems not faced head-on, he had discovered to his personal cost, never went away—they just got out of hand.

'Wait for me by the lift,' he instructed her, 'I will need to discuss rearranging my schedule.'

'Really, Matt. There's no need to put your entire day on hold! Just let me go home and we can both discuss this when it's sunk in and…and we're both calmer.'

'I'm perfectly calm. In fact, given the situation, I couldn't be calmer.' Nor was he lying. The fog was beginning to clear and a solution was presenting itself. It was the inevitable solution, but already he was coming to terms with it. He was rising to the occasion and that, for him, was something of which to be proud. She would discover soon enough that he was a man who shouldered his responsibility—even when, as in this instance, it was occasioned by something out of his control.

Strangely, he didn't feel as cornered as he might have expected.

Tess regarded him helplessly. He could be as immovable as a block of granite. This was one such occasion. 'Then we'll go to a café. Or a coffee shop. Or even just find a bench somewhere.' When he nodded, she gave a little sigh of resignation and left him slipping on his jacket, shutting down his computer, getting ready to face one of the most important conversations of his life.

It was pointless pushing the button. He was with her in less than five minutes. He had told her that he was calm and he looked calm. Cool, calm and composed. If nothing else, he was brilliant when it came to hiding his feelings. In fact, he could have been nominated for an award, judging from the performance he was putting on as he depressed the button and they took the lift down.

There was a coffee shop two blocks away, he was

telling her. It would be relatively quiet at this time of day.

When she asked him, stiff and staring straight ahead like a mannequin, what he had told his secretary, he shrugged and said that he had intimated some sort of situation with his new nanny. Nothing new there, he had implied to her. It had been a thirty-second conversation. His secretary wasn't paid to ask intrusive questions.

As the lift door purred open, Tess thought that anyone listening to their impersonal, polite conversation would have been forgiven for thinking that there was absolutely nothing amiss.

Matt continued to talk to her as they walked towards the coffee shop.

He certainly didn't think he had overreacted to a word she had said, but he had still managed to scare her—and that didn't sit right with him. To think that she had looked at him with those wide green eyes and effectively informed him that she didn't want to be in his company without the safety of an anonymous public around her had shocked him to the core.

It was essential to put her at ease. Talking about nothing in particular as they covered the short distance to the coffee shop was step one in that procedure.

Once there, he installed her at a table away from the window and any possible distractions and ordered them both something to drink and eat—although when he appeared with two lattes and a selection of pastries Tess glanced at him and blushed.

'To be honest, I've gone off coffee,' she confessed. 'And food in general. I have morning sickness that lasts all day, pretty much.'

Which made it all so real that his eyes were drawn to her still flat stomach. His baby! Unlike the Matt of ten years ago, this Matt was finding it strangely pleasurable to contemplate impending fatherhood—even with the dilemmas involved. There was much to be said for maturity.

'I can get you something else. Name it. Whatever you want.'

'You're suddenly being nice. Why?'

Matt sat down and helped himself to a cinnamon roll. 'If you think that I reacted too strongly, then I apologise, but this has come as a shock. I've been very careful when it comes to making sure that...accidents never happen...'

Tess hung her head in guilty shame. And, as luck would have it, this 'accident' had occurred with a woman who had never been destined to be a permanent fixture in his life. He might not have lasted the course with Vicky, but Tess couldn't imagine that he would ever have accused *her* of staging a pregnancy for his money.

'However,' Matt continued, interrupting her train of thought before it had time to take hold and plunge her into further depths of misery, 'there's no point dwelling on that. We're both facing a problem and there are always solutions to problems. Have you told anyone about...this situation?'

'I've only just found out myself!' Claire didn't have a clue as to what was going on. She would be in for a double shock. Tess shuddered just thinking about it. When she paused to consider her parents, her mind went blank. Beyond that, there were so many practical concerns that she hardly knew where to begin—and here he was, cool as a cucumber, working it out as though it was a maths question with an easy answer.

'Well, sooner rather than later, that's going to have to change. Your parents are going to have to know, for a start.'

'Yes, I *realise* that...'

'How do you think they're going to react?'

'I...I haven't thought about it. Yet.'

'And then there's the question of money.' He watched her carefully, but she was obviously still mulling over the thought of breaking the news to her parents. He knew that she was very close to them. He could see where her thoughts were going. 'Fortunately for you, I am prepared to take full responsibility for this. I think you know where this is leading.'

Cinnamon roll finished, Matt looked at her over the rim of his mug and said nothing until he had her full and undivided attention.

'We will be married. There is no other option.'

He waited for signs of relief and gratitude. Now that his proposal had been made, he decided that things might have been considerably worse. Their relationship might have come to an end, but that end had been prematurely engendered by the fact that she had given him an ultimatum—by the fact that time had not been on their side. Yes, he had certainly concluded that she was not his ideal match, at least on paper, but his thinking had had to change and change it had. Never let it be said that he wasn't blessed with an ability to get the best out of a thorny situation.

Relief and gratitude were taking their time, and Matt frowned at her. 'Well? We're going to have to proceed quickly. I will break it to my parents, and then arrangements can be made for a wedding. Something small would be appropriate, I think you'll agree.'

'Are you *proposing* to me?'

'Can you think of a better solution?' Matt was prey to a one-off, very peculiar feeling. He was a knight in shining armour, she the damsel in distress. He had never been given to fanciful notions of this nature, but he was now, and a sensation of general wellbeing spread through him with a warm glow.

Her eyes glistened and he whipped out his handkerchief—pristine white.

'This is everything I ever dreamed of,' Tess said bitterly. 'And I'm not going to embarrass you by bursting into tears in the middle of a coffee shop, so you can have your handkerchief back.'

'I guess it is,' Matt concurred.

'All my life,' Tess continued in a driven undertone that finally caught his attention, 'I've dreamt of a man proposing to me because he has no choice. What girl wouldn't want that? To know that a guy who doesn't love her, and in fact was glad to see the back of her, is big enough to marry her because she's pregnant!'

For a few seconds Matt was stunned into speechlessness. Twice in one day so far he had been lost for words! Tess wondered whether a world record had been set.

'Furthermore,' she carried on, 'haven't you learnt *any* lessons from your past?'

'You're losing me. Correction. You've *lost* me.' Having leant forward, he now flung himself back in the chair and gave her a scorching look from under his lashes. 'I can't think of a single woman who wouldn't be jumping up and down with joy at this juncture! Not only am I *not* walking away, I'm positively offering a solution. You are having my baby. You will therefore be protected—as will our child. With my ring on your finger you will never need or want for anything in your life again. And what *lessons*,' he added belatedly, 'are you talking about?'

'I'm talking about your ex-wife, Matt! Catrina?'

'What about her?'

'You married her because she fell pregnant. You married her out of a misguided sense of responsibility.'

'I married her because I was young and foolish. Her pregnancy had very little to do with it.'

'Look…' She took a few deep, calming breaths. 'I understand that you want to do the right thing but the right thing, isn't for us to get married.'

'You're telling me that a stable home life for a child is unimportant?'

'You *know* that's not what I'm saying,' Tess cried in frustration. 'Of *course* a stable home life is very important for a child! But two people living under the same roof for the wrong reasons doesn't make for a stable home life. It makes for…for bitterness and resentment. It wouldn't be right for both of us to sacrifice our lives and a shot at real happiness because I happen to have fallen pregnant.'

Matt was finding it hard to credit that she was turning him down, but turning him down she was. Only days ago she had been desperate to prolong their relationship, and now, when he was offering her the chance to do so, she was throwing it back in his face as though he had insulted her in the worst possible way! On some very basic level, it defied understanding.

'You're not being logical.'

'I'm being incredibly logical. I won't marry you, Matt. I know I wanted us to carry on seeing one |another—I know I would have stayed here a while longer if you had wanted me to—but I've had time to think about that, and you were right. It would never have worked out. We just aren't suited, and we're not going to become magically suited just because I made a mistake and fell pregnant.'

Matt felt the ground shifting awkwardly under his feet.

'You won't be returning to Ireland.' He delivered this with brutal certainty. 'If you think that you're going to make your bid for happiness across the Atlantic, then you're going to have to think again.'

A shot at real happiness? He pictured her having her shot at real happiness with one of those sappy guys she claimed to be attracted to and it was a picture that made him see red. He wasn't going to get embroiled in a long debate about it, however. Reluctantly he admitted that he was in a very vulnerable place. The second he had arrived at his solution to their problem, the very minute he had understood what would have to be done and had reconciled himself to the inevitable with a great deal of largesse, he had expected her to follow suit.

'Then I guess we'll have to talk about arrangements,' she said heavily.

Matt shook his head in the impatient gesture of a man trying to rid himself of something irritating but persistent.

'I would never deprive you of having a bond with

your child,' she continued gently. 'I know what you went through with Samantha.'

'So what are your suggestions?' When it came to the art of compromise, his skills were remarkably under-developed, but now Matt understood that compromise was precisely what he would have to do. Until he could persuade her round to his point of view. Legitimising their relationship made perfect sense to him, but he knew that he would have a lot of ground to cover. He had sidelined her, and she wasn't going to let him forget that—even though circumstances had now irrevocably changed.

Like a dog with a bone, he chewed over her assumptions that they were better off apart, that they were ill suited to one another. She seemed to have forgotten very quickly just how compatible they had been—and not just in bed. This about-turn in his thinking was perfectly acceptable to Matt. Things were different now. Instead of trying to spot the possible downsides, she should be trying to see the definite upsides. As he was! He was prepared to make any necessary sacrifices. Why shouldn't she?

'I could stay on in Manhattan…'

'That's non-negotiable.'

'Maybe live with Claire until I find myself a flat and a job.'

'Have you heard a word I said?' Matt looked at her incredulously. 'You won't be working. There will be no need. Nor will you be rooming with your sister.' His face registered distaste. 'If you're hell-bent on not accepting my proposal, then a suitable place will be found. Somewhere close. *Very* close.' He scowled, still disgruntled with the way his plans had been derailed. 'With regards to my work, I know that you want to contribute financially, but there will be no need for you to think that I come as part of the package.'

'Why are you so determined to put obstacles in my way!'

'I'm not putting obstacles in your way, Matt. You accused me of having ulterior motives in going to bed with you...' Tess felt her voice wobble, just thinking back to that hurtful accusation.

'I apologise,' he inserted quickly. 'You have to understand that it's my nature to be suspicious. I was just taking a step back and voicing possibilities.'

'There's no point trying to backtrack now,' Tess told him stiffly. 'You said what you said in the heat of the moment but you meant every word. I'm not happy about the thought of living off you, and I won't do it.'

'Most women would kill for what you're being offered,' Matt intoned with intense irritation.

'I'm not *most women*, so don't you go bundling me up in the same parcel as everyone else!'

'What job are you going to get?'

'I want to go into teaching. I told you. I'll investigate the process.'

Matt instantly determined that, whatever the process was, he would make sure that he decided it. He would not envisage a life with his child being raised separately while Tess vanished off to teach other people's children. She should be with her own, keeping the home fires burning for him, looking after Samantha...

It was a comfortable image. Seductive even.

'Now—' Tess stood up '—I feel really drained. It's

been stressful for me too, believe it or not, and I have a lot of things to be thinking about. So if you don't mind I'm going to head back to the apartment. I'll be in touch with you tomorrow.'

He was being dismissed! Control had been completely wrested from his possession, and for once he was in the position of having to grit his teeth and take it.

'What time? I could send Stanton for you. We can have lunch. Dinner, if you prefer. There's still a lot to discuss…'

'I'll…I'll let you know…' Tess said vaguely. She had so much to think about. Was she doing the right thing? He had offered marriage. Was it fair to the baby growing inside her that she turned him down? Her head felt as though it would burst.

They both needed space to think, and she wouldn't let him call the shots. That was a dangerous road which she had already travelled. Matt Strickland didn't love her. He never had and he never would, and the arrival of a baby wouldn't change that. And without love how could she marry him? That thought infused her with strength.

'Perhaps the day after tomorrow,' she amended. 'And then we can meet up and talk this over like two adults. Once we've done that, we can start sorting out the practicalities. This sort of thing happens to loads of people. We're not unique. We can both deal with it and move on.'

CHAPTER NINE

TESS returned to her sister's apartment to find that nothing in life ever went according to plan. The answer-machine was blinking furiously and there were five messages. Four were from her sister and one was from her mum. Her mother's message, delivered in an awkward, stilted voice—her *I'm-leaving-a-message* voice—informed her that her father had been rushed to hospital with a suspected heart attack. 'Everything will be fine, we're sure,' her mother had added as an afterthought. 'No need for you to come back home early. Our Mary is on top of things. It's wonderful to have a doctor in the family.'

The remaining messages were from Claire, repeating what their mother had communicated and adding that she was at the airport and would be in the air by the time Tess got the message. Then she demanded, 'Don't you ever answer your cell phone?'

There were eight missed calls and several text messages. Her cell phone had been innocently forgotten and was still in the kitchen, on charge.

The thoughts that had been driving her crazy on the trip back to the apartment now flew out of her head, replaced by panic. Her father was *never* ill. In fact, Tess

didn't think that he had ever registered with a doctor—
or if he had he had been a once-in-a-lifetime patient. If
her mother had seen fit to call, then it must be serious.
That was the path her logic took. It also advised her to
get on the next flight out.

She flung some things in a hand luggage bag, and
on the way to the airport reflected that getting out of
the country for a while was probably the best thing that
could have happened. Away from Manhattan, she would
have time to think in peace. She would phone Matt in a
few days and arrange to meet with him just as soon as
she judged that her father was fit and fine.

Not seeing him would be the biggest act of kindness
she could give herself, because seeing him earlier on
had just reconfirmed what she had already known. He
wreaked havoc with her peace of mind. The second she
laid eyes on him it was as if an electric charge had been
plunged into her, and it didn't matter how much she tried
to think herself out of feeling that way, she was helpless
against his impact.

Some time away from him—even a few days—would
allow her to build up some defences. She would have to
face the unappealing reality that her life was going to
change for ever. Not only would she have a permanent
tie with Matt, but she would be condemned to follow
the outcome of his choices through the years. She would
have to watch from the outside as he became involved
with other women, shared his life with them, introduced
them to Samantha and to their own child. However much
he wanted to take on responsibility, she'd had to release
him from a sacrifice that would have destroyed them

both, and it wouldn't be long before his relationship with her became purely functional.

She would have to learn to deal with that. She would get a job when the baby was born. Not immediately. First she would check out colleges and see what might be required of her. Those weeks of teaching Samantha had bolstered her confidence. She would start her academic climb with a positive outcome in sight. In time, she would get a job and meet someone else. Someone more suitable.

When she began to think about this mystery man, waiting just around a mythical corner, her thoughts became vague, and she had to stop herself from making the sweeping assumption that no one could ever possibly compete with Matt.

As soon as she landed in Ireland she phoned her mother who, like her, had a habit of forgetting her mobile phone—leaving it on counters, in the bedroom, sometimes on top of the television. Because, 'If it's important, whoever it is will call the proper phone.' There was no reply.

Exhausted after her long flight over, and greeted with a damp, unappealing Ireland which seemed so much quieter and so much less vibrant after the excitement of New York, Tess took a cab back to her home.

The buzz of the city was well and truly left behind as the taxi meandered along the highway and then trundled along narrow streets surrounded by great stretches of countryside, as though the cab driver had all the time in the world.

He talked incessantly, and Tess made a few agreeable

noises while allowing her thoughts to wander like flotsam and jetsam on an ocean current. She pictured her father lying grey-faced and vulnerable on a hospital bed. Mary would know exactly what was going on, and would give her a more realistic assessment than either her mother or Claire. When she thought of her father being seriously ill she began to perspire, and switched her thoughts to her own problem. Although she would be seeing her entire family, she would not be able to breathe a word about her condition. She would have to wait until things calmed down a bit—then she would break the news. The very last thing either of her parents needed was yet more stress. Maybe she would wait until she returned to Manhattan. She hoped her mother wouldn't expect her to stay on.

It was yet another possible complication that she once again shied away from facing. Life as she once knew it now seemed simple in comparison, but looking around her as the taxi drew into the small village where she had, until recently, lived with her parents, Tess wondered how she hadn't itched to fly the coop long ago. Everything was so *small* and so *static*. They drove past the village hall, the shops, the cinema. Several miles away there was a bigger town, where she had always gone with her friends, but even that seemed rural and placid in comparison to the vigour of Manhattan.

The house was empty when she arrived, but signs of occupation were everywhere to be seen. Mary's jacket hung on the banister. Claire's bag had been dumped in the hall and lay half open, with items of clothing spilling out.

The immediacy of the situation grabbed Tess by

the throat, and all thoughts of Matt were temporarily jettisoned.

The next few hours were a blur of activity. She was deeply, deeply exhausted, but her body continued operating on autopilot. She contacted Claire, then drove her mother's car to the hospital—and that felt very strange after a diet of public transport, taxis and Matt's private chauffeur.

'He just complained of feeling a bit out of breath,' her mother whispered, drawing her to one to whisper. 'The old fool.' Her eyes had begun watering but she soldiered on and blinked her tears away. 'Never had a day's illness in his life, so he didn't want me to call the doctor. Thank the Lord I did! They say it's just a scare. He's going to be fine. But he'll have to give up some of his favourite foods. He's not going to like that. You know your dad.'

It was late by the time Tess's body finally caught up with. One minute she was chatting with her sisters and her mother in the kitchen, then she was having her shower, slipping into a nightie, and then her head hit the pillow and she disappeared into sleep as though tranquillised.

And that continued to be the case for the next three days. She settled into a routine of sorts—back in her old bedroom, sharing the bathroom with Mary and Claire and bickering with them about the length of time they took whenever they ran a bath. Her father was improving steadily and had begun to complain about the hospital food, which seemed a good sign.

Lurking at the back of the gentle chaos and the cosiness of the familiar was Matt's dark, brooding presence, and the pressing situation with which they had yet to deal. But every time Tess reached for the phone to call him her hand faltered and she began sweating, and then she'd postpone the conversation which she knew would inevitably have to be made. After the second day he began to leave messages on her mobile, and missed calls were registered. Tess decided to give it until the weekend to get in touch. The weekend would mark five days out of contact.

Mary would be returning to London and Claire would be going with her, taking a few days off to remain in the country and using the opportunity to import Tom, so that they could do some shopping and also meet the parents if she deemed that her father was up to it. She had already e-mailed her resignation and seemed to have no regrets about losing her high-flying job in Manhattan because Tom would be transferring to London. Between her father's improving health and Claire's exciting news Tess was happy to sideline herself in the background, where she could nurse her own worries in peace.

Which was precisely what she was doing in her room, with her tiny, very old television turned on very low, telling her about unexpected flooding in Cornwall, when her mobile went and an unknown number was displayed.

At the very height of his frustration Matt had invested in a new phone, with a new number, because after days of trying without success he could think of no other way of getting in contact with her.

He'd hesitated to telephone her sister. What excuse could he possibly give? Tess had been adamant that she would break the news to her family in her own time.

Already dealing with having his perfectly formulated plan to marry her turned on its head, the last thing he needed would be to arm her with more grounds for grievance.

Over a period of three days his mood had travelled on a one-way road from poor to appalling. He couldn't get her out of his mind. Then he'd begun to worry. What if she had been taken ill? Been in an accident? Was lying somewhere in a hospital, unable to get in touch? The surge of sickening emotion that had filled him at the thought of that had been shocking—although, as he had shakily reminded himself, perfectly understandable given her condition. He was a man of honour. He *would* be shaken to the core at the thought of the mother of his child falling ill and being unable to get in touch with him.

But before he began ringing round the hospitals in the area he'd had the last-minute brainwave of buying a new phone—one with a new and unrecognisable number— just in case she simply wasn't answering his calls.

The second he heard her voice at the other end of the line he felt a spasm of red-hot anger envelop him like a mist. He realised that he had been *worried sick* about her.

'So you *are* alive,' were his opening words.

On the other side of the Atlantic, Tess sat up in bed. The sound of his voice was like a shot of adrenaline, delivered intravenously.

'Matt...I've been meaning to give you a call.'

'Really? When?' It was just as well that she wasn't within strangling distance, he thought with barely suppressed fury. 'In case you haven't noticed, I've made several hundred calls to you over the past few days. *Where the hell are you?* I've been to the apartment four times and no one has been there!'

'I needed to have a little time to myself.' She glanced around her furtively, half expecting to see him material- ise out of thin air, so forceful was his personality even over a telephone thousands of miles away.

'I'm sick to death of hearing what *you* need!' He had to stop himself from roaring down the line. There was no place for anything less than civilised behaviour in their situation, but the woman brought out a side to him that he hadn't known existed and one which he found difficult to control. Not even with Catrina, at the very height of their dysfunctional marriage, when revela- tions had been pouring out from the woodwork like termites, had he felt so uncontrollably responsive. Where with Catrina he had taken refuge from his problems by burying himself in his work, with Tess that was no solu- tion. However hard he tried, it was impossible to focus. 'Running away isn't the solution! Where *are* you?'

'I'm…' Two things stopped her from telling him the truth. The first was the knowledge that to confess that she was on the other side of the Atlantic, having taken off without bothering to let him know, would make him even angrier than he already sounded. The second was the fact that she *couldn't* let him know where she was. He was her problem in America, and with her father still recuperating there was no way that she wanted him to intrude and possibly risk jeopardising her father's recovery. How would her parents react if he phoned the house and gave the game away? Let slip that she was pregnant? Single and pregnant by a man who wasn't going to be her husband? Her parents would have to be gently eased into that, and this was not the right time.

'I'm out of New York. Just for…for a few days. I know we have stuff to talk about, and I'll give you a call just as soon as I return.'

'Where. Are. You?'

'I'm…'

'If you don't tell me where you are,' he said in a calmer voice, 'then I'll do some investigative work and find out for myself. You would be surprised how fast I can get information when I want it.'

'I told you—'

'Yes, I know what you told me, and I'm choosing to ignore it.'

'I'm back home,' Tess confessed, 'in Ireland. My dad got rushed into hospital and I just had to get to the airport and fly over.'

Matt paused. 'Rushed into hospital with what?'

'A heart attack scare. Look, I'm sorry—'

'And is he all right?' Matt interrupted tersely.

'On the mend. We're all very relieved.'

'Why didn't you say so in the first place? No. Better question. Why didn't you answer one of my five hundred calls and *tell* me that?'

'I had a lot on my mind…and I wanted to have some space to think…'

Across the water, alarm bells started ringing.

Matt was in no doubt that her initial reaction to hearing about her father would have been to hop on the first flight out. Although he was close enough to his parents, they had always been highly social and very much involved in their own lives. Tess, on the other hand, was fiercely attached to her parents and her sisters. He assumed that she would not have broken the news about her pregnancy to them—not given the circumstances.

But *why* hadn't she picked up any of his phone calls? Or returned any of them?

Space to think amongst her tightly knit family unit, back on her home turf, allied itself, in his head, with her desire to find happiness with someone else. It was not a happy alliance. With the comforting familiarity of her village around her, how long before she started contemplating the prospect of foregoing the stress of the unknown in New York? He was certain that her parents would react kindly to her pregnancy. Perhaps a small moral lecture, but they would weather the news and immediately provide support.

New York would fast become a distant memory. She might nurse some scruples about running away, but how long before she recalled the adverse way in which he had reacted to news of the pregnancy? How long before she started thinking of his insinuations about the financial benefits of having his baby—his implication that she might have engineered an agreeable financial nest egg for herself? Would she take time to step back and consider *his* side of the story? See where *his* perfectly understandable concerns stemmed from?

Not for the first time, Matt wondered why she couldn't have been one of the scores of willing women who would have been *overjoyed* at a marriage proposal from him and the financial security for life it entailed. But then the thought of Tess falling into line with one of those women was laughable.

She was telling him now about how much it was helping, being back in Ireland.

'So when exactly do you expect to be back here?' he cut in. Now that his brain had taken off on another tangent, like a runaway horse, he was alert to that shade of hesitation before she answered, and was composed and understanding when she mumbled something about as soon as she could—though she couldn't very well leave her mum on her own immediately. Not with Mary and Claire both gone.

He rang off shortly after.

There was a considerable amount of work for him to do. Meetings with important clients, bankers, lawyers. It only took a few phone calls to rearrange that situation.

His next call was to his mother, who would cover for him at home in his absence, ensuring that Samantha had a familiar face when he wasn't around. She had only just started at her new school and, whilst everything seemed to be progressing with startling ease, he still felt better knowing that she would return to the apartment and someone who actually had a vested interest in whether she did her homework or not.

Then he called Samantha, who had to be fetched out of her class and was breathless when she picked up. Amidst the turmoil, her moment of disappointment when he broke the news that he would be out of town for a couple of nights was a light on the horizon.

His calls completed, Matt informed his secretary to get him on the first flight out to Ireland.

He was thinking on his feet—something he was excellent at. He left his office with instructions for his flight details to be texted to him within the hour, and then he was heading back to his apartment, packing the minimum of things, fired up by an urgency to *act*.

He didn't know whether Tess would have run away to find her space to think had she not been called on an emergency, but now that she *had* left the country he wasn't going to hang around to find out whether her return was on the cards.

Tess Kelly was unpredictable in the extreme. There were also hormones rushing through her body. He wasn't completely clueless about pregnancy. Under the influence of her hormones, she was capable of pretty much *any* rash decision!

As fresh thoughts superimposed themselves on already existing ones, his decision to go to Ireland seemed better and better by the second.

Having checked out the paperwork which she had dutifully filled in at her time of employment, he had easily ascertained her parents' address. The only question was whether he would show up unannounced on the doorstep, or get to see her via a more roundabout route.

Respecting the situation concerning her father, Matt arrived in Ireland intending to settle himself into a local hotel and then consider his next step forward. His intention was blocked when he discovered that there was no hotel in the village, which was much smaller than he might have expected.

'Where *is* the nearest hotel?' He impatiently directed his question to the taxi driver, who seemed quite pleased to have delivered his fare to the middle of nowhere.

'Depends on what sort of hotel you're looking for.'

Fed up, Matt decided to take his chances on going directly to her parents' house, and he handed the driver a slip of paper on which he had scribbled the address. He would deal with whatever problem arose from his decision with his customary aplomb.

It was a matter of fifteen minutes before the taxi was pulling up in front of a Victorian house with a pristine front garden and enough acreage to just about avoid being overlooked by the neighbours.

The flight had been long and tiresome, even in first class, but Matt was raring to go. He felt as though he had spent the past few days sitting on his hands, and that just wasn't his style. He was confrontational by nature.

He was prepared for anything and anyone as he pressed the doorbell and waited.

Not for a moment did it occur to him that no one would be home, and the sound of hurrying footsteps rewarded him for his confidence.

Tess had been looking forward to a bit of peace and quiet. Claire had left not an hour ago, and shortly after that her mother had gone to the hospital, leaving Tess to tidy up the house, which hadn't been touched properly since her father had been taken into hospital.

She had no idea who could be at the door. She debated not answering and hoping that the caller would eventually get the message and disappear, but she couldn't do it.

Pulling open the door, dressed in old clothes which she had worn as a teenager—faded track pants and an old tee shirt that should have been thrown out a long time ago—Tess half wished that she *had* ignored the bell, although for a few heart-stopping seconds, she didn't quite believe her eyes.

Matt was larger than life—dramatic against the crisp Irish scenery and the quietness of the rural backdrop.

'You look surprised to see me.'

He remained on the doorstep and looked at her. Her caramel-coloured hair was pulled up into a scruffy ponytail, and her clothes looked as though they had seen better days, but even so he still found it a strain to keep his hands to himself. He always knew when she wasn't wearing a bra, and she wasn't wearing one now. He could make out the slight hang of her breasts, and the tiny peaks where her nipples were jutting against the soft jersey of her tee shirt.

'Are you here on your own?' he asked, when she made no attempt to break the silence. 'I didn't want to crash land on you, Tess, but I felt that it might be better all round if I came here instead of waiting for you to return to America.'

'I haven't told anyone about us!' she breathed. 'There's no one at home now, but it would have been a disaster if you'd come two hours ago!'

'Oh, I don't think so,' Matt drawled, running out of patience. 'Sooner or later everyone is going to have to know, and ducking and pretending that that time isn't going to come won't solve anything. Are you going to invite me in?' He held out his hand and gave her a duty-free carrier bag from the airport. 'A book for your father—it's the latest one by that guy you told me that he likes—and a scarf for your mother.'

Tess stepped aside and watched warily as he entered the hallway. As happened everywhere he went, he dominated his surroundings and she couldn't wrest her eyes away from him. The sight of one of his designer holdalls in his hand broke the spell.

'How long are you planning on staying?' she asked, dismayed.

'I'm staying until you're ready to come back to America with me.'

'You mean you came all the way here to escort me back to New York? Like a kid who has run away from home?' Annoyed with herself, because her excitement levels had rocketed the second she had clapped eyes on him, thereby proving that all her hard work over the past few days had been for nothing, Tess was ready to pick a fight. Did he think that he could do just as he pleased? What did that herald for their future? Would she be relegated to being told what to do at a moment's notice, just because he could? Rich, beautiful Catrina from another powerful family had been able to assert her own terms, even if they had been unfair. *She*, on the other hand, had no such power behind her, so where exactly would she stand?

'Well, you may be here longer than you think.' Tess folded her arms. 'Claire and Mary have both left for London, and someone has to stay with Mum until Dad's back home. Maybe even longer. Who knows? She's going to need lots of help.'

'And you're going to volunteer for the post without breathing a word to either of them about your condition? I can't allow that.'

'You can't *allow* it?' Tess looked at him incredulously. 'Since when do you have a say in what I do and don't do?'

'We've been over this.' So he *had* been right to get on a plane and pursue her. She had no intention of hurrying back to New York. 'And I can't allow it because you're in no kind of condition to start doing heavy manual chores around the house. I will ensure that there is someone here to take the strain off your mother—'

'You'll do nothing of the kind!' Tess cried. 'She won't even know that you've been here!'

'And how do you figure on keeping me a secret?' Matt grated. 'Are you going to lock me away in a room somewhere and feed me scraps of food through a hole in the door? Because I'm telling you right now that's the only way you're going to be able to keep me out of sight. I didn't come here to have a fight with you!'

'No, you came to cart me away!' *You don't care about me*, she thought, as furious resentment rose to the surface and threatened to spill over. *You would have happily turned your back and never seen me again, but now here you are, suddenly concerned for my welfare because I happen to be pregnant with your child!*

'If needs be,' Matt confirmed with implacable steel. 'In the process, I intend to stay until I meet your parents and tell them what's going on.'

Tess blanched. 'You can't. Dad's not well.'

'What do you think will happen if you break the news to him? I'm tired of playing games with you over this, Tess. You're twenty-three years old. You're sexually active. You got pregnant. Which bit of that do you imagine would affect them most?'

Tess chewed her lip and looked away.

'Well?' Matt pressed. 'Do you think that they will

collapse on the spot if they find out that you've had a relationship.'

'It wasn't a relationship.' She knew exactly where the sticking point was with her parents—her charming, old-fashioned parents, with their old-fashioned ways and gentle moral code. 'They won't like the fact that I'm pregnant…they won't like it that I'm going to be a single mother. Neither of them can deal with that shock right now. You have to trust me.'

'I'm staying, Tess—and you can always spare them the shock of your being an unmarried mother, can't you? Think about it. Think about how happy they would be if they knew that their daughter was pregnant but was going to *marry* the father of her child…'

CHAPTER TEN

TESS looked at Matt in disbelief. 'I need to sit down,' she said shakily. She walked on legs that felt like wood into the comfortable sitting room and sank onto a squashy sofa, tucking her feet under her.

For a few moments Matt strolled through the room, barely noticing the pictures in the frames, the ornaments, all the reminders of a life greatly enhanced by children. His attention was focused on Tess. She looked small and vulnerable, huddled on the sofa, but Matt wasn't going to allow himself to feel sorry for her.

She had fled to Ireland without bothering to call him, she had ignored every phone call and message he had left for her, and she had as good as admitted that she had no intention of hurrying back to New York.

'That's blackmail.' She raised huge, accusing eyes to his and his mouth tightened.

'It's problem-solving. You're terrified that your parents are going to be disappointed in you, and I'm showing you that there's no need for that.'

'I've spent ages telling you why it would be a bad idea.'

'Yes. I heard all the reasons you churned out.' He sat heavily on the sofa, depressing it with his weight, and

Tess shifted awkwardly to avoid physical contact. 'You don't see the need to marry me just because we made a mistake. Life's too short to be trapped in a marriage for the wrong reasons. You want to spread your wings and find your soul mate.'

'You're twisting everything I said.'

'Tell me which bit you think I've got wrong. The trapped bit? The soul mate bit? Were you *ever* going to return to Manhattan? Or did you come back here with good intentions only to decide that you would erase me out of your life?'

'Of *course* I was going to return to New York! I'm not irresponsible! I want you to have a real bond with this child.'

'You're one hundred percent irresponsible!' Matt snapped. He looked at her with glowering, scowling intensity. 'You refuse to marry me. You refuse to acknowledge that a child needs both parents. You witnessed first-hand the hell I went through gaining Samantha's trust—trust that should have been mine by right but was destroyed by a vengeful ex-wife.'

'I can't bear to think of you putting up with me for the sake of a child.' Tess defied the suffocating force of his personality to put across her point of view. She thought of her parents and how they would react to the thought of her living a single, unsupported life in New York. Based on their experience, children should be born into a united home. How would they ever understand that love and marriage didn't necessarily go together? They were savvy enough when it came to the rest of the world, but she had a sinking feeling that they would be a lot less savvy when it came to their own offspring.

The fact that Claire was excitedly due to be married to the man of her dreams would make it all the harder for them to understand how she, Tess, had managed to become embroiled in the situation that she had.

Matt was offering her a way out, and for a split second she desperately wanted to take it. It wouldn't be ideal—no one could say that—but it would solve a lot of problems.

She pulled herself up short when she remembered how her cotton-candy daydreams and pointless, optimistic fantasising had landed her where she was now. She had fallen in love with him and dared to hope that time would work it's magic and miraculously *make* him love her. It hadn't, and she would be a complete fool to forget that. Marry him, she told herself sternly, and she would witness the slow build-up of his indifference. He would have affairs, even if he kept them under wraps for the sake of maintaining a phoney front, and she would never, ever be able to give herself a chance at finding someone who could care for her.

'Don't try and get into my head, Tess.'

'I know you.'

'I'm willing to make the sacrifice. Why aren't you? You were happy with me once,' he said brusquely. 'We got along. It's ridiculous for you to assume that we can't make a go of it.'

'If we could have made a go of it—if you had *wanted* to make a go of it—you would have asked me to stay. You would have been prepared to make a go of it then.'

Matt hesitated. 'This is too big for wounded pride

to come into the equation. Anyway, maybe I made a mistake.'

'Mistake? What kind of mistake?' She looked at him suspiciously. She had dared to hope so many times that the prospect of daring to hope again was literally exhausting. 'Since when does Matt Strickland *ever* make mistakes?' she muttered, and he gave her a crooked smile that made her heart flip over. 'I don't say that as a compliment,' she qualified quickly, before that smile made her start to lose ground. 'It's important to make mistakes. People learn from their mistakes. I made mistakes growing up. I've learnt from them.'

'Did you make a mistake with me?'

Tess flushed. 'If I could turn back time, I—'

'That's not what I'm asking. I'm asking if you think you made a mistake with me. I don't want an answer based on hypothesis.'

He was no closer to her now. In fact, he was leaning back, looking at her with brooding, narrowed eyes, and still she felt as though she was being touched.

'Because I don't think *I* made a mistake with *you*. I think the mistake I made was to let you go.'

Suddenly the air seemed close and the room too small. The breath caught in her throat and her skin was on fire.

'Don't you dare!' She stood up, trembling, and walked towards the window. Outside, the scene was peaceful. The carefully tended garden was ablaze with flowers. However, Tess was oblivious to the colourful summer landscape. Her heart was beating so hard that if she held her breath she was sure she would be able to hear it.

When she turned around it was to find him standing so close to her that she pressed herself against the window-ledge. His proximity brought her close to a state of panic. She trusted *him*. She just didn't trust *herself*.

'Don't dare…*what*? Come close to you? Why not?' He shoved his hands into his pockets. If he didn't, he knew what he would do. He would reach out and touch her, maybe just tuck that stray strand of hair behind her ear. Hell, her eyes were wide and panicked, and he hated seeing her like this. He clenched his jaw and kept his hands firmly tucked away. 'Why fight me?' he muttered, and dark colour slashed his cheekbones. 'Why fight *this*?'

'I don't know what you're talking about, and I don't need you to try and undermine me. I know what you're doing.'

'Tell me. What *am* I doing?'

'Everything it takes to get what you want,' Tess heard herself say with unaccustomed bitterness. 'You've come here so that you can take me back to New York because you don't trust me. I'm sorry I didn't phone you, and I'm sorry I didn't answer your messages, but I've needed to take a little time out and I've been worried sick with Dad being in hospital. Not that you care. The only thing you care about is making sure that I'm in place, and you'll do whatever it takes to get me there—even if it means blackmailing me into doing what you want. You know what it could do to my parents in the situation they're in if you dump this news on them, but you'd go right ahead and do it if you thought it would get you what you want! And you expect me to *want* to commit myself to you? When everything you do just confirms that you're arrogant and ruthless and only care about what you want?' She drew in a deep breath and braced herself to continue. 'Don't even think of telling me that you made a mistake throwing away what we had!' Her voice was shrill and unforgiving. 'It's easy to say that now. Do you really think that I'd believe you?'

'You're upsetting yourself.'

'I'm not upsetting myself! *You're* upsetting *me*.'

'I don't want to do that. I…I never want to do that.' With an effort, Matt pushed himself away from her and returned to sit on the sofa. Like a slow motion sequence in a film, every mistake he had made with her rose up with reproving clarity.

He had been attracted to her, and without a second thought he had seduced her into his bed. He had accepted the gift of her virginity without bothering to question the devil in the detail, and then, when she had suggested remaining in New York, he had run a mile. Conditioned to identify himself through his work, and accustomed to always ensuring that it was placed at the top of the agenda, he had reacted to her reasonable requests about where their relationship was heading by backing away.

To compound his sins he had greeted news of her pregnancy with suspicion—only to further raise her guard and drive her away by insisting on trying to determine what she should do and what she shouldn't.

Had he even *once* thought about stepping back and taking stock of how he actually felt?

Not in the habit of doubting his ability to manage situations, Matt was shaken to the core at the realisation that he had blown it. She might tremble the second he got near her, but a physical response wasn't enough. It had never been enough. And yet he knew that if he told her that now she wouldn't believe a word he said, and he couldn't blame her.

Tess looked at him uneasily. For once his deepening silence didn't seem to indicate anything ulterior. He wasn't even looking at her. He was staring into space and his expression was unreadable.

She took a hesitant step away from the window, but it was only when she was standing in front of him that he raised his eyes to hers.

'I've screwed up,' he said bluntly. He raked his fingers into his hair and lowered his eyes. 'Of course I'm not going to blackmail you into anything.'

'You're not?'

'Sit. Please? And that's not a command. It's a request.'

Tess, caught off guard by this strangely unsettling and subdued side to him, perched primly on the edge of the sofa, ready and willing to take flight at a moment's notice—although her hands wanted to reach out, and she wanted to lace her fingers through his. Frankly, she had to resist the powerful urge to do anything necessary to bring a smile to his lips, even if that smile was laced with cynicism. This was not a Matt she was accustomed to seeing, and it disconcerted her.

'You think I'm trying to take advantage of you? I'm not.' Matt felt as though he was standing on the edge of a precipice, arms outstretched, about to fling himself over the side in the wild hope that he would be caught by a safety net. He also felt very, very calm. 'I've done so many things wrong that I don't even know where to begin to try and explain myself, and I fully understand that you probably won't believe a word I say to you. Frankly, I wouldn't blame you. I entered into a relationship with you for the sex—pure and simple. I've been bitten once, and I've lived my life since then making damn sure that I wouldn't be bitten again. Every woman I've ever been with since Catrina has been like Vicky. It was easy never to become involved. My personal relationships were effectively, just extensions of my working life, with sex thrown in.'

Tess, all ears, found that she was holding her breath. With his walls breaking down, this was a vulnerable Matt laying his soul bare. She knew that instinctively, and she wasn't going to break the spell. Every word wrenched out of him was like manna to her ears. If she wasn't being hopelessly enthralled, she would be slightly ashamed.

'I should have questioned what it was I saw in you when you came along, but I didn't. I've always had absolute, unwavering control in my personal life. How could I expect that what I had with you would be any different?'

'And it was? Really? How different?' Tess cleared her throat and blushed sheepishly. 'It's important, you know—to…um…let it all out…'

'In that case, it's very kind of you to let me talk,' Matt murmured wryly. '*Very* different, in answer to your question. You made me a very different person. I did things with you that were all firsts—although at the time I hardly recognised it. I stopped work for you. Yes, I went to meetings—I organised deals, I met with the usual lawyers and bankers and hedge fund directors—but for the first time in my life I couldn't wait to get back to the apartment. I managed to persuade myself that that was because my relationship with my daughter was finally beginning to take shape. Of course that was part of the reason. You were the other part. You made leaving work behind easy.'

Tess allowed herself a little smile of pure joy, because whatever came out in the wash, nothing would ever erase the warm pleasure that his admission was giving her, and like a kid in a toy shop she didn't want the experience to end. When would she have the opportunity to visit that place again?

'When you asked to prolong our relationship, I reacted out of habit and instinct. Both told me to walk away. I didn't bother to question it, and once it had been done pride entered the equation. But you never left my head. It was as though you had become stuck there. No matter what I did, you followed me everywhere I went—a silent, nagging reminder of what I'd thrown away.'

'But you would never have said a word if I hadn't shown up in your office and told you that I was pregnant,' Tess said ruefully.

'Wouldn't I?' Matt caught her eyes and held her gaze. 'I'm inclined to think that I would have. I'm inclined to think that I would have been right here, in this place, doing what I'm doing now, even if you hadn't made life so much easier for me by falling pregnant.'

'But it was unplanned. You were furious. You *blamed* me!'

'I've never had any lessons in being in love. How was I to know what to say and how to react?'

'Being in love?' Her voice trembled, and her hands trembled too as he took them in his.

He stroked her fingers with his thumb. Sincerity blazed from his eyes. 'If I'd ever known true love,' he admitted gruffly, 'I might have recognised the symptoms. But nothing prepared me for you, Tess. Looking back, I can see that Catrina was just an expectation I fulfilled without thinking too hard about it. You were the unexpected. You crash-landed into my life and everything changed overnight. I didn't come here to take you away against your will, and I'm sorry that that was the impression I ended up giving.'

'You love me?' She repeated it with wonder, trying it out on her tongue for size and liking the way it felt. Too good to be true. But when she looked at him she knew that he meant every word of what he had said. 'I love *you*,' she whispered. 'I slept with you because I loved you. You were everything my head told me I shouldn't want, but you crash-landed into my life as well…'

'I want to marry you, Tess. I don't want to marry you because you're having our baby. I want to marry you because my life isn't complete unless you're in it. I want to go to sleep with you beside me every night, and I want to wake up in the morning with you right next to me.'

With a sigh of contentment, Tess crawled onto his lap and closed her eyes, happy to be enfolded in his warmth and to feel his fingers gently stroke her hair.

'I've never been so happy in my entire life,' she confessed. 'I think I might cry, given half a chance.'

'Will you marry me as soon as possible?' he breathed. 'I know you probably don't want to take the attention away from your sister, but I don't know how long I can wait. I want you to flash my ring on your finger so that every man out there knows that he's not to come within ten feet of you unless specifically given permission.'

Tess laughed into his shoulder, and then wriggled so that she could look up at him.

'That's ultra-possessive…'

'I'm an ultra-possessive man,' he growled, 'and don't ever forget it.' At last he felt free to touch her, to feel the wonder of her body that was slowly going to be transformed with his baby in it. He pushed his hands up under her tee shirt and groaned as the rounded curves of her breasts filled them. He stroked her nipples, and the familiar feel of them hardening under his touch was beyond erotic.

'Is there any chance that a family member might surprise me in the middle of making love to you?' he questioned in a shaky undertone. 'Because if there is, then we're going to have to get to your bedroom quickly. I love you and I want you and I need you. It feels like it's been years…'

Upstairs, on her small double bed, they made love with sweet, lingering slowness. To Matt it really did feel as though it had been years since he had touched her, even though it had been only a matter of a couple of weeks.

He touched her everywhere. He kissed and nuzzled the breasts that would enlarge over the months, and suckled on nipples that would darken and distend. When he came into her, her slippery sheath brought him to an almost immediate orgasm. Never had making love been such a liberating experience—but, then again, never had a woman unlocked him in the way she had...

They were married less than two months later. It was a quiet and very romantic ceremony, at the local church where her parents had been members of the congregation for ever. Matt's parents and a handful of close friends made the journey, and of course Samantha was the centre of attention and as excitable as it was possible to be.

Tess had never doubted that her parents would embrace Matt as a member of their family, and they did. She was more surprised and thrilled that his parents were just as warm and welcoming towards her. Maybe it was because they could see the devotion on their son's face whenever he looked at her, and the love on his daughter's face at the prospect of Tess becoming her stepmother.

Small but subtle changes took place over the ensuing months. They continued to live in Matt's vast penthouse apartment, which was convenient for Samantha's school, but they also bought a country house of their own, and spent most weekends there. Tess hadn't abandoned the prospect of a career in teaching, although she was now going to wait until the baby was born and then take everything slowly and in her stride. The fact that both Matt and Samantha had one hundred percent belief in her was a huge encouragement.

Tess had never thought that such happiness was possible, and her feelings of contentment must have transmitted themselves to her baby, for little Isobel was born without drama. Eight and a half pounds of apple-cheeked, green-eyed, black-haired, good-natured little girl.

She could only smile and agree when Matt, as he was fond of doing, told them that at long last he was where he had always wanted to be—surrounded by beautiful females who had finally succeeded in domesticating him.

THE SECRETARY'S
BOSSMAN BARGAIN

RED GARNIER

Red Garnier is a fan of books, chocolate and happily-ever-afters. What better way to spend the day than combining all three? Travelling frequently between the United States and Mexico, Red likes to call Texas home. She'd love to hear from her readers at redgarnier@gmail.com. For more on upcoming books and current contests, please visit her website at: www.redgarnier.com.

This book is dedicated to the fabulous Desire™ editors, who provide endless wisdom, advice and inspiration.

Krista, Charles and Shana—
Thank you for the gift of writing for your line.

And to Diana Ventimiglia, who believed in me since the beginning. You're fondly remembered.

One

She was ready to beg him.

Virginia Hollis shuddered. She wrapped her arms around herself and stared out the back window of the sleek black Lincoln as it wound along the darkened streets of Chicago. People strolled down the block, hands in their pockets, chins neatly tucked to their chests to shield their faces from the biting wind. Men held cell phones to their ears; women struggled with their shopping bags. One glimpse made it seem like such a regular evening. An ordinary night.

But it wasn't ordinary. It couldn't be.

Because Virginia's world had stopped turning.

The men who'd knocked on her door this morning had had a message for her, and it had not been a kind one.

She inhaled deeply and glanced at her simple black dress and the delicate strappy heels on her pink-toed feet. It seemed important for her to look nice—not just respectable, but sophisticated, noble—because the favor she was to ask was anything but.

And she could think of no one else to ask but *him*. God. Just thinking of humiliating herself like this in front of *him* made her stomach churn.

Nervously, she tugged on the pearl strand draped around her neck and tried focusing on the city again. The pearls were smooth under her fingers, genuine and old, the only thing Virginia had been able to salvage from her mother's belongings.

Her father had lost it all.

Bet by bet, he'd lost the cars, the antiques, the house. Virginia had watched with a combination of helplessness and rage. She'd threatened, screamed, pleaded with the quickly aging man, all to no avail.

There was no stopping him. No stopping the gambling.

There was nothing left now.

Nothing but her.

And she could not, *could* not, turn a blind eye to those men—to the threat they posed. To the threat they had succinctly delivered. No matter how much she frowned upon what her father did, and no matter how many times she'd promised never again to speak to him about it and he continued gambling anyway, he was her father. Her only family.

Once he'd been a businessman. Respected, admired even. Now it saddened her to think what she'd become.

Virginia didn't know how much he owed. She'd rather not know. All she knew was the deal she'd struck with those three surly men that morning. She had a month to come up with one hundred thousand dollars, during which time they would leave him alone.

In her wildest dreams, Virginia had never imagined coming up with that amount of money, on such little time. But while *she* couldn't, Marcos Allende could.

The little hairs on her arms pricked to attention at the thought of him. Her boss was a quiet, devastatingly handsome man. Some said he was gifted; his touch was that of a Midas. While Virginia had only been his assistant for a year—his third of three assistants, because it seemed one alone couldn't handle the daunting task of having him as boss—in that length of time, she had seen enough of him to agree.

The man was out of context.

He was bold, ruthless and proud. Single-handedly, he'd spotted, bought and righted troubled companies, and he'd created an empire. He inspired respect and admiration among peers and fear among his enemies. Judging by the overwhelming number of phone calls he received from the female population of Chicago, Virginia could tell they adored him. And in Virginia herself, the man inspired things she dared not consider.

Every morning when she stepped into his office, he would study her with that dark, compelling gaze and disturb every inch and atom of her body with the hot intimacy in his eyes. She would always try to act professionally, to look away when his stare became inappropriately long. But his eyes had a way of undressing her, of speaking in silence, of summoning visions in her mind about him and her and skin and sweat. Yet tonight she was on her way to him for one purpose only, and she reminded herself that her visit to his lair at such a late hour might not be welcome.

With his assistants he was always the firm, quiet boss, but Marcos Allende was reputed to have a hell of a temper, one she might witness tonight for the very first time.

Her stomach clenched when the car pulled into the ample driveway of one of the Windy City's most luxurious apartment buildings, situated on the heavily trafficked Michigan Avenue. A uniformed valet opened the door.

She mumbled a quick "thank you" and stepped out of the car, walking into the sumptuous apartment building with an eerie calm that belied every one of the roiling emotions inside her.

She made no eye contact with the people milling around the area, but instead focused all of her attention on the polished bronze doors at the far end of the lobby.

"Mr. Allende is expecting you."

An elevator attendant waited for her. He slipped a card into the top slot inside the confined elevator space and lit the top *P* before stepping out with a bow. "Good evening, madam."

The doors closed and Virginia stared at her blurry reflection.

Oh, God, please let him help me. I'll do anything. Anything...

Long seconds later, the doors rolled open to reveal the penthouse—a vast room with black granite floors, dimly lit and lavishly furnished. The walls could've been covered in crisp green bills and screamed the owner's net worth just as loudly. To a mortal, his place seemed as inaccessible in price as the owner was claimed to be in character.

Virginia stepped inside. A pair of elegant, willowy bronzes flanked the entry and a massive oil painting with vibrant black brushstrokes hung at the end wall. Before she could absorb the rest of the opulent area, as though drawn by some unknown force of nature, her gaze landed on him. He stood next to the bar at the far end of the living room. He was as elegant and unmoving as the designer furniture surrounding him. Dark, tall, detached. He faced the window, his broad back filling the shoulders of his jacket. Her heart thumped as she took a step forward, the click of her heels on granite magnified in the silence.

"I trust you had a fine ride."

Her flesh pebbled at the hum of his voice. So husky. So mellow. As though he were no threat to anyone. The crackling energy around him dispelled the notion fast.

"I did. Thank you for sending a car, and for seeing me on such short notice," she said quietly.

Starting to shake inside, she advanced toward the living room, stepping lightly across a plush Persian rug. He didn't turn. Virginia wasn't certain she even wanted him to. Every time their gazes met, a bolt of electricity would shoot through her. Sometimes he didn't even need to speak. His eyes did it for him. And in her mind, he said the wickedest things to her.

Now here she was, in his apartment, ready to face that bold, virile man she'd fantasized about. Ready to beg him.

Never mind Virginia had her modestly successful life, which she'd tried to live by the book. Never mind she'd paid her bills on time and tried first and foremost to stay out of trouble. Never mind anything but what had to be done. Saving her father. Doing anything she had to, to make him safe again.

She could've sworn Marcos read her thoughts just now, for he whispered, "Are you in trouble, Virginia?" While still gazing out the window as though mesmerized by the tiny flicker of city lights.

She swallowed, eyeing his back. "It appears I am."

"And you came to ask for my help?"

A ball of unease settled in the pit of her stomach, and the words seemed to be wrenched from her throat. "I do need your help, Marcos."

He turned, and she was rendered motionless by the sheer black power of his stare. "How much?"

Her heart pounded faster. His face was so exquisitely masculine, and there was something so naughty about him—his attitude, his dark good looks, his accent—that a dormant part of her found thrilling and frightening at once. Every inch of his Latin blood showed in his bronzed skin, the very masculinity oozing from his pores.

His inquisitive gaze traveled with interest down the length of her body until she could bear no more. She lifted her chin with pride, though the way she wrung her hands before her wasn't all that convincing. "I—I don't expect anything for free. I wanted to see you about an advance. A loan. Perhaps I could do more work for you. Special projects."

His eyelids dropped as he sighted her lips. "You're very pretty tonight, Virginia."

The low seduction in his words made her heart clench in a fistful of thrill. She fought the thrill, telling herself he was a sexy, virile man—and that he must look at all women this way. Which was why they called him. All. The. Time! When those eyes were on her, he made her feel like the sexiest woman alive—like the only woman alive.

"I'm trying to raise…" She paused, summoning all her courage. "I'm trying to raise one hundred thousand dollars. Can you help me?" she asked him then, lowering her face. As she spoke, she felt so…so cheap…so humiliated to be asking for money…

"Is that all you need?" he asked softly. As though it were nothing. A paltry sum. And to him, with all his billions, of course it would be.

He surveyed her in silence. "May I ask why you need it?"

Her gaze flicked up to his, and she shook her head. She couldn't bear it.

His lips twitched and the corners of his eyes crinkled, almost—*almost*—managing to make him less threatening. "You won't tell me?" he prodded.

"If you don't mind," she mumbled. She tugged the hem of her dress to her knees when his gaze ventured to her legs and lingered. "So there's nothing I could do for you? In exchange for this…incredible salary?" God. She couldn't even say the amount it seemed so out of reach.

He laughed, and Virginia didn't think she'd ever heard him laugh before. The sound resembled the roll of distant thunder.

He set his glass on the nearby bar and signaled to the twin leather couches. "Sit."

She sat. Her back was stiff and straight as she tracked his lithe moves around the room. How could a big man move with such grace? How could—

"Wine?"

"No."

He poured two glasses nonetheless. His hands moved skillfully—too skillfully not to notice—and brought one to her.

"Drink."

She grasped the fluted glass and stared at a faraway bronze sculpture, trying not to breathe for fear of what his scent might do to her. He smelled so amazingly good. Earthy and musky and male. She drew in a shaky breath until he dropped onto the couch across from hers.

When he stretched his arms out behind him, he made the couch appear small, his wide frame overwhelming the bone-colored leather designer piece. Under his jacket, the dress shirt he wore was unbuttoned at the top, gifting her with a view of smooth, bronzed skin and a polished gold cross.

She wanted to touch him. She wondered what that bronze skin would feel like under her fingers, if his cross was cold or warm…

Suddenly sensing his scrutiny, she raised her chin and smiled.

Lifting one black brow, Marcos opened his hand and signaled to her. "You're not drinking."

Virginia started, then obediently sipped. "It's…good. Very…um, rich."

"Have I ever bitten you?"

She almost choked on the wine, blinked, and then, then she saw the smile. A prime smile. Rare, like everything valuable, higher on one end than the other.

"I can see this is difficult for you," he said, with a glimmer of warmth in his eyes.

"No. I mean, yes. It is." He had no clue!

He set his glass aside, crossed his arms over his chest, and snuggled back as if to watch a movie. "You don't trust me?"

Her heart skipped a nervous beat.

Trust him? She respected him. Admired him. Was in awe of him and, because of his power, even a little afraid of him. And maybe, she realized, she trusted him, too. From what she'd seen, Marcos—quiet, solid, heart-of-gold Marcos—had proved to be nothing but a champion for his people. A lion protecting his cubs. When Lindsay, assistant two, had been weeping for months after her twins were born, Marcos had hired an army of nannies and sent her off to a second honeymoon in Hawaii with her husband.

Lindsay was still talking about Maui.

And when Mrs. Fuller's husband passed away, the over-wrought woman had cried more tears reminiscing about all that Marcos had done to support and aid her family than she had cried at the funeral.

No matter how humiliating this was, how awful her situation and having him know it, she knew, like nothing in her life, he was as steady as a mountain.

Holding his gaze, she replied in all honesty. "I trust you more than I trust anyone."

His face lit in surprise, and he scraped his chin between two blunt fingers. "And yet you don't tell me what troubles you?"

The thought that he—the man she most honored, esteemed—would know her life was in such shambles squished her heart like a bug. "I would tell you what I need the money for if I thought it mattered, and I would tell you if that is the only way you'll give it to me."

With an expression that would befit a lone hunting wolf,

Marcos rose and strode over, then pried the glass from her fingers. "Come with me."

Unnerved that she couldn't even begin to guess the thoughts in that unique, labyrinthine mind of his, Virginia followed him down the wide, domed hallway of his penthouse, becoming acutely aware of his formidable frame next to her.

And she couldn't help but wonder if maybe she wasn't a little bit the fool for trusting him after all.

Predatorily, Marcos studied her profile, her nose, the untamed, unruly bounce of her curls. She bit her lip in nervousness. Where was he taking her?

Visions of a bedroom flicked across her mind, and her cheeks flamed hot.

He opened the last door for her, and Virginia entered the darkened room, shamed at her own quickening pulse.

"Your home office?" she asked.

"Yes."

He flicked on the light switch, and the room burst to life. Bookshelves lined three of the four walls. A Turkish rug spread across the sitting area. Five glossy wood file cabinets formed a long, neat row behind his desk. No adornments. No picture frames. No distractions. As fine in taste as the rest of his apartment, with a state-of-the-art computer perched atop a massive desk, his office screamed two words: *no nonsense.*

"I like it." She strode inside, the knowledge that this was his private, personal space making her blood bubble. Her fingers itched with the overwhelming urge to organize the stacks of papers on his desk.

"I know about your father, Miss Hollis."

Dread sunk like a bowling ball in her stomach. "You do?"

She spun around, and when he stepped into the room, Marcos achieved the impossible: he made it shrink in size.

"You do not exist in the world I do without being cautious about everyone who comes into your inner circle. I have a dossier on everyone who works in close proximity with me, and I know every detail of their lives. Yes, I know about his problem."

"Oh."

What else did he know?

He passed her as he crossed the room, and she stifled a tremor as if he'd been a cool hurricane wind. "Why didn't you come to me before?" he asked, matter of fact.

"I'm here now," she whispered.

Halting behind his desk, he shoved the leather chair aside and leaned over the surface. His shirt stretched taut over his bunched shoulders and his eyebrows pulled low. "How bad is it?"

"It… The gambling comes and goes." Flushing at his scrutiny, she turned to busy herself with the books on the shelves, and then said, as if he'd expertly unlatched a closed door which had been near bursting with secrets, "He's out of control. He keeps betting more than what he has and more than I could possibly earn."

"Is that the only reason you're here?"

His voice grew so textured, a jolt of feminine heat rippled through her. She spun around—shocked by the question. Shocked by the answering flutter in her womb.

Her breath stopped.

His gaze. It was open. Raw. Revealed a galvanizing wildness, a primitive hunger lurking—lurking *there*—in the depths of his eyes, like a prowling beast.

Pent-up desire rushed through her bloodstream as he continued to stare. Stare at her in a way no man, ever, should look at a woman and expect her to survive. "Is that the only reason you're here tonight? Virginia?"

As if in a trance, she moved forward on shaky legs, closer to his desk. "Y-yes."

"You want nothing else? Just the money?"

How to talk? How to think? Breathe? Her heart felt ready to pop from the pressure of answering. "N-nothing."

In the back of her mind, she vaguely realized how simple and unassuming her needs sounded as she voiced them. When they were not. They were tangled. They had grown fierce with his proximity. Out of reason, out of context, out of *control*.

"Will you help me," she murmured as she reached the desk, and somehow the plea sounded as intimate as if she'd asked for a kiss.

"I will." Deep and rough, the determination in his answer flooded her with relief.

He was going to help her.

In her soaring mind, Marcos was mounted on a white charger holding up a flag that read "Virginia."

And she...well, hers might be a banner. A neon sign. A brand on every inch of her body and possibly her heart. Marcos Allende. God, she was a fool.

"I don't expect something for nothing," she said. Her voice throbbed even as a tide of relief flooded her.

It was as if some unnatural force drew her to him, pulled her to get closer and closer. Did the force come from him? From her? If it weren't for the desk—always the desk between them—where would she be?

No. The obstacle wasn't a desk. It was everything. Everything. Nothing she could ever arrange or fix or clean.

Marcos raked one hand through his hair, then seized a runaway pen and thrust it into an empty leather holder. "I'll give you the money. But I have a few requests of my own."

"Anything," she said.

His gaze was positively lethal. His hands—they made fists. "There's something I want. Something that *belongs* to me. Something I must have or I'll lose my mind with wanting it."

A shiver ran hot and cold down her spine.

He wasn't speaking of her—of course he wasn't—but nonetheless, she felt something grip inside her as though he were. What would it feel like for Marcos to want her so fiercely? "I...understand."

"Do you?"

He smiled bleakly at her, then continued around his desk.

He swept up a gemstone globe from the edge and spun it around, a lapis lazuli ocean going round and round. "Here." His finger stopped the motion, marking a country encrusted in granite for her eyes. "What I want is here." He tapped.

Tap tap tap.

She stepped closer, longingly lifting a fingertip to stroke the length of the country he signaled. Travel had seemed so far down the line of her priorities she hardly gave any thought to it now.

"Mexico," she whispered.

His finger slid. It touched hers. He watched. And she watched. And neither of them moved. His finger was blunt and tan, hers slim and milky. Both over Mexico. It wasn't even a touch, not even half a touch. And she felt the contact in every fiber of her lonely, quivering being.

He turned his head, their faces so close that his pupils looked enormously black to her. A swirling vortex. He whispered, as though confessing his every hidden desire and sin, "I'm after Allende."

She connected the name immediately. "Your father's business?"

"The business he lost."

He set down the globe, and again, his finger. This time the back of it stroked down her cheek. Marcos touching her, Marcos looking so strangely at her, oh, God. He smelled so good she felt lightheaded.

"And you believe I can help?" she asked, one step away

from him, then two. Away from his magnificent, compelling force, away from what he made her want.

He scraped a restless hand down his face. "The owner has managed it poorly and contacted me for help." A tiny muscle ticked at the back of his jaw. "I'm usually a sucker for the ailing, I admit, but things are different in this case." Disgusted, he shook his head. "I do not intend to help her, you understand?"

"Yes." She didn't understand, exactly, but rumors around the office were that *no one* mentioned Allende to Marcos unless they wanted their head bitten off.

He paced. "I'm taking it hostilely if I have to."

"I see."

"I could use an escort."

Escort.

"I need someone I can count on. Most of all—" he crossed his arms and his enigmatic black gaze bored into hers "—I need someone willing to pretend to be my lover."

Lover.

Her hands went damp and she discreetly wiped them at her sides. "Lover." When his long steps brought him over to her, she instinctively backed away until her calves hit a small ottoman.

Unperturbed, Marcos headed over to the bookshelf, his strides sure and unhurried. "Would you be interested in doing this for me?"

Her head whizzed with unwelcome, naughty thoughts. Thoughts of Mexico and Marcos. Martinis and Marcos. Mariachis and Marcos. "Yes, definitely." But what exactly did he mean by *pretend?* "So what would you expect of me, for how long?" An unprecedented thrill was trickling along her veins.

He rummaged through the books, moving tome after tome. "A week as my escort in Monterrey, and perhaps some work after hours until I'm able to close. I'll be sure to handle your…little problem."

"That's all?"

He shot her a look of incredulity. "That's not enough?"

She just smiled. And waited.

And watched.

The muscles under his shirt flexed as he reached the top shelf and pulled out a huge leather volume.

"Maybe your company at the Fintech dinner?" he continued, winged eyebrows flying up. "Would you mind? Going with me?"

She fiddled with her pearls, unable to stop fidgeting. "You… I can always arrange a date for you."

His lips curved upward as he waved the heavy book in her line of vision as easily as if it were a mere piece of paper. "I don't want a date, Miss Hollis. Here. You can take this—a bit about Monterrey, if you'd like." He set it on the ottoman. He had a lovely, lazy kind of smile, and she felt it curl her toes.

"I feel like I'm robbing you blind," she said, lifting the shiny book.

He paused in the middle of the room and stared at her with his deep gypsy eyes. "If I allowed it, it wouldn't be robbery, would it."

She saw his cool, brief smile and flattened the book tight against her breasts when they pricked. Traitors. But he'd smiled three times tonight. Three. Or more? Three or more just had to be a record.

"You're an asset to my company," he continued in an unnaturally husky voice, stalking back around the desk. "A week of your time is valuable to me. You're hard-working, smart. Loyal. You've gained my trust, Virginia, and my admiration—both difficult feats."

A feathery sensation coursed along her skin. She was certain he used that same self-assured tone in his meetings, but she wondered if it had the same thrilling effect on the members of his board.

When she couldn't seem to find anything useful to do other than ogle stupidly, she automatically did what she always did to cure herself. She set the book aside and began arranging the papers at the edge of his desk—from a messy pile to a neat pile. "T-thank you for the compliments. I enjoy working at Fintech very much. And for you…of course. Which is why I don't want to jeopardize my position."

She continued arranging, aware that he was doing nothing—nothing—but towering a few feet away and watching her. Like he did in the office sometimes. He would stop what he was doing and watch with those black, exciting eyes.

"What will we say at the office?" she rambled.

Gossip could be ruthless at Fintech. To think Lindsay or Mrs. Fuller might believe she'd done something un-professional to land a business trip with Marcos gripped her with unease.

When Marcos didn't reply, she looked up and caught the wicked sparkle in his eyes. She had the strangest sensation that he'd been staring at her bottom. "We will say that I ordered you to accompany me, of course. You are my assistant, after all."

His brows drew together and he peered at her hard, as though daring her to argue with him.

But a pang struck her right where it hurt; she knew she could never be more than an assistant to him. He was Marcos Allende. He could be Zeus himself, he was so unattainable.

Virginia was dreaming if she wanted more than a seat outside his office. Dreaming if she thought the desire in his eyes was for her. Dreaming to think that, even if it were, he'd do something about it and she'd dare let him.

No. She could not, would not allow herself to continue

harboring those foolish nightly fantasies about him. The daily ones had to go, too. It was hopeless, and it was hurtful, and it was stupid. He was offering her an assignment.

When the pile couldn't be a more perfect tower, she straightened it with as much dignity as she could muster. "I'd be happy to be your escort."

He nodded slowly. "Good. Great. Excellent." His voice was strangely terse, so utterly rich it seemed to sink into her body until it pulsed inside of her. "I knew we'd come to an agreement, then."

Dealing with a tumult of emotions without betraying herself proved difficult. Excitement warred with worry, gratitude with desire.

One week with him in Mexico. Playing his escort, his *lover*—a role Virginia had slipped into plenty of times in her mind. But this would be real, a real pretense, where she—inexperienced and naive in the ways of men—would pretend to be lover to a hunk, god and legend. Where she could even seize the moment, do something reckless she would no doubt come to regret and plant a kiss on the lips of the man who was unknowingly responsible for Virginia not wanting others. Did she dare? Did she fly? Did she have magic powers?

Was there even the possibility of being a good pretend lover to him after he'd dated actresses, duchesses, centerfolds?

Growing more and more unsettled at her new assignment, she picked up the book, *Monterrey: Tras el Tiempo,* and headed for the door, stealing one last glimpse of him. "Thank you, Marcos. For…everything. Good night."

"Virginia." When she was halfway down the hall, he caught up and seized her wrist, urging her around. His clasp sent a shiver skidding up her arm. "It's a five-hour flight. I mean to leave tomorrow afternoon. Can you be ready by then?"

Ready, she thought wildly.

She could be a virgin Mayan princess prepared her whole life for this ultimate sacrifice, be an Anne Boleyn laughingly led to her beheading, and she would *still* not be ready for Marcos Allende.

But she smiled. Her nod came out jerky.

He seized her chin and raised it slightly. She sucked in a breath at the contact, and the tips of her breasts brushed against his chest. "Will you be ready, Virginia?" he persisted.

Her legs quivered. All kinds of things moved inside her body. His breath was hot and fragrant on her face, and his lush, mobile mouth was so close, a moan rose to her throat, trapped there. Like the wanting of a year, trapped there.

How would he *feel* against her? His mouth? His hands?

He was so hard all over, so unlike any other man she'd known. He made her feel safe and protected and special, but he also made her burn, frightened her with the way she needed *something* from him more than she could possibly bear or understand.

She suppressed a shiver. "I'll be ready," she assured, a nervous excitement flourishing in her breast as she took a healthy step back. "Thank you. I know…I know you could ask someone else to do this for you. And I doubt you'd have to pay for her company."

His eyes smoldered, and his face went taut with some unnameable emotion. "Yes, but I want you."

I want you.

A ribbon of hope unfurled inside her. It feathered from the top of her head down to the soles of her feet. She didn't trust it. Marcos didn't mean the words the way they had sounded to her ears. Ears starved for anything he ever said to her.

She told herself, firmly, until it was embedded in her brain, that Marcos wanted someone trustworthy, someone biddable, and his lionlike instinct surely prodded him to help her.

And, oh, how she had wanted to be different. To him. Not

charity. Not like his stepbrother, a reckless playboy Marcos had to rescue time after time—not like all the strangers and friends who called him every day, seeking his counsel, his power, his help.

Everyone wanted something of Marcos Allende, for underneath the hard exterior lay a man with a strong, solid heart of gold. His faith in people was inspiring, his ruthlessness rivaled only by his mercy. Marcos…took care of you. And those early mornings when Virginia had stepped into his office to find his broad shoulders bent over the desk, his shirt rolled up to his elbows, his silky black hair falling over his forehead, his voice husky and his eyes tired from lack of sleep, her heart had ached with wanting to take care of that big, proud warrior. *Who gives you back what you give, Marcos Allende?*

Is there anyone out there who takes care of you for a change?

Now she determined that whatever he wanted, she would give. "You won't regret it, Marcos," she softly promised. "Helping me, I mean."

His lips twitched. That amused smile did things to her stomach, but it didn't seem to reach his eyes. Those remained hooded, unreadable. He ran the back of one finger down her cheek, the touch sparking fire. "It is I who hopes you never regret this visit."

Two

"Your new lover?"

Silent, Marcos stood at the living room window and broodingly watched the car pull away with Virginia inside it. From the penthouse, the Lincoln looked like a sleek black beetle, slipping into the intermittent traffic before the apartment building.

The pressure in his chest mounted with the distance.

His blood still pumped hot inside his veins and his head swam with a thousand thoughts, all of them X-rated.

"Or a mistress maybe?"

Twisting around, he faced his newest guest, the inquisitive Jack Williams—ex-corporate spy and now self-made millionaire. He was helping himself to a bag of nuts he'd obtained from the bar.

"My assistant," Marcos said tonelessly, swirling his newly poured Scotch in his hand. The cubes clinked in the glass.

Jack had arrived promptly at eleven as promised—the tall, blond Texan was never late, and, like a golden retriever listening to a particularly silent whistle, he had cocked his head when he spotted Virginia almost in Marcos's arms. As she whispered goodbye, Marcos's own instincts had flared to life and whispered that she wanted to stay.

But when "Williams the Bastard"—as the press had dubbed him—said he'd deliver, he delivered. And unfortunately what Marcos expected couldn't wait.

Still, he couldn't allow his friend to get the wrong impression of her, so he lifted his glass in a mocking toast. "She makes good coffee."

Jack popped an almond into his mouth and munched. "Aha. In bed?"

Marcos crossed the living room and headed back into the office, Jack trailing behind him.

Cranky, frustrated and exhausted, he set the glass atop a stack of papers on his desk and sank into the high-backed leather seat. "I'm not that man, Jack. Never mix business with pleasure, remember?"

But Virginia's sweet, fragrant scent lingered in the air. A torment to his straining body. A mockery to his words.

He respected his employees, took pride in being regarded as a man with moral fiber. And yet when it came to Virginia Hollis, it seemed he was reduced to the instincts of a caveman.

His friend's smooth, easy chuckle coming from the threshold somehow cranked up his frustration. "I remember. But the question is: do *you?* Should I have fetched a spoon, buddy? You looked ready to eat her."

Marcos would have scoffed. He certainly didn't welcome the canny twinkle in Jack's eye. But then he remembered the desperate urge he'd had to kiss Virginia…the exquisite scent of her skin, so close to his…the surprisingly fine feel of her in his arms, stirring and enticing beyond belief…

His chest cramped with emotion as he dragged a hand down his hot face. "Perhaps the old adage is true, and some rules are meant to be broken—especially if you're the moron living by them."

"Don't go there, Marcos." Jack pushed away from the door, dead serious. "I've been there. Not fun, man. Not fun for you, definitely not fun for her. Office affairs always end badly—no matter how well you plan them when you begin."

Marcos pondered the massive, crowded bookcase on the wall across from him. A near bursting sensation was lodged in the pit of his gut. He didn't want to hurt her. Hell, he hadn't wanted to *want* her.

Diablos, but he'd been sexually frustrated since the day he'd hired her. She was demure, desperate and determined, and Marcos had feared she'd be a distraction. But he hadn't counted on the fact that his primitive response to her would reach such a fever pitch.

"I've never gotten involved with an employee in my life— but she's different, Jack. And yes, I am aware of how that sounds."

Reclining in his seat with a grimace, he opened his cuff buttons and rolled up his sleeves.

He was actually considering, perhaps he was even past considering and had already made up his mind, giving them both what they'd wanted for months.

He was a man, flesh and blood like all the others. There was only so much he could stand. And Virginia...no matter how energetically she tried to conceal her reactions to him, she responded. Viscerally, primitively—a woman underneath the tidy assistant after all. A sweet, lovely woman who knew instinctively when a man wanted her. No, not wanted— Marcos *burned* for her.

And now he'd asked—practically demanded—she spend a week with him. Pretending to be his lover. At a time when all his energies, all his attention, needed to be on the one prize he'd sought to gain for so long.

Allende.

He hadn't been certain whether to ask her as escort. She was too much a temptation to play lovers with, and in order to successfully achieve his goals, focus was key.

But tonight the lovely Virginia—alone and financially abandoned by her family, something Marcos could identify with—had turned to him for help.

Tonight, as he'd gazed into her bright, fierce eyes, he couldn't deny himself any longer.

He wanted her.

He'd offered her a position for a week, true, but that was merely a guise for what he really wanted to do.

Her powerful effect would linger with him long after he left his office at night. He thought of her continually, every hour. He relived their encounters in his mind sometimes, enjoyed hearing her laugh at Lindsay's antics when his office doors were parted. He could not push her image away at night and loathed to see her in trouble when she seemed to seek so little of it for herself.

He'd made a mental list long ago with plenty of valid reasons to leave her alone.

She was an innocent, he was not. She was vulnerable, he could hurt her. She was his employee, he was her boss. There were dozens of reasons to stay the hell away from Virginia.

The ways she'd looked at him tonight pulverized them all.

"Here. I have just the thing to cheer you up." Jack stepped outside and returned rummaging through his leather briefcase. He yanked out a manila folder and held it out. "There you go, big man. Your wish is my command."

Marcos plucked the file from his hand and immediately honed in on the name printed across the tab. Marissa Galvez.

He smiled darkly. "Ah, my rainmaker. Everything here, I assume?"

"Everything on Marissa and her sleazy little deals. She's quite a busy little bee. You'll find it to be riveting reading. Took me a while, as you can see—but I did give you my word to have it ready by tonight."

Marcos skimmed through the pages, not surprised that the file was as thick as the woman was scheming.

Marissa Galvez. A shaft of anger sliced through him. The lady had hopes of a reconciliation before discussing numbers?

Of course she did. She read *Forbes*. Was smart enough to realize the son was worth more than the father she'd left him for, not thousands or millions, but billions. She knew the company, which should have rightfully been *his,* was prime for takeover and it wouldn't take much but a few savvy connections to learn it had been Marcos who'd been buying the outstanding stock.

Unfortunately, insulting Marissa's renewed interest in him wouldn't do to accomplish his goals. But a beautiful, smiling lover would slowly and surely take care of her dreams of reconciliation—and let them get down to the real business at hand.

Allende. *My company.*

"Mind telling me how you're going to convince the delectable woman to sell? Without succumbing to her request for some personal attention before discussing numbers?" Jack queried.

Marcos lunged to his feet, waving the evidence in the Texan's face. "With this. It's my game now, my rules." He met his friend's sharp, blue-eyed stare and his lips flattened to a grim, strained line. "Allende is in a vulnerable position. Sooner or later, she'll have to sell."

"Not to you, she doesn't."

Marcos shrugged disinterestedly. "She knows she's game for a hostile takeover. And she knows I'm the shark after her.

She wouldn't have called if she didn't want to get on my good side."

And I've got my pretty, green-eyed "lover."

"Will she?"

And her pretty little mouth. "What?"

"Get on your good side?"

"When you start wearing a tutu, Jack. Of course not."

Distaste filled him as he recalled her phone call. Dangling Allende up to him like bait, proposing they discuss it in her bed. She'd played with him as a naive, noble, seventeen-year-old boy, but it would be an ice age in hell before she played with the man.

"She called because she wants you back," Jack pointed out.

"Fortunately, I have an escort," he said and headed to the window, a part of him somehow expecting to see the Lincoln. "Being I will be conveniently taken, we'll have to forego the personal and get down to the numbers."

"I see now. So the lovely lady is key."

Those eyes. Big, bright, clear green, and so expressive he thought she'd pummeled his gut when she'd looked at him so adoringly. She made him feel…noble. Decent. Desperate to save her ten times over in exchange for another worshipful gaze.

When she'd called to request a moment of his time only hours ago, he'd allowed himself a brief flight of fantasy. He fantasized she'd been ready to succumb to him, ready to admit what already threatened to become inevitable. Even as he allowed himself the luxury of the fantasy, he knew she was too cautious and respectable for that.

It was up to him now. What was he going to do?

He shot Jack a sidelong look. "Marissa will get what's coming to her." And Virginia…

Jack swept up his briefcase with flair. "The devil on a Falcon jet, yes." He saluted from the threshold and flashed his signature I'm-Jack-the-Ripper grin. "I'll let you pack, my friend."

"My gratitude to you, Williams. And send the bill to Mrs. Fuller this week, she'll take care of it."

When Jack said an easy "will do" and disappeared, Marcos swallowed the last of his Scotch, his eyebrows furrowing together as he thought of the demure strand of pearls around Virginia's neck tonight. His woman wouldn't wear such little pearls. She'd wear diamonds. Tahitians. Emeralds.

With a swell of possessiveness, he brought to mind the lean, toned form of her body, watched countless times across his office desk, countless times when it had been by sheer determination that he'd forced his scrutiny back to his work.

A size six, he predicted, and promptly pulled his contact list from the top drawer and flipped through the pages.

If she was playing his lover, then one thing was certain: Virginia Hollis would look the part.

In the quiet interior of the Fixed Base Operator which specialized in servicing company jets, Marcos stood with his hands in his pockets. He brimmed with anticipation and gazed out the window from the spacious sitting area while the Falcon 7X jet—a sleek, white dove and one of his faster babies—got fueled.

He'd like to blame his simmering impatience on the deal he was about to negotiate. But the truth was, his assistant was late, and he was impatient to see *her*.

Now a door of opportunity was wide open for them. An opportunity to interact outside the busy, hectic pace of his office. An opportunity to step out of their roles and, if they chose to, temporarily into a new one.

She'll pretend to be my lover.

That she had accepted to aid him in this manner made

him feel heady. For how long would they be able to pretend and only pretend? Three days, three hours, three minutes?

In the back of the room, the glass doors rolled open. The sounds of traffic sailed into the building and Marcos swung around. To watch Virginia stroll inside.

A balloon of protectiveness blossomed in his chest.

The only thing untidy about his assistant today was her hair. Wild, windblown and uncontrollable. The ebony curls framed a lovely oval face and eyes that were green and clear and thick-lashed. Hauling a small black suitcase behind her, she paused to store a bag of peanuts in the outside zippered compartment. The mint-green V-neck sweater she wore dipped sexily to show the barest hint of cleavage. His mouth went dry.

She straightened that agile body of hers and swiped a wave of ebony curls behind her shoulder. The scent of citrus—lemons, oranges, everything that made him salivate—wafted through the air as she continued hauling her suitcase forward. Christ, she was a sexpot.

"Virginia," he said.

Her head swiveled to his. "Marcos."

He smiled. The sight of her face, warm in the sunlight, made his lungs constrict. She wore no makeup except for a gloss, and with her curls completely free, she was the most enchanting thing he'd ever seen.

Licking her lips as he came forward, she pulled the suitcase up and planted it at her feet—a barrier between their bodies. "You got a head start on me," she said. She spoke in a throaty, shaky voice that revealed her nervousness.

He eyed her lips. Burnished a silky pink today, inciting him to taste.

"I apologize, I had some last-minute work out of the office."

Dragging in a breath, he jerked his chin in the direction of the long table down the hall, offering coffee, cookies, napkins—all that Virginia liked to toil with. "Fix yourself coffee if you want. We'll board in a few minutes."

"You? Coffee?"

Somberly he shook his head, unable to prevent noticing the subtle sway of her skirt-clad hips as she left her compact black suitcase with him and walked away.

He was fascinated. By the sweet-smelling, sexy package of Virginia Hollis. Five feet four inches of reality. Of *pretend* lover.

Cursing under his breath, he snatched her suitcase handle and rolled the bag up to his spot by the window. The pilots were storing his luggage, consisting mostly of shopping bags from Neiman Marcus.

He crossed his arms as he waited for their signal. The file the infallible Jack Williams had given him last night provided him with more than enough ammo to persuade Marissa to sell, yet even the knowledge of emerging victorious didn't make this particular task any easier. You could crush a bug in your fist and it still didn't mean you would enjoy it. But Allende—a transport company on its last breath, flailing for help—had his name on it.

It was his. To resuscitate or to murder.

Virginia drew up beside him and he went rigid, inhumanly aware of her body close to his. She was a subtle, scented, stirring presence.

Without so much as moving his head, he let his eyes venture to the front of her sweater. The fabric clung to the small, shapely, seductive swells of her breasts. A wealth of tenderness flooded him. Virginia had come dressed as his assistant in the sweater, her typical knee-length gray skirt, the simple closed-toe shoes with no personality. "I'm afraid this won't do," he murmured.

A smile danced on her lips as she tipped her face up in bewilderment. She seemed animated today, no more the worried siren begging for his assistance last night. "What won't do?"

Virginia. With her perfect oval face, creamy, elegant throat and bow-shaped morsel of a mouth that invited him to nibble. It really seemed easier to stop breathing than to continue saying *no* to those marshmallow-soft lips. "The sweater," he said quietly, signaling the length of her body with his hand. "The skirt. The sensible shoes. It won't do, Miss Hollis."

She set her coffee cup and napkin on a side table, then tucked her hair behind her ear. "I did pack a few dresses."

"Did you." His eyebrows furrowed together as he surveyed her pearls. "Designer dresses?"

"Why, no."

He raised his hand to the pearl necklace. "How attached are you," he whispered, trailing his finger across the glossy bumps, "to wearing these?"

She watched him for a moment, a telling wariness in her voice. "They were Mother's."

"Pretty. Very pretty." The pent-up desire that blazed inside him textured his voice. "You see, my lover…might wear something else." He was playing with fire. He didn't care. "My woman—" he plucked a pearl between two fingers "—would wear Tahitians. Diamonds. Emeralds."

Her eyes danced. "Are you afraid I won't look presentable?"

He dropped his hands and shot her a dead-serious look. "I'm afraid you will look too much like my assistant and not my lover."

But she kept on smiling, kept on enchanting him. "I see."

He frowned now. "Understand me, Virginia. If I'd wanted to be seen with my assistant, I'd have brought Mrs. Fuller."

This made her gasp, and the gasp did not make his scowl vanish. He nodded towards the Falcon. "Your new wardrobe is in the plane. There's a room in the back. Change."

Three

Of all the highhandedness, of all the *arrogance,* of all the bosses in the world—she had to be in debt to *Marcos.* Undoubtedly the most complicated.

While the jet motors hummed in the background, Virginia slipped into the slinky patterned dress inside the windowless little room at the back of the plane. Damn him. She had agreed to his request, but how was she supposed to reply to his autocratic commands? Worse, the clothes were divine. She couldn't in her right mind stay annoyed at a man with such exquisite taste. Her knight in shining armor.

Enthralled by how slight and satiny the dress felt against her body, she ran three fingers down the length of her hips, wishing there was a mirror to let her visually appreciate the dress's exquisite, plunging back. *And how is this necessary to his plan?* she wondered.

Gathering her courage with a steady intake of breath, she forced herself to step outside.

Throughout the tasteful wood and leather interior, the air

crackled with the suppressed energy of his presence. His head was bent. His powerful, well-built body overwhelmed a cream-colored, plush leather seat, and his hair—abused by his hands during the flight—gleamed in the sunlight as he read through a massive leather tome. He was clad all in black, and the short-sleeved polo shirt he wore revealed tanned, strong forearms corded with veins. Watching him, big and proud and silent, completely engrossed and unaware of her gaze, she felt like sighing.

With a quick mental shake, she walked down the wide plane aisle, noting the screen embedded in the wood-paneled wall behind Marcos's seat. The electronic map showed the plane just three red dashes away from the little dot of Monterrey. At least one more hour.

As she eased in between their seats, intent on taking her place across from him, one huge hand shot out and manacled her wrist. She was spun around, and she gasped. Then there was nothing to pry those glimmering eyes away from her, no shield from the scorching possessiveness flickering in their depths.

"No," he rasped, his voice hoarsened by how little he'd spoken during the flight.

A melting sensation spread down her thighs, his accent too delicious to not enjoy. *No, don't sit yet,* she thought he meant, but she couldn't be sure. No one could ever be too sure of anything with Marcos. Maybe it was *no* to the dress!

Aware of her chest heaving too close to his face, she tried to pry her wrist free but failed miserably. "I changed. Wasn't that what you wanted?"

He cocked his head farther back and stared, his grip loosening slightly. "You're angry at me."

"I…" She jerked her chin toward the book on his lap, wanting, needing him to remove his hand. "Please. Read."

For a woman who'd strived to become invisible for years, the last thing she felt now was unseen. The filmy Issa London dress hugged her curves subtly, the wrap-around style tied with a bow at her left hip. The fabric felt so feminine she became utterly conscious of her body—and how he peered at it in interest.

"You approve of the clothes I bought you, *amor?*" he said huskily.

Amor? A jolt went through her at the endearment. Panicking, she tugged with more force and whispered, halfheartedly, "You can let go of me now."

His gaze pierced her, his unyielding hand burning her wrist. By the way his touch spread like a wildfire, her boss may as well have been touching her elsewhere. Where her breasts ached, where the back of her knees tingled, where her nerves sparkled and where she felt hot and painfully aware of being empty.

He released her. So abruptly she almost stumbled.

Still reeling, Virginia sank into her seat like a deflated balloon. Her pulse thundered. Her hands shook as she strapped on her seat belt.

His intense regard from across the aisle became a living, breathing thing. "Does a man's interest offend you?" he asked silkily.

Blushing furiously, she propped her purse on her lap. "Did you know Monterrey has over five million people now?" She shoved the maps she'd printed at the office and lists of Spanish words back in her purse.

He slapped the book shut and let it drop with a resounding thump at his feet. "Would *my* interest offend you, Virginia?"

She squinted at him, expecting a laugh, a chuckle, a smile at least.

He was perfectly sober. Excruciatingly handsome and sober.

Oh, no. No, no, no, he wouldn't do this. She was prepared

to do a job, but she was not prepared to allow herself to become a man's…plaything.

No matter how much she fantasized about him in private.

With a nervous smile, Virginia shook a chastising finger at him, but it trembled. "Mr. Allende, the closer we've gotten to Mexico, the stranger you've become."

Silence.

For an awful second, her blatant claim—part teasing and part not—hung suspended in the air. Virginia belatedly bit her lip. What had possessed her to say that to her boss? She curled her accusing finger back into her hand, lowering it in shame.

Sitting in a deceptively relaxed pose, he crossed his arms over his broad chest and regarded her with an unreadable expression. Then he spoke in that hushed, persuasive way of his, "Do you plan to call me *Mr. Allende* when you're out there pretending to be my lover?"

Self-conscious and silently berating herself, Virginia tucked the skirt of her dress under her thighs, her hands burrowing under her knees. "I didn't mean to insult you."

"I'm not insulted."

She racked her brain for what to say. "I don't know what came over me."

He leaned forward with such control that even a glare might have been more welcome by her. "You call me Marcos most of the time. You call me Marcos when you want my favors. Why now, today, do you call me Mr. Allende?"

She looked away, feeling as if her heart were being wrung. He spoke so quietly, almost pleadingly, that he could be saying something else to her—something that did not smack her with misery.

Because I've never been alone with you for so long, she thought.

She hauled in a ragged breath and remained silent.

The plane tilted slightly, eventually coming in for a landing as smoothly as it had flown. Its speed began to ease. If only her hammering heart would follow.

They taxied down a lane decorated with large open plane hangars, and she fixed her attention on the screen behind him, resolved to smooth out the awkwardness. "Do you believe Allende will be a safe investment for Fintech?" she asked. She knew it was all that remained of his past. His mother had passed away long before his father had.

"It's poorly managed." He extracted his BlackBerry from his trouser pocket and powered it on. "Transport vehicles have been seized by the cartels. Travel is less safe these days in this country. For it to become successful, strict security measures will need to be put in place, new routes, new personnel, and this will mean money. So, no. It isn't a safe investment."

She smiled in admiration as he swiftly skimmed through his text messages. He oozed strength. Strength of mind, of body, of purpose. "You'll make it gold again," she said meaningfully, still not believing that, God, she'd called him *strange* to his face!

He lifted his head. "I'm tearing it apart, Virginia."

The plane lurched to a stop. The engines shut down. The aisle lit up with a string of floor lights.

Virginia was paralyzed in her seat, stunned. "You plan to destroy your father's business," she said in utter horror, a sudden understanding of his morose mood barreling into her.

His hard, aquiline face unreadable, he thrust his phone into his pocket and silently contemplated her. "It's not *his* anymore." His face was impassive, but his eyes probed into her. "It was meant to be mine when he passed away. I built it with him."

This morning, between phone calls, coffee, copies and errands, she'd gotten acquainted with Monterrey from afar. Learned it was a valley surrounded by mountains. Industrial, cosmopolitan, home of the wealthy and, at the very outskirts of the city, home of the poor. Indisputably the most prominent part of northern Mexico. Conveniently situated for Allende Transport, of course, as a means to import, export and travel—but also conveniently situated for those who imported and exported illegal substances. Like the cartels.

Allende wasn't a bouquet of roses, she supposed, but she'd never expected Marcos willingly to attempt to destroy it.

"You look as if I'd confessed to something worse," he noted, not too pleased himself.

"No. It's only that—" She checked herself before continuing this time. "That's not like you. To give up on something. You've never given up on Santos no matter what he does."

His intense expression lightened considerably. "My brother is a person—Allende is not."

Mightily aware of how out of character this decision was, Virginia ached to remind him he'd dedicated his life to helping companies in crisis, had taken under his wing businesses and even people no one else had faith in but Marcos, but instead she rose to her feet. Unfolding like a long, sleek feline just awakened to the hunt, Marcos followed her up. And up.

"Virginia, this isn't Chicago." He loomed over her by at least a head. His face was impassive, but his eyes probed into her. "If you want to sightsee, you'll be accompanied by me. Too dangerous to be alone here."

Dangerous.

The word caused gooseflesh on her skin.

Remembering her research on the city, she peered out a window as two uniformed *aduanales* and twice as many armed *militares* marched up to the plane. She'd heard military men customarily accompanied the Mexican customs agents but she was still floored by the intimidating sight. The copilot unlatched the door up front and descended to meet them.

She couldn't see much of the city at this late hour, but what she'd read online had mesmerized her. She would have even thought the setting romantic if his careful warning weren't dawning on her. "Dangerous," she said. "What must it be like for the people who live here?"

"Difficult." He rammed his book into a leather briefcase and zipped it shut. "Kidnapping rate has risen alarmingly during the last couple of years. Mothers are lifted outside the supermarkets, kids out of their schools, members of both government and police are bribed to play blind man to what goes on."

A rope of fear stretched taut around her stomach. "That's so sad."

She took one last look out the plane window. Nothing moved but the Mexican flag flapping by the customs building.

"It looks so calm," she protested.

"Under the surface nothing is calm." As he stood there, over six feet of virile overpowering man, he looked just a tad tired, and human, and so much sexier than behind his massive desk. He looked touchable. *Touchable.*

Under the surface nothing is calm. Not even me.

"Mrs. Fuller said you grew up here," she remarked as she eyed the fruit assortment on a table near the front of the plane.

"From when I was eight to eighteen," he answered. He stared, mildly puzzled, as she grabbed two green apples and slipped them into her purse.

"In case we get hungry," she explained sheepishly.

His eyes glittered with humor. "If you get hungry, you tell me and I'll make certain you're fed."

"What made you leave the city?" Leave a place that was beautiful and deadly. A place that gave out the message: Don't trust. You're not safe. And the one that had built a man like Marcos Allende, with an impenetrable core.

He braced one arm on the top wood compartment, waiting for the pilots to give them leave to descend. "Nothing here for me. Nothing in España either."

She loved the way he pronounced that. España. The way his arm stretched upward, long and sinewy, rippling under his black shirt before he let it drop. Somber, he gazed into her eyes, and the concern she saw in his gave her flutters. "Are you tired?"

"I'm fine." *You're here,* she thought.

The look that came to his eyes. The way he appraised her.

Virginia could've sworn there could be no flaw in her entire body. Nothing in this world more perfect to those dark, melted-chocolate eyes than she was.

His eyes fell to her lips and lingered there for an electric moment.

"Virginia." He closed the space between them. One step. All the difference between breathing or not. All the difference between being in control of your senses and being thrust into a twister.

He leaned over as he pried her purse from her cramped hands. His fingers brushed the backs of hers and a sizzle shot up her arm.

"Why are you nervous?" The low, husky whisper in her ear made her stomach tumble. She felt seared by his nearness, branded, as though he were purposely making her aware that his limits extended to breaching hers. She felt utterly… claimed. "You've fidgeted all day."

So he had been aware of her?

Like…a predator. Watching from afar. Planning, plotting, savoring the prey.

Why was this exciting?

His breath misted across the tender skin behind her ear. "Because of me?"

Her muscles gelled. *Because I want you.*

She took a shaky step back, singed to the marrow of her bones but smiling as though she was not. "I always get a charge after being rescued."

"Ahh." He drew out the sound, infusing it with a wealth of meaning. "So do I. After…rescuing." He swung his arm back so her purse dangled from one hooked finger behind his shoulder.

When the pilot announced they were clear, he signaled with an outstretched arm toward the plane steps. "Ladies first."

She warily stepped around his broad, muscled figure. "I admit I'm not used to your silences still."

His gaze never strayed from hers as she went around. "So talk next time," he said. "To me."

Right. Next time. Like he inspired one to make intimate revelations. And like he'd have another company to take over with the help of a "lover."

As both pilots conversed with the customs officials, Virginia stopped a few feet from the gaping doorway. Warmth from outside stole into the air-conditioned cabin, warming her cool skin. But she found she couldn't descend just yet.

She'd do anything to get her father out of his mess, yet suddenly felt woefully unprepared to play anyone's lover. Especially Marcos's lover. No matter how much she ached for the part and planned to get it right.

She pivoted on her heels to find him standing shockingly close. She craned her neck to meet his gaze. "Marcos, I'm going to need you to…tell me. What to do."

He wore an odd expression on his face, part confusion and part amusement. The smile he slowly delivered made her flesh pebble. "You may step out of the plane, Miss Hollis."

Laughing, she gave an emphatic shake of her head. "I mean, regarding my role. I will need to know what you suggest that I do. I'm determined, of course, but I'm hoping to get some pointers. From you."

His lids dropped halfway across his eyes. He lifted a loose fist and brushed his knuckles gently down her cheek. The touch reached into the depths of her soul. "Pretend you want me."

A tremor rushed down her limbs. Oh, God, he was so sexy. She was torn between latching on to his tempting, unyielding lips and running for her life. "I will, of course I will," she breathed.

A cloak of stillness came over her—so that all that moved, all she was aware of, was his hand. As he trailed his thumb down to graze her shoulder and in a ghost of a touch swept a strand of hair back, he swallowed audibly. "Look at me like you always do."

"How?"

"You know how." There was so much need in his eyes, a thirst she didn't know how to appease, which called to a growing, throbbing, aching void inside of her. "Like you care for me, like you need me."

"I do." She shook her cluttered head, straightening her thoughts. "I mean, I am. I *will*."

She shut her eyes tight, fearing he would see the truth in them. Fearing Marcos would realize she'd been secretly enamored of him all along. Since the very first morning she'd stepped into his office, she had wanted to die—the man was so out of this world. So male. So dark.

And now…what humiliation for him to discover that, if he crooked his finger at her, Virginia would go to him.

He chuckled softly—the sound throaty, arrogant, male. "Good."

His large hand gripped her waist and urged her around to face the open plane door a few feet away. She went rigid at the shocking contact. Longing flourished. Longing for more, for that hand, but on her skin and not her clothes, sliding up or down, God, doing anything.

Dare she dream? Dare she let herself long just a little,

without feeling the remorse she always did? Like she could indulge in a healthy fantasy now and then?

She wiggled free, sure of one thing: dissolving into a puddle of want was not what she should be doing just now.

"But…what do you want me to do, exactly?" she insisted, carefully backing up one step as she faced him. His eyebrows met in a scowl. He didn't seem to like her retreating. "This is important to you, right?" she continued.

"Señor Allende, pueden bajar por favor?"

Spurred to action by the voices on the platform, Virginia descended the steps. Marcos quickly took his place beside her.

They followed two uniformed officials toward a rustic, one-story building rivaled in size by Marcos's jet. A small control tower, which looked abandoned at this hour, stood discreetly to the building's right. A gust of hot, dry wind picked up around them, bouncing on the concrete and lifting the tips of her hair.

Virginia grabbed the whirling mass with one hand and pinned it with one fist at her nape. Marcos held the glass doors open for her. "No need to pretend just now, Miss Hollis," he said. "We can do that later."

His eyes glimmered dangerously with something. Something frightening. A promise. A request.

Her heart flew like the wind inside her, bouncing between her ribs, almost lifting the tips of her feet from the ground. Warily she passed through the bridge of his arm, one word's haunting echo resounding in her mind. And for the dread that began to take hold, it might have been a death sentence.

Later.

Fifteen minutes later, after a brisk *"Bienvenidos a Mexico"* from the *aduanales*, they were settled in the back of a silver Mercedes Benz, their luggage safely tucked in the trunk.

"A Garza Garcia, si?" the uniformed driver asked as he eased behind the wheel.

"Por favor," Marcos said.

His palm tingled. The one he'd touched her with. The one that had reached out to cup the lovely curve of her waist and caused Virginia to back away. From his touch.

Frowning, he checked his watch—it was ten past midnight. Wanting had *never* been like this. You wanted a watch, or a house, or money, but wanting this particular woman was no such whim. It was a need, something pent-up for too long, something so valued you were hesitant to have, or break, or tarnish, or hurt.

The car swerved onto the deserted highway and Virginia tipped her face to the window, lightly tugging at the pearls around her neck.

"You had a decent trip, Señor Allende?" their driver asked.

"Yes," he said, stretching out his legs as far as he could without bumping his knee into the front seat.

Miles away, the distant core of the city of Monterrey glowed with lights. The sky was clear and veiled with gray, its shadow broken by a steady stream of streetlights rolling by.

"It's lovely here." Virginia transferred her purse to the nook at her feet then tapped a finger to the window. "Look at the mountains."

Her skin appeared luminous upon every brisk caress of the streetlights, and in the shadows her eyes glittered uncommonly bright. They sparkled with excitement.

He felt a tug at his chest. "I'll show you around tomorrow in daylight," he said curtly.

Her eyes slid over to his, grateful, alive eyes. "Thank you."

A heroic feeling feathered up his chest, and he pushed it aside.

During a lengthy quiet spell, the driver flicked on the radio and soft music filled the interior of the car. Virginia remained way over on the other end of the seat.

Not near enough…

He studied her figure, becoming fixated on the rounded breasts swelling under her clingy dress, the curve of her thigh and hip and small waist. Swirly black bits of hair tickled her shoulders. Her long, shapely legs had a satin shine to them, inviting him to wrap them around his body and spill days and weeks and months of wanting inside her.

He whispered, in a low murmur that excluded the driver, "Are you afraid of me?"

She stiffened. Pale, jade-green eyes rose to his for a second before her lashes dropped. "No. Why would you ask?"

Her shyness brought out the hunter in him, and it took effort on his part to keep under control. Go slowly with her… His heart began to pound. He patted his side. "You could come a little closer."

Ducking her head to hide a blush, she smoothed her hands along the front of her dress. Then she flicked a tiny knot of fabric from it. "Just haven't traveled in ages."

"You cringe at anyone's touch, or merely mine?"

She blinked. "Cringe? I'd never cringe if you…touched me."

The words *touched me* hovered between them like a dark, unleashed secret, an invitation to sin, and when Marcos at last responded to that, the thick lust in his voice was unmistakable. "You moved away when I urged you out of the plane. And when I helped you into the car."

"I was surprised." Her throat worked as she swallowed. Her eyes held his in the darkness. "I told you to tell me what to do."

She was whispering, so he whispered back.

"And I asked you to come closer just now."

A tense moment passed.

In silence, Marcos once again patted his side, this time more meaningfully.

After a moment's debate, Virginia seemed to quickly make up her mind. Thrusting out her chin at a haughty angle, she began to edge toward him. "If you're thinking I'm not good at this, I'll have you know I can pretend just fine."

Her scent stormed into his lungs. His nostrils twitched. His heart kicked. His temperature spiked.

Cautiously, as though petting a lion, she turned his hand over and set her cool, small palm on his. She gingerly laced her fingers through his. Lust kicked him in the groin at the unexpected touch. His head fell onto the back of the seat, a groan welling up in the back of his throat. Crucified by arousal, he dragged in a terse, uneven breath, squeezing his eyes shut.

She inched a little closer, tightening her grip. Her lips came to within a breath of his ear. "Does that satisfy you, Your Highness?"

He didn't let it show, the emotion that swept through him, but it made his limbs tremble. He said, thickly, "Come closer."

He wanted to jump her. He wanted all of her, right here, right now.

He inhaled deeply, his chest near bursting with the aroma of her. Clean, womanly, sweet. "Closer," he said, hearing the growl in his own words.

When she didn't, he glanced down at their joined hands. Hers was tiny and fair, nearly engulfed by his larger one. He ran the pad of his thumb along the back of hers, up the ridge of her knuckle, down the tiny smooth slope. She felt so good. And he felt eighteen again. "Soft," came his trancelike murmur.

Transfixed, she watched the movement of his thumb, her breasts stretching the material covering them as she inhaled. He dipped his head and discreetly rubbed his nose across the shiny, springy curls of her hair. Christ. Edible. All of her. He could smell her shampoo, wanted to plunge all ten fingers into her hair, turn her face up and kiss her lips. Softly, so he could savor her breath, go searching deep into her mouth.

Ducking his head so the driver wouldn't hear him, he whispered, "You might try to appear to enjoy my touch."

Their bodies created a heat, a dark intimate cocoon in the confined car interior, enhanced by the warmth of their whispers. "Marcos…"

His hand turned, capturing hers as she attempted to retrieve it. "Virginia."

Their gazes held. Like they did across his office, over the tops of people's heads, in the elevators. Those clear, infinite eyes always sought out his. To find him looking right back. Their fingers brushed at the pass of a coffee mug, a file, the phone. At contact their bodies seemed to flare up like matches—tense, coil, heat up the room. Even with a wall separating them, his awareness of her had escalated to alarming levels. And she'd been more fidgety with him than she had in months.

"We're pretending, remember?" he said, a husky reminder.

Pretend. The only way Marcos could think of that wouldn't involve her feelings, or his. The only way they might be able to—hell, what was this? It had been going on so long it felt like surrender—without anyone hurting in the end. Without their lives changing, breaking or veering off in separate ways because of it.

"Yes, I know."

"Then relax for me." Lightly securing her fingers between his, he delved his thumb into the center of her palm with a deep, intense stroke, aware of her audible intake of breath as he caressed. "Very good," he cooed. "I'm convinced you want me."

"Yes." Her voice was but a whisper, hinting at how the

sinuous, stroking circles of his thumb affected her. "I mean… I'm trying to…appear that I do."

But she seemed as uncertain and startled as a mouse who didn't know where to run to, and Marcos was very much taking to the cat's role. He wanted to play, to corner, to taste.

He glanced up. "Don't tax yourself too much, hmm."

Her warm, fragile fingers trembled in his. The excitement of a new country had left her eyes, replaced by a wild, stormy yearning. "I'm trying not to…get bored."

His thumb went deep at the center then eased back. "Hmm. Yes. I can see you're fighting a yawn." His eyes ventured up along the top of her head, taking in its gloss. "You have pretty hair. Can I touch it?"

He did. It felt soft and silky under his fingers, tempting him to dig in deeper, down to her scalp.

She made a sound in her throat, like a moan. A hunger of the worst, most painful kind clawed inside him. She had a way of staring at him with those big eyes like he was something out of this world. It was a miracle he'd resisted her this long.

"A man," he gruffly began, massaging the back of her head as he greedily surveyed her features, "would be lucky to make you his."

Her eyes sealed shut so tightly she seemed to be in pain. She squirmed a little on the seat and, unbelievably, came nearer. "You don't have to convince me. I'm already pretending."

Her breasts brushed his rib cage, and the heat of her supple body singed his flesh through their clothes. He intensified the strokes of his fingers. "A man would be lucky to make you his, Virginia," he repeated.

Her lashes fluttered upward, revealing her eyes. Pale green, ethereal. Distrustful. "What are you doing?"

His gut tightened. *What does it look like I'm doing?* He

wanted to yank her onto his lap, feel his way up her little skirt, and kiss her mouth until her lips turned bright red. Her face blurred with his vision. With his need. He had to force himself to leave her hair alone.

She exhaled a string of broken air, then relaxed somewhat, shifting sideways on the leather seat. Facing him. Her smile faded. "Who are we fooling, Marcos, with this charade?"

"Marissa Galvez, Allende Transport's owner."

And maybe you. Definitely me.

He retrieved her hand from where it had gone to wring the hem of her dress and secured her wrist in his grip as he raised it. He turned it over and set a soft, lingering kiss at the center of her palm. A tiny, breathless gasp came from her.

"We must practice," he murmured, gazing into those deep, bottomless eyes.

"Oh." She shivered. Not moving away, and not moving closer, she allowed him to drag his lips along her open palm. She watched him through her lashes, her lips shuddering on each uneven breath.

"And why must we fool her?" Her question was a silky wisp.

"Because she wants me," he huskily answered. She tasted divine. Her skin was smooth and satiny under his lips, and he predicted every inch of her body would feel just like it. Perfect. "It wouldn't do to insult her." Against his mouth and lips, he felt the vibrant tremor that danced up her arm. Emboldened by her response, thirsting for more, he opened his mouth and gently grazed his teeth at the heel of her palm. "I happen to want someone else."

"I'm sure—" she began, swallowing audibly. "I'm sure you can have anyone you want."

"If I want her bad enough and put myself to task, yes." His lips closed and opened against her hand. Before he could restrain himself, he gave a lick at her palm. Pleasure pummeled through him. "And I've grown to want her…bad," he strained out, swallowing back a growl.

"Oh, that was…" Her hand wiggled as she tried prying it free. "I don't think…"

"Shh."

He held her wrist in a gentle grip and raised his head. He watched her expression soften, melt, as he whisked the pad of his thumb across her dampened palm, getting it wet. He lifted the glistening pad of his thumb to her lips, his timbre coated with arousal. "Pretend you like it when I do this."

A sound welled in the back of her throat as he stroked. She nodded wildly, her lips gleaming at each pass of his thumb. "Yes, yes, I'm pretending," she breathed.

He'd never seen a more erotic sight, felt a more erotic sensation, than playing with Virginia Hollis's quivering pink lips in the back of a moving car. "Umm. Me, too. I will pretend…you're her."

"Aha."

"And I very much want her." God, he enjoyed her unease, enjoyed seeing her pupils dilate, her breath shallow out.

"O-okay."

His thumb continued glancing, whisking, rubbing, right where his mouth wanted to be. He bent to whisper, to conspire together, just him and her. "Let's pretend…we're lovers, Virginia." His voice broke with the force of his desire, came out rough with wanting. "Pretend every night we touch each other…and kiss…and our bodies rock together. And when we find release—"

"Stop!" She pushed herself back with surprising force, sucking great gulps of air. "God, stop. Enough. Enough pretending tonight."

He tugged her closer. They were breathing hard and loud.

"You should kiss me," he said gruffly.

"Kiss you." She absently fingered his cross where it

peeked through the top opening of his shirt. He went utterly still—the gesture too sweet, too unexpected, too painful.

Her fingers reached his throat, then traced the links of the thick chain.

Too aware of this now, he dropped her hair and squeezed her elbow meaningfully. "Virginia. Your mouth. On mine."

They'd had foreplay for a year—with every glance, every flick of her hair, every smile.

She drew back and laughed, a choked, strained sound. "Now?" She couldn't seem to believe her eyes and ears, seemed stumped for words to deny him.

The car halted at a stoplight. A few cars drove up beside them. Marcos went still, glancing at her quietly until their car continued.

He had never wanted to feel a body as much as he wanted to feel hers.

And her mouth—he'd give anything to taste that mouth, was being for the first time in his life reckless, selfish, for that very mouth. A mouth that promised all the innocence he'd never had, trust, beauty, affection he'd never had.

Without any further thought, he pulled her close. "One kiss. Right now."

"But you're my boss," she breathed, clutching his shirt collar with a death grip. But her bright, luminous green eyes gazed up at him. And those eyes said yes.

Her lips were plush, parted, eager for his. He brought his thumb back to scrape them. "Just pretend I'm not him."

"But you *are* him—"

"I don't want to be him, I want to be…just Marcos." Their relationship had been wrapped in rules, limited by their roles. What if Virginia had been just a woman? And he just a man? She would have been his, might still be his. "Only Marcos."

The passing city lights caused slanted shadows to shift across her face—she looked splendid, wary, wanting.

"A kiss is harmless, Virginia." His vision blurred with desire as he stretched his arm out on the seat behind her and dipped his head. Their breaths mingled, their mouths opened. "People kiss their pets. They kiss their enemies on the cheeks. They kiss a letter. They even blow kisses into the air. You can kiss me."

"This is a little unexpected."

"God, I'd hate to be predictable." His arm slid from the back of the seat and went around her shoulders, loosely holding her to him. His fingers played with the soft, bouncy curls at her nape. His accent got unbearably thick—like his blood, a terse string of lust flooding his veins. It took concentration to give her a smile meant to disarm. "Stop thinking about it and kiss me."

Her curls bounced at the shake of her head. "We don't have to kiss to pretend to be…together. I can pretend convincingly without kissing."

No kissing? Christ, no. He had a fascination with her mouth, the delicate bow at her upper lip, the ripe flesh of the bottom one. He'd been kissing that mouth for days, weeks, months, in his mind.

"You're wrong, *amor*." He bussed her temple with his lips, aware of his muscles flexing heatedly under his clothes, his skin feverish with pent-up desire as she continued clinging to his shirt. "We must kiss. And we must kiss convincingly."

"I— You didn't mention this before."

He caressed her cheekbone with the back of one finger and noted the frantic pulse fluttering at the base of her throat. Christ, once again she was fixated with his mouth, and he wanted to give it to her. Now. Right now. Slam it over hers, push into her, taste all of her. "Kiss me, Virginia. Kiss me senseless." He barely held himself in check with his ruthless self-discipline.

She hesitated. Then, in a burdened breath, "Only a kiss."

His heart rammed into his ribs at the realization that she had agreed. To kiss him. *Ay, Dios.*

He urged himself to ease back on the seat and stifled the impulse to take matters into his own hands. He was a second away from losing his mind. A second away from tearing off her clothes, the necklace at her throat, his shirt, everything that separated them. Still, he wanted to be sure, sure she wanted this. Him. Them.

He groaned and said, "Kiss me until we can't breathe."

"I... The driver could see us." She sounded as excited as he, and the breathless anticipation in her voice plunged him even deeper into wild, mad desire.

"Look at me, not him."

"You're all I'm looking at, Marcos."

He didn't know who breathed harder, who was seducing whom here. She laid her hands over his abdomen. He hissed. The muscles under her palms clenched. His erection strained painfully.

Her hands slid up his chest, a barely there touch. *Fever.* She cradled his jaw with two cool, dry palms...and waited. Hesitant, inexperienced. In a ragged plea, she croaked, "Close your eyes."

He did. Not because she asked, but because her fingers lovingly stroked his temple, down his jaw. Her hands drifted lower and curled around his shoulders, rubbing along the muscles so sensually he gritted his teeth. This was murder.

She had to stop. She had to go on.

"Do it. Do it now." The helpless urgency in his voice startled him as much as the other emotions coursing through him. Arousal ripped through him like a living beast.

Then he felt the warm mist of her breath on his face, sensed the nearness of her parting lips, heard through the roaring in his ears her tremulous whisper. "I'm a bit out of practice—"

He didn't let her finish. He reached out and slipped a hand beneath the fall of hair at her nape and hauled her to him. "Virginia," he rasped, and slammed her mouth with his.

Four

Virginia had meant for a quick kiss. Only a taste. A taste to satisfy her curiosity. Her need. A taste because she could not, could never, deny this man. But when he pulled her down and his mouth, so strong and fierce and hungry, touched hers, there was no stopping what came over her.

They'd been panting, laughing; he'd been teasing her, had pulled her onto his lap. Pretending had been so easy, but now...now this mouth, this man, the hands gripping the back of her head, were too real. Rough. Raw. Devastating.

She moaned helplessly as he slanted his head, murmuring something indiscernible to her, and his warm, hot tongue came at hers, and his hard need grew larger and stronger under her bottom, and the realization that he really *wanted her* barraged through her.

He began to take little nips, and those lush, sure lips moving against hers set off the flutters in her stomach, the fireworks in her head. *"Sabes a miel."*

He spoke in an aroused rasp against her lips. She clung to

his neck and tried not to moan as his warm breath slid across her skin, heating her like a fever.

"Te quiero hacer el amor," he murmured, running his hands down the sides of her body, his fingers brushing the curves of her breasts, his chest heaving with exerted restraint. *"Toda la noche, te quiero hacer el amor."*

She had no idea what he said, but the words pulsed through her in a wave of erotic pleasure. Her breasts swelled heavy, her nipples in such pain she pressed them deeper into his chest and she opened her mouth wide, moving instinctively against him, and she knew this was wrong, so wrong, would not happen again, which surely must be why she incited it. "What are you saying to me…" she murmured into him.

His breath was hot and rapid against her. "I'm saying I want to make love to you. All evening, all night." He groaned and twisted his tongue around hers as their lips locked, the attachment intense, driven, absolute.

She sucked in a breath as his palms engulfed her straining nipples, felt his desire in every coiled muscle, in the rough way his palms kneaded, the thrusts of his tongue as his mouth turned ravenous on hers.

He groaned, appearing decidedly out of control for the first time since she'd known him. He stroked the undersides of her breasts with his thumbs and whisked his lips along the curve of her jaw, and she cocked her ear to his nibbling lips, shuddered when he murmured to her. "Your gasps tear me to pieces."

"Marcos…"

She was hot and burning inside.

He made a grinding motion with his hips, and her thighs splayed open as he desperately rubbed his erection against her.

His tongue plunged into her ear, wet, hot, sloppy. "Stop me, Virginia." One determined hand unerringly slipped through the V of her dress and enveloped her breast. "Virginia. Stop me, Virginia."

He squeezed her flesh possessively, and when his palm rubbed into her nipple, her eyes flew open in shock. The feel was so delicious, so wrong, so *right,* she hid her heated face against his neck and almost choked on the sounds welling at the back of her throat. Sensations overpowered her body, her mind struggling to comprehend that this was really happening with Marcos Allende.

"That's your hotel up ahead, sir."

Swearing under his breath, Marcos gathered her closer. His ragged breaths blasted her temple. He squeezed her. "We'll finish this upstairs."

Virginia pushed back her rumpled hair. Upstairs? God, what were they even doing?

Chuckling at the look on her face, Marcos bussed her forehead with his lips as his gentle hand stroked down her nape, trembling slightly. "I should've known we'd be combustible," he murmured.

The Mercedes pulled into a wide, palm tree–lined hotel driveway and Virginia fumbled for her purse while Marcos stepped out and strolled to her side, reaching into the car and helping her to her feet.

His glimmering, dark gaze didn't stray from her face, not for a second. *We kissed,* his dark eyes said. *I touched you. I know you want me.*

And for an insane second, all she wanted was to forget why she was here and who she was and be swept away by this one man, this one night, in this one city.

As though discerning her thoughts, Marcos cupped half of her face in his warm palm, and his eyes held something so wild and bright it almost blinded her. "Upstairs," he said again.

The promise plunged into her like a knife as he moved away to discuss something with the chauffeur, and Virginia stood there like someone in a hypnotized state, watching his big, tanned hands at his sides. Hands she'd felt on her.

She gritted her teeth, fighting the lingering arousal tickling through her. He was playing with her. He was *pretending*. He was a man who'd do anything to win—and he wanted Allende.

Marcos seemed oblivious to her frustration when he returned, slowly reaching behind her, his fingers splaying over the small of her back as he led her up the steps.

She followed him and no, she wasn't imagining him naked, touching her, kissing her in the exact way he'd just done—no, no, no. She studied the beautiful hotel and the potted palms leading to the glass doors with the intensity of a scientist with his microscope.

The lobby and its domed ceiling made her lightheaded. It was so…so… God, the way he'd touched her. With those hands. As if that breast were his to touch and his hand belonged there. How could he pretend so well? He'd been so hard he could've broken cement with his…his…

"Do you like it, Virginia?" he asked, smiling, and signaled around.

She gazed at the elegant but rustic decor. "The hotel? It's beautiful."

His eyes twinkled, but underneath it all, he wore the starved look of a man who'd hungered for a very long time and intended to feast soon. He looked like a man who could do things to her she didn't even imagine in fantasies, like a man who would not want to be denied.

And he would be. He had to be.

"It's very…charming," she continued, anything to steer her mind away from his lips, his mouth, his gaze.

They wound deeper into the marbled hotel lobby. A colorful flower arrangement boasting the most enormous sunflowers she'd ever seen sat on a massive round table near the reception area.

Virginia could still not account, could not even fathom, that she'd just kissed him. Her!—woefully inexperienced, with her last boyfriend dating back to college—kissing Marcos Allende. But he'd been cuddling her, whispering words so naughty she could hardly stand the wanton warmth they elicited. No matter how much resistance she'd tried to put up, he was the sexiest thing on the continent, playing some sort of grown-up game she had yet to put a name to, and Virginia had been close to a meltdown.

It had all been pretend, anyway. Right?

Right.

Trying to compose herself, she admired his broad back as he strolled away, the shoulders straining under his black shirt as he reached the reception desk and leaned over with confidence, acting for the world as if he were the majority stockholder of the hotel. The two women shuffling behind the granite top treated him as if they agreed.

Virginia quietly drew up to his side, her lips feeling raw and sensitive. She licked them once, twice.

A lock of ebony hair fell over Marcos's forehead as he signed the slip and slid it over the counter. "I requested a two-bedroom suite—it would appease me to know you're safe. Will this be a problem?" Facing her, he plunged his Montblanc pen into his shirt pocket, watching her through calm, assessing eyes.

She saw protectiveness there, concern, and though her nerves protested by twisting, she said, "Not at all." Damn. What hell to keep pretending for a week.

"Good."

In the elevator, as they rode up to the ninth floor—the top floor of the low, sprawling building—his body big and commanding in the constricted space, the silence whispered, *we kissed.*

In her mind, her heart, the choir of her reason, everything said, *kiss kiss kiss.*

Not good, any of it. Not the blender her emotions were in, not her tilting world, not the fact that she was already thinking, anticipating, wondering, what it would feel like to kiss again.

Freely. Wildly. Without restraint.

She would have to stall. Abstain. Ignore him. God. If she did something to compromise her job, she would never forgive herself. And nothing compromised a job like sex did. And if she compromised her heart? She stiffened, firmly putting a lid on the thought.

Mom had loved Dad with all her heart—through his flaws, through his odd humors, through his drunken nights, through all the good and bad of which there was more of the latter, her mother had loved with such steadfast, blinded devotion Virginia had secretly felt...pity.

Because her mother had wept more tears for a man than a human should be allowed to weep. Appalling, that one man could have such power over a woman, could take her heart and her future and trample them without thought or conscience.

Even on her deathbed, sweet, beautiful, dedicated Mother had clutched Virginia's hand, and it seemed she'd been hanging on to her life only to continue trying to save her husband. "Take care of Dad, Virginia, he needs someone to look out for him. Promise me, baby? Promise me you will?"

Virginia had promised, determinedly telling herself that if she ever, ever gave away her heart, it would be to someone who would be reliable, and who loved her more than his cards, his games and himself.

No matter her physical, shockingly visceral responses to Marcos, he was still everything she should be wary of. Worldly, sophisticated, ruthless, a man enamored of a challenge, of risks and of his job. The last thing she pictured

Marcos Allende being was a family man, no matter how generous he'd proven to be as a boss.

Down the hall, the bellhop emerged from the service elevator, but Marcos was already trying his key, allowing her inside. He flicked on the light switch and the suite glowed in welcome. Golden-tapestried walls, plush taupe-colored carpet, a large sitting area opening up to a room on each side. *"Gracias,"* he said, tipping the bellhop at the door and personally hauling both suitcases inside.

Virginia surveyed the mouthwatering array of food atop the coffee table: trays of chocolate-dipped strawberries, sliced fruit, imported cheeses.

A newspaper sat next to the silver trays and the word *muerte* popped out in the headline. A color picture of a tower of mutilated people stared back at her.

Marcos deadbolted the door. The sound almost made her wince. And she realized how alone they were. Just him. And her.

And their plan.

Suddenly and with all her might, Virginia wished to know what he was thinking. Did he think they'd kiss again? What if he wanted more than a kiss? What if he didn't?

Feeling her skin pebble, she shied away from his gaze, navigated around a set of chairs and pulled the sheer drapes aside. The city flickered with lights. Outside her window the hotel pool was eerily still, the mountains were still, the moon still. She noted the slow, rough curves and the sharper turns at the peaks, lifted her hand to trace them on the glass. "Do you come here frequently?" she asked quietly—her insides were not still.

"No." She heard the sunken fall of his footsteps on the carpet as he approached—she felt, rather than saw, him draw up behind her. "There wasn't reason to."

He could be uttering something else for the way he spoke so intimately. Inside, a rope of wanting stretched taut around her stomach and she thought she would faint. The proximity of his broad, unyielding hardness sent a flood of warmth across her body, and the muscles of her tummy clenched with yearning. His body wasn't touching hers; there was just the threat of the touch, the presence that created a wanting of it.

In the darkness of her bedroom, very late at night, she'd wondered if Marcos was as ruthless when he loved as when he did business. And if his kiss…was as dark and devastating as his eyes had promised it would be.

It was. Oh, God, it was.

The air seemed to scream at her to turn to him and *kiss*.

The close contours of his chest against her back, the scent of him, were an assault to her senses. He laid his hand on her shoulder, and the touch was fire on his fingertips. "This is a safe neighborhood—I won't lose sight of you, Virginia."

But outside the danger didn't lurk. It was in her. It was him. She locked her muscles in place, afraid of leaning, moving, afraid of the magnetic force of him, how it felt impossible not to turn, touch. "What was it like for you when you were young," she said, softly.

His hand stroked. Fire streaked across her skin as he drew lazy figures along the back of her arm. "It wasn't as dangerous back then. I grew up in the streets—I kept running away with my father's workers, looking for adventure."

Did he move? She thought he'd grown bigger, harder, nearer. She sensed his arousal, the thundering in his chest almost touching her back. Or was it her heart she heard?

He lowered his lips and briefly, only a whisper, set his mouth on her neck. A sharp shudder rushed through her. "Now even bodyguards aren't safe to hire," he whispered on her skin. "Wealthy people have armored cars and weapons instead."

She closed her eyes, the sensations pouring through her.

"No-man's-land?" Just a croak. A peep from a little bird who couldn't fly, would willingly be lured in by the feline.

He made a pained sound and stilled his movements on her. "Were you pretending just now when you kissed me?"

Oh. My. God. They were actually discussing it.

Her nod was jerky.

Marcos hesitated, then huskily murmured, "Do you want to…?"

She sank her teeth into her lower lip to keep from saying something stupid, like yes. "To what?"

His whisper tumbled down her ear. "You know what."

"I don't know what you mean." But she did. Oh, dear, she did.

"Kiss…" Thick and terse, his voice brimmed with passion. "Touch…"

Shaking like a leaf in a storm, she wiggled free and walked around him, her insides wrenching. "I told you I could pretend just fine."

Heading for the couch and plopping down, she surveyed the food once more, but her eyes didn't see anything.

Was she supposed to stay strong and resist what her body and heart wanted when she had a chance to have it? Was she supposed to say no and no and no?

Marcos plunged his hand into his hair. "That was *pretense?*"

"Of course." He sounded so shocked and looked so annoyed she might have even laughed. Instead, her voice grew businesslike. "So you left. And your father stayed here? In this city?"

For a moment, he released a cynical laugh, and when he gradually recovered, he roughly scraped the back of his hand across his mouth as if he couldn't stand remembering their kiss. Reluctantly, he nodded. "You're good, Miss Hollis, I'll give you that."

"What made you leave here?" she asked, blinking.

One lone eyebrow rose and this time when he laughed, she knew it was at her attempt at conversation.

"Well." Propping a shoulder against the wall and crossing his arms over his chest in a seemingly relaxed pose, Marcos exuded a raw, primal power that seemed to take command of the entire room. "Allende Transport was taken. By my father's…woman. It was either her or me—and he chose her. But I promised myself when I came back…the transport company would be mine."

His voice. Sometimes she'd hear it, not the words, just the bass, the accent. Marcos was larger than life, large in every single way, and Virginia could pretend all she wanted but the fact was, she'd be stupid to forget her position. And she had to make sure the car incident would never again be repeated.

"Marcos, what happened here and in the car was—"

"Only the beginning."

She started. The beginning of what? The end? She ground her molars, fighting for calm. "We were pretending."

"Aha."

"Yes," she said, vehemently. "We were."

"Right, Miss Hollis. Whatever you say."

"You asked me to pretend, that's what I'm here for. Isn't it?"

His silence was so prolonged she felt deafened. Was she here for another reason? A reason other than what he'd requested of her? An intimate, wicked, naughty reason?

She could tell by the set of his jaw that if he had a hidden agenda, he wouldn't be admitting to it now.

Walking off her conflicting emotions, she fixed her attention on the food. The scents of lemon, warm bread, cheeses and fruit teased her nostrils, but her stomach was too constricted for her to summon any appetite. Usually she'd be wolfing down the strawberries, but now she wiped her hands on her sides and put on her best secretarial face. "At what time should I wake up tomorrow?"

"We have a late lunch, no need to rise with the sun," he said.

She signaled to both ends of the room, needing to get away from him, wishing she could get away from herself. "And my room?"

"Pick the one you like."

She felt his gaze on her, sensed it like a fiery lick across her skin.

She went over and peered into a room: a large, double-post bed, white and blue bedclothes. Very beautiful. She went to the other, feeling his eyes follow. The lamplight cast his face in beautiful mellow light. He looked like an angel that had just escaped from hell, like an angel she wanted to sin with.

"I guess either will do," she admitted.

She smiled briefly at him from the doorway, and although he returned the smile, both smiles seemed empty.

And in that instant Virginia was struck with two things at once: she had never wanted anything so much in her life as she wanted the man standing before her, and if his lips covered hers again, if his hands touched her, if his eyes continued to look at her, she would never own her heart again.

She said, "Good night." And didn't wait to hear his reply.

The room she chose was the one with coral-pink bedding and an upholstered headboard. She didn't question that, for appearances, he would wish him and his "lover" to appear to share a room. But she quietly turned the lock behind her.

As she changed, she thought of what she had read about Marcos and Monterrey. She arranged the clothes in the large closet, each garment on a hanger, and eyed and touched the ones he'd bought her.

She slipped into her cotton nightgown, ignoring the prettier garments made of silk and satin and lace, and climbed into bed. Awareness of his proximity in the adjoining room caused gooseflesh along her arms. A fan hung suspended from the ceiling, twirling. The echo of his words feathered through her, melting her bones. *I'll pretend...you're her.*

She squeezed her eyes shut, her chest constricting. *It's not you, Virginia,* she firmly told herself.

She touched a finger against her sensitive lips and felt a lingering pleasure. And in her heart of hearts, she knew she was. She was her, the woman Marcos wanted. She'd dreamed of him in private, but dreams had been so harmless until they came within reach.

Marcos Allende.

Wanting him was the least safe, most staggering, worrying feeling she'd ever felt.

And one thing she knew for certain was that to her, Marcos Allende was even more dangerous than his beautiful, deadly city of Monterrey.

Sleep eluded him.

The clock read past 1:00 a.m. and Marcos had smashed his pillow into a beat-up ball. He'd kicked off the covers. He'd cursed and then he'd cursed himself some more for thinking one kiss would be enough to rid himself of his obsession of her.

Then there was Allende.

He had to plan, plot, leave no room for error. He had to stoke his hatred of Marissa, to be prepared to crush her once and for all.

But he could not think of anything. Memories of those kisses in the car assailed him. The fierce manner in which his mouth took hers and her greedy responses, the moans she let out when he'd touched her. How his tongue had taken hers, how she'd groaned those tormenting sounds.

He lay awake and glared at the ceiling, his mind counting the steps to her room. Twenty? Maybe fewer. Was she asleep? What did she wear to sleep? Was she remembering, too? Jesus, what a nightmare.

He shouldn't have asked her there.

He'd thought nothing of Allende, nothing of tomorrow, but had kept going over in his mind the ways she'd kissed him and the ways he still wanted to kiss her.

He sat up and critically surveyed the door of his room. He wanted her to give in. Wanted something of hers, a stolen moment, something she hadn't planned to give him, but couldn't help but relinquish. She was cautious by nature. She'd fear ruining everything, all she'd worked so hard for, all she'd tried to achieve. A steady job, security, respect. Could he guarantee this would remain solid when they were through? Could they even continue working together—flaring up like torches like this?

Their kiss had shot him up into outer space; obviously he still couldn't think right. In his drawstring pants, he climbed out of bed and slipped into his shirt.

He meant to review his numbers once again, ascertain that the amount he planned to offer for Allende was low, but fair enough to secure it.

Instead he ignored his files and found himself standing outside his assistant's bedroom door, his hand on the doorknob, his heart beating a crazy jungle-cat rhythm.

He turned the knob, smiling at his certainty of her, her being always so…orderly, having locked it against him.

His heart stopped when he realized Virginia Hollis's door was unlocked. Now all that kept him from Virginia Hollis were his damned scruples.

Five

"Sleep well?"

"Of course. Wonderfully well. And you?"

"Perfectly."

That was the extent of their conversation the next morning over breakfast. Until Marcos began folding his copy of *El Norte*. "A favor from you, Miss Hollis?"

Virginia glanced up from her breakfast to stare into his handsome, clean-shaven face. *A kiss,* she thought with a tightness in her stomach. A touch. God, a second kiss to get rid of that haunting memory of the first.

With her thoughts presenting her the image of him—Marcos Allende—kissing her, she flushed so hard her skin felt on fire. She toyed with her French toast. "Nothing too drastic, I assume?" she said, some of the giddiness she felt creeping into her voice.

"Drastic?" he repeated, setting the morning paper aside.

She shrugged. "Oh, you know…murder. Blackmail. I don't think I could get away with those."

Eyes glinting with amusement, he shook his head, and his smile was gone. His elbows came to rest on the table as he leaned forward. "What kind of boss do you take me for?"

One I want, she thought. *One who kissed me.*

Those broad, rippling muscles under his shirt could belong to a warrior.

God just didn't make men like these anymore.

She'd lied. She hadn't slept one wink.

If she'd been camping out in the dark, naked, within ten feet of a hungry lion, maybe she'd have been able to sleep. But no. She had been within a few feet of her dream man, and her lips had still tingled from his kiss, and her body seemed to scream for all the years she hadn't paid attention to letting someone love it.

After lying on the bed for what felt like hours, for some strange reason she had bolted to her feet and rummaged through the stuff he'd bought…and slipped into something sexy. A sleek white silk gown that hugged her like skin. Heart vaulting in excitement, she'd unlocked the door. Returned to bed. And waited. Eyeing the door.

The knob had begun turning. Her eyes widened, and her pulse went out of orbit. She waited minutes, minutes, for the door to open, and yet the knob returned to place again. Nothing happened. He changed his mind? Her heart sped, and then she flung off the covers and stepped out of bed.

The living room was empty—silver in the moonlight. And then, torn between some unnamable need and the need for self-preservation, she'd quietly gone back to bed.

Now, looking like a well-rested, sexy billionaire, he asked what kind of boss she took him for.

"One who's never bitten me," she blurted, then wished to kick herself for the way that came out sounding. Like an invitation. Like…more. Damn him.

He chuckled instantly, and Virginia pushed to her feet

when she totally lost her appetite. He followed her up, uncurling slowly like he always did.

"I like the dress," he said, studying the fabric as it molded around her curves. It was a very nice dress. Green, to match her eyes, and one from a designer to please His Majesty.

"Thank you, I like it, too."

His gaze raked her so intimately she felt stripped to her skin. There was a silence. Her heart pounded once. Twice. Three times. Virginia couldn't take a fourth.

"Name your favor," she offered.

Eyes locked with hers with unsettling intensity, he wound around the table, and his scent enveloped her—not of cologne and definitely not sweet—but so intoxicating she wanted to inhale until her lungs burst inside her chest.

Gently, he seized her chin between his thumb and forefinger, tipping his face back to hers. An unnamable darkness eclipsed his eyes, and an unprecedented huskiness crept into his voice. "Just say, 'Yes, Marcos.'"

Her breath caught. His voice was so ridiculously sexy in the morning. Virginia pulled free of his touch and laughed. "You," she accused, tingles dancing across her skin. "I don't even know what I'm agreeing to."

His arms went around her, slow as a boa constrictor, securing her like giant manacles. "Can't you guess?"

Something exploded inside her body, and it wasn't fear.

Lust. Desire. Everything she didn't want to feel.

His breath was hot and fragrant on her face, eliciting a little moan she couldn't contain. Oh, God. He felt so hard all over, so unlike any other man she'd known.

His voice was gentle as he tipped her chin up. "Yes to my bed for a week, Virginia. Say yes."

Was he insane? "Wow," she said, almost choking on her shock. "I've never had such a blatant come-on."

The determination on his face was anything but apologetic. "I don't want to play games with you." He studied her forehead, her nose, her jaw. "I intend to please you. I've thought of nothing else. Tell me," he urged, caressing her face as he would a porcelain sculpture. "Are you interested?"

Interested? She was on fire, she was frightened, confused and scared, and she hated thinking, realizing that she was no match for him.

She should've known that if Marcos ever made a move for her, he'd come on like he always did—strong, like a stampeding bull charging to get his way. Her breasts rose and fell against his chest as she labored to breathe. Her legs were so weak they couldn't support her, and she remained standing only by her deathly grip on his arms. "One week?"

"Seven days. Seven nights. Of pleasure beyond your imagining."

"A-and what if I can't give you this pleasure you want?"

"I will take any pleasure you can give me, Virginia. And you will take mine."

There was no mistaking. His deep, sexy voice was the most erotic thing she'd ever heard. "A-and if I say I'm not interested?"

He chuckled softly—the sound throaty, arrogant, male— melting her defenses. "If that is what you wish." His gaze pierced her, as though searching for secrets, fears. "You haven't wondered about us?" He lowered his head and skimmed her lips lightly, enough to tease and make her shiver when he retracted. "You unlocked your door last night, and I was so close to opening it, you have no idea."

"Oh, God," she breathed.

His lips grazed hers from end to end. "You wanted me there, you wanted me in your room, your bed."

"I—I can't do this."

His hands lowered to the small of her back and pressed her to his warm, solid length. "You can. Your body speaks to me. It feels soft against mine, it molds to me. Say it in words."

There was no escaping his powerful stare, no escape from what raged inside her. "I can't, Marcos."

Growling, he jerked free and for a blinding second she thought he was going to charge out of the room, he seemed so frustrated. Instead he carried himself—six feet three inches of testosterone and lust and anger—to the window and leaned on the frame. "The first moment I set eyes on you, you planted yourself in my mind. I'm going insane because once, Virginia, once I was sure you were crazy about me. So crazy. You can't help the way you look at me, *amor*. Perhaps others don't notice, but I do. Why do you fight me?"

Her eyes flicked up to his and she was certain her anxiety reached out to him like something tangible. His muscles went taut. "Do I get an answer?" he demanded.

She smiled, shaking her head in disbelief. "You're proposing we mix business and pleasure."

He wanted her desperately, she realized. Like she'd never been wanted before. And she might enjoy allowing herself to be wanted like this.

So, with a pang of anticipation in her left breast, she said, "I'll think about it over lunch."

The floral arrangement in the lobby had been replaced with one chock-full of red gerberas and bright orange tiger lilies bursting amidst green. They navigated around it, Marcos's hand on her back.

"If you want everyone to know you're nervous, by all means, keep fidgeting."

"Fidgeting? Who's fidgeting?"

He grabbed her trembling hand and linked his fingers through hers, his smile more like a grin. "Now no one. Smile, hmm? Pretend you like me."

Her pulse skyrocketed at the feel of his palm against hers, but she did not reject the touch and held on. *This should be easy. Easy,* she told herself. One look at her and everyone would think she was in love with him.

Impulsively she breathed him in, feeling oddly safe and protected. They'd had a wonderful morning, talking of everything and nothing as he accompanied her to the shopping mall across the street. The morning had flown by in casual conversation, which had been a good thing particularly when the night had seemed endless to her.

Now they entered the restaurant. Past the arched foyer entrance stood the most beautiful woman Virginia had ever seen. Tall and toned, blonde and beautiful. Her lips were red, her nails were red. She was clad in a short leather jacket teamed with a white miniskirt and a pair of heels Virginia was certain only an acrobat could walk on. Her face lit up like a sunbeam when she saw Marcos, and then it eclipsed when she saw Virginia.

She swept to her feet and came to them, her walk as graceful as the swaying of a willow tree. All other female eyes in the restaurant landed on Marcos.

"You're bigger." Her eyes became shielded, wary when they moved to her. "And you're...not alone."

In one clean sweep, Marissa took in the entire length of Virginia's knee-length emerald-green designer dress.

Marcos drew her up closer to him and brought those inscrutable eyes of his down on Virginia, his gaze sharpening possessively. "Virginia Hollis, Marissa Galvez."

He gave Virginia such a male, proprietary look she felt stirrings in all manner of places in her body. Nervous, she offered the woman a nod and a smile. Marissa's hand was slim and ringed everywhere. They shook hands and took their seats.

The awkwardness had a strange beat—slower somehow, and heavy like lead.

Over the sunlit table, Virginia tentatively slid her hand into Marcos's, sensed him smile to himself, then felt him give her a squeeze of gratitude which Marissa might have taken as affection. A silence settled. Every minute was a little more agonizing. Marcos's thumb began to stroke the back of hers, causing pinpricks of awareness to trail up her arm. Sensations of wanting tumbled, one after the other. What would it be like if this were real? Sitting here, with such a man, and knowing the name of the shampoo he showered with and the cologne he wore?

Marissa's blue eyes shone with a tumult of emotions. "Why didn't you come to him? He begged you to."

Virginia's spine stiffened. Whoa. That had been quite a hostile opening line. But then what did she know?

Marcos answered coolly, reclining easily in his upholstered chair. "I did come."

"A day too late."

The corners of his lips kicked up, but the smile was hard somehow, and it didn't reach his eyes. The air was so tense and dense it was scarcely breathable. "Perhaps if he'd really sent for me, I'd have come sooner—but we both know it wasn't him who summoned me."

Surprise flickered across the blonde's face. "Why would he not call his son on his deathbed?"

"Because he's an Allende."

She made a noncommittal sound, rings flashing as she reclined her chin on her right hand. Her eyes dropped to Virginia and Marcos's locked hands over the table, and finally the woman shrugged. "He died with his pride—but I could see him watching the door every day. He wanted to see you. Every time I came in he…" She faltered, pain flashing across her face as she lowered her arm. "He looked away."

Marcos was idly playing with Virginia's fingers. Did he realize? It seemed to distract him. Comfort him, maybe. "He didn't want to see you, Marissa?"

Her eyes became glimmering blue slits. "He wasn't

himself those last days." She smiled tightly. *"No se que le paso, estaba muy raro."*

Even as Marcos replied in that calm, controlled voice, Virginia sensed his will there, incontestable, allowing for nothing. "You ruin your life for a woman—I suppose you're bound to have regrets. And to be acting strange," he added, as though referencing the words she's said in Spanish.

A waiter dressed in black and white took their orders. Virginia ordered what Marcos was having, wishing she could try everything on the menu at least once but embarrassed to show herself as a glutton. When the waiter moved on, Marissa's eyes wandered over her. She tapped one long red fingernail to the corners of her red lips.

"You don't look like Marcos's type at all," she commented matter-of-factly.

Virginia half turned to him for a hint of how to answer, and he lifted her hand to graze her knuckles with his lips, saying in a playful murmur that only she seemed to hear, "Aren't you glad to hear that, *amor?*"

She shivered in primal, feminine response to the smooth touch of his lips, and impulsively stroked her fingers down his face. "You didn't see your father before he died?" she asked quietly.

His eyes darkened with emotion. "No," he said, and this time when he kissed the back of her hand, he did so lingeringly, holding her gaze. Her temperature jacked up; how did he do this to her?

The moment when he spread her hand open so her palm cupped his jaw, it felt like it was just them. Nobody else in the restaurant, the hotel, the world.

"You'd never abandon your father," he murmured as he held her gaze trapped, pressing her palm against his face. "I admire that."

Her chest moved as if pulled by an invisible string toward him. Had she ever received a more flattering compliment?

His pain streaked through her as though she'd adopted it as hers, and she ached to make him feel better, to take the darkness away from his eyes, to kiss him…kiss him all over.

She stroked his rough jaw with her fingers instead, unable to stop herself. "Perhaps he knew you loved him, and he understood you kept to your pride, like he did," she suggested.

"Marcos? Love? He wouldn't know love if it trampled him," Marissa scoffed and frowned at Marcos, then sobered up when he swiveled around to send her a chilling look. "It's my fault anyway. That you left. I've paid dearly for my mistake, I guarantee it," she added.

He didn't reply. His gaze had dropped to where his thumb stroked the back of Virginia's hand again, distracting her from the conversation that ensued. He seemed to prefer that touch above anything else. He kept stroking, caressing, moving her hand places. He put it, with his, over his thigh, or tucked it under his arm. Longing speared through her every single time he moved it according to his will. He genuinely seemed to…want it. Was he pretending? When his eyes came to hers, there was such warmth and heat there.… Was he pretending that, too?

Marissa mentioned Allende, and Marcos, prepared for the discussion, immediately answered. His voice stroked down Virginia's spine every time he spoke. Her reaction was the same: a shudder, a quiver, a pang. And she didn't want it to be. She didn't want to have a reaction, she shouldn't.

While the waiter set down their meals, she thought of her father, of how many times he'd disappointed and angered her, and she thought of how hurt she'd have to be in order not to see him again. Sometimes she'd wanted to leave, to pretend he didn't exist to her, and those times, she would feel like the worst sort of daughter for entertaining those thoughts.

Marcos wasn't a heartless man. He stuck by his brother

no matter what he did. *My brother is a person, Allende is not,* he'd told her. But his father had been a person, too. What had he done to Marcos to warrant such anger?

She had her answer fifteen minutes later, after she'd eaten the most spicy chile relleno on the continent and swallowed five full glasses of water to prove it. She excused herself to the *baño* and was about to return to the table when she heard Marissa's plea from the nearby table filter into the narrow corridor. "Marcos…if you'd only give me a chance…"

"I'm here to discuss Allende. Not your romps in my father's bed."

"Marcos, I was young, and he was so…so powerful, so interested in me in a way you never were. You were never asking me to marry you, never!"

He didn't answer that. Virginia hadn't realized she stood frozen until a waiter came to ask if she was all right. She nodded, but couldn't make her legs start for the table yet. Her chest hurt so acutely she thought someone had just pulled out her lungs. Marissa Galvez and Marcos. So it was because of a woman, because of her, that Marcos had never spoken again to his father?

"You never once told me if you cared for me, while he… he cared. He wanted me more than anything." Marissa trailed off·as if she'd noticed Marcos wasn't interested in her conversation. "So who is this woman? She's a little simple for you—no?"

He laughed, genuinely laughed. "Virginia? Simple?"

Virginia heard her answering whisper, too low to discern, and then she heard his, also too low, and something horrible went through her, blinding her eyes, sinking its claws into her. She remembered how difficult it was as a little girl to cope with the whispers.

The father is always gambling…they say he's crazy…

Now they talked about her. Not about her father. About her. She didn't hear what he said, or what she said, only felt the pain and humiliation slicing through her. Her father had put her in this position once more. No. She'd put herself in it. Pretending to be lovers with a man she truly, desperately wanted…and then looking the fool in front of someone she was sure had really been his lover.

Jealousy swelled and rose in her. She had no right to feel it, had never been promised anything, and yet she did feel it. Their kiss yesterday had been glorified in her mind and she'd begun to wishfully think Marcos had wanted to be with her this week. Silly. She'd even told herself she might like sharing his bed for a week.

She felt winded and strangely stiff when she reached the table. She sat quietly. She focused on dessert, tried to taste and enjoy, and yet her anger mounted, as if she really were his lover, as if she had anything to claim of him.

When he reached for her hand, it took all her effort, it took her every memory of having gone to beg him for help that evening, not to pull it away.

If she weren't sitting she'd be kicking herself for being so easy. She sucked in air then held it as he guided that hand to his mouth and grazed her knuckles with his lips.

Her racing heart begged for more, but Marcos's kiss was less obvious than last night, more like a whisper on her skin. Every grazing kiss he gave each knuckle felt like a stroke in her core.

A slap in the face.

They say her father's crazy…

By all means, Virginia would pull her hand away in a few seconds. She just wanted…more. More hot breath and warm lips on the back of her hand. More fire between her legs. A place so hot and moist it could only be cooled by—

Something moved.

His phone.

His lips paused on her for a breathless second before he

set her hand back on her lap and whispered, "It's the office. I have to get this."

Virginia made a strangled sound which was supposed to be an agreement and clearly sounded more like a dying woman. She watched his dark silhouette move between the tables and disappear down the hall so quickly. She already missed him. She scanned her surroundings. Everybody was eating, carrying on conversations. The world hadn't stopped like she'd thought because of those tiny kisses on her knuckles.

She sank back in her seat, agitated when Marissa watched her. She brought her hand to her mouth, the one he'd kissed, and closed her eyes as she grazed her lips in the exact same places his lips had touched.

Eyes popping open to meet the other woman's canny gaze, she straightened, readjusted the hem of her knee-length dress, and mentally cursed this pretense from here to Alaska and then to Mars. Was he seducing her? Or was this all for Marissa's sake?

"So," Marissa said. "You love him."

Virginia was about to jump in denial, frantic to save herself from this accusation, which of course implied that she was stupid, needed therapy and more, and then she realized he was counting on her to pretend that she did.

Love him.

"I…" Her lips couldn't form the words *I love him*. Her tongue seemed to freeze. Seemed to want to say only one thing, and that was *I hate him*.

She hated him and this stupid plan and how he touched her and how well he pretended to want her.

So instead she nodded, and let Marissa think what she would.

His powerful scent reached her long before he sat down beside her again. Virginia stared straight ahead like a horse with blinders. And just to prevent any more stoking of the staggering anger building inside her, she tucked her hands under her thighs. There. See if the man could touch her knuckles now.

She remained quiet the rest of the meal.

She heard Marissa invite them to a party the next day while she considered Marcos's offer.

She told herself she didn't care to know what kind of offer he'd made.

Six

Something had changed.

Virginia had changed. She was different, and yet, it was all the same with him. The twisting sensation in his gut, the demented beat of his heart, the itch in his hands, the coiling want in his body.

Alert, clever, perceptive and spirited…now his assistant seemed to be struggling to comprehend what she'd witnessed as they reached their rooms.

They'd had such an enjoyable time this morning, he'd been certain he knew where they were heading tonight.

He wasn't sure anymore.

He wasn't sure of anything—very unlike an Allende.

He took her to the middle of the living room and just stood there, his jacket in one hand, looking at her. His every muscle felt stiff and pained, his hard-on merciless, and when he moved the slightest bit, arousal lanced through him. He set his jacket aside and felt as if the air was being squeezed out of his lungs. She was disappointed he'd been such a bad son to his father? He'd lost her admiration? Her respect?

His insides twisted at the thought. He stepped forward, toward her, his thoughts congested, tangled like vines. The heat of her angry breaths made his insides strain in his want to drink it, feel it, appease it. It sent him teetering into an aroused state he couldn't fathom, much less understand. Eyeing her in silence, he tugged at his tie, stripping it from his neck, breathing harshly.

"I'd say that went well."

She tilted her head, her eyes fierce, something there marking him as loathsome. "She didn't believe us for a moment, that we…" She turned away as if disgusted. "She didn't buy it."

He narrowed his eyes—watching the tantalizing rise and fall of her chest. How would they feel to the touch? Soft. Yes, God, soft and small. Perky? Yes, that, too. His mouth watered. "Whether she believes it or not is of no consequence now."

Her eyes flashed a glittery warning. "You wanted to make her jealous."

"Jealous," he repeated, puzzled by the accusation. "Is that what you believe?"

She shoved her hair back from her forehead. "Yes, it is. And I'm sorry I disappointed, Marcos."

His blood raged hot and wild. He'd never seen her like this. Almost out of control, begging for…something he wanted to give her. Suddenly he'd give anything to hear her utter his name in that same haughty, do-me tone. He'd do anything to just…bury this ache inside her.

"I look at her and feel nothing—not even anger anymore. I didn't want her jealousy, but I didn't want her insinuating herself into my bed either."

"Because you want her there. Otherwise you wouldn't need me standing between you!"

He grabbed her arms and jerked hard, spurred by every ounce of pent-up desire in him, harbored for too long. "Listen to you!" She slammed against him with a gasp. Her eyes flamed in indignation and his body roared to life, singed by her lushness, her mouth so close. "There's only one woman I want in my bed—one. And I've wanted her for a long, long time."

"Then go get her!"

He backed her toward the bedroom. "Oh, I will—and I'll have her right where I want her." He dragged her closer and pulled her dress beneath her breasts and her scent, sweet and warm, washed through his senses. He seized a nipple with two fingers and pushed her breast up to his mouth and sucked.

He paused briefly to say, "The thought of you has me tied into knots. I want to taste you. For you to give me your lips, feel my body in yours. I want you coming with my name on your lips, coming over and over, with me."

She caught his head and moaned. He could see the needs, the emotions, rising in her and darkening her eyes to storms. His hands caught her wrists and pinned them over her head and tightened. "Share my bed."

"Marcos…"

A throbbing sensation pulsed through him, aching in his erection, his chest, his head. His voice grew hard, fierce as his cheek pressed against hers and he murmured in her ear. "I won't beg, not even for you, I won't ask again, Virginia. I have a craving for you…it's running wild and out of control. You share this craving. You crave me, you crave me so much you tremble with the force of it. Don't deny us. Don't deny me."

His breathing was ragged, hers wild. The gleam of defiance died out in her eyes as she gazed at his lips. He groaned and pulled her head to his as he swept down. His kiss was bred by passion, rampant with lust. The raging desire threatened to consume his mind, his sanity. He was undone by her kiss, her taste. His mind raced, his thirst for her sweeping through him. Her response was wholehearted, fiery, and it almost sent him to his knees. Her mouth sipped, her hands took what he wanted to give her. He called upon restraint but there was only passion here. Over and over he thought of being gentle, over and over her answer was to intensify, demand more.

He grabbed her and thrust her onto the bed, bouncing, and he was ripping at his shirt.

She climbed to her knees, her hands on her dress, fumbling to unbutton.

He whipped his shirt off, meeting her glimmering green gaze, stripping naked. "Do you want me?"

"Yes."

He unbuckled his belt and sent it slapping to the floor. "Lie back."

His heart thundered as he waited for her to, aware of the erection straining before her, listening to her sharp inhale. She backed away, her dress riding up to show her blue panties. And she was… There were no words. That lacy blue stuff looked delicious on her.… He wanted to use his lips to pry it off, his teeth… No, he couldn't wait; he needed to feel her skin.

He fell on her and trapped her under him, yanking her arms up, his pelvis arching into her. "You'll take what I can give you, all of it, *amor*."

"Yes."

She struggled against him, but he tamed her with his mouth, pinning her with his weight, stretching out naked on top of her. He grabbed her hair and held her still, and it felt like silk between his fingers. "I'm going to love doing this with you."

She sighed and rubbed against him like a cat. "I'll pretend to like it."

Her voice was husky, full of longing, inviting him to do

things to her. He cupped the full globes of her lace-covered breasts, dragging his teeth across that delectable spot of skin, licking the curve between her neck and shoulder. "Oh, you will. I'll make sure you do." Her nipple puckered, and he pinched to draw it out even more. "This little nipple pretends very well."

She lay back, all skin and hair and woman, drawing him to her warmth. Her arms were around him, her hands on his back, kneading the bunched-up muscles. He shuddered. He could lose himself in those eyes, in that body, in her, and he demanded, "Say 'Marcos.' Whisper my name to me."

"Marcos."

She wasn't sure from what part of her had come this determination, this courage or this desperate want, she only knew she needed him. He annihilated her mind, her senses. She hadn't realized what she'd do, how she'd fight to be with this one man until she'd seen Marissa.

She hadn't yet finished saying his name, a word that echoed the passion roaring through her, and he was there already, growling "Virginia" and taking her mouth in a fierce kiss. A flock of butterflies exploded in her stomach when their lips met. Her head swam as the flames spread, his tongue thrusting precisely, strongly, fiercely inside, emotion hissing through her, weakening her, overwhelming her.

Growling, he deepened the kiss as he tugged the bow loose at her hip, and she felt the fabric of her dress unfurl until it opened and hung at her sides. "It's important your body becomes familiar with my touch. All of it. You want Marissa to believe us, don't you? If you want others to believe it you have to believe it yourself. Your body has to know to respond when I touch it."

A strangled sound echoed in the silence and in the back of her mind Virginia realized it came from her. He cupped one lace-encased breast. Oh, it was so wonderful. So bad. So everything. She'd stop him in a minute…in one more minute…no, she'd not stop him, not tonight, maybe not ever.

Utterly possessing her lips, he slid his free palm down the flatness of her stomach and below. "It's important I know your curves…the texture of your skin…"

She could feel every sinew of his muscles against her. His fingers…sliding downward. Deep, forgotten places inside her clenched in waiting for his touch. Opening her mouth, she flicked her tongue out to his. "Marcos."

"Here you are. Soaked."

His voice grew husky. Desire trembled there. His hand between her legs began to slide under her panties. She arched involuntarily when he feathered a finger across the soft, damp spot at the juncture of her thighs. Every pink, throbbing part of her pinged at his touch. She moaned in her throat and sank back deeper into the bed as he caressed more deliberately.

She'd never known a touch could feel like fire, spread through her until every inch throbbed and burned. Involuntarily she moved her hips, filling his palm with the dewy softness between her legs.

"Marcos…" It was a plea, and it carried in it the fright she experienced in what he made her feel.

"Shh." His lips grazed her temple. "Open up to me." His free hand tugged at her bra and bared her left breast to him. Her disbelieving gaze captured the instant the rosy peak of her nipple disappeared between his lips. A thrilling jolt rushed through her as the moist heat of his mouth enveloped her. Her head fell back on a moan.

Instinctively she reached up to cup the back of his head, cradling him with the same gentle care he used to suckle her breast. He groaned profoundly in his throat and continued to fondle her with his mouth, lips nipping, tongue swirling, mouth suckling.

His hand moved lightly, expertly, his fingers unerringly

fondling her through her panties. Hot little shivers rushed through her.

One long finger began to stroke her dampness. Open her with little prods of the tip.

She squirmed in shock, a little in agony, seeking ease for the burn growing inside her. "I hurt." Blindly, her parted mouth sought more of the warmth of his lips. He penetrated her. With his tongue. His finger. She arched and cried out, shocked by the sensation. An explosion of colors erupted behind her eyelids. His mouth melded to hers harder. Skin, heat, ecstasy.

Her skin felt damp while every cell in her body felt hot and tingly. With a low growl, he delved a hand into her hair and pulled her head back, moving his mouth up her neck. It was damp and velvety on her flesh, licking as though her skin were his only sustenance. In her ear he rasped, "I'm filling you."

"Yes." Against his throat.

"You crave me to fill you." His finger was thrusting, possessing—his body incredibly hard against hers. "You need me to take away the hurt."

Pleasure ripped through her, and her back arched helplessly as she moaned. "You make me reckless, Marcos, you make me…"

"Burn." He opened his mouth. Giving her the mist of his breath. "I can't believe how ready you are. How slick. Are you pretending? Are you, *amor?*"

"No."

He gave her his tongue. She could hear the soaked sounds his touch caused and felt embarrassed and aroused all at once. "Shh. Take my finger," he huskily murmured, the graze of that finger so bare and fleeting across her entry she mewled with a protest to take it in again. "Soon I'll give you two. Do you want two?"

"No," she lied. Her body ruled now, screamed, shivered against his.

"Hmm." He inserted the first, then the second deeply. "I'll pretend that was a yes."

Her thoughts scattered. "Marcos, please…"

"My God, you're responsive." His hands continued to work their magic as he looked down on her. "You were jealous for me."

The burn intensified. The clench in her womb unbearable. "Yes," she breathed, closing her eyes.

His groan sounded like a growl. "I like that."

"Marcos."

He was watching her, the effects of what he did to her. Every time she gasped, or let go a little moan, his face tightened with emotion—and alternately, something clenched tightly in her. She'd never known the extent of her passion, was surprised at how shamelessly she took pleasure from him.

Gently, he pried her fingers away from his neck and brought her hand between their bodies. "Touch me."

"Where? Where do I…"

"Here." He shifted over her. The sheets slid well below his hips and their every inch, shoulder to hips, became perfectly aligned. The very hardest part of him pushed against her hand. "Feel me," he strained out. "Feel how I want you. This isn't for her, Virginia, this is for you."

He ground his hips against hers unapologetically. When she let go, his rigid length grazed her moistness through her panties. They groaned at the contact. He pressed closer, ground himself harder, wide and long against her. She wanted to die.

By the erratic heaves of his chest, Virginia suspected even though he was larger and more powerful, he was as defenseless to their chemistry as she was. Under her fingers, his skin was warm and slightly damp. Shyly, she continued to explore him, sifting her fingers through the dark hair at his nape, amazed at the soft texture.

His hands covered her breasts. The calluses on his palms were palpable through the lace, and her breast swelled ripely under his kneading.

Turning her cheek into the pillow, she let her eyes drift shut as she fought the intimacy of it all, the swelling tenderness that washed over her as he touched her. It was difficult to imagine that he was not her lover and she wasn't entirely, completely, indisputably his.

Burying his face between her breasts, he gnawed at the tiny bow at the center of her bra. She felt the unmistakable graze of his teeth on her skin. He used them to scrape the top swell of her breast and a very startling whimper escaped her.

His mouth shifted to the peak, pointy and obvious under the fabric, and he licked her. The hot dampness of his tongue seeped into her skin. She shuddered. A thrilling heat fanned out from her center.

He reached around her and unhooked her bra. When he peeled it off her, she instinctively covered herself with her palms.

"I want to see." He pried her hands away and placed them on his shoulders. His dark, heavy-lidded eyes regarded each of her breasts with interest. His breath fanned across one exposed nipple. "So pretty."

She drew in a ragged breath as he brushed the little bud with the pad of his thumb. It puckered under his finger. If possible, his eyes darkened even more. "Do you want my mouth here?"

"I d-don't know."

He swiped his tongue across the tip. "Yes, you do." He closed his eyes and nuzzled her with his nose. "Do you want my mouth here?"

"Yes."

He licked gently. "Like that."

"Yes."

He grazed with his teeth. "Or like that."

She squeezed his shoulders, staring to shiver. "B-both."

He nibbled using his lips then drew her fully into his mouth. "Hmm. Like a raspberry."

Her eyes shut tight. The sensation of being devoured entirely by his mouth had her melting.

Could he say something wrong, please? Could he not lick her…like that? Could his hands be smaller, less thorough, less hot, less knowing?

Turning to suckle her other breast, he delved one hand between her legs and slipped into her panties. "I want my mouth here, too," he murmured, searching her pliant folds with strong, deft fingers.

She gasped and thrashed her head, seized by a mix of shame and pleasure as he unerringly found, opened, invaded that most intimate part of her. "N-no…no mouth there."

"But I can touch?"

Quivering and warm, she sensed him watching her as he gently eased one finger into that moist, swollen place that craved him.

She gulped back an enormous clog of emotion. "Yes."

"Chiquita." It was a reverent whisper, full of wonder as he stretched her. *"Chiquita mia."*

She arched, shamelessly offering herself. As he continued his foray inside her, a marvelous pressure gathered at her core.

His nostrils flared. "One minute," he rasped as he searched under her dress for the silken string of her panties. She was weightless on the bed when he tugged them off her legs. "And I put us both out of our misery."

His chest gleamed bare when he leaned over her, his shoulders bunched with tension as he grasped her calves.

He stared into her eyes, his expression tight as he guided her legs around his hips. "Hold on to me. Don't let me go."

The way he asked to be held made her think she'd never let him go, she'd make him love her, she'd hold on to him.

He pulled her to his hips and she felt him, hot and thick and rigid, pressing into where she was pliant and damp. A wildness raged inside her when he ducked his head to suckle a breast—suckle hard the instant he pushed in. She bucked up to receive him, urging him in with her hands and legs.

They moaned in unison when he entered, their breaths mingling as he angled his head to hers, their lips so close that all he had to do was bend his head an inch to capture her mouth and the whimper that followed when he was fully inside her.

"Yes," he growled.

"Yes," she breathed.

A fullness took her, bringing the discomfort of being stretched more than she could bear, and then he was moving inside her and the unease transformed to pleasure. Waves and waves of pleasure.

And in that instant she loved what he did to her, how he brought her every cell and atom to life, how he offered her ease. Ease for this wanting.

She'd longed for that ease more than anything.

As he moved in her, touched and kissed her, she gave encouraging sounds that seemed to tear out from within her—and he continued. Taking. Giving. Expertly loving her.

Braced up above her, his arms rippled with tension, his throat strained, his face was raw with the semblance of pleasure. All were memorized in her mind.

Vaguely, in her blanked, blissful state, she knew sex would never again be like this. Would a man ever live up to this one?

A sound that was purely male vibrated against her ear as he placed his mouth there to whisper, "Come for me."

Moving deftly, he pushed her higher and higher, murmuring carnal, unintelligible words in Spanish that melted her bones like the silk and steel thrusts of his body. *Mia. Suave. Hermosa. Mia. Mia. Mia.*

All Virginia could say was "Marcos." In a plea, a murmur, a moan. *Marcos.* Over and over again. *Marcos* as he increased his pace, driving faster, more desperately into her. Vaguely she felt the warmth of him spill inside her, the convulsions that racked his powerful body as ecstasy tore through them both, the pleasure consuming, making him yell, making her scream, scream "Marcos."

"Marcos" as he kissed her breasts, her lips, her neck. "Marcos" as the pressure spread. "Marcos" as she shattered.

Seven

Darkness: it was hard to leave it. But a strong, familiar scent wafted into her nostrils. Tempting. Tantalizing. Beckoning her awake. Coffee. Yes. Strong and rich and ready. Virginia stirred on the bed. She stretched her arms first, then her legs, sighing when it hurt pleasantly to do both.

"...in an hour...yes...we'll be there..."

Virginia bolted upright on the bed when she recognized that particularly deep baritone voice. Her head swam. *Lips tugging at her nipples, fingers pinching, touching, pleasuring...whispers...* A throb started between her legs. She squeezed her eyes shut and swung her feet until her toes touched the carpeted floor. *Calm down.* She would not, could not, panic.

Sunlight glowed in the living room, making her squint as she entered. He stood by the window in his shirt and slacks. His raven-black hair looked damp from a recent bath. He held one arm stretched above his head, his tan hand braced on the windowsill. His was a solid presence in the room.

Sturdy as an ox, that was the way he looked. That was the way he was.

"Good morning," she muttered.

He turned, smiled.

She set her coffee on a small round table beside the desk and lowered herself to a chair, Marcos coming forward and kissing her forehead.

"Did you order the entire kitchen contents up here?" she whispered.

He stroked her cheek. "I wanted to be sure I ordered what you liked."

A blush was spreading up her neck because she remembered cuddling against him after she'd gone on and on saying *please*. God, no.

His eyes were full of knowledge, of satisfaction of having loved his lover well and hard for a night. Her skin pebbled with goose bumps as she realized he was remembering everything they'd done through the night: the kissing, the laughing, the kissing, the eating cheese and grapes on the carpet, the kissing.

They had made love until Virginia thought she'd pass out from bliss.

And hours before waking up, when she had cuddled in and draped one leg across his hips, he had made slow, lazy love to her again, and whispered words to her in Spanish she could only dream of finding the meaning of.

He lifted her chin, studying her. "Did I hurt you last night?"

With a small smile, she tugged on the collar of her pajama top and showed him his bite. His forehead furrowed.

"That has to be painful."

"Only in the most pleasurable way."

Settling down, she took a healthy sip of coffee, then set the cup back down. "What?" she pressed.

He was looking at her strangely.

"What?"

"You begged me to take you last night."

"And?"

"And I liked it."

Her stomach muscles contracted. Suddenly her lips felt puffy and sensitive as she remembered just how thoroughly he'd kissed her. "Marcos, this will be very complicated in Chicago."

"It doesn't have to be."

A thousand butterflies fluttered in her chest. "You expect we can keep this up?"

"We touched. We made love four times in one night. Do you expect we can stop by Monday?"

They'd touched. His tanned, long hands had been somewhere in her body, and hers had been somewhere in his. She couldn't bear to remember. "What do you…suggest?"

"Nobody has to know about us. And my suggestion is to continue."

Her body trembled. Little places zinged and pinged as though reminding her just, exactly, where his hands had been. "Continue."

He leaned against the window and his hand slowly fisted high up on the windowsill. "I swear I've never seen anything lovelier than you, naked. Your breasts."

She closed her eyes, sucking in a breath, willing herself not to remember what he'd done there. How he'd squeezed or cradled or…

"Marcos…"

"You cried out my name when I was inside you."

Oh, God. Yes, she had, yes, she had. Had she no honor? No pride when it came to him? No digni—

"I couldn't sleep for wanting to take you again." He smiled sadly. "You kept cuddling against me and I kept growing hard. I had to…shower."

Wrapping her arms around her shaking frame, she asked, "Do you want to?"

"To what?"

"Make love to me again."

And he said…

"Yes."

Her stomach exploded. He wanted her. Still. More than yesterday? Marcos still wanted her. But they couldn't continue in Chicago. They couldn't.

His arm fell at his side as he spun around and pinned her with a smile. "Eat up, though. We're going sightseeing."

She set down her coffee mug before she spilled it all over herself. "Really?"

"Of course. Really. We're flying over the city on a chopper first. Then we'll lunch downtown."

"A chopper."

"Are you concerned?"

"Actually, no. Excited."

She dug into the eggs, the waffles and the tea.

Marcos was piling his plate as though he hadn't been fed since his toddler years. "Would you like a tour of Allende," he asked casually.

Allende. She grinned. "I thought you'd never ask."

It occurred to her she had never imagined she could ever have one of these mornings with Marcos. Such a lavish, elegant hotel suite and such a clear, sunny day outside, a beautiful morning. Like husband and wife. Talking. Smiling. Laughing as they enjoyed breakfast. But they were boss and assistant, embarking on what had to be wrong. The air around them was charged with sexual tension. Really, it could very well be lightning in there.

"Did she…agree to your bid?" Virginia asked, breaking the silence. This watching him eat was a little too stimulating to her mind.

He popped a grape into his mouth. "She will."

"She didn't seem interested in even discussing business."

"It's a game." His eyes skewered her to her seat. "She wants me to demand Allende and I won't."

"So you'll play this for the entire week."

"Not likely." He spread cream cheese atop his bagel. "I'll leave with an offer and let her think it over."

Were he any other man, Virginia was sure a woman like Marissa could handle him. But he was Marcos. Nobody could think straight with him near and he was as manageable as a wild stallion to a child. "If she rejects your offer?"

He diverted his attention from his tower of gluttony and selected a newspaper among the three folded ones, calmly saying, "She's not getting a better one, trust me."

He yanked open *El Norte*. "What angered you? Yesterday?"

The cup paused halfway to her lips then clattered back down on the plate. "I heard you...discussing me. I've always found that annoying."

Slowly he folded the paper and set it aside. The intense stare he leveled on her made her squirm. Those gypsy eyes, they did magic in her. Black magic.

"You're blushing."

"I'm not."

But her face felt hot and so did other parts of her.

His jaw tightened and a muscle in his cheek flexed. "Is it the attention? You do not like this?"

She drew in a deep breath because unfortunately there was no brown bag she could cover her face with. She had to pretend he was hallucinating. "It's the whispering behind my back."

"You cannot control what people whisper." He popped a piece of his bagel into his mouth and then picked up the paper again.

"You are wrong." How could he think that? "You can

control your actions. You can give them no cause to...to whisper."

"You'd let gossip hurt you, Virginia?"

His voice was full of such tenderness she actually felt it like a stroke. "You've never been hurt by words before?"

Once again, the paper was lowered. This time his eyes burned holes through her. "I said words to my father. I'll bet my fortune that yes, they hurt."

Something distressed her. His gaze. His tone. "You wish you took them back?"

He considered with a frown. "No. I wish he'd have taken them for what they were. The words of a wounded boy determined to break him."

She had never known Marcos to be cruel. But he could be dangerous. He was predator, and he had been wounded. "You could never make amends with him?"

His smile was pantherlike, almost carrying a hiss. "Because of her."

"Marcos," she said again after a moment, even more alarmed at the harsh set of his jaw and ominous slant of his eyebrows. "Marcos, why do you want to destroy the company? You could make amends with it. Save it, mend it."

"It would take too much effort." He waved her off with a hand, went back to the paper. "Eat up, *amor,* I'm eager to show you the city."

"You're eager to get back and have your way with me," she quipped.

He threw his head back and gave out a bark of laughter, his expression so beautiful her heart soared in her chest. "So we understand each other, then."

He couldn't tear his eyes away from her.

She was the same woman he'd wanted for so long, and yet she had become someone else. A sexy woman who was comfortable in his presence, smiling, laughing, open to speaking her mind.

Eyes sparkling as the helicopter touched the ground, Virginia pulled his headphones down to his neck. "That's Allende?" she yelled through the rotor noise.

He glanced out the window, squeezing her fingers with his. Impossible, but her excitement was rubbing off on him. "That's it, yes."

Once they climbed out of the helicopter, Marcos surveyed the vast industrial building that sat on two hundred acres of land. It was smaller than he remembered it—but then he'd been so much younger.

The sun blazed atop their heads. Virginia's raven mane gleamed. And in that moment Marcos didn't see how aged the building appeared, or notice the grease on all the trucks and carriers that were parked in endless rows across the parking lot. He saw his father and himself, discussing the delivery schedule. A strange heaviness settled in his chest, weighing him down.

"Are we going in?"

Pulled from his thoughts, he looked at his assistant. How she managed to stand there—sexy and innocent—while he felt so unsettled was beyond him.

Bracing himself for whatever greeted him inside, he led her toward the double glass doors beneath a metal sign that read *Transportes Allende*.

Within minutes the two guards unlocked the door and ushered them in. Marcos and Virginia were free to roam the old wide halls. An attractive blush tinted her cheeks as she eagerly drank in her surroundings.

There was nothing to say about the structure, except that it was bare bones, obsolete and old. *Horrible*.

New installations were a must. A more recent fleet of carriers to strengthen their position as a link to the U.S. market. New—

"This is terribly spacious," she said, leaning a hand on a red brick wall that served as a room division.

Marcos reined himself back. What in *the hell* had he been thinking?

He didn't want to restore the company to its former glory; he wanted it gone.

He frowned darkly while Virginia swayed her hips and went peeking from room to room. All were vacated for the morning under Marcos's instructions. An encounter with Marissa was the last thing he'd wanted today—and thankfully she was smart enough to have obliged.

Virginia tucked her hair behind her ear, her forehead creasing as she peered up at the rafters on the ceiling.

Rather than notice the paint was peeling off the walls and making a list of fixing that—Miss Hollis was probably already cataloguing that for him, in any case—Marcos focused on her reactions.

Something warm and fuzzy stirred in him. Virginia would be a pitiful poker player. Her expressions were too untrained for intrigue—and her father's past had given her a loathing for the game.

"My first office," he said then, without tone.

She spun around in the doorway as he spoke, wide-eyed. "This one? With the view of the front gate?"

He followed her into the small space and tried to see it through her eyes, old and dirty and cluttered, but then it just appeared like what it was: a promising place in need of some attention.

Marcos could've kicked himself for mentally volunteering to give it some TLC. No. Hell, no.

He wouldn't.

All he wanted was to eliminate it, like wiping out his past in one fell swoop. Swoosh. Gone. Presto!

But judging by the interest that swam in Virginia's eyes,

she approved of the place, too. "It fits you somehow," she said. "Rough around the edges."

They shared a smile.

The fuzzy feeling inside him grew to incredible proportions.

"How many transport units does it have?" she asked. "Approximately?"

He watched her sail to the window. His eyes tracked her progress for a moment and then he followed her.

She was peering through the blinds, scanning the vast loading area, when he came up behind her.

He buried his face in the side of her neck and enveloped her in his arms, biting back a groan. "There are two thousand and forty cargo carriers—plus hundreds of smaller units for simpler deliveries."

She smelled of a soft, powdery fragrance, her hair scented with his travel shampoo. The combination flew up to his head like an aphrodisiac.

He'd never imagined the days they spent together would be like this. Lust and desire constantly had him on edge, true, but there was also the delightful peace and pleasure of her company.

Gently, he guided her around to face him. "As soon as we land in Chicago, I will have the funds transferred to your personal account. I want those men out of your and your father's lives so you can be at peace. Agreed?"

A shadow descended, veiling her eyes. Inch by inch, her smile disappeared.

He cupped her face between his palms. "Something wrong with that?"

Clearly something was. She averted her gaze and gnawed on her lower lip. "Thank you, no, it's all fine. That's our arrangement, right?"

Pretend, she didn't say. But his mind supplied it.

When Marcos did not deny this, Virginia lowered her

face and drew away, suddenly looking very young and very vulnerable. She hugged herself tight. "I'd forgotten I'm being paid for this, that my father's bad habits brought me here."

Marcos knew that a woman like her didn't easily fall into a man's bed. Was she regretting that she had? Or only the circumstances that had brought her there?

A host of male instincts assailed him, urging him to embrace her, take her, appease her, seize the instinctive role of a man and protect her.

With a surge of dominant power, he grasped her shoulders and gave a gentle clench. "You're worried he won't stop gambling—that this will only be a temporary relief from your problem."

She nodded. "I am."

Virginia had been calling her father every day. His insides wrenched in protest at the knowledge of her suffering because of a reckless old man on a suicide mission. "How long since your father had a real job?" They strolled back into the hall, side by side.

"Since Mother died. Several years ago."

They came into the last office—his father's old office. Virginia probably didn't know it had been his because of its ample size, or maybe she suspected, Marcos didn't know. All he knew was that he couldn't bear to look around but at the same time couldn't leave it.

He crossed the wood floor, now covered with a shaggy white rug, and touched the window as he gazed outside. "He's been like this ever since? Your father?"

"It's gotten out of control recently."

Circling around the desk, he stroked the blunt edge with his fingers—he used to sit there and listen to his father talk on the phone. Thoughtfully, he asked, "Has he tried to even get a job?"

"He did. He's tried, but of course he's found nothing. At

least that's what he says, but I suspect his pride won't let him accept the kinds of jobs that have been offered to him."

He frowned. "Sometimes you have to take what you can get."

"I agree." She toed the plush ends of the rug with the tip of her high heels. "I just feel he was hoping for someone to give him a chance at what he used to do. He was a good manager except he spoiled his chance."

Second chances, Marcos thought. People spoke of them all the time, but in reality nobody offered them.

His father hadn't offered it to him.

Nor had he offered one to his father.

Gradually, he allowed his surroundings to filter into his mind. A snapshot of Marissa beside the dormant computer. Frilly female things atop the desk. And he realized with a sinking heart that Marissa had taken possession of his father's office.

There was no picture of the old man who'd raised him. The soccer posters—vintage ones that his old man had collected—were no longer on the walls. She'd taken everything, that heartless witch. *Everything!*

"This is your father's office?" Virginia watched him, and the pity in her eyes made him desperate to eliminate it.

"Not anymore." He smiled tightly, snatching up her hand. "Come on, let's go. The office staff is coming in later."

He escorted her outside. Thinking of how it was too late for his father and him—but maybe not for hers. Marcos's old man had not been a gambler, but his quest for a woman had trampled his own son.

It seemed unfair a child should sacrifice their happiness for a parent. Marcos had not been willing.

He'd *never* accept as a stepmother a woman who'd months before been his lover, *never* accept as a stepmother a woman who was so obviously playing his father for a fool. After numerous heated arguments where Carlos Allende refused to admit his son's view as true, Marcos had packed his bags and left. But Virginia?

When her father fell into that dark gambling pit once more, what was this generous, loyal creature going to do? And what would he be willing to do to help her?

She loved Mexico.

There was something deliciously decadent about the time they spent during the following days poking around little shops, eating in restaurants, walking the city.

This afternoon, as Virginia's heels hit the marbled floors of the awe-inspiring MARCO museum, she drew in a deep, reverent breath. This was a luxury she'd never allowed herself before. She'd rarely allowed herself outings to relax or to stimulate the mind; she'd always been so consumed by worry.

Now she wove through the paintings on exhibit, feeling Marcos's presence next to her, and felt like she'd stepped into an alternate reality.

Every painting that caught her eye, every sculpture she viewed with the eyes of a woman who had suddenly acquired sight. And hearing. And touch. The colors were vibrant, and the themes were all passionate. Even death seemed passionate.

At night, Marcos took her out to eat in a small café just blocks away from the city plaza. After salad, tacos and fries, they walked arm-in-arm through the throng of people.

She'd never felt so safe.

She was in a dangerous city, surrounded by a language she did not understand and among unique, intriguing people, and she felt utterly safe. Her world felt so distant. Her father's debts, the threats, the fact that things could get worse. Nothing mattered when these long, sinewy, rock-hard arms were around her.

She felt, for the first time in her life, protected. *Secure.*

During their ride back to the hotel, she caught Marcos watching her with those eyes and that knowing smile, and a sneaky little voice whispered to her. It accompanied them to their rooms, nestling somewhere deep inside her.

This is as real as real gets, Virginia Hollis. Can you make him see it?

No, she doubted that she could. He viewed the world with the eyes of a man. While she, with those of a woman.

As she struggled to tame her welling emotions, Marcos grasped her chin between his thumb and forefinger and tipped her head back. "Who does he gamble with? Do you know?"

It took a moment for her to grasp his train of thought. She shook her head. "I don't know."

Marcos hadn't dropped the subject of her father for days. It was as though he were intent on avoiding the topic of his own parent and was focusing instead on fixing the troubles of hers.

Shrugging off his shirt, his eyes held hers in the lamplight, his voice a mellow rumble. "You said his gambling put you in this position. In that bed right behind you. My bed. Did you mean it?"

She considered the question at length, and though she'd needed to save her father no matter what, she also softly admitted, as she pulled off her short-sleeved sweater, "I think I brought myself here."

She tossed her sweater aside, then her bra. Even in the flickering shadows, she caught the tightening flex of his jaw and throat. That her nakedness affected him made her smile and move close to him. Her palms hit the smooth velvet of his chest and her fingers rubbed upward. "What do you say about that, Mr. Allende?" she whispered.

With slow deliberation, he turned his head toward hers. As his fingers ventured in a languorous caress up her back, his mouth grazed her cheek and his sweet, hot breath coasted across her skin. "I say you're the sexiest little thing I've ever seen. Miss Hollis. And I want you to promise me—whatever happens between us, you're coming to me if your father's ever again in trouble."

"No, Marcos."

"Yes. You are. I'd make you give me your word you'll not pay debts that aren't yours, but I know that'd be unfair to ask of you. You feel responsible for him, I respect that. Now please understand I feel responsible for you."

Her toes curled at the proprietary gleam in his eyes. "But you're not."

"You're my employee."

"You have thousands of employees."

His knuckles caressed her nipples, and her body flared to life at the touch. "But only one who's been my lover."

The words lingered in the air for a heated moment. She was ready to give up. Just wanted to kiss. Could almost hear the seconds ticking as their time together ran out.

"No contest?" he queried then, sensing his victory.

She yielded, shaking her head, wrapping her arms around him. "None."

By the time their lips touched, she was holding her breath, parting her lips for his smiling mouth to take. He seized them softly and began to entice and torment her with nips and nibbles and gentle little suckles she felt down to the soles of her feet.

When he lowered her to the bed, his mouth became more demanding, spreading fire through her veins. And as his tongue forayed hard and hot inside her, one hand traveled up her ribcage to knead one waiting, throbbing breast with long, skillful fingers. *"Chiquita."*

He scraped his whiskers across her chin, and she sighed.

She was his lover for a week.

She was nothing more and she would never be more.

Braced up on one arm, he used his free hand to unbuckle her slacks. He pulled the zipper low and pulled them off her. His thumb touched the elastic of her panties and made slow, sinuous circles before he eased it down.

Lover for a week. That's all.

Discarding her panties, he urged her down on the bed and rained haphazard, unexpected kisses across her torso. On her shoulder, her tummy, then feasted on the tip of one breast. Virginia dropped her hand and absently caressed the back of his satiny black head as it moved, imagining what it would be like to suckle a baby. Their baby.

She'd always wanted a family.

Virginia, lover for a week!

As he kissed a path down her belly, it struck her with a sweet wrenching pain that she had never sensed her dream of a family so far out of reach. At first the desire had been tucked aside to help her father resurface from his grief. Now it had come to the forefront of her mind and it mocked her.

Because she had become lover to this man.

This enthralling black-haired Spaniard.

And every man in her future would always be compared in her mind to Marcos Allende. Every bed she slept in would not be this one. And she dreaded, doubted there would be a man in this world to kiss her the way he did. Touch her like this, just like *this*.

Realizing his mouth was approaching somewhere dangerous, she squirmed under him. "If you knew what I was thinking," she spoke up at the ceiling, "you'd leave the room."

He lifted his head and met her gaze, his voice frighteningly solemn. "Don't give me your heart, Virginia."

Oh, God. She squeezed her eyes shut. *Don't fall in love with him, don't fall in love with him,* don't fall in love with him. She scoffed, yanked her arm free as she sat up. "What? You think you're all that and then some? That I cannot resist you? I'll have you know…my heart…was not part of our bargain. You're the boss and I'm the…employee and this is…an arrangement."

One callused palm ran up and down the side of her leg. "And yet it's easy to forget who we are here, isn't it? Easy to get confused."

She frowned over the concern in his voice and grabbed his head, defiantly pulling his lips to hers.

Lovers. That was all.

This is as real as real gets, Virginia Hollis. Can you make him see it?

They came to understand each other. Too well, maybe. They talked, but not of the future. They talked, but not of themselves.

They pretended, as they'd agreed to do.

"Did you enjoy yourself this week?"

Riding to the airport in the back of the Mercedes, Virginia sat curled up against Marcos's side and laid her cheek on his shoulder. It was strange—how instinctively she sought this place, and how instinctively Marcos wrapped his arm around her shoulder to offer it to her.

She didn't care if she shouldn't do this, only knew within hours she wouldn't dare. So she did it now.

"It's been wonderful," she admitted and trailed off when he brushed his mouth across her temple and placed a soft, almost imperceptible kiss there. "Unexpected and…surreal and wonderful."

He held her so tight, so intimately, and whispered against her hair, "We should've done this before."

Going pensive at the note of lingering lust in his voice, Virginia played with the buttons on his shirt while Marcos checked his phone and made a call to the office. As he spoke into the receiver, she stole a glance at him.

His voice rumbled in her ear, and his arm around her

was absently moving up and down her bare arm. She'd been unable to keep from staring at him all week, and had been secretly delighted that most times he'd been checking up on her, too.

When he hung up, he gazed out the window at the passing car lights and said, "You'll wire yourself the money from my account and take care of your problem straight away. Promptly, tomorrow morning."

A command. As an authoritative man and, also, her boss.

"Understand?"

She hadn't noticed she'd flattened her hand on his chest until his own big one came to cover hers. She watched their fingers entwine. Lovers' fingers.

God, she'd done the most reckless thing. Look at her— draped all over her boss. Imagine if this ever got out? If people knew? Worse of all, her tummy was in a twist because she loathed for it to stop. And it had to—tonight. "Yes, I'll take care of it right away," she murmured, and on impulse took a good long whiff of his familiar scent.

"I've been thinking." Marcos turned her hand around for his inspection and his thumb began to slowly circle the center of her palm. "I'd like to offer your father a job."

"A job?"

"I figure if he realized he could be useful, he'd break the cycle of vice he seems to be stuck in."

She thought about it, still resting her cheek against his chest, feeling utterly contented and yet dreading tomorrow when that feeling could be replaced with unease. "Why?" she asked then.

He quirked an eyebrow, then narrowed his eyes. "Why what?"

She fingered the heavy cross at his throat. "Why… him?"

"Why not?"

She shrugged, but her heart began to flutter at the prospect. "Maybe he's just hopeless." As hopeless as she was. How would she bear Monday at the office? She was terribly in lust with the man. He was an extraordinary lover, made her feel so sexy and wild she wanted to take all kinds of risks with him, and now he offered her father this incredible lifeline?

"Maybe he is hopeless," Marcos agreed, chuckling.

But no, he was not hopeless, no one was. A smile appeared on her face. "Or maybe he will want one more chance." And maybe she could handle Monday after all.

She'd survived so far, had feigned not to want Marcos for days and weeks and months. Now she'd act as though nothing had happened. As though when he looked at her, her insides didn't leap with joy, and when he smiled at her, her stomach didn't quiver.

He smiled at her then, causing all kinds of happenings in her body, and stroked her cheek with his warm hand. "I've looked into him. He was a smart, dedicated man, and he could be one again."

Virginia contemplated his words, pleased that Marcos was smart enough to look past her father's mistakes and see the hardworking man underneath. And a plan formed in her mind. Her father had managed a large chain store so successfully that, if everything hadn't gone downhill after her mother's death, he'd be CEO by now.

"You know, Marcos," she said quietly, straightening on a burst of inspiration, "I think he might enjoy coming to Mexico."

Silence fell. The car swerved to the left and into the small airport driveway. Virginia remembered the look of grim solemnity in Marcos's face during their tour of Allende and she plunged on.

"He might even enjoy working at Allende," she said. She tossed the bait lightly, hoping to plant some kernel of doubt in him so he'd reconsider his decision regarding the company's future. But he went so still, she almost regretted it.

He stared at her with a calculating expression, then gazed out at the waiting jet. "Maybe."

Neither said another word, but when he pulled her close, ducked his head and kissed her, she fought not to feel a painful pang.

This was where they'd first kissed.

It only made sense it would be where they had their last.

Eight

She was tidying up his office the next morning when Marcos halted at the doorway. The sight of Virginia fiddling with the coffeemaker froze him, then heated up his blood.

As she poured a cup—black, as he liked it—the plain buttoned-up shirt she wore stretched across her breasts in a way that made watching feel like purgatory.

"Good morning."

She glanced up with a soft gasp. "Marcos—Mr. Allende." And there went her breasts again, swelling, pert and lovely as she took a little breath.

His heart thudded as they stared at each other, the words lingering in the air. *Mr. Allende.*

A word meant to erase everything that had happened in Monterrey, Mexico.

Having never expected she would make it this easy, he stepped inside and pulled the doors shut behind him. "Good morning, Miss Hollis."

He really could do this.

They'd pretended to be lovers before.

Now they would pretend they never had been.

Black coffee mug cradled against her chest, Virginia stared at him with the glazed wariness of a woman who feared that a man knew her secrets. "Can I get you anything, Mr. Allende?"

You.

He bit off the word, pulled off his jacket and tossed it onto the L-shaped sofa before he started for his desk. His head buzzed with thoughts of her. Her, smiling up at him from her place on his lap. She had an obsession with tidiness, and it showed. His office was pristine. She was a tidy little box, his Miss Hollis. Who would've known she'd be such a wanton in bed? So uninhibited? So sexy? So addictive?

"I hear you arrived home safely," he said, his groin stirring at the memory of their lovemaking. *Dammit, don't go there, man.*

"Yes, thank you." She flashed him one of those smiles that made his thoughts scramble. "And I caught up on my sleep a little."

"Excellent. Excellent."

His body clenched at her admission, for *he* hadn't had a wink of sleep since their return. He kept remembering her, innocent, cuddled up against him.

Diablos, he had never imagined he'd once again look at Monterrey with longing. Now he did.

He longed to be there with his assistant for another week where he knew exactly what to do with her.

Lips thinning in disgust at his own erotic thoughts, he took the coffee cup from her hands when she passed it to him and dismissed her with a wave. No use in delaying their parting. "That will be all. Thank you, Miss Hollis."

And with a painful wrench of mental muscle, he tore his eyes away and pushed her from his mind.

He had a business to take over.

* * *

Chicago felt different. The wind was the same, the noise, the traffic, and yet, it felt so different. She'd had to face Marcos at the office again today. Yesterday, their nonchalance toward each other had been so borderline pathetic she'd felt nauseated by the time she got home.

This morning, unable to stomach coffee, she made her way down the hall. The door to the extra bedroom where her father had been sleeping for the past couple of months was shut, and Virginia pressed her palm against it for a long moment, wondering if she should wake him. Let him know she was leaving for work. That everything had been taken care of and his debt absolved.

She decided she would call later instead and carried her small black duffel bag outside where the taxi waited, remembering Marcos's offer to give her father a job.

It had been easy then, to accept anything he'd wanted to give her. They'd been…involved. Now, Marcos Allende could calmly forget about it, as he'd forgotten the rest.

Worst of all was it hurt.

Even when she'd expected it.

As she stepped onto the amazingly busy Fintech nineteenth floor, Virginia hoped every employee would be in their usual flurries of movement and therefore too busy to notice she was fifteen minutes late.

But notice her they did.

The very moment her heels hit the carpet, a quiet spread throughout.

For the second day in a row, people glanced up from the copy machines. Behind their desks, heads lifted. The fact that everyone, everyone in the vast open space, knew and had probably discussed the fact that she had spent a week with Marcos in Monterrey became brutally evident. Deep inside, where all her fears were kept in a tight little bundle, she heard something.

They say she's his lover...

Had someone spoken that? Was she putting words and thoughts into their mouths because of her own regrets?

Dragging in a calming breath, she crossed the sea of cubicles, then went down the art-packed hallway. At the far end, to the right of the massive carved doors that led to Marcos's office, three identical rosewood desks stood. She slid in behind hers. The savvy Mrs. Fuller, who'd been with Marcos "longer than his mother has," was quick to make her way around her own tidy work place and greet Virginia. "He's very strange today," the older woman said, wide-eyed. "He smiled at me and he said 'thank you.'"

The words didn't diminish the kernel of fear settled in the pit of Virginia's stomach. If she so much as stepped out of her boundaries this week and onward...if she was fool enough to even remind him of Mexico...she dared not think of who would be sitting behind her desk next week.

"Then the deal must be going in his favor." Virginia attempted a teasing smile as she turned to get settled.

Lindsay, a young redhead near Virginia's age who'd also become her friend, drew up next to Mrs. Fuller. Their expressions were those of genuine excitement. "How was Mexico?" the older woman asked as Virginia sank into her chair and gazed at the top of her desk. A picture of her mother. A fake orchid. Her yellow markers sticking out of a silver can.

"Was it hot? I hear it's sweltering this time of year," Mrs. Fuller insisted. Virginia hadn't seen the woman yesterday since they'd reached Fintech later than normal.

"Yes," Virginia said, having no other answer to give a woman who was known through the entire building as levelheaded and kind.

As Mrs. Fuller's concerned gray eyes bored into the top of Virginia's head, she wished she could have been spared this encounter with even more fervor than she'd wished to avoid her last one with the dentist.

"He's been gazing out the window all morning, and with so much to do, that is so unlike him," Lindsay confessed under her cinnamon-scented breath. "And he asked me where you were."

Virginia was spared having to reply when the phones began their usual music. Struck as though by lightning, both Lindsay and Mrs. Fuller were spurred to action. They jumped behind their desks and began tackling the calls.

Ignoring the telephone ringing equally obnoxiously on her desk, Virginia tucked the duffel into the nook under the computer. She would not, could not, think of his mood meaning anything. Their deal would be over soon, after the Fintech dinner, and they would forget Mexico. He had promised it would not affect her job.

Inspecting her drawers and taking out her personal notepad and the colored clips she'd bought in a burst of secretarial enthusiasm, Virginia felt her throat close at the sudden memory of her mother. That hopeful light always in her eyes. Her warm, caring smile. She had always had a saying to cheer Virginia up. Would she have one for Virginia today? One about there always being something better out there? Better than Marcos?

"Miss Hollis, I hear you were out with the boss?"

She started in surprise. Fredrick Mendez, one of the youngest accountants, had propped his hip onto the corner of her desk and was eyeing her with a combination of amusement and mock despair.

"For a week," she stressed as she straightened in her chair.

"That's too much, Miss Hollis. Too much time without you. So, did you bring me a key chain?"

"Did you ask for one?"

"All right, at least show us some pictures," Fredrick

insisted. But when Virginia's usual friendly smile just would not come, he fell to his knees and clutched a hand to his chest. "Oh, Virginia, thy eyes shalt truth reveal—"

"Am I running a circus here, Mendez?"

The deep, clear voice, but most of all, the distinguished accent, struck Virginia like a cannon blast.

Her eyes flew to locate the source. Inches away, exiting the conference room and on his way to her, Marcos Allende was a sight to behold. Power and sophistication oozed from his every pore. His stride was slow and confident, his expression perfectly composed. And his every step kicked up her heartbeat. Six of his top lawyers followed.

Upon realizing who'd spoken, Fredrick's pale complexion turned in the space of a second to a tomato-red. He jumped to his feet and smoothed a hand along his polka-dot tie. "No, sir. I was just welcoming Virginia back on our behalf."

"Our?" He said the word as though Fredrick had no right to include himself in something he hadn't been invited to.

Turning to where Virginia sat with perfect poise behind the desk, Marcos thrust his hands into his pockets and silently contemplated her. "Don't you have work to do other than hound Miss Hollis," he said softly, and there was no doubt whom he addressed.

Fredrick took off with a mumbled "Yes, sir."

Without removing his eyes from her, he also said, "Brief me on the new stipulations when they're in."

In unison, the lawyers expressed their agreement and dispersed.

Without the buffer of their presence, there was nothing to pry those jealous black eyes from hers, no shield from the scorching possessiveness flickering in their depths.

Suddenly breathless, Virginia wondered if the blouse she wore today might be too white, or a little sheer? If her skirt was too short, her hair too unruly, the silver hoop earrings inappropriate for Fintech?

Meanwhile Marcos was the epitome of the worldly businessman.

He filled his black Armani like it had been tailor-made for those broad, square shoulders, which tapered down to his lean waist and narrow hips.

God! She could not believe the dark, breathtaking creature before her was her lover from Mexico.

Suddenly, as their gazes held, their eyes screaming with something dark and sinful, Virginia was certain the entire room thought she had slept with him. *They say she's his lover...*

Please, God, let no one ever know.

"Marcos," she said, moderating her tone. "I'm sorry I'm late, but I—"

Hands planted on the desk, Marcos stretched his arms out and in a single fluid move leaned forward. As his face neared her, Virginia saw Mrs. Fuller's eyes turn to saucers, and Lindsay almost fell back in her chair.

When the tip of his nose almost touched hers, she could focus on nothing else but six feet three inches of Marcos Allende. He ducked his head.

"Do you remember our deal?"

The murmur couldn't have been heard by anyone else. But she felt as if the clock, the world, stopped.

The feel of his breath on her face sent a torrent of warmth through her singing veins. "Yes, of course, I remember."

He leaned back a bit, regarding her as though he expected the same illumination he seemed to have experienced to have struck her, too. "After-work hours were included, weren't they?"

She couldn't explain the thrill she experienced, this inspiring and overwhelming happiness. He was asking for more, more from her, and not until this moment when she had his full attention had she realized how thirsty she'd been for it. "They were. Why do you ask? Is it that you need some assistance?"

His smile, slow in reaching completion, was meltingly sexy. "I do."

They say she's his lover...

She was plunging into a bottomless pit where surely there was nothing but heartache, and still, her blood was thrilling in her veins. "I'm always happy to be of assistance."

He gazed directly at her—the intent in his eyes unmistakable. "Be certain you present yourself at my apartment this evening. There's much to do."

She flushed beet-red, and scribbled in a yellow Post-it, *Is this what I think it is?*

He read it and tucked the note into his jacket, not before stroking her thumb with his, and sent her a look of such emotion and longing she almost wept. "Six p.m. sharp, Miss Hollis. I'm afraid it's an all-nighter."

He'd already started for his office when she blurted, "I can handle all-nighters."

"Good. This one's particularly hard."

When the doors closed shut behind him, whispers erupted, and Mrs. Fuller jumped to her feet and raced toward her in a flurry of mortification.

"Virginia. Please don't tell me this is what I think it is."

Heart pumping irregularly, Virginia grabbed her notepad. "I'd better go. The sales projections start in a few minutes and Marcos will want my notes." Oh, God, they had seen and heard all that, hadn't they?

Virginia, like putty in his hands. Marcos, suggesting she go to his place to...to...behave wickedly.

But the woman caught her by the shoulders and clenched tight with her fists, her face stricken. "Oh, sweetie, please say it isn't so!"

"Mrs. Fuller," Virginia said in a placating voice, patting

one of her hands for good measure. "I don't know what you mean, but there is nothing going on here, *nothing!*"

"Yes, there is. I've seen the way you look at him. You're a sweet young girl, an innocent little lamb, and Marcos is…a wolf! He's emotionally detached and you can't possibly—"

Virginia turned her head to hide her blush only to catch half the office staring at them. But Lindsay was smiling in glee behind her desk and sticking her thumbs up as though Virginia had just won the lottery.

Lowering her voice to a whisper, Virginia confessed, "I can handle wolves. I can handle a pack of them, I promise you. And this is nothing like what you think."

"Vee. Sweet, sweet Vee." Mrs. Fuller's hands trembled when she framed her cheeks between them. "I adore Marcos like a son. He has been a kind boss to me, and when my poor Herbert died…" She sighed, then shook her perfectly coiffed head and got back on track. "But he is not the kind of man a woman like you needs. There hasn't been a single woman in his history he's kept around for more than a month. You'll end up with a broken heart and even lose your job."

That her last comment struck a nerve was a given.

"I'm not losing my job for anything." Virginia forced a smile to her face and much needed courage into her heart. She wanted him. She wanted him so bad she had to have him, would seduce and remind him. "He's my boss, and he wants me to assist him, and so I will. Please don't worry, Mrs. Fuller, or your heartburn will act up. I'll be fine. And be sure everyone, *everyone* knows there's nothing going on here."

But even as she stepped into the projection room, she couldn't help wondering how well they'd be able to hide it for as long as it lasted.

And what would happen to her when it was really, truly finished.

Nine

After the longest work day of his entire life, and one during which he'd gotten exasperatingly little work done, Marcos arrived home to find her waiting in his living room.

Of course. His assistants had his key code—why shouldn't she be here?

With the sun setting behind her, her feet tucked under her body on the couch, and a book spread open on her lap, Virginia Hollis was a welcoming sight.

When he stepped out of the elevator that opened into the penthouse, she came to her feet, her hands going to her hair—to her rich, curly black hair, which was deliciously tousled as though she'd been running her fingers through it all day.

He fisted his hands at his sides, his mouth going dry. Good God. She wore drawstring pants and a button-up shirt with little ice cream cones. The colorful, almost childish pattern was also stamped all across the pajama pants. And on her, that weathered, warm-looking thing was the sexiest garment he'd ever had the pleasure of gazing upon.

He hadn't intended to sleep with her. Or had he? He'd wanted to see her, damn it. And now he could hardly believe what she was so obviously offering to him.

When he finally spoke, his voice came out rougher than he'd anticipated. "Have a good day?"

She set her book on the side table. Nodded. Then, "You?"

God, this was so domestic he should be climbing back into the elevator right about now. And getting away from there as fast as he could.

Why didn't he?

Because his hands itched to touch her. His guts felt tight and he was hot and hard with wanting her. He'd wanted to drag her into his office today, feel his way up her little skirt, kiss that mouth until her lips were bright red. He couldn't stay away, had now determined he was a fool to.

She wanted him, too.

Removing his jacket, he draped it across the back of a chair, nodding, as well.

"I brought my notes," she said quickly. "Just in case."

He gazed into eyes that were green and bottomless, and slowly advanced. "Good. Notes are important," he offered in return, and because he had missed the enticing, arousing sight of her all day, he gruffly added, "What else did you bring me, Miss Hollis?"

The soft smile that appeared on her lips trembled. Her hands smoothed her pajamas all along her hips and his eyes greedily swept up and down the length of her. "I like that… thing you're wearing." More than that, he was warming up to the idea of tearing it off her and licking her like vanilla ice cream.

"Thank you." She signaled at his throat. "I—I like your tie."

He wrenched it off, tossed it aside, then closed the space

between them. "Come here," he said quietly, wrapping an arm around her waist and drawing her flat against his body. "Why are you so shy all of a sudden?"

She set her hands lightly on his shoulders, barely touching him. "I—I don't know. I shouldn't have slipped into my pajamas."

Lust whirled inside him. She had a way of staring at him with those big eyes, like he was something out of this world. And she felt soft and womanly against him, her scent teasing his lungs as he buried his face in her hair. "I've wanted this, Virginia. God, how I've wanted this."

As she tipped her head back to him, he covered her lips with his.

Employing every ounce of experience and coaxing power at his disposal, he began to feast on that little mouth, drink of her honey.

Hesitantly she dipped her tongue into his mouth and a pang of longing struck in his core at how sweet she tasted, how entirely she succumbed and fitted her body to his.

In his need, he didn't hear himself, the way his voice turned hoarse with longing as he spoke to her, cupping the back of her head gently. *"Delicioso...besame...dame tu boca..."*

She tasted of warmth and hunger, and responded like a woman who'd thought of him all day—wanted him all day.

Just as he had thought of ways of devouring her, too.

The kiss went, in the space of three seconds, from a hard quest to a need that left no room for finesse. While he took thirsty sips of her mouth, his hands went places, one to cup a plump buttock, the other to work on her shirt.

Her eager hands tugged his shirt out of the waistband of his pants and slipped inside, making him groan when her cool, dry palms caressed his chest up and down.

He imagined lifting her, wrapping her legs around him and taking her, and she jumped as though she were thinking the same thing, kissing him like no woman had ever kissed him before. She curled one shapely leg around him, and his hands went to his zipper.

"Damn." He halted, then set her slowly on her feet. Restless, as he drew back, he rubbed the straining muscles at the back of his neck.

They were breathing hard and loud.

Her hand flew up to cover her moist, glistening lips. "I... I'm sorry. I didn't mean to bite you."

That little bite had made him want to bite her back, in every place imaginable. Damn. He rubbed his face with both hands, his blood thrumming in his body. He'd undone three buttons of her pajama top, and the flesh of one breast threatened to pop out.

Marcos regarded the creamy flesh while an overwhelming urge to dip his fingers inside the cotton and weigh that globe in his hand made him curl his fingers into his palm.

"Marcos?"

He jerked his eyes away, stared at the top of her head. "I had a long day." *And I thought of nothing but this moment.*

He'd been out of his mind with jealousy at the sight of her flushed cheeks, that clown Mendez begging at her feet. How many men had stared at her, wanted her, like Marcos did?

Oblivious to the rampant storms of his thoughts, Virginia followed him down the hall and into the bedroom. He was a mass of craving and thirst and he'd never felt so perilously close to losing control before.

Crossing the length of the room, he braced a hand on the window and gazed out at the city. If she ever dared make a fool of him...if she ever dared so much as look at another man while she was with him...

"Marissa was after me for years."

A quiet settled, disturbed by the rustle of her clothes as she moved around. "I'm sorry."

Yes. Well.

So was he.

Such humiliation, the way she'd played him. "I didn't know my father wanted her," he said, unable to conceal the disgust in his voice, "until they were already...involved."

When he turned, she was standing by the bathroom door. She'd grabbed a brush and was pensively running it through her hair. The lights shone on the satin mass.

Entranced, Marcos watched the curls spring back into place after a pass, and he wanted to plunge his fingers through that hair and wrap it in his hands.

"Don't do that."

She stopped. It took him a moment to realize the hoarse, ragged plea had come from him. She lowered her arm.

"Do what?"

The cotton molded to her chest, rose and dipped in the most attractive places. Aware of how hard he was, how hot under his clothes, he feared his own instincts when she set the brush on the nightstand and directed her full attention on him.

"I'm not Marissa," she said, coming toward him.

He liked how candid she was. How she smiled with her eyes. How she walked. Talked. No, she was not Marissa.

Getting a grip of his thoughts, he shook his head. "I didn't say that." But it would be worse with her. If she ever hurt him. Deceived him. Betrayed him. He'd never trusted so fully, had never felt so many things at once.

"Marcos," she said softly. Her eyes were examining his stiff shoulders, the stony mask on his face, as she halted before him. He was shocked at the raw emotion shining in her eyes. Not only desire. But tenderness. Concern. Caring.

Caring that tugged at some little strings inside him.

Caring that begged him to care, too.

Damn.

She was his lover. He had a right to touch her, take her,

come with the pleasure of being inside her. It was all this was. Lust.

Lust lust lust.

"Never—" He could hardly speak as he lifted a hand to her silky, raven hair. She gasped at the touch, went very still.

"—ever—" he said gruffly, and tangled his fingers, fisted that lovely hair in his hand, using his knuckles to push her head up to where his lips waited "—lie to me."

He took her gasp, rubbed her lips farther apart, and traced their seam with his tongue. They were flavored with toothpaste and mint, and they were wet and hot. "Never lie to me with this mouth."

He licked into her, and she moaned. "I love this tongue, never lie to me with this tongue."

She inhaled a ragged breath and his tongue followed its path inside her, searching deep. In one instant her hands curled wantonly around his wrists, went higher up his arms, opening around the width of his biceps. Her fingers bit into his shirt and skin.

It was instinct, need, something fierce he couldn't understand, that pressed him to slam her back against the wall, take her, make her his mistress. It was so consuming to him, this passion, he was afraid if he followed it, he would break her apart. Or maybe he would break apart, feeling this—for her. With her.

Was this what his father had felt for Marissa? Was this why he'd given everything for her, everything to her? Let her slowly finish him off...so long as she kept on kissing him, looking at him, touching him like this?

When a cell phone rang, he tore his mouth away and she fumbled in a purse she'd left by the nightstand to answer. "Yes?"

His hand flicked the buttons of his shirt as she walked away and softly spoke into the receiver.

His heart rammed into his ribs, his blood a thick, terse boil in his veins. He was losing his head—and he didn't like it. He considered retiring to his study to work, put distance between them. No. No. He wanted her. He walked forward, shrugging off his shirt.

"Yes…yes, I didn't want to wake you…and yes, I'll see you…um…I'm working late and I don't know how long I'll be—" Silence. A soft, very soft, "Good night."

She came back, smiled.

"You're spending the night," he said, rendering it a statement when in fact he wanted confirmation. She was seducing him—in her pajamas, brushing her hair, staring with those green, green eyes.

Gritting his teeth against the flaring lust, he readied himself briskly, his erection springing free.

He grabbed her hand and put it on himself. If that didn't tell her, show her, how far gone he was, then he didn't know anything anymore. Still, he recalled Monterrey, all those nights with her, the days, and gruffly spoke. "You're staying the night here—with me."

She nodded and met his gaze, her eyes bright and fiery. She stroked his chest with soft, fluttering hands, dragging her lips across his jaw, his chin. "I want you in me, Marcos."

A primal hunger had overtaken his mind, his senses, until he felt as instinctive as an animal. An animal tantalized by the nearness of his mate. "You came to seduce me, didn't you? You like being at my beck and call. You came to please me, service me."

Smiling, she stepped back, and her hands went to her shirt, and Marcos watched as she began to unbutton it farther. Her fingers pulled another button free, then the next, and his eyes flicked up to hers. "I'm crazy about you," he rasped.

Virginia didn't seem to hear the truth in his words, the worry they carried. He felt out of control, and he didn't like it.

"C-can I try something with you?" she asked hesitantly, easing her top off her shoulders.

He nodded, mute with desire and anticipation.

"Would you stay still, please?" she asked.

"What are you going to do to me, Miss Hollis?" he asked in a guttural voice. He fisted his hands at his sides, watching her hands like a man about to die under them. He stood utterly still, admiring her flesh as she revealed it. His voice was barely audible, his eyes on the gentle curves of her breasts as she stepped out of her pants and at last stood as naked as he.

"Just don't move, okay?"

So he waited, his chest expanding on each breath. She trembled when she stepped closer. "Can I touch you?"

He swallowed thickly. "Please."

He sucked in a breath when she set her hand on his chest and began kissing his neck, his ear, his jaw. His breathing became a wild thing. He was motionless as her hands began to roam down his chest. She hesitated at his waist.

His jaw clamped, his nostril flared, when she wrapped her hand around him.

"Is this okay?"

Ecstasy surged through him in a tidal wave. His breath made a strange whistle. "Yes."

"Do you want—"

His head fell, forehead against hers. "Just keep touching me."

She eased her fingers between his parted thighs, to gently cup him in her palm. She began to rub.

He hurt under her stroking hand. His mind spun with images of her and him, losing themselves in his bed like he'd wanted to. His hands idle at his sides, he softly, so softly, said, "You're not pregnant, are you, *amor?*"

She tensed for a moment, and he frowned. He reached down and pried her hand away.

"Are you? We didn't use protection the first time, and I'd like to know if there were consequences."

Ignoring him, she took his shoulders in her little hands and urged him down on the mattress. "The only consequence is this, Marcos. Me. Wanting more."

He sat there, on his bed, like a man in hypnosis, and watched her straddle him.

They kissed.

Marcos was dying with pleasure, his body rocking as he feasted from her lips, lips that were soft and warm against his, lips that were wide open for his tongue to search in deep, so deep. Her sex cradled his hardness, her legs twined around him as tight as her arms while he ran his hands up her sides, into her hair, groaning at the way she whimpered his name. Marcos. All he could say was, "Virginia." Oh, Virginia.

He pulled roughly at her hair.

"Why?" His voice was a cragged sound.

"I…I don't know what you're talking about."

"Why do you look at me like this? What are you playing at?"

Watching him through heavy, sooty lashes, she kissed his nipples, his abs. She was smiling—teasing him with her teeth. Her tongue. Driving him out of his mind. Out. Of. His. Mind. "Must it be a game for you to enjoy it, Mr. Allende?" she purred. "Must we play at another pretense for you to let me in?"

He snatched her hair to halt her wandering mouth, suddenly trembling with thirst for not only her body, but for something else. Something he'd always, always, seen and sensed and tried to grasp in her eyes. "Are you trying to drive me insane?" he demanded.

She pulled free and lovingly cupped his jaw, kissing him softly on the lips. "I'm trying to make you remember."

He framed her face, engulfing it between both hands, and before he took her lips in the hard, hot way his screaming soul demanded, growled, "I'm trying to *forget*."

Ten

"With luck, the negotiations will advance, then my lawyers will fly down to…" Marcos trailed off as Virginia strolled into his office the next morning, bringing those long legs with her, her raven curls bouncing with each tiny step her tapered, knee-length skirt allowed.

She stopped to check discreetly on the coffeemaker—directly in Marcos's line of vision. A bolt of lust arrowed to his groin. *Marcos, oh, please, more, more.*

Her gasps of last night echoed in his head.

This morning they'd gone at each other like—hell, like two wild animals—before they'd separately headed for the office. He'd asked her to buy something special to wear to the Fintech dinner, to splurge. She hadn't seemed to be impressed. He wanted to please her, to give her something, and yet the only thing Virginia Hollis seemed to want was him.

Damn, he was totally taken—in a way not even Marissa had taken him before. Virginia's moans, her body, writing against his, with his. It maddened him. Heated him. Excited him. Appalled him.

Aware of the abrupt silence in the vast carpeted space, a quiet that magnified her noises as she innocently fiddled with spoons and cups, Marcos jerked his eyes back to the open proposal and tapped his Montblanc pen against the sales projection chart. He cleared his throat. "Where was I?"

"Allende. Marissa Galvez. Negotiations," Jack said, sprawling on a chair across from his desk.

"Of course." He dropped his pen and lounged back in his high-backed leather chair, stacking his hands behind his head. He met the Texan's electric-blue stare. "As soon as negotiations take on a serious note I'll call in the cavalry and we—"

Virginia leaned down to refill Jack's coffee, and her proximity to the man made Marcos's jaw clamp in anger. He felt ridiculously jealous. Yes, *diablos,* he was totally had.

"We'll close," he finished tightly, and slapped the proposal shut. She had no idea, no idea.

Or was she doing this on purpose?

The sunlight that streamed through the floor-to-ceiling windows of the Art Deco building shone over her loose hair. But she was frowning, he realized then, somehow worried, and the noose tightened around his neck.

"Miss Hollis," he said. Last night's seduction? That ridiculously simple but mouthwateringly sexy outfit? Was all this some sort of plan of hers?

She spun, shocked as if from out of her thoughts. "Yes?"

He reclined in his seat and crossed his arms. She was pale this morning. Guilt assailed him. He hadn't let her sleep much, had he? "I was telling Mr. Williams about Monterrey."

She spared a fleeting glance at Jack's lean, jeans-clad figure, and he shot her one of his disarming grins. "How nice," she said absently, and lifted the glass coffeepot to Marcos. "More coffee?"

He shook his head, searching for warm emotions in her expression, all of which usually showed on her face as she experienced them. There were none this morning either.

Her desperation last night, her need, her wanting…he'd felt them all. He'd throbbed with every one of them. Today she looked distant. Why?

I'm not Marissa…

His body clenched. No. No. She was not. Virginia was even more dangerous.

"Marissa Galvez is flying in this weekend," he then offered. Why did he offer this information? Because deep down, her words continued to pull at his heartstrings. *Mend Allende. Make it gold again.*

Did he dare? Did he even want to?

"Oh. How nice. I'm sure she'll be more agreeable this time."

The reply was so noncommittal and so lacking in generosity of feeling that he frowned. When the carved oak doors shut behind her, Jack murmured, "I see."

"Hmm?" Marcos took a long, warm gulp of coffee.

"I see," Jack repeated, propping a shiny lizard boot atop his knee.

He drank again, savoring the scent, the warmth of her coffee. Was she sick? "Mine, Jack."

"Yes, I see."

Marcos grunted. Jack wouldn't even begin to comprehend the pain of his sexual frustration. The looks she gave him— tenderness, desire, admiration, respect. When would he tire of her? He'd expected to tire within the week, and yet it had been over a month now. He could not get enough of her. Was she tiring of him? Good God, was that a possibility?

His friend's dry chuckle wafted in the air. "I assume your

plan worked with Marissa. She no doubt thought you were taken with Virginia."

Marcos pushed to his feet and headed to the wide bay window, his coffee cradled against his chest. "My bid has been rejected, Jack."

Silence.

His chest felt cramped with anger, frustration. "She controls the board and somehow made sure they declined."

"Ahh. Then I assume we're getting hostile? Why are we even discussing Allende if not?"

"We are getting hostile." He spun on his heel. "If we could."

Jack made a scratching noise. "Meaning?"

Damn Marissa and her sneaky ways. Marcos had discussed for the tenth time the purchase of her shares, and she still held off selling to him. In the back of her warped mind, she no doubt believed she could bend Marcos like she'd bent his father—who else would save her company but the son? What else would ensure her continued ownership but marriage?

No. She wouldn't get away with it, not anymore, and yet even in the midst of this surety, the fact that a woman would have power over his future made his blood boil.

"Meaning I must pressure her to sell, Williams. She's flying to Chicago this weekend—I invited her to the Fintech dinner. As long as she owns the majority of the shares, a hostile takeover is close to impossible. She must sell, and she must sell to *me*."

"Pardon my slowness, but you invited her to Chicago?"

"I want Allende, Jack."

"You want to kill it," Jack added.

Marcos absently scanned the busy sidewalks below. "And if I don't?"

Jack's usually fast retorts seemed to fail him this time.

Marcos's mind raced with every new discovery he'd made about Hank Hollis today. The man had lost his way—not unusual after the heartache of losing a beloved wife, Marcos supposed. But he'd been visiting AA meetings, seemed to be struggling to get his life back on track. He'd been a risk-taker on the job, and ruthless when it came to disciplining those beneath him. Years ago, he'd pushed his chain of stores, every single one of them, to be better, more efficient, and the admirable numbers he'd produced for them didn't lie.

"What if I told you," Marcos began, "that I'd save Allende. What if I told you I've found a man to do the dirty work— one who's driven and who's thirsty to prove something to someone?" *Maybe he'd enjoy coming to Mexico.*

"Marcos, I'm on your board as a professional, not as a friend. The same reason you're on mine."

"Of course."

And Virginia would be free of the pain her father had been causing. She would be free to be with him. Marcos.

"Well, as both, I have to tell you," his friend continued in a thickening drawl. "It's that damned prodigal apple. Any opportunity man *or* woman has to get a bite out of it, ten out of ten times, they *will*."

"Amen."

"I'm serious."

He swung around. "All right. So we get to play gods and kick them out of the kingdom. New management, new rules, no thieving, no blackmailing, no mafia."

"I agree. But who's heading new management?"

His eyebrows furrowed when he realized there was no clear space on his desk to set down his cup of coffee. The last fifteen years of his life—hard, busy years—were in this desk. A heavy oak Herman Miller, the first expensive designer piece he'd bought after his first takeover. It was old—he was superstitious—and it was a keeper and it was *packed*. The surface contained no photo frames, no figurines, nothing but a humming computer and piles and piles of papers that would later go into a roomful of file cabinets. He planted the mug over a stack of papers. "You are," he flatly repeated.

Jack's gaze was razor sharp. "Me."

His lips flattened to a grim, hard line as he nodded. "You. And a man I consider may be hungry to prove himself."

Jack hooked his thumb into his jeans pocket. "Go on."

Marcos folded into his chair, grabbed a blue pen and twirled it in his hand as he contemplated. "I negotiate for Marissa's shares and agree to allow her to stay in the company temporarily, while you and Hank Hollis will get the ropes and start a new team."

"Hank Hollis." His eyes narrowed to slits. "You're not serious."

He smiled the very same smile the Big Bad Wolf might have given Little Red Riding Hood. "Oh, but I am."

Hank Hollis would redeem himself in Virginia's eyes, right along with Allende. Marcos would make sure of it.

If Virginia had had any worries regarding her poor emotional state for the past twenty-four hours—other than having stupidly, blindly, foolishly fallen in love with Marcos Allende—she now had more proof for concern.

Pale-faced, she walked into the long tiled bathroom to stare for the twentieth time at the sleek white predictor test— the third one she'd used today—sitting next to the other two on the bathroom sink.

Pink.

Pink.

Pink.

All three were *pink*.

Of course. Because when it rained, it *poured*. Because when one thing went terribly wrong, *everything* went wrong. Because when your world collapsed on top of your head, really, *nothing* you could do would stop the crash.

Letting go her breath while the sting of tears gathered

in her eyes, she leaned back on the white tiles lining the bathroom walls and slowly, weakly, dragged her body down its length until she was sprawled on the floor.

She was very, undeniably pregnant.

With Marcos's baby.

There could be no more solid proof of her naïveté. She'd walked into his penthouse one evening with little in the way of emotional shields, without protection and without standing a chance. She might as well have torn out her heart and offered it in her hand. What had she expected would come out of it? Of all those pretend kisses, the laughter, the moments she could not forget?

Did she think he would say, "Step into my life, Virginia, I want you in it forever?"

Did she think he would say, "Marry me, *amor,* where have you been all my life?"

Oh, God. Covering her face with her hands, she considered what he would do when he found out about this.

A vision of him suggesting something bleak made the bile hitch up in her throat. She choked it back and shook her head, wrapping her arms around her stomach, speaking to herself at first, then below at the tiny little being growing inside her.

"I have to tell him." And when a wealth of maternal love surged through her, she ran a hand across her stomach and determinedly whispered, "I have to tell him."

Maybe she was more of a gambler than she'd thought. He might be furious, and he could turn her away, but still she found herself righting her hair and her clothes in front of the mirror, preparing for battle. Gathering up all the tests in the plastic bag from the drugstore and stuffing it in her purse, she once again headed back to Marcos's office.

She knocked three times. "Mr. Allende?"

His friend Jack seemed to have left already, and now, as she entered, Marcos pulled up a file from a stack on his desk, studied it, set it back down, rubbed his chin then finally stared at her.

"Close the door," he said, all somber.

She couldn't read that expression. She tried for flippant and saucy. "I'm under orders to spend a lot of money on anything I fancy."

"Are you now." He frowned. "Who is this man who orders you around? Seems to me you should run far and fast away from him, Miss Hollis."

The unexpected smile he shot her made her grin. "Did I mistakenly put whiskey in your coffee?" she asked, nearly laughing.

His eyes sparkled. "You might want to sit on my lap while you investigate."

She approached his desk, thinking about the baby, his baby, growing inside her body. "I was wondering if you were busy tonight. I'd like for us to talk."

"Virginia." He leaned forward and gently lowered her to his lap. "You have me. I'm at your disposal every night."

"Marcos…" The words *I want more* faltered in her throat.

He must have misinterpreted her concern, for Marcos dropped his hands to his sides and sighed. "Nobody knows about us, Virginia, please don't fret. I'm trying to keep things running smoothly. My office won't be abuzz with gossip, I won't allow it."

Gossip. Could everyone be gossiping? Whispering? Her stomach clenched in dread. "But you keep stealing touches and people are noticing." That much was true. And soon… how would she hide a pregnant belly?

Marcos boldly raked her figure with his gaze, reclined in his seat and said, "Then I should give these people something more to do."

She blinked, then realized he was teasing her, and she

forced her lips into a smile. But it wasn't funny. Soon they'd notice she was pregnant. Soon she'd be waddling around.

He scraped two fingers across his chin as he studied her. "You look worried."

She couldn't do this here—she felt as emotionally stable as a compass gone berserk. "Maybe the Fintech dinner isn't such a good idea," she suggested.

"It was part of our arrangement, Miss Hollis."

She swallowed and snatched up his files, deciding to postpone this for…tonight. Tomorrow. Never. "The projection room is ready."

"You have your notes?"

"Of course. And yours."

He stormed down the long hallway with her, and as people smiled at her in a "Yay, you" kind of way, her unease grew tenfold.

During the meeting, Virginia tried to concentrate on the images flicking on the projection screen. Sales charts with numbers. But Marcos sat unbearably close.

"Is it the dinner?"

She stiffened. "What?"

"Why you're worried. Is it?"

"I… No."

"The outfit? You're afraid you won't find one you like?"

She shook her head. "No."

He leaned forward. He tapped her pad. "Reading your notes here. 'Colorful charts.' Very observant, Miss Hollis. Now why are you worried? Tell me."

She attempted to take more notes but her mind was elsewhere.

"Now, you see the hedge fund study we just passed?" he said when she, apparently, was not going to talk. "We lost a little, but the fund was heavily invested in metals, as well, and the gold price has been rising, so we closed with a positive number nonetheless."

"Yes, I understand. You lose some and win some. Like… gambling."

He chuckled. "Indeed. It's all a game of risk, Miss Hollis. You weigh the benefits against the risk. And decide how to move forward. You may lose, but at least you played the game. Or you may win…and the prize is exquisite."

She did the exercise in her mind. Risk—her job, her self-respect, her body to a pregnancy, her heart…no, it was too much to bear to even think it. Benefit—save her father, who didn't deserve saving, and share a wonderful week with the most wonderful, wonderful man.

She would have liked to think that if she remained cool and aloof, she would not be risking anything. If she behaved like her usual self, there was no reason the office would speculate. If she ignored his scent, his lips and his eyes, and the fact that she'd fallen in love with him, then she could settle for the benefits. Eventually.

Except already, there was a child.

Their child.

And she wouldn't be able to hide his growing presence much longer.

Eleven

"That's supposed to be a dress?"

She sensed Marcos at the doorway, actually heard a whoosh of air as though the sight of her had stunned him, and she continued tugging the fabric down her hips, her legs, carefully avoiding his gaze as she stepped into it.

"Hello? Fintech dinner? You said buy something to dazzle them. Splurge. Buy the dress of your dreams." *Before I blow up like a balloon and have your bastard baby.*

"The key word was *something*," Marcos growled, "That is nothing."

In the middle of his spacious, carpeted closet, standing before a mirror in a satiny green dress that was making her smile and Marcos frown, Virginia flicked her hair and scoffed at his words.

His glare deepened. "I'm not taking you looking like this."

"Excuse me?"

"I'm serious."

"This is all I have, I spent a fortune on it. You told me—"

"I don't care what I said. I am saying right now, I'm not taking you…into a party with half the city…in that…that scrap."

"Don't be absurd, it's perfect."

A muscle ticked in the back of his jaw. He grabbed her arm and pulled her close. "Do you have any idea what a man thinks of…at the sight of you in that dress?"

"I thought it was elegant, but seductive, if I'd thought it was—"

He grabbed her by the waist and pressed her to him, and the shock of feeling every lean, hard inch of him against her made her gasp. "He thinks of peeling it off with his teeth. He imagines your breasts without the satin over them, and he imagines you, wrapped all around him, with your hair all across his bed."

Her bones melted inside of her.

Marcos, in a tuxedo, was easily the sexiest thing she'd ever seen. She wanted to beg him to peel the dress off her fevered body with his teeth and to wrap her limbs around him with his weight crushing her on the bed.

She tipped her face back, remembering an entire month of making love to Marcos.

In the morning. At midnight. Evenings when he got home. Coupled with those memories, she had others of him with the morning paper spread across the table, coffee cup in hand. Him shaving. Him taking a shower. With her.

She could not remember a thought that didn't make her tummy constrict.

Feeling her thighs go mushy, she stroked her fingers up his cleanly shaven jaw. "You're so handsome," she whispered.

His eyes roved her face, cataloging her flushed cheeks, the telling glaze in her heavy-lidded eyes. "I want you." His hands tightened, and she became excruciatingly aware of his erection biting into her pelvis. His eyes were so hot they were like flames. "I want you every minute of every godforsaken day and it's making me grumpy."

When she gasped, he let her go. A muscle flexed in the back of his jaw as he clenched hard. He shook his head. "Damn."

It took an effort to stand on her own two feet while quietly nursing the sting of his rejection, but she thrust her chin up with a little dignity. "This is all I have to wear."

God, she had turned into a wanton. She only wanted to touch and touch and touch him. To be kissed until her breath left her.

Flushing, she pulled open the carved-wood closet doors and began to rummage through the shoe rack.

Marcos paced the area and raked a hand through his hair. "The pearls have to go."

She straightened, a hand coming to stroke a smooth pebble at her throat. Her father had stripped out every material memory of her childhood, of her mother, the life they'd once had. He'd pawned her mother's engagement ring. The pearl earrings to match the necklace she always wore. He'd sold off the nice clothes, even the locket they'd given Virginia as a little girl.

"Are they too old-fashioned?"

"They're not you."

He pulled out a box from a drawer, and she blinked. The box was sky-blue in color, with a silken white bow on top. As his long, tanned fingers tugged the edges of the bow and the shimmering ribbon unfurled in his hand, the unmistakable words *Tiffany & Co.* appeared.

Within seconds, he'd opened a velvet box and held up the largest, most dazzling diamond necklace Virginia had ever seen. Its sparkle was blinding. Its sheer magnificence just made her breath, her brain, her everything scatter.

The piece was worthy of old Hollywood, when the women

would wear their finest evening dresses and most impressive jewels for the night. A large, oval-shaped green pendant hung from rows and rows of large, brilliant diamonds that fell like curtains and lace in the most exquisite workmanship Virginia had ever set eyes on.

"I… It's lovely."

"It's yours."

She shook her head. "I can't."

But he stepped behind her and began to fasten it around her neck. His lips grazed the back of her ear as his fingers worked on the clasp. When he was done, he turned her around to face him. "You're mine to spoil. It's yours. Tomorrow. Next week, next month, next year. It's yours."

This was him, announcing, in a way, that he was sleeping with her. No one who saw her would have any doubt. Why would he do this tonight? Why would she allow it?

She experienced a horrible urge to touch him, an even more intense one to ask him to hold her, but that would only bring the tears gathering in the back of her eyes to the forefront. She didn't understand these tears, or the desperate sensation of having lost before she'd even fought for him.

Her eyes dropped to his chest as she felt a blush creep up her cheeks. His cross lay over his chest, glinting bright gold against the bronzed skin. His breath stirred the hair at the top of her head. The warmth of his body enveloped her.

His hands framed her jaw, lifting her face to his. "I bought you earrings and a bracelet, too."

As he seized her wrist with his long, tanned fingers, she watched the thick cuff bracelet close around her. Oh, God, no wonder mistresses were always so sexy and smiling, when all their men treated them just like this!

"I can't," she still said. Because it felt so wrong. So intimate. So personal. It made her mind race with thoughts she did not—should not—think of. She was lying to him, or at least, withholding something important.

And it felt so odd, the weight of the diamonds and the forest-green emerald on her. It felt like a chain around her neck—Marcos's chain on her. And her baby. And her future.

You're mine to spoil...

"I insist, Virginia," he sternly said, and drew her at arm's length to take in the visual.

Self-conscious, Virginia dropped her gaze and tugged at a loose curl on her shoulder. The dress hugged her body like a lover's embrace, the jewels refracted thousands of little lights and for the first time in her life Virginia felt like a fraud. A woman desperate to be anyone, anyone, that the man she loved could love.

"I don't know what to say."

His chuckle was full of arrogance, but it made her melt all the same. "Then get over here."

When he drew her close and kissed her with a passion that buckled her knees and had her clinging to his shoulders, she didn't say anything at all. But her mind screamed, "We're having a baby!"

"Marcos, I'd like to talk to you, tonight."

He fixed his powerful eyes on her, his face unreadable. He seemed to have forgotten about the dress, and she wondered if he'd been jealous. Marcos wasn't surrounded by the aura of relaxation of a man who'd spent an entire night feasting on his lover, but with the tension of one who wanted more. The air felt dense between them. "I have other plans for tonight," he admitted.

She could not even smile at that. "Still, I'd like for us to talk."

He cradled her face, forced her to meet his gaze. "What is it?"

The concern in his eyes, the gentleness in his voice, only made her crave his love with more intensity. She did not want to crave it with such intensity, did not want to feel the emptiness growing inside her, realizing she lacked his love at the same time as their baby grew bigger.

Their agreement was over once she accompanied him to the Fintech dinner. And maybe they would be over, too.

She drew in a tremulous breath. "After the party."

"All right," he said, smiling. "In fact, there's something I'd like to speak to you about, too."

Inside the lavishly decorated lobby of the glass-and-steel skyscraper smack in the center in Michigan Avenue, Marcos guided Virginia through the throng of people, nodding to a few. "That's Gage Keller, he's a developer. His company, Syntax, owns half of Las Vegas now. The young woman with him is his wife."

"Second, I presume?"

He grinned. "More like sixth."

He brought her around to where a group of men and women stood by a spectacular ten-foot-tall wine fountain. "The woman drowning in jewels over there is Irene Hillsborough; she owns the most extensive collection of Impressionist art in the States. Old money, very polite."

"Very snotty?" Virginia added when the woman lifted her head to stare at her then promptly glanced away.

An appreciative gleam lit up his eyes as he smiled down at her and patted her hand. "How perceptive."

"Allende." A bearded middle-aged man Marcos had presented her to just moments ago—Samuel...something— came back to slap his back. "Haven't seen much of Santos lately. What is that troublemaker up to?"

"I wouldn't know," Marcos said with a rather bored intonation, then uncharacteristically offered, "You can ask him later if he shows." He steered Virginia away, and an immediate image of Santos—surely gorgeous and bad, so bad—made her ask, "Santos is coming?"

"If only to be a pain in the ass, yes." He said it so decidedly, so automatically, her eyes widened in surprise.

He then urged her around, and a woman with silvering hair and an ecstatic look on her face was fast winding her way toward them.

"That would be Phyllis Dyer," he continued, "the director of donations and—"

"Marcos," the woman said, lightly laying her hand on his shoulder as she kissed one cheek, then the other. Her voice quivered with excitement. "Marcos, I can't thank you enough for your generosity. I heard from the Watkinson Center for Children today and they were all wondering why the early Christmas. It was so kind of you, as usual."

Marcos gave her a curt nod. He then brought Virginia forward. "May I present Virginia."

The woman's soft gray eyes went huge. "Oh, well, how lovely to meet you. I believe this is the first time I have had the pleasure of meeting one of Marcos's girls." To her, she leaned forward to whisper, "This one's a keeper, darling, if you know what I mean."

"Oh, I'm not his… I'm actually his—"

After a bit more small talk, Phyllis left with an encouraging pat on Virginia's shoulder, and Virginia ventured a glance at him. "Why didn't you tell her I was your assistant?"

Tucking her hand into the crook of his arm, he guided her toward the sweeping arched doors that led out into the terrace. He didn't answer her.

Stepping past an elegant trellis, he led her across the terrace, illuminated with flickering gas lanterns that lined the perimeter.

When he loosened his hold on her, Virginia stepped forward and leaned on a cement banister and gazed out at the fountain. A breeze stirred the miniature trees in the nearby planters, the chilly air making her flesh pebble with goose bumps.

Unconsciously, she rubbed her arms up and down, listening to the soft piano music audible through the speakers. Somehow, the notes couldn't completely mute the faint rustle of water.

She drew in a steadying breath. "Aren't you up for a speech soon?"

Through the corner of her eye, she followed his movements as he set his wineglass on the flat surface of a stone bench. "Yes."

She gasped at the feel of his hand, warm and strong, curling around hers, tugging her forward. In a haze, she found herself slowly but surely gravitating toward him, captivated by the play of moonlight on his features and the gentle, insistent pull of his hand.

"I want us to dance, and I had a feeling you'd say no if I asked you in there."

"Dance," she parroted, mesmerized.

He smiled. Manly appreciation sparkled in his eyes as he curled his arm around her waist and pulled her even closer. *"Te ves hermosa, ven aqui."*

Anything Marcos told her in Spanish Virginia did not understand, but she felt the words so deeply, as though he were telling her a secret her instincts knew how to decode.

Both arms enveloped her and their bodies met in a visceral move, seeking a fit of their own volition. Surrounded by the piano music, feeling the cool breeze on her skin beside the fountain, Virginia suddenly wondered if she would ever experience this again. Everything. What he made her feel. The flutters inside her when she became the sole focus of those pitch-black eyes.

"Marcos," she began to protest.

"Shh. One dance."

Her involuntary squirms only made him tighten his grip on her, press her closer, urge her to move against his tall, hard body in a very slow, sensual dance. He trailed one hand up her back and delved into her hair, his fingers caressing her scalp in a light, hypnotic massage.

His hands shifted on her back, splaying wide, keeping her flat against his solid length. Virginia remembered when they had been sweaty and hot and needing each other last night. She trembled at the memory and he tightened his hold on her. She knew, sensed, felt, that he also remembered.

His eyelids drooped suggestively as he ran his knuckles down her cheek. His lips hovered over her mouth and lightly skimmed side to side. "I can't wait to take you home with me."

A feeling unlike any other bloomed inside her. She trembled down to her knees as she fought to quell it, afraid of what would happen if she set it free.

"Take me home...like a stray?" she ventured. Was this the full-moon fever? Her hormones? She'd never thought love could feel like this. So total. So powerful.

Marcos let go a rich, delicious chuckle. "More like the loveliest treasure."

She guided her fingers up his taut, hard-boned face, not daring to hope that he might...

"What is it you wanted to tell me tonight? You said you wanted to speak with me, too?"

His smile didn't fade, but a soft tenderness lit up his eyes. "Can't you guess, *chiquita?*"

"Can you give me a hint?"

He nodded, calmly explained, "It's about us."

The tender but possessive way he held her, the warm, admiring way he gazed down at her, prodded her on. "Is there...an us?"

A tingle drummed up and down her body where they touched.

His eyes went liquid, hot with tenderness as he tipped her face back. "You tell me."

I'm pregnant with your baby. She could not say it, needed to know what he had to say first.

He stroked her cheek with one knuckle. "I know what a woman like you wants," he said softly. "I can't give it to you, Virginia, but I'd like…" He trailed off when they heard a sudden noise.

Virginia's stomach tumbled with the need to hear the rest. What had he meant to say? For a single disconcerting moment, she worried he'd sensed the sudden, alarming, fragile emotions she was struggling with and this made her even more determined to hide them.

Next she heard the echoing footsteps of someone approaching. Virginia trembled when Marcos released her, her heart gripping when she spotted Marissa. Her hair streamed behind her, and her smile was provocative. And suddenly Virginia felt very small and very pregnant.

To Marcos, with wry humor, Marissa handed her arm as though he'd asked her to dance, and slyly purred, "I hope I'm interrupting something."

Bad form. Bad, bad form.

Marcos couldn't make his proposition to Virginia here. *Diablos*—where was his head? On Allende? No, it was not even there, and Marcos was shocked at the discovery.

Somewhere during the past month…somewhere between a headache, when Virginia had smoothed his hair off his brow and "knew the perfect thing to take care of that headache" for him…somewhere between one morning and another, when they sipped coffee in silence…somewhere between the sheets, when he was lost inside of her in a way he'd never thought humanly possible…somewhere between one of her million kinds of smiles…somewhere between an exchange of files…something had happened.

Marcos had let down his guard. He'd allowed himself to trust a woman, fully and completely, in a way he'd sworn he'd never trust another human. He'd allowed her to filter his mind, his thoughts, to the point where his goals had shifted... shifted and shifted until he no longer knew if they were his or hers.

"I need your help."

Marissa's soft, pleading words registered out on the terrace, and yet his eyes followed Virginia's lovely figure as she glided back into the crowded room. He'd noticed the frustration in her jade-green eyes when she stepped away, saw her struggling to hold her temper in check. She was a curious one, his Virginia. No doubt she craved to know what he'd planned to say. He smiled to himself as she wound her way away from him, into the room, her bearing as regal as a queen's.

She was wearing the most amazing, breathtaking, heart-tripping dress he'd ever seen, and he was dying to take it off her.

"Should we talk inside?" he asked curtly, shifting his attention back to Marissa, who in turn was eyeing him speculatively.

"Of course."

He led her into the decorated space. An orchestra played. Couples danced in harmony to the tune. Amongst the round tables, people mingled.

Heading toward the conference hall at the south end of the lobby, they crossed the room. He greeted several acquaintances, nodded his head at a few more and kept a close eye on Virginia. Her hair fell down to cover part of her face. Her profile was exquisitely feminine, like a doll's.

Taking in her visage, he felt a slow, throbbing ache spread inside of him, and contrary to most of the aches she gave him, this one had nothing to do with physically wanting her.

When he secured Allende, he could mend it, and he could mend her father along with it. He could give her safety and peace and pride.

The intensity with which he wanted to give this to her shocked him to his core.

Whereas before Virginia Hollis had been something to be observed but not touched in his office, a Mona Lisa behind glass, she was more real to him now than his own heartbeat. She was flesh and bones and blood. She was woman.

His fierce attraction to her, kept tightly on a leash, had spiraled out of control the moment he'd put his lips right over hers, or perhaps the moment she'd called him and Marcos had known, in his gut, he was going to have her.

Fierce and unstoppable, the emotions raged within him now, under his muscles, and the urge to cross the room and sweep her into his arms became acute.

With an effort, he tore his eyes away from Virginia, tried to steady the loud beat of his heart.

A man, notoriously tall, athletic and dark, with a smile that had been known to break a woman's heart or two, caught his attention.

Santos Allende was the only person in the world who would not wear a tie to a black-tie event. As he ambled over, he lifted a sardonic brow at the same time he lifted his wineglass in a mock toast. "Brother."

Marcos nodded in greeting, drained his drink, and introduced Marissa and Santos even though they needed no introductions. They loathed each other.

"How's the hotel business?" Marcos asked him without even a hint of interest.

"Thriving, of course."

Though Santos was irresponsible and wild, Marcos held no antagonism towards his brother, and usually regarded his exploits and antics with amusement. Except tonight he wasn't in the mood for Santos. Or anyone else.

Too smart for his own good sometimes, Santos chuckled at his side.

"So. Is that one yours?" Santos lifted his glass in Virginia's direction, and Marcos gazed at her again. His chest felt heavy and his stomach tight.

"Mine," he confirmed.

"I see." Santos smiled and rammed a hand into his pants pocket. "Mistress or fiancée?"

"Mistress," he snapped.

But his mind screamed in protest at those words.

Would she agree to his proposition to become his mistress? Live with him, be with him? She'd turned his world upside down, inside out, in over a month. He wanted her every second of the day—not only sexually. Her laugh brought on his laughter, her smiles made him smile, too. He was…he didn't know what. Enraptured. Charmed. Taken.

By her.

"That would make her your first mistress, eh, brother?" his brother asked. "No more fiancées after Marissa here."

Marissa whipped her attention back to Marcos. "You mean she's just a fling? Your girlfriend?"

He set the glass down on the nearby table with a harsh thump. "Unless you want me to leave you in prison the next time you're there, don't push it, little brother."

And to Marissa, with a scowl that warned her of all kinds of danger, "I say we've played games long enough, you and I, and I'm not in the mood for them any longer. You have something I want. The shares that belonged to my father—I want a number and I want it now."

She's his submissive, been like this for years…

Old lover demanding she be fired…competition… Allende…

Allende and Galvez…

It was easy at first, to pretend she hadn't caught bits and pieces of the swirling conversation. But after she'd heard it over and over, ignoring the comments popping up wherever she went became impossible.

It hurt to smile, and to pretend she wasn't hearing all this. But then, he'd taught her to pretend just fine, hadn't he? And she was doing quite well. Had been commending herself all evening for remembering people's names and keeping up with their conversations. And smiling her same smile.

But when the whispers were too much, she pried herself away from a group of women and strolled around the tables with her mind on escaping, finding Mrs. Fuller, Lindsay, a friendly face, but even they seemed engaged in the latest gossip.

She stopped in her tracks and frowned when a young man approached. He was over six feet tall, lean but muscled. He moved with slow, lazy charm, his smile oozing charisma. Rumpled ebony hair was slicked back behind his ears, his hard-boned face and striking features prominent. Laser-blue eyes sparkled with amusement as he halted before her and performed a mock bow.

"Allende. Santos Allende."

He spoke it the way Agent 007 would say, "Bond, James Bond," and it made her smile. So he was the elusive Santos.

"Virginia Hollis."

Drawing up next to her, he signaled with a cock of his head, a glass of red wine idle in his hand. "The bastard looking at you is my brother."

"Yes, I'm his assistant. You and I have spoken on the phone."

Santos had the looks of a centerfold, the kind that modeled underwear or very expensive suits like Hugo Boss, while Marcos had the very appearance of sin.

As if reading her mind, his lips quirked, and he added, "He didn't mention that."

"He mentioned me?"

Her eyes jerked back to Marcos; it seemed they couldn't help themselves. She always caught herself staring at him.

He was weaving toward the hallway with Marissa. When Marcos ducked his head toward her, Virginia's stomach clenched with envy and a sudden, unexpected fury.

He glanced back over his shoulder and when their gazes collided, a strange wildness surged through her. His face was inscrutable and his tuxedo was perfectly in place; only an odd gleam in his eyes spoke of his inner tumult. And in her mind, Virginia was positively screaming at him. *Everybody knows! Everybody knows I'm your stupid...silly...*

No. It was her fault, not his.

She'd wanted him, and she'd gambled for the first time in her existence. She knew his scent, the feel of his hair, the sounds he made when he was in ecstasy with her.

She knew his mouth, his whispers, knew he slept little but that he would remain in bed beside her, watching her.

She knew he liked to put his head between her breasts, knew he made a sound of encouragement when she stroked his hair.

But she did not know how to make this man love her.

This man with all these secrets, all of the locks and bolts around his heart.

He wanted Allende. To destroy it. He wanted her. To play with.

She was just his toy. Something to fool around with. Once, she might have jumped with glee. But now she wanted so much more from him, thought there could be no greater treasure in this world than to be loved by him.

"So did the affair come before he hired you or after?"

Santos phrased his question so casually and with such a playful gleam in his eyes that Virginia could only blink.

He grinned and shrugged his shoulders. "I'm sorry, I'm just terribly curious. I have to know."

Cheeks burning with embarrassment, Virginia ducked her head and tried to get away. "Excuse me."

With one quick, fluid move, Santos stepped into her path

and caught her elbow. "Marissa wants him, you do realize this?"

She stepped back, freeing her arm from his, hating that it was so obvious, so transparent on her face. "I can't see why you think I'd care."

But his curling lips invited her to mischief. "She offers something my brother wants very badly. What do you offer?"

She frowned. "I wasn't aware this was a competition—"

"It's not." He tipped her chin up, those electric-blue eyes dancing with mirth. "Because I think you've already got him."

When she hesitated, he bent to whisper in her ear, sweetening the offer with words she found she could not resist.

"My brother is very loyal, and if you managed to steal his heart…no ten businesses would top it."

But Virginia knew that one business, one woman did— when she heard the news announced later in the evening that Fintech would be taking over Allende.

Twelve

They rode to the penthouse in dead, flat silence. Marcos seemed engrossed in his thoughts, and Virginia was deeply engrossed in hers.

It took her ten minutes, while he made phone calls to Jack and his lawyers, to pack the meager belongings she'd once, mistakenly or not, left in his apartment.

She was calmer. Immobile on a tiny corner of the bed, actually, and staring at the doorway, nervously expecting him to come in any minute. But calmer.

Though she didn't know whether the nausea inside of her was due to the pregnancy or to the fact that she would not be sleeping with Marcos for the first night in over a month.

She just couldn't do this any longer. Every little word she'd heard tonight had felt like whiplashes on her back; she could not believe her colleagues would speak this way about her. And then Marcos…offering her a necklace, but not his love. Him telling his brother she was his…his…

No.

She refused to believe he would refer to her as something tacky. But the truth, no matter how painful, was the truth. Virginia was his assistant—one of *three*—and she was sleeping with her boss. It didn't matter if she'd spent the most beautiful moments of her life with him. It didn't matter that every kiss, every touch, she had given with all her might and soul. It didn't matter that she'd loved him before and loved him now.

She was sleeping with her boss, and she'd never be respected if she continued. She'd never respect *herself*.

If only she were able to tuck her determination aside for a moment and enjoy one last night with him. The last night of a month she would not ever forget. The last night with the man she had fallen in love with, the father of her unborn child.

Drawing in a fortifying breath, she left the bedroom and went searching for him.

She'd heard him in his office, barking orders to Jack over the phone, laughing with him, even—he was not concealing his delight over his deal.

The door of the study was slightly ajar, and she slipped inside in silence.

He sat behind his desk at the far end. He looked eerie behind his computer, concentrated, the light doing haunting things to his face. Her stomach clenched with yearning. "Marcos, may I talk to you?"

He stiffened, and his head came up. Her breath caught at the devastating beauty of his liquid black eyes, and her heart leapt with a joy that quickly became dread when he remained silent. There was lust in those orbs, desire, and she seized on to that with all her might before he jerked his gaze back to the computer. "I'm very busy, Virginia."

She tugged at the hem of her dress, uneasy of how to proceed. She tried to sound casual. "Marcos, I thought we could discuss…something. I may not spend the night and I really feel it's important—"

"Jesus, do we have to do this now?" His hands paused on the keyboard, then he dropped his face and rubbed his eyes with the heel of his palms. "I'm sorry. Right. Okay. What is it, Virginia?"

Her eyes widened at his condescending tone. The thought that he'd always put Allende and his business before her made her stomach twist so tight she thought she would vomit. She'd forgotten she was his plaything. If she produced money maybe he'd give her five minutes now?

"We were going to discuss…us." Her voice trembled with urgency. "At the dinner, you mentioned wanting to say something."

He leaned back, his expression betraying no flicker of emotion, no hint of what was going through his mind. "Can't us wait a day? Hmm?"

"No, Marcos, it can't."

He sat up straighter, linked his hands together, and kept silent for what felt like forever. His calm alarmed her. He was too still, too composed, while his eyes looked…indulgent. "What is it you want to say to me?" he at last asked.

Suddenly she felt like young Oliver Twist, begging, "Please, sir, I want some more." And she hated him for making her feel like that.

Her voice broke and she swallowed in an attempt to recover it. "Look, I realize what kind of arrangement we have," she began. "A-and maybe it was good for a time. But things change, don't they?"

He nodded, his entire face, his smile, indulgent.

She dragged in a breath, trying not to lose her temper. "Marissa, Marcos."

"What about Marissa?" His eyes were so black, so intense, she felt as though they would burn holes through her.

Are the rumors true? she wondered. *Did she force you*

into a marriage bargain only so you could once again own Allende? "You loved Marissa. Do you love her still?"

A frustrated sound exited his throat as he flung his hands over his head. "I'm not discussing Marissa now, of all times, for God's sake!" he exploded.

But Virginia plunged on. "I think it very tacky to jump around from bed to bed, don't you?"

His eyebrows drew low across his eyes, and he nodded. "Extremely."

To her horror, her throat began closing as she pulled her fears out of her little box and showed them to him. "She hurt you, and maybe you wanted to use me to hurt her back—" Why else would he want Virginia? She was not that smart, not that special, not that beautiful, either!

She tried to muffle a sob with her hand and couldn't, and then the tears began to stream down her cheeks in rivers. With a muffled curse, he rose and came around the desk, walking toward her. His face and body became a blur as he reached her, and though she tried to avoid his embrace, her back hit the wall as she tried escaping.

He bent over her, wiped her tears with his thumb. "Don't cry. Why are you crying?"

The genuine concern in his voice, the soul-wrenching tenderness with which he cradled her face, only made the sobs tear out of her with more vigor. "Oh, God," she sobbed, wiping furiously at the tears as they streamed down her face.

When he spoke, he sounded even more tortured than she was. "Don't cry, please don't cry, *amor*." He kissed her cheek. Her eyelashes. Her forehead. Her nose. When his lips glided across hers, she sucked in a breath of surprise. He opened his lips over hers, probed her lightly with his tongue, and said, in a tone that warned of danger, "Please give me ten minutes and I'm all yours. Please just let me…"

When he impulsively covered her mouth, she opened for

the wet thrust of his tongue, offering everything he didn't ask for and more. His kiss was hot and avid, and it produced in her an amazing violence, a feeling that made her feel fierce and powerful and at the same time so vulnerable to him.

The possibility that he was feeling some kind of pity for her made her regain some semblance of control. She pushed at his wrist with one hand and wiped her tears with the other. "I'm all right."

"You're jealous." He took her lips with his warm ones, nibbling the plump flesh between words. "It's all right. Tell me that you are."

She shook her head, not trusting herself to speak.

"I was when you danced with Santos," he rasped, "jealous out of my mind. Out. Of. My. Mind." His teeth were tugging at her ear, and he was making low noises of pleasure as his hands roamed up her sides, following her form, feeling her.

She dragged her mouth across his hair, softly said, "I can't do this anymore, Marcos."

He froze for a shocked moment.

In one blindingly quick move, he lifted her up and pressed her back against the wall, pinioning her by the shoulders. "Is this your idea of getting my attention?"

Her heart thundered in her ears. "I can't do this any longer. I want more." *A father for our child. A man who'll always stand by me. Someone who cares.*

A nearly imperceptible quiver at the corner of his right eye drew her attention. That was all that seemed to move. That and his chest. Her own heaving breasts. They were panting hard, the wild flutter of a pulse at the base of his throat a match to her own frantic heartbeat. "What more do you want?" His voice was hoarse, more a plea than a command.

She grasped the back of his strong neck and made a sound that was more frustrated than seductive. "More! Just more, damn you, and if you can't figure out it's not your money then I'm not going to spell it out for you."

He stared at her as though what she'd just said was the worst kind of catastrophe. Then he cursed in Spanish and stalked away, plunging his hands into his hair. "You picked the wrong moment to share your wish list with me, *amor*."

"It's not a long list," she said glumly. She felt bereft of his kisses, his eyes, his warmth, and wrapped her arms tightly around herself. "We said we'd talk, and I think it's time we did."

"After midnight? When I'm in the midst of closing the deal of my life?"

"I'm sorry about the timing," she admitted.

She swallowed hard for some reason, waiting for him to tell her something. He didn't. His back was stiff as he halted by the window. His breaths were a frightening sound in the room—shallow, so ragged she thought he could be an animal.

But no, he wasn't an animal.

He was a man.

A man who had ruthlessly, methodically isolated his emotions from the world. She did not know how to reach this man, but every atom and cell inside of her screamed for her to try.

But then he spoke.

"Virginia." There was a warning in that word; it vibrated with underlying threat. It made her hold her breath as he turned. There was frustration in his eyes, and determination, and his face was black with lust. "Give me ten minutes. That's all I ask. Ten minutes so I can finish here and then you'll get your nightly tumble."

His words jerked through her, one in particular filling her with outrage. *Tumble!*

She began to quake. A chilling frost seemed to seep into her bones.

Stalking around her, he fell back into his chair, was sucked back into his computer, and began writing.

"Tumble," she said.

He set down the pen and met her gaze. The man was mute as wallpaper.

She signaled with trembling fingers. "For your information." She wanted to fling her shoe at his face, to shred every single paper on the pile she'd neatly organized atop his desk, but she clenched her eyes shut for a brief moment. "I do not want a tumble!"

Several times, Virginia had imagined how their parting would be.

Not even in her nightmares had she imagined this.

She couldn't bear to be in the same room with him, didn't dare glance up to make note of his expression.

Stricken by his lack of apology, she choked back words that wanted to come out, hurtful things she knew she would regret saying, words about being sorry she'd met him, sorry she loved him, sorry she was pregnant by him, but staring at the top of his silky black hair, she couldn't. Instead she said, "Goodbye, Marcos."

And Marcos…said nothing.

Not *goodbye*. Not *chiquita*. Not *amor*.

But as she waited by the elevator, clutching her suitcase handle as though it was all that kept her from falling apart, a roar unlike any other exploded in his study. It was followed by an ear-splitting crash.

The clock read 1:33 p.m.

He had what he wanted, Marcos told himself for the hundredth time. Didn't he? And yet the satisfaction, the victory, wasn't within reach. Perhaps because what he really wanted was something else. Someone else.

The pressure was off his chest—the lawyers were currently sealing the deal. Allende for a couple of million. Marcos now owned every single share of stock in the company, had recovered every inch and centimeter and brick and truck of what Marissa had taken from him.

It had not taken much at all to bend her to his will; the woman had nothing to bargain with. Marissa had to sell or she'd go bankrupt. She'd held no more attraction for him, as she'd thought, no temptation. After a few harsh words from him and a few tears from her, there had finally been a bit of forgiveness between them.

And with that, everything had changed. By her admittance to defeat, she'd unwittingly granted Marcos the opportunity to color his past another shade that wasn't black.

He felt…lighter, in that respect. But heavy in the chest. So damned heavy and tortured with a sense of foreboding he couldn't quite place.

"You needed me, Mr. Allende?"

His heart kicked into his rib cage when Virginia strolled into his office five minutes after he'd issued the request by phone.

Yes, I need you. I do. And I'm not even ashamed to admit it anymore.

Dressed in slimming black, she held a manila file in her hand, and a few seconds after she closed the doors behind her, Marcos spoke. "You left before the ten minutes were over."

Silently she sat and fiddled with her pearls, her eyes shooting daggers at him when she spared him a glance. "I realized you wanted your space, so I indulged you."

Those last words came barbed, as though he'd once spoken them in sarcasm and she were flinging them back at him. She looked tired, his Miss Hollis, he noted. As though she'd slept less than an hour and tossed around for all the rest. Like he had.

He didn't understand her anger very well. But they'd had plans to speak afterward, had been sleeping together so delightedly he hadn't expected the loss of her last night to affect him like it had. Were ten minutes too much to ask?

"Ten minutes, Miss Hollis. You can't even grant me that?"

"You were being—" As though offended by her own thoughts, she bolted upright in the chair, spine straight. "Something of a jerk."

He choked. "Jerk! This spoken by an opinionated little brat I've spoiled rotten?"

The blow registered in her face first, crumpling her tight expression. Marcos raked his fingers through his hair and shot up to pace his office.

He felt like celebrating with her, like marking this momentous day in his career with something even equally outstanding for him personally. But somehow he sensed he had to make amends with her first.

Virginia had wanted him last night. First, he'd been occupied with Marissa. Who'd deceived and lied to him. And who had become so insignificant in his life, he'd forgiven her. After he got what he wanted from her.

All this, thanks to Virginia.

Suddenly, Marcos felt a grieving need to explain, to placate her, to restore the sparkle in her pretty green eyes. Staring around his office, at the papers scattered across the desk, he quietly admitted, "Virginia, I want to make you a proposition."

Her slow and deep intake of breath was followed by a dignified silence. This was not the way he'd intended to ask her and yet suddenly he had to. Here. Now. Had to know she would belong to him, only him.

They were fighting, the air between them felt electric, charged with anger and lust and something else he couldn't quite place. Something fuzzy and warm that made him feel close to her even when she annoyed him.

He strode over to her chair and bent, put his palm on her

bare knee, and said, with fervor, "Would you be my mistress, Virginia?"

The way she automatically breathed the word *no,* he'd have thought he'd slapped her. Her eyes shone with hurt and her mouth parted as though she wanted to say something else but couldn't. "No," she said again, on another breath, this one made of steel.

"I don't think you understand what I'm saying," he said gently, stroking her knee and moving his hand up to clasp hers where it rested on her lap.

"Don't!" She said it in such a fierce voice that he halted. Even his heart stopped beating. She shook her curls side to side, her face stricken. "Don't touch me."

What was this? What was this?

He caught her face in one hand, his heartbeat a loud, deafening roar in his ears. "Darling, I realize you might have misinterpreted my interests in speaking to Marissa, which I assure you were only business. It's you I want, only you. And I'm very prepared to give you—"

"What? What will you give me?" She stood up, her eyes shooting daggers at him. "Do you even realize that the only thing I've been pretending all this time is that I don't love you?"

His heart vaulted, but his voice sounded dead as he stepped back. The confession felt like a bomb dropped into his stomach. "Love."

She chose to look out the window. And at last handed him the file. "Here's my resignation."

She set it atop his stacks and started for the door, and Marcos tore across the room like a man being chased by the devil. He caught her and squeezed her arms as his paralyzed brain made sense of her words.

"If you're telling me you love me," he said through gritted teeth, "look at me when you say it!"

She wrenched free. "Let go of me."

He caught her elbow and spun her around, and she screamed, *"I said don't touch me!"*

Worried the entire floor may have heard that, he let go of her. His chest heaved with the cyclone of feelings inside of him. He curled his fingers into his hands and his fingers dug into his palms, his knuckles jutting out.

"You want me," he growled.

"No." She backed away, glaring at him.

"You tremble for me, Virginia."

"Stop it."

"You want me so much you sob from the pleasure when I'm inside you."

"Because I'm *pretending* to enjoy your disgusting *tumbles!*" she shot. She was flushed and trembling against the wall, her nipples balled into little pearls that begged for his mouth. But in her voice there was nothing but pain.

"Pretend? When the hell have we pretended?" He crushed her against him, squeezed her tight even as she squirmed. "We're fire, Virginia. You and I. Combustion. Don't you understand English? I'm asking you to stay. With me. And be my mistress," he ground out.

Did she even realize he'd never in his life said this to a woman before? When her lashes rose and her gaze met his, the damaged look in her eyes knocked the air out of him. He didn't expect the slicing agony lashing through him at her next words.

"I'm not interested in being your mistress."

When she disengaged from him and pulled the doors open, he cursed under his breath, raked a hand through his hair. All noise across the floor silenced, and he immediately grabbed his jacket, shoved his arms into it as he followed her to the elevator.

He pushed inside before the doors closed, and she turned her face toward the mirror when he demanded, "Do I get two weeks to convince you to stay? I want you here. And I want you in my bed."

"You want. You need." Her voice quivered with anger, and its tentacles curled around him so hard he could've sworn it would kill him. "Is that what you wanted to speak to me about? Becoming your…*mistress?*"

His heart had never galloped this way. His plans had never veered off so unexpectedly, so decidedly. Their gazes met. Hers furious. His…his burned like flames. He grabbed her shoulders. The need inside him was so consuming he saw red. "Say yes. Christ, say yes now."

But the way she looked at him wasn't the same way she always did. "Do you think that's what I want?" she asked, so softly he barely heard through the background elevator music. "Did I ever give you the impression I would…settle for…such an offer?"

Stunned that she would look at him like he was a monster, he took a step away from her, and another. His body burned with the want to show her he meant not to punish but to love her with every graze of his lips and every lick of his tongue.

And he said, out of desperation, impulse, the exact second the elevator halted at the lobby floor, "I love you."

And the words, magic words, ones he'd never, ever said before, didn't have the effect he'd predicted.

Her laugh was cynical. "See, you're so good at pretending, I don't believe you."

And she spun around and walked away, out of the elevator, away from him, away from it all.

Stunned, he braced a hand on the mirror, shut his eyes as he fought to make sense of the rampaging turmoil inside him.

What in the hell?

Thirteen

Alone in his Fintech offices, motionless in his chair, Marcos stared out the window.

The nineteenth floor was empty. It was 3 a.m. But there was no power on this earth, no way in hell, that he'd go back alone to his apartment. His penthouse had never felt so cold now that Virginia Hollis was gone. The sheets smelled of her. He'd found a lipstick under the bathroom sink and he'd never, ever felt such misery. The sweeping loneliness that had accompanied that unexpected find was staggering.

He'd stormed out of his home and now here he was, inside his sanctuary. The place where he evaluated his losses and plotted his comebacks. Where he'd conquered the unconquerable and ruthlessly pursued new targets. Where, for the last month, he'd spent countless hours staring off into space with the single thought of a raven-haired temptress with pale, jade-green eyes.

And now he stared out the window, blinded to the city below, and he told himself he did not care.

He told himself that a month from now, he would forget Virginia Hollis.

He told himself this was an obsession and nothing more. He told himself the gut-wrenching, staggering throb inside him was nothing. And for the hundredth time, until the words rang true and his insides didn't wince in protest every time he thought them, he told himself he did not love her.

But it was a bluff. A farce. A lie.

Virginia had her money. Their arrangement had culminated at the Fintech party and had left him with an overwhelming sense of loss he couldn't quite shake. She'd left him wanting. Wanting more.

Marcos, I love you.

She hadn't said it in exactly those words—but in his mind, she did. And he'd never heard sweeter words. More devastating words. Because suddenly, and with all his might, he wanted to be a man who could love her like she deserved.

The pain in her eyes—he'd been the one to put it there. Touch of gold? He scoffed at the thought, thinking he destroyed anything he touched that had life. He'd put that misery in Virginia's eyes and he loathed himself for it.

His proposal, what he'd offered her, not even half of what he'd truly wanted from her, sickened him.

All along, he'd wanted her. He was a man accustomed to following his gut, and he did it without a conscience. He knew when he saw land and wanted it. He knew what he looked for when he bought stocks. He knew, had known from the start, he wanted Virginia in his bed, under his starved, burning body. But now, clear as the glass before him, he knew what else he wanted from her.

He wanted it all.

He wanted a million dances and double that amount of her smiles.

He wanted her in his bed, to see her when he woke up, to find her snuggled against him.

He wanted to pay her credit card bills and he wanted her with a baby in her arms. His baby. His woman. His *wife*.

Mia. Mia. Mia.

He'd been alone his entire lifetime, pursuing meaningless affairs, convincing himself that was enough. It had all changed. Slowly, almost imperceptibly, but surely, ever since the day he'd hired Virginia Hollis.

Now he had broken her heart before she'd truly admitted to having lost it to him. He should've treasured it. Tucked it into his own and never let it go.

Sighing, he pushed his chair around and stared across his office. A dozen plasma TV screens hung on the wall to the right. They usually enlivened the place with noise and light, but were currently off. They lent a gloom to the area that Marcos found quite the match to his mood.

In fact, a morgue was quite the match to his mood.

He stalked outside, and made his way to a sleek wooden desk. Her items were still on it. He scanned the surface—polished to a gleam, all orderly, all her, and he groaned and let his weight drop into her chair.

Her rejection felt excruciatingly painful. Not even the day Marissa Galvez had stared up at him from his father's bed had he felt such helplessness.

What in the devil did she want from him?

As he stroked a hand along the wood, he knew. Deep in the closed, festering pit of his emotions, he knew what she wanted. Damn her, she'd been playing him for it! Seducing him, delighting and enchanting him, making him love and need and cherish her.

And now he couldn't even remember why he had thought she didn't deserve everything she wanted. Because she was a woman, like Marissa? Why had he thought his bed would be enough for everything she would lack? Had he grown so heartless that he would rob her of a family?

He began opening and closing the desk drawers, looking for some sign of her. Something—anything—she might have left behind.

For the first time in his life, someone else's needs seemed more important than his, and he loathed the overwhelming sense of loss sweeping through him like an avalanche.

If he had an ounce of decency in him, if he was not the unfeeling monster she thought him to be at this moment, Marcos would let her go.

And just when he was certain it was the right thing to do, just when he was determined to forget about her and all the days they'd pretended and all the ways they'd been both wrong and right for each other, he spotted the boxes crowded into the back of her bottom drawer.

And the three test strips. All of them had the same result.

"Nurse, is my father out in the hall?"

Virginia had been transferred to a small private room in the west hospital wing, where she'd slept for the night hooked up to an IV drip, and this morning the one person she longed to see hadn't yet made an appearance. She wanted to go home already—she felt tired, cranky, lonely—and still the nurse kept delaying her departure.

The balmy-voiced nurse fidgeted around the bare room, organizing the trays. "I believe he's outside. I'm sure he'll come in shortly."

Virginia sighed, the sensation of having been run over by an elephant especially painful in her abdomen and breast area. She cupped her stomach. Amazing, that the baby already had its heartbeat. Amazing that just as she left its father, the baby had tried to leave her body, too.

"Virginia?"

She went completely immobile when she heard that.

There, wearing a severe black turtleneck and slacks, stood Marcos Allende in the doorway. Her heart dropped to her toes. She felt the urge to snatch the sleek red carnation her father had set on the side table and hide her pale, teary face behind it, but she was too mesmerized to pull her eyes away. Large, hard, beautiful—Marcos's presence seemed to empower the entire room, and she suspected—no, knew—everyone in this hospital must be feeling his presence.

He stood with his feet braced apart, his arms at his sides, his fingers curled into his palms. And something hummed. Inside her. In her blood, coursing through her veins.

"An acquaintance, miss?"

The nurse's tone gave a hint of her preoccupation. Did she feel the charge in the air? Was the world twirling faster? The floor falling?

Virginia nodded, still shocked and overwhelmed by this visit, but as she stared at the sleek-faced, long-nosed young woman, she hated her mind's eye for gifting her with another, more riveting image of Marcos's dark, cacao gaze. His silken mass of sable hair. Long, tanned fingers. Accent. Oh, God, the accent, that thick baritone, softly saying *Miss Hollis*...

"I'll leave you two for a moment, then."

Oddly close to being devastated, Virginia watched the nurse's careful departure, and then she could find no excuse to stare at the plain white walls, no spot to stare at but Marcos.

If she had just been torpedoed, the impact would have been less than what she felt when he leveled his hot coal eyes on her. He stood as still as a statue.

Why didn't he move? Was he just going to stand there? Why didn't he hold her? Why was he here? He was angry she quit? Angry she hadn't collected her items? Did he miss her just a little bit?

She sucked in a breath when he spoke.

"I'm afraid this won't do."

The deep, quiet, accented voice washed over her like a waterfall. Cleansing. Clear. Beautiful.

Oh, God. Would she ever not love this man?

She pushed up on her hands, glad her vitals were no longer on display or else Marcos would know exactly how hard her heart was beating. "Marcos, what are you doing here—"

He looked directly at her as he advanced, overpowering the room. "I had to see you."

She sucked in breath after breath, watching him move with that catlike grace, his expression somber. Her body quaked from head to toe. The unfairness of it all; he was so gorgeous, so elegant, so tempting. So unreachable. And she! She was so…so beat-up, tired, drained. Hospitalized. Oh, God.

Her lips trembled. As if she weighed next to nothing, he bent and gently scooped her up against him, and Virginia liquefied.

I almost lost our baby, she thought as she wound her arms around him and buried her face in his neck.

He inhaled deeply, as though scenting her. Then, into her ear, his voice ringing so low and true it tolled inside of her, "Are you all right?"

Only Marcos could render such impact with such softly spoken words. Her entire being, down to her bones, trembled at his concern. And then came more. It was just a breath, whispered in her ear, and he whispered it with fervor.

"I love you."

Her muscles clenched in protest, and her head swiveled to her father's when she spotted him at the open doorway. The weathered man's face was inscrutable and his suit was perfectly in place; only the ravaged look in his eyes spoke of what he'd done.

He'd told Marcos about the baby?

"You lied to me, you left me, and yet I love you," Marcos

continued, his voice so thick and gruff, as though he were choking.

After the fear, the cramps and the possibility of losing her baby, Virginia had no energy. She just wanted him to speak. The sturdiness of his hard chest against hers gave her the most dizzying sensation on this earth. She'd thought she'd never feel his arms again and to feel them around her, holding her so tight, was bliss.

She didn't realize she was almost nuzzling his neck, breathing in his musky, familiar scent, until her lungs felt ready to explode.

"Do you think we could pretend," he whispered into the top of her bent head, "the past two days never happened, and we can start again?"

More pretending? God, no! No more pretending.

But she refused to wake up from this little fantasy, this one last moment, refused to lift her face, so instead she rubbed her nose against the side of his corded neck. A strange sensation flitted through her, like the soaring she felt when she played on the swings as a child.

His voice was terse but tender as he wiped her brow with one hand and smoothed her hair back. "And our baby?"

Shock didn't come close to what she experienced. Her nerves twisted like wires. "P-pardon?"

"You lost our child?"

For the first time since Marcos had come through that door, Virginia noticed the red rimming his eyes, the strain in his expression. Even his voice seemed to throb in a way she'd never heard before.

She moved not an inch, breathed no breath, as her mind raced to make sense of his question. Then she glanced out the small window, not at what lay beyond, just at a spot where Marcos's face would not distract her. "What makes you say that?" she asked quietly, her fingers tugging on themselves as she scanned the room for the possible culprit behind this misunderstanding. Her father.

"Look at me." Marcos's massive shoulders blocked her view as he leaned over the bed rails. His breath stirred the top of her head as he scraped his jaw against her hair with absolutely no restraint, and then he spoke so passionately her middle tingled. "Look at me. We'll have another baby. I've always wanted one—and I want one with you." He seized her shoulders in a stronghold, his face pained and tortured as he drew away and forced her to meet his gaze. "Marry me. Today. Tomorrow. Marry me."

"I— What do you mean *another* baby?" After many moments, she pinned Hank Hollis with her stare. "Father?"

Wide-eyed, her father hovered by the opposite wall, shifting his feet like an uncertain little boy. He opened his mouth, then snapped it shut, then opened it again, as if he were holding on to great words. "I told him you'd lost the baby."

She gasped. What a horrible thing to say! "W-why? Father! Why would you do that?"

The man rubbed the back of his neck, pacing the little room. "So he'd leave. You said you didn't want any visitors."

While the honest words registered in her foggy mind—the first protective thing her father had done for her in ages—Virginia stared at the aging man. Her heart unwound like an old, twisted shred of paper.

For years, she had been so angry at this man. Maybe if she hadn't changed, become pregnant, fallen in love, she'd still be. But now—she didn't want resentment or anger. She wanted a family, and she'd take even one that had been broken.

Virginia leveled her eyes on the beautiful, thick-lashed cocoa ones she'd been seeing in her dreams and straightened up on the bed, clinging to that fine, strong hand. "Marcos,

I'm not sure what he told you, but I'd like to assure you I'm all right. And so is the baby."

When she pictured telling Marcos about a child, she hadn't expected an audience, nor having to do it in a hospital room.

Still. She would never, in her life, forget this moment.

Marcos's expression changed, metamorphosed, into one of disbelief, then joy. Joy so utter and pure it lit his eyes up like shooting stars.

"So we're expecting, then?"

The term *we* coming from his beautiful mouth made her giddy with excitement.

He smiled, and it was brilliant, that smile, that moment.

Did this please him? Yes! She'd bet her life on it.

She nodded, her heart fluttering madly, a winged thing about to fly out of orbit. "I'd like to go home now," she admitted, and although her father stepped forward to offer assistance, the words weren't meant for him.

She gazed up at Marcos—quiet and mesmerizing—as she eased out of the hospital bed with as much dignity as she could muster.

His attention was no longer hard to bear. She wanted it; she wanted him.

Virginia Hollis knew this man. Inside and out, she knew him. How true he was to his word. How dedicated. How loyal. And how proud. She didn't need any more proof than his presence here, his touch, the look in his eyes and the promise there.

Rising to her full height, she linked her fingers through his and squeezed, feeling flutters in her stomach when he smiled encouragingly down at her. "Yes, Marcos Allende. I'll marry you."

Epilogue

The day arrived three months before the baby did.

Walking up to the altar, with the music shuddering through the church walls, Virginia had eyes only for the dark, mesmerizing man at the far end of the aisle. Tall and smiling, Marcos stood with his hands clasped before him, his broad shoulders and solid arms and steely, stubborn jaw offering love and comfort and protection.

Virginia was certain that nobody who watched him would be blind to the way he stared at her. Least of all she.

They shared a smile. Then her father was letting go of her arm.

Soon Marcos was lifting the flimsy veil to gaze upon her face and into her eyes, eyes which she used to fervently tell him, *I love you!*

Their palms met, their fingers linked, and the moment they did he gave her a squeeze. She felt it down to her tummy.

I, Virginia, take thee, Marcos, to be my lawfully wedded husband...

When he spoke his vows, the simplest vows, to love and cherish, her eyes began to sting. By the time the priest declared them man and wife, she was ready—more than ready—to be swept into his arms and kissed.

And kiss her he did. The priest cleared his throat. The attendants cheered and clapped. And still he kissed her.

Virginia let herself take her first relaxed breath once they were in the back of the limo. Gravitating toward each other, they embraced, and tiny tremors of desire spread along her torso and limbs. She'd had this fool idea of waiting to be together again until they married—and she was dying for him to touch her.

As they kissed, Virginia found her husband already dispensing with her veil. "There we go," he said contentedly. "Enjoy the dress because I assure you, it is coming off soon."

Actually relieved to be without the veil and anxiously looking forward to Marcos dispensing with the dress, she leaned back on the seat and cuddled against him. "I never knew these things were so heavy," she said. The skirt ballooned at her feet but thankfully there was no volume on top to keep her away from the man she most definitely intended to jump at the first opportunity.

"Come here, wife." He drew her close as the limo pulled into the street and the city landscape slowly rolled past them. Staring absently outside, Virginia sighed. His arms felt so good around her, being against him so right. Being his wife.

Both protectively and possessively, Marcos pressed her face to his chest and with his free hand, reached out to rub her swelling stomach. She'd noticed the more it grew, the more he did that. "How is my little girl today?" he asked against her hair.

Her eyebrows drew into a scowl. "We're having a boy,"

Virginia countered. "A handsome, dashing boy like his daddy. No girl would kick like this little guy does, trust me."

"Your daughter would, you saucy wench," he said with a rolling chuckle. "And my instincts tell me we are having a plucky, curly-haired, rosy-cheeked daughter. She'll run my empire with me."

Virginia smiled against his chest and slid a hand up his shirt to find the familiar cross lying at his throat and play with it. "Father keeps asking how many grandchildren we plan to have, he's obsessed with wanting it to be at least three."

Marcos laughed, and that laugh alone warmed her up another notch.

"Ahh, darling," he said. "He can rest assured we'll be working on that night and day." The praise in his words and the suggestive pat on her rear filled her with anticipation of tonight and future nights with her complex, breathtakingly beautiful, thoroughly giving and enchanting husband.

"He's so changed now, Marcos," she admitted, feeling so relaxed, *so* happy.

"His work in Allende has been impressive, Virginia. Even Jack is amazed."

"And you?"

He snorted. "I got to say to the moron 'I told you so.'"

She laughed. Then she snuggled closer and said, "Thank you. For believing that people can change. And for forgiving that little fib he told you at the hospital."

He nuzzled the top of her head. "He was trying to protect you—he didn't know me yet, and I respect that. Your father deserved a second chance, Virginia. We all do."

She sighed. "I'm just glad he's put all his efforts into making the best of it. And I'm proud of you, dear sir, for being wise enough to put the past behind you and keep Allende."

And for being most decidedly, most convincingly, most deliciously in love with her.

* * *

The band played throughout the evening, and the guests at the reception laughed and danced and drank. Hardly anyone would notice the groom had kidnapped the bride, and if they did, Marcos sure as hell didn't care.

He still could not understand why Virginia had gotten it into her head to play hard-to-get leading up to the wedding, and even less could he comprehend why he had obediently complied.

But now in the cloaked shadows of the closet, he had Virginia right where he'd always wanted her. In his arms. His mouth feasted on her exposed throat while his hands busily searched her dress for access—any access—to the smooth, creamy skin beneath.

"Careful!" Virginia screeched when he yanked on the delicate zipper at the back and an invisible button popped free.

He laughed darkly and maneuvered through the opening. "You're not wearing it again, *reina*. I could tear it apart and dispense with all this silliness." The guests had been crowding them for hours when all Marcos wanted was to be with his bride. Now his hands stole in through the opening at the small of her back, where he instantly seized her cushy rear and drew her up against him. "Come here. You've been teasing me all night."

"How kind of you to notice."

"Hmm. I noticed." He kissed the top of her breasts, all evening looking lush and squeezable thanks to Christian Dior, and then used his hands to gather the volume of her skirts and yank most of them back.

She automatically wrapped her stockinged legs around him when he pressed her against the wall. "You're incorrigible," she said chidingly, but he could hear the smile in her voice and the little tremble that said how very much his wife wanted to be ravaged by him.

He brought his hands up front and lowered them. "I'm open to being domesticated."

"Luckily I'm open to attempting that daunting task. In fact—no, not the panties!" A tear sounded, Virginia gasped, and his fingers found what they were looking for.

"Bingo," he purred.

"Oh, Marcos." Slipping her hands under his jacket and around his shoulders, she placed fervent little kisses along his jaw. "Please."

With a rumbling chuckle, he found her center and grazed it with his fingers. "Please what, *chiquita?*"

Against his lips, she mumbled, "You know what, you evil man."

"Please this?"

"Yes, yes, that." She left a moist path up his jaw and temple, and in his ear whispered, "I was aching to be with you all day."

"Shame on me." He turned his head and seized her earlobe with his teeth, tugging. "For keeping you waiting."

"I adore what you do to me."

He groaned at the husky quality of her voice. "No more than I, darling." Unable to wait, he freed himself from his trousers and, grasping her hips, began making love to her.

A whimper tore out of her, and she clutched his back with her hands.

"Chiquita." He wound his arms around her and was in turn embraced and enveloped by her silken warmth, completely owned and taken by the woman who had single-handedly stolen his heart.

No matter how quiet they tried to be, they were groaning, moving together. Marcos closed his eyes, savoring her, his wife and partner and mate and woman. When she exploded in his arms with a gasp, crying out his name into his mouth, he let go. Gripping her hips tighter, he muttered a choked, emotional *te amo* then let out a satisfying, "Hmm."

"Hmm," she echoed.

Inconspicuous minutes later, the bride and groom exited the closet. The ballroom brimmed with music and laughter, most of the guests who remained being the people closest to them.

With an appreciative eye, Marcos noticed the bride looked deliciously rumpled. Her cheeks glowed bright, and the fancy hairdo she claimed had taken endless hours to achieve had become magnificently undone.

As if reading his thoughts, she shot him a little black scowl. "I'm sure that everyone who sees me now will know—" she rose up to whisper into his ear "—that you just tumbled me in the closet. Really. Is that how your wife should expect to be treated, *Señor* Allende?"

Smiling into her eyes, he lifted her knuckles to his lips. "My wife can expect to be treated with respect and admiration and devotion."

With a dazzling smile, she let him drag her to the dance floor when a compellingly slow song began. "I believe this dance is mine," he said, and meaningfully added, "So is the one afterward."

She stepped into the circle of his arms, finding her spot under his chin to tuck her head in and sliding her arms around him. "You are a greedy fellow, aren't you?"

His lips quirked, and his eyes strayed toward the arched doorway, where his little brother stood, barely visible through the throng surrounding him. "With Santos around, I don't plan to let you out of my sight."

Virginia laughed. "He's already told me everything. Even about the time you broke his nose and chin. I swear that man loves to make you out as the ogre." She glanced past her shoulder and wrinkled her little nose. "Besides, he seems pretty busy with the two he brought tonight…and the dozen others he's trying to fend off."

Grateful that for the moment the guests were oblivious

to them as they danced amidst so many familiar faces, Marcos ran a hand down her back and glanced at the firm swell between their bodies. "How do you feel?" he asked, somber.

She smiled as she canted her head back to meet his gaze. "I feel…perfect." She kissed his lips and gazed up at him with those same green eyes that had haunted him. Their sparkle surpassed the blinding one of the ring on her finger, and her smile took his breath away—like it did every day. "You?" she asked.

His lips curled into a smile, and he bent his head, fully intending to take that mouth of hers. "A hundred thousand dollars shorter," he baited. He touched her lips, and his smile widened. "And I've never felt so lucky."

* * * * *

MILLS & BOON®

Need more New Year reading?

We've got just the thing for you!
We're giving you 10% off your next eBook or
paperback book purchase on the Mills & Boon
website. So hurry, visit the website today and type
SAVE10 in at the checkout for your exclusive

10% DISCOUNT

www.millsandboon.co.uk/save10

MILLS & BOON®

Why not subscribe?
Never miss a title and save money too!

Here's what's available to you if you join the
exclusive **Mills & Boon Book Club** today:

✦ *Titles up to a month ahead of the shops*
✦ *Amazing discounts*
✦ *Free P&P*
✦ *Earn Bonus Book points that can be redeemed
 against other titles and gifts*
✦ *Choose from monthly or pre-paid plans*

Still want more?
Well, if you join today we'll even give you
50% OFF your first parcel!

So visit **www.millsandboon.co.uk/subs**
or call Customer Relations on 020 8288 2888
to be a part of this exclusive Book Club!

SUBS_2014